Between the Sheets

Colette Caddle

LARGE PRINT

Oxford

First published in Great Britain 2008
by
Simon & Schuster UK Ltd.

Published in Large Print 2009 by ISIS Publishing Ltd.,
7 Centremead, Osney Mead, Oxford OX2 0ES
by arrangement with
Simon & Schuster UK Ltd.

British Library Cataloguing in Publication Data
Caddle, Colette.
    Between the sheets.
    1. Women novelists - - Family relationships
    - - Fiction.
    2. Separated women - - Fiction.
    3. Dublin (Ireland) - - Fiction.
    4. Large type books.
    I. Title
    823.9'2–dc22

ISBN 978–0–7531–8334–2 (hb)
ISBN 978–0–7531–8335–9 (pb)

Printed and bound in Great Britain by
T. J. International Ltd., Padstow, Cornwall

For my three wonderful men

Acknowledgements

As always my warmest thanks to all those that helped get this book from an idea in my head to a place on a shelf.

First I must thank Ian Chapman and everyone at Simon & Schuster, for their usual professionalism. I must single some people out, though, for a special mention.

There were times when it felt that I would never finish this story, and I was tempted to change the title to Thank God That's Over! For practically carrying me across the finishing line, thank you to my lovely editor Suzanne Baboneau and the talented and patient Libby Vernon.

My sincere and heartfelt gratitude to the voice of reason, my agent and friend Sheila Crowley and all the team at AP Watt.

To a copyeditor extraordinaire, thank you Clare Parkinson. To Lizzie Gardiner and Ami Smithson for a wonderful cover — they say you don't judge a book . . . but we all know the truth!

To the many people involved in getting my book to stand out from the crowd — Amanda Shipp, Nigel Stoneman and their teams in marketing and publicity.

To Julie Wright, Charlotte Robertson, Grainne Reidy and all the UK sales team for getting the book out there. Also to Gill Richardson and Gill Hess for

everything they do to sell my books in Ireland —
believe me, it's a lot!

Thanks to the distributors and shop staff everywhere
who get my books on the shelves.

And to you the reader for taking the book back off
again — my humble gratitude.

And finally, thanks to the Caddles and the Lynotts.
To my wonderful mother who has been completely
neglected while I wrote this book but as supportive as
ever. To my beloved sons who remind me daily of
what's really important in life. And to Tony whose
tolerance knows no bounds.

CHAPTER
ONE

Victor Gaston watched as Bobbi released the clip on her hair, allowing it to tumble in Titian curls around her shoulders. "I must say I'm not used to this. My pilots are usually quite gruff and very hairy."

She laughed as he reached up to pull off her tie and slowly open the buttons of her starched white shirt. "At Prestige Airlines we aim to please. Do you know that you can even specify which pilot you want?"

"I definitely want you," he groaned, pulling her down on to his lap.

"We don't have long," she warned. "I'm flying to Vienna in an hour."

"Then, Captain, prepare yourself for take-off," he said, his mouth coming down hard on hers . . .

"Dana, couldn't you at least pretend that you're interested?" Gus hissed in his wife's ear.

Dana De Lacey snapped back to the present and realized that the speaker had finally come to the end of his long, tiresome story. She quickly joined in the round of polite applause and flashed her husband an apologetic smile. "Sorry, but he was particularly boring," she whispered back.

When Gus replied he too was smiling, but there was a steely note in his voice. "The Society of Architects' Dinner is only once a year and it will all be over in an hour. I don't think that's too taxing even for you."

"I said I'm sorry." Dana suppressed a sigh and smiled ingratiatingly at the elderly man opposite. God, Gus was grumpy tonight. In fact he'd been a right grouch for weeks and had gone completely mad when she'd tried to wriggle out of tonight's dinner.

They had been sitting in the kitchen of their large farmhouse in west Cork at the time and she had been nursing a bad hangover. She'd only got out of bed at noon and then it was just to crawl downstairs and curl up on the sofa. After some persuasion, Gus had made her a cup of camomile tea and she'd sipped it gingerly as he sat working on his laptop at the old oak kitchen table.

"How come you're not sick?" she'd complained, taking in his bright eyes and healthy colour. "You had just as much to drink as I did." They had been out to dinner with a local builder who was also a good friend and it had turned into a long night.

"A pint of water before bed and a three-mile jog this morning," he'd replied with a smug grin.

She'd shuddered. "Masochist."

He'd laughed. "We should go for a long walk along the beach; that would make you feel better."

She'd shaken her head as she checked her watch. "I need to go and pack. I want to get the four o'clock train back to Dublin."

His fingers had paused over the keyboard and he'd stared at her. "Oh, come on, Dana, stay a few more days. The weather forecast is excellent and we could do with a bit of downtime, just the two of us."

"Sorry, but I have too much to do."

"You can write here," he'd protested.

"You know I can't."

He'd looked past her at the sun glinting on the blue waters of Bantry Bay. "I can see that it might be hard to find inspiration."

"Ha ha. It's because I don't have my stuff around me, you know that."

"I know that," he'd agreed.

"I'm sorry for being so anal." She'd smiled apologetically. "Please don't let's fight, I'm really not up to it."

"I'm not going to," he'd promised, sounding resigned. "I won't be back in Dublin for a few days. I have some business to attend to down here."

"So much for downtime!" Dana had retorted, and as she'd stretched and risen to her feet she'd missed the look of annoyance that crossed her husband's face. "Shall I book a taxi to take me to the station or will you drive me?"

"Of course I'll drive you."

"Thank you." She'd put a hand on his shoulder as she passed.

He'd reached up to cover it with his own. "I wish you'd stay."

She had bent to drop a kiss on his head and he'd pulled her close. "Next time," she'd promised. "Don't stay down here too long; that bed feels very empty without you."

"I'll be back at the weekend and don't forget we're going out on Sunday night."

She'd frowned. "We are?"

"It's the Architects' Dinner, Dana." He'd shaken his head impatiently. "I told you and Sylvie about it weeks ago. It's in your diary."

"Do I have to go?" she'd moaned. "Tom and Ashling will be there; you don't need me as well."

"Ashling is having a lot of back pain at the moment so they're bowing out this year." His eyes had hardened. "Don't let me down, Dana; it's only once a year."

"All right, all right, I'll go."

The atmosphere had been tense as they drove to the station and Gus had hardly responded when she'd kissed and hugged him goodbye. Things hadn't been much better since he'd got back. She hadn't a clue what was wrong. He was usually such a good-humoured man.

And now here she was at the dreaded dinner, and it was every bit as boring as she'd anticipated. How, she wondered, did a man as charismatic and dynamic as her husband have anything in common with these people? She looked around and tried to imagine any of the grey, two-dimensional characters in this room being as creative and innovative as Gus, and couldn't. It was no wonder he and Tom won award after award; they were without doubt in a league of their own. She turned her head slightly so she could study Gus, and smiled at the attentive way he was listening to the president's speech. God, he did look sexy tonight. The dark-blue velvet dinner jacket complimented his eyes, and wearing it with the open-necked white shirt and jeans he looked both cool and sophisticated. It was this effortless and unconscious style, confidence and lazy grin that had attracted her from the moment they met.

She could still recall the electricity between them that first day. She had just bought the farmhouse in Cork, except then it had been a damp and dark stone building with nothing going for it but its amazing view. Her agent, Walter Grimes, had thought she was completely mad but said if she insisted on proceeding with the venture, she should at least hire a good architect. And so, after talking to his numerous contacts in the UK and Ireland, he'd introduced her to Gus Johnson of the esteemed Johnson and Cleary Architects in Dublin.

Dana smiled now at the memory of how she'd felt when Gus had first taken her hand in his. His grasp had been cool and firm and when he had smiled into her eyes, her heart had skipped a beat. From that moment, Dana didn't really care what kind of an architect he was, he had the job. Within weeks they were an item, he moved in two months later and they'd married the following year. They had made a striking if incongruous couple. While Gus was tall, with red-blond wavy hair, blue eyes and a smattering of freckles across his nose, Dana was tiny, sallow-skinned and had huge, black-brown eyes. "Little and large," he'd joke when she'd go up on her tiptoes to kiss him. "Beauty and the beast," she'd retort.

The speeches were over now and people were starting to circulate. The blonde across the table was laughing too loudly at something Gus had said and Dana found herself automatically putting a possessive hand on his arm. She leaned close to him, her lips almost touching his ear. "Can we go now? I'm tired and I just want to have you all to myself."

Gus sighed. "Fine, we'll go."

He helped her to her feet and Dana smiled around the table, her eyes finally connecting with the blonde's. "Goodnight, then, lovely to meet you all."

As they crossed the foyer, her mood already lightening, she said, "Let's go to a club."

"I thought you were tired."

"I've got a second wind." She smiled up at him, her eyes twinkling mischievously.

He didn't return her smile. "I have an early start."

Dana's shoulders slumped as she followed him back to the car. "You're just no fun lately, you know that?"

As they drove home in silence, Dana's thoughts once again turned to *The Mile High Club*, her nineteenth novel. The main character, Bobbi Blackwell, was now in the cockpit, expertly flying the private plane to Vienna, her skin still tingling from the touch of her new lover. Victor Gaston was turning out to be a good character, Dana thought. He was sexy and funny and she was quite pleased with the way he and Bobbi worked together on the page. All in all, the novel was going quite well, which was a relief as her publishers were talking about using it to launch their Passion imprint in the UK and Ireland. Dana was excited at the thought of finally being in print in her own country but at the same time she wondered if Ireland was ready for her brand of spicy literature and the exploits of Bobbi Blackwell both on and off the ground. Her agent assured her it was. "Your books may be a little raunchy but they still have class and humour. You are the perfect way for Peyton Publishing to introduce their Passion imprint to Europe. You're their number-one author in that genre, you're local and you're beautiful too."

Though Dana was grateful for Wally's encouraging words she wasn't sure she believed them. Her work might go down okay in the UK but she wasn't at all sure how it would be received in Ireland. She was the daughter of a famous and acclaimed Irish poet and the first thing the press would do was compare father and daughter, and she would be found lacking.

When she had started writing she had taken her mother's maiden name, De Lacey, in the hope that people wouldn't make the link between her and the lauded Conall O'Carroll. But Ireland was a small place and you couldn't keep a secret like that for long.

It irked her that no matter how much she tried to escape the man, he still seemed to encroach on her life. She didn't often get mentioned in the papers, but, when she did, her name was always linked with his. Would *The Mile High Club* change that or would she spend all her days in his shadow? Only time would tell.

★ ★ ★

"Dana?"

Realizing that Gus had pulled into their driveway and turned off the engine, Dana stretched like a cat, climbed out of the car and slowly followed him inside. "Bed?" she asked, pausing at the bottom of their sweeping staircase and smiling suggestively. Working on sex scenes always got her in the mood and she'd based more than a few of them on her own love life with Gus.

He flung his keys and phone on the hall table and turned towards the kitchen. "I need a drink."

"I'll have a spritzer," she called after him and went on up to the large master suite. Going through to her dressing room, she undressed, took off her make-up and then slipped into a simple sheath of chocolate-coloured silk. "Not bad for thirty-seven," she murmured, appraising her reflection in the floor-to-ceiling mirror. She was arranging herself in a suitably alluring pose on their king-size bed when Gus walked into the room.

"Come and sit down." She patted the bed invitingly.

Gus handed her the wine and sat down on the edge of the bed with his back to her.

She put her glass on the bedside table and, moving closer, slid her arms around his waist. Her fingers deftly opened the buttons of his shirt and she slipped a hand inside to caress the smooth skin of his chest. "I've been thinking about doing this all night," she told him.

Gus pushed her hand away. "Don't."

Slightly taken aback, Dana sat back against the pillows and reached for her drink. "What's going on,

8

Gus? You've been like a bear with a sore head for days, no, weeks. Is it work?"

He shook his head and, standing up, crossed over to the window.

"Then what? Oh, come on, Gus, talk to me."

He chuckled softly. "Funny, I thought that was my line."

"What do you mean? What are you talking about?"

"I can't do this any more," he said, not moving.

She stared at his back, at the slump of his shoulders, and heard the resignation in his voice. "Do what?"

"This." He made a gesture at her and then himself. "Us. I've tried but I just can't do it."

Dana set her glass down carefully. "Is this some sort of joke?"

"I wish it was."

"Is there someone else?" she asked, her voice even but her stomach twisting into a painful knot.

"No, of course not," he said crossly.

"So what is all this about? Are you having a midlife crisis, is that it?" She forced a laugh. "Shall I buy you a Harley or a red sports car or maybe we could dye your hair —"

"Dana —"

"Look," she hurried on, thinking that as long as she kept talking she could sort this. "I know I'm not the easiest person to live with and that maybe sometimes you fancy other women, but that's okay."

"I don't!" He shot her a curious look. "But wouldn't it bother you if I did?"

She shrugged. "You're a red-blooded, handsome man and I realize that you must have urges . . ."

"You make me sound like a character from one of your books," he groaned.

She smiled affectionately. "No, you're much sexier."

He shot her a despairing look and turned back to the window. "I think I should move out," he said quietly.

"What?" she exploded.

He drained his glass and turned back to face her. "It's for the best."

She stared at him, waiting for him to burst out laughing and tell her this was all a prank, albeit a slightly sick one, but his expression remained grim. "You say you are going to leave me and that it's for the best and you're not even going to tell me why?"

He seemed to consider the question carefully before answering. "When I met you I was completely knocked for six. You were so beautiful and funny and I couldn't believe my luck when you agreed to marry me."

"We were meant to be together," she agreed tearfully.

He carried on as if she hadn't spoken. "I loved you so much and I thought that as the years passed we would grow closer and our relationship would get stronger and deeper." He looked straight into her eyes.

"And it has," she said urgently. "I adore you, you're everything to me. You're my best friend."

"Really?"

She nodded fervently.

He smiled, his eyes holding hers. "Would you trust me with your deepest, darkest secrets?"

She smiled back nervously. "Of course."

Gus just watched her, his eyes sad.

Dana hugged her arms tightly around her. "So, what now?"

"Now I'd better go," he said quietly and walked over to the door.

"And that's it!" She flung up her arms in frustration. "And may I ask, are you going for good, or just planning to take a sabbatical from our marriage?" Her voice was rising but she didn't care now. "Or are you deserting Tom and your company too? Possibly to go walkabout in the bush or were you thinking of trekking through the Himalayas?"

He didn't move from his position by the door. "This is hardly the time for sarcasm."

"No," she said, feeling deflated and hopeless. "I suppose it isn't."

"I don't know where I'm going," he admitted. "I hadn't planned any of this; it just sort of happened."

Dana went to him and cupped his face in her hands. "Then let's pretend it didn't. Don't go, Gus," she whispered. "You love me, I know you do."

For a moment she saw doubt in his eyes, but then it was gone.

"I'm sorry, Dana," he said with finality and took her hands away. "I'll find somewhere to stay and then I'll come back for my stuff."

She stiffened. "No! If you're going," she said, her voice shrill, "you can take it all right now."

"Dana, be reasonable —"

"Reasonable?" she cried. "You want me to be reasonable? Okay, then, let me help you pack." She ran to his dressing room and started taking armfuls of clothes from the rail. "Where would you like these, in a case? Or should I just chuck them out of the window and save you lugging them downstairs?"

He gripped one of her wrists. "Dana, stop."

She swallowed back her tears and looked up into his eyes, searching for some sign of hope, but his expression was closed and unyielding. She shoved the clothes into his arms. "I mean it, Gus, take your things now or I swear I'll burn them." And turning on her heel, she flew out of the room and down the stairs to her office.

She waited for him to come after her, to bang on the door to tell her it was all a terrible misunderstanding, but all she heard was his steady tread on the floorboards above as he packed his bags. Sinking into her chair, she drew her knees up under her chin and started to tremble.

There was light in the sky when Dana awoke, a dreadful crick in her neck and pins and needles in her toes. Apart from the energetic dawn chorus outside there was an eerie stillness about the house and she let out an involuntary gasp as memories of the previous night came flooding back. Rising from her crouched position she made her way slowly into the hall and climbed the stairs, pausing for a second before throwing open the bedroom, door. She crossed the room to Gus's wardrobe but she could see, without even going in, that he'd taken everything except clothes destined for the charity bag. "Oh, Gus, why?" she whispered as the tears rolled down her cheeks. Stumbling back into the room Dana crawled on to the bed and buried her face in his pillow.

Hours later it was the sound of the hall door closing that woke her. Immediately she was up and running for the door. "I knew you'd be back," she called gaily. "I knew it was all a mistake —"

She pulled up short at the sight of Iris McCarthy looking up at her from the hall, a bewildered look on the woman's face.

"But, Mrs Johnson, I always come on Monday mornings at ten."

Dana felt the tears well in her eyes. "Yes, sorry, of course you do," she managed. "I'm sorry, Iris. It's just I don't feel very well. I think I'll stay in bed today."

"Of course, Mrs Johnson. Shall I answer the phone if it rings?"

"No! No, that's okay."

"Very well, then. Can I get you anything?"

Dana shook her head. "No."

Iris nodded. "Then I'll get on with the laundry."

Dana went back into her bedroom and closed the door. Sinking down on to the bed she reached for the phone and with shaking hands called Gus on his mobile but it went straight to the answering service. After a moment's hesitation Dana dialled his office number instead.

"Good morning, Johnson and Cleary, can I help you?"

"Ann, it's Dana. Could you put me through to Gus, please?"

"Oh, hello. I'm afraid he's not here this morning. Why don't you try him on his mobile?"

Dana swallowed hard. "Yes, I'll do that, thank you."

When the phone rang thirty minutes later, Dana pounced on it. "Gus?"

"Sorry to disappoint you." It was the unmistakable drawl of her agent, calling from London. "It's disgusting, after all these years, that you still get excited when your husband phones," he teased.

Dana swallowed hard. "Hi, Walter."

"So, how goes it, darling?"

"Yes, wonderful," Dana replied, hoping he couldn't hear the tremor in her voice.

"I thought you'd still be asleep after your exciting evening."

"What do you mean?" she demanded, wondering how he could possibly know.

"It was the Architects' Dinner last night, wasn't it?"

"Oh, yes. Yes, that's right."

"So how did it go?"

"Oh, you know, the usual." Dana forced a small laugh. "Listen, Wally, I'm in the middle of a difficult passage —"

"Then you get right back to work," he told her. "I just wanted to tell you to expect a call from Ian Wilson."

"Who?"

"My PR guy in Dublin. I told you about him, remember?"

14

"Yes, of course."

"He's going to get to work on your publicity and wants to have a chat with you first."

"That's a little premature, surely? I mean, Gretta hasn't even said they're definitely going ahead yet."

"It's only a matter of time," Walter said confidently, "and I want your name on everyone's lips. If that doesn't convince your editor that you're the obvious author to launch their new venture, nothing will. Now you get back to that keyboard, my darling, and I'll talk to you later in the week."

Dana hung up and was trying to decide whether or not to leave a message on Gus's answering service when the phone rang again. "Hello?"

"Hello, Mrs Johnson, I'm phoning from your telephone company. I wonder if you have a few minutes —"

"I don't," Dana snapped and hung up. For the rest of the morning she paced her room or just sat staring out into the garden. It was after three when the phone rang again. She snatched it up and clutched it to her ear. "Hello?"

"Hi, honey, how you doin'?"

She groaned inwardly at the sound of her editor's voice. "Oh, hi, Gretta."

"Hey, girl, you don't sound so good," the New York editor said sharply. "Everything okay?"

"Everything's fine," Dana soothed. "It's just that I'm at a rather crucial point in the story —"

"Then I won't interrupt you. It's just been a few days and I wanted to check in."

It had only been Friday when they last talked, Dana thought irritably. Sometimes Gretta was just too pushy.

"How is *The Mile High Club* these days?" Gretta said with a throaty chuckle.

"Well, I can't say from experience —"

"I don't believe that for a moment, not with that gorgeous man of yours."

"Yes, well, appearances can be deceiving," Dana said miserably.

"Are you sure you're okay?"

"Yeah, really, Gretta, everything's fine and the book's going great. I'm just a bit preoccupied."

"I love the way you get so involved in your books," the editor said happily. "If you need a sounding board, just call, okay?"

"I will, thanks."

As Dana put the phone down there was a gentle knock on the door, and Iris came in. "I thought you might like a little snack," she said, setting a small tray down on the table by the window. Dana looked without interest at the sandwich but took a grateful sip of the strong hot coffee.

Iris studied her, a worried frown creasing her brow. "You're very pale. Maybe we should get the doctor out to have a look at you."

"There's no need, Iris, I'll be fine after I've had some rest."

"Then at least let me answer the phone for you," Iris insisted.

Dana sighed. "Yes, okay, then, thank you. But if Mr Johnson calls, put him straight through."

Iris smiled. "Of course. I'm sure he must be worried about you."

Dana blinked back her tears. "I doubt that."

"Don't be silly, the man is mad about you. Now when you've finished your coffee, try to get some rest; I always think it's the best medicine."

"Thanks, Iris," Dana said, feeling even more tearful at the woman's kindness.

"You're welcome." The housekeeper left, closing the door quietly behind her.

It was nearly six o'clock when Dana woke again and Iris was long gone. The tray had disappeared and in its place was a note of her phone messages. At the bottom Iris had written: Mr Johnson didn't call.

And, Dana realized with certainty, he wasn't going to.

CHAPTER
TWO

Sylvie was painting her toenails when the buzzer at the gate went. She continued painting and cursed under her breath when it buzzed again. Bloody Iris. It was an ongoing battle between them as to whose job it was to answer the door. When the buzzer went a third time, Sylvie carefully replaced the top on the nail polish and went into the hall. "Yes?"

"Hi, it's Ian Wilson. We spoke earlier on the phone?"

Sylvie frowned as she pressed the button to let the man in and went to open the door.

Ian parked his rusty Fiat Uno alongside Dana's BMW and jumped out. "Sylvie?" he asked, crossing the driveway.

She nodded.

"Nice to meet you."

She took his hand and stood back to let him in and then led him into the sitting room. "Like I said on the phone, I'm afraid there's no possibility of you seeing Dana today."

"That's fine," he said easily, folding his tall frame into an armchair. "I just thought you could give me a bit of background information."

"Is there any point? She hardly leaves her room these days so I can't see her agreeing to do any interviews, can you?" Sylvie sat down opposite him and crossed one long leg over the other. "You've had a wasted journey."

Ian's eyes rested appreciatively on her legs. "Oh, I wouldn't say that."

Sylvie rolled her eyes. "You are very forward, you know that?"

He grinned. "Well, I do work in publicity."

"And what exactly does that involve?"

"I make sure that everyone knows who Dana is, what she does, and then, hopefully, they buy her books."

"She's already known; her dad's a poet, you know."

"Conall O'Carroll, yes, I know. But I'm going to make her famous in her own right not just because she's somebody's daughter."

"And how do you do that?"

He shrugged. "Get her lots of interviews, make sure she goes to all the right parties, is seen with the right people — that sort of thing."

Sylvie's eyes widened. "And you do that for a living?"

He laughed. "It's not quite as easy as it sounds. So, tell me, what's wrong with Dana, or is she the kind of diva that regularly takes to her bed?"

"No way, she's usually a very hard worker but her husband walked out on her three weeks ago and she hasn't written a word since."

Ian's lips twitched. "I hope you're not as frank and open with everyone."

Sylvie's eyes narrowed. "I'm not stupid. Walter told me that I should tell you everything."

"Quite right too. So why did the husband leave?"

"I've no idea. I don't even know where he's gone, although he might be staying in their home in Cork. He loves it there."

"With his business in Dublin, that's unlikely. He's probably shacked up with a new girlfriend."

"Why do you assume that there's another woman?"

He shrugged. "There usually is."

Sylvie sighed. "I hope you're wrong. Whatever the reason, she's devastated. I can't remember her going so long without writing before. Gretta will not be impressed."

"Gretta?"

"She's Dana's editor in New York," Sylvie explained.

"Ah yes, Peyton Publishing. Walter's told me all about them. So does this Gretta know what's going on?"

"No. She's been calling every couple of days but Dana won't take her calls and it's hardly my place to tell her."

Ian frowned. "Walter needs to have a word with your boss. This is no time to make your publisher nervous."

Sylvie rolled her eyes. "She won't talk to Walter either and, honestly, you'd think it was my fault the way he goes on. He can be such a bitch sometimes."

"He has his moments. And she hasn't told you anything about what happened?" Ian pressed. He hadn't counted on having to deal with a recently separated author, but maybe he could turn it to their advantage. Journalists got bored publicizing new books but they loved a good human interest story, especially if it involved rich, attractive and flawed individuals.

Walter had given him a short, potted history on Dana and Gus and was pleased when Ian told him that he had already heard of the couple. Anyone who read the property and financial pages in the newspapers had heard of Gus Johnson and Tom Cleary. Their partnership was one of the leaders in Irish architecture and they were usually involved in all the most lucrative contracts. Dana wrote cheap chick-lit but was only published in the States and her main claim to fame had always been the fact that she was the estranged daughter of Conall O'Carroll. Once she got together with Gus, however, that had changed. They made a very attractive couple and were usually photographed when they attended charity events. Of course the caption would still say "Dana De Lacey, daughter of Conall O'Carroll". It was his job to change that.

"Are you listening to me?" Sylvie asked crossly.

He smiled apologetically. "Sorry, what was that?"

"I was saying that Dana isn't talking to me or anyone else. Mind you," she frowned, "Iris seems to have her ear."

"Iris?"

"The housekeeper," Sylvie explained. "She's worked here for years."

Ian brightened. "Is she here today?"

"In the kitchen, but you're wasting your time, she won't tell you a thing."

"You underestimate the Wilson power of persuasion." And with a wink, he was gone.

"Iris?"

The woman with the straight grey hair and equally straight back looked up from her ironing. "Yes, can I help you?"

Ian stretched out his hand and smiled. "Ian Wilson. How do you do?"

Iris watched him with sharp eyes as she briefly put her hand in his.

"I came to see Ms De Lacey but apparently she's not receiving visitors at the moment."

Iris said nothing and returned to her ironing.

"I wouldn't trouble her only Walter Grimes asked me to look in; it's about increasing her publicity in Ireland. That's my job, you see."

"Indeed." The housekeeper didn't look up.

He bit his lip; she was a tough nut, this one. "I hear she and Mr Johnson have separated. I was very sorry to hear that. They made a lovely couple."

The iron paused briefly but Iris remained silent.

"I'm sure the last thing that Dana wants at the moment is to discuss her private life so if I could just get a few facts about the break-up, I could issue a press release."

Iris set the iron down and looked up at him. "Why? What's it got to do with her work?"

"Not a lot," he agreed, "but the public always want to know the details of celebrities' lives."

"I'd say it's the reporters that want to know that information, not the public."

"Yes, perhaps you're right," he said, his smile growing more forced. "Nevertheless —"

"Are you asking me for information about Mr and Mrs Johnson?"

"Well, yes, some background would be great —"

"I can't help you, Mr Wilson."

"But, Iris —"

"Please see yourself out. I need to finish my work."

"Told you," Sylvie said, seeing his defeated expression.

"Don't worry, I don't give up that easily."

"What else can you do?" Sylvie retorted.

"Oh, I don't know, take her out on the town and get her photographed in one of those classy nightclubs."

Sylvie smirked. "You haven't even managed to get her out of her room yet."

"No, but you will."

"Me?"

"Yes. You're going to go up there and talk her into going out and I'll make sure that her picture appears in the paper the next day."

"And why on earth would she agree to that?" Sylvie stared at him as if he'd lost his mind.

"Because it would be a wonderful way to make her husband jealous."

"Maybe, but I doubt she'd agree."

"You doubt I'd agree to what?"

The two whirled around to see Dana standing in the doorway.

"Dana!" Sylvie jumped guiltily to her feet. "This is the PR consultant, Ian Wilson."

He smiled and reached out to shake her hand. "It's an absolute pleasure to meet you, Ms De Lacey."

She nodded curtly and then turned a questioning gaze on her personal assistant. "So what were you saying?"

"We weren't gossiping, Dana, honest," Sylvie said hurriedly.

"I was just saying that I thought a night out on the town was probably what you needed after your, er, break-up and it would kick-start our publicity campaign."

"How?" Dana asked.

"I'd make sure that you were photographed and that your picture appeared in one of the tabloids."

"I told him you weren't in the mood for socializing," Sylvie chipped in.

Dana looked from her back to Ian and smiled slowly. "I don't know. Maybe it's not such a bad idea. It's been ages since I went out without . . ." Dana faltered for a second, "since I had a night out. Where do you suggest we go?" she asked Ian.

"Lobo," he said without hesitation.

"Where?" Dana frowned.

"It's the club to go to if you want to be seen," Ian explained. "There are always photographers hanging around."

"That sounds perfect."

Ian grinned delightedly. "Really?"

Dana shrugged. "What have I got to lose?"

24

"You may be quizzed about Mr Johnson," he warned.

Dana stiffened. "What do you mean?"

"Well, they probably don't know that you've split up yet but they may, so you should be prepared."

Dana's face fell. "Maybe it's not such a good idea."

"It's only a matter of time before the press find out you're separated," Ian said gently. "If you tell them up front it will be easier. If they think there's more to it than that, they'll be nosing around both you and your husband until they get some kind of a story."

"But why would they be interested in us?" Dana protested, tearfully.

Ian smiled sadly. "This is Dublin. You know how tiny the celebrity circle is. The press are always looking for someone or something to talk about, and you and Mr Johnson are a very attractive and successful couple. Like it or not, Dana, you're news. You also have to remember that we're going to need the media if — no, when — we start to promote your book. We really can't afford to alienate them."

"Make the most of it," Sylvie urged, as doubt clouded Dana's face. "Just imagine Gus's reaction if he saw a photograph in the paper of you looking gorgeous and happy; that would show him."

Dana smiled. "Okay, then. You will come with me, won't you, Sylvie?"

"Try stopping me," her PA said eagerly.

"Thanks. Let's do dinner first; I'm going to need a couple of drinks going to face reporters."

"Make sure it's only a couple," Ian warned.

Dana's eyes narrowed. "I'm not stupid. I'm going upstairs for a bath, Sylvie. No calls."

"Walter really needs to talk to you," the girl called after her, "and Gretta was on again."

Dana, already halfway out of the door, didn't stop. "They'll just have to wait. I can't deal with them right now."

Ian rushed out into the hall after her. "I need to talk to you about some engagements I have lined up over the next few weeks."

"What?" Dana stopped.

"Walter said I should get started without you," he apologized.

She shook her head, her eyes sad. "I'm sorry, not now." And she hurried upstairs, leaving him to stare after her.

Still, at least he'd convinced her to go out tonight, that was something. Now he'd have to make sure that she was photographed. He stuck his head back into the office. "Nice to meet you, Sylvie."

"And you." Sylvie smiled happily.

"Make sure you go to Lobo, okay?"

"We'll be there," she promised, already wondering if there was an outfit in her wardrobe that would help land her a millionaire rock star or property developer.

Dana shut the bedroom door and leaned her head against it with a weary sigh. She'd rather stick pins in her eyes than go out tonight but she couldn't stay in her room forever and she did like the idea of showing Gus that she wasn't a crumbling heap without him —

except, of course, that she was. She walked over to the mirror and stared at her reflection. She barely recognized the dejected, mournful character that stared back at her. This wouldn't do. It wouldn't get her man back. Tonight she would go out and she would smile and look happy if it killed her. And tomorrow she would get back to work.

Striding purposefully into her wardrobe, Dana began to flick through the rails looking for something that would tell the world she was doing just fine without Gus Johnson. Tears rolled down her cheeks as she looked at dresses that reminded her of happier times. Tonight, she realized, was going to involve the performance of a lifetime.

"This is a great place, isn't it?" Sylvie said, looking around her, wide-eyed.

"The food is good too, you should try some." Dana looked pointedly at Sylvie's smoked-chicken salad that she had been pushing around her plate for the last ten minutes.

"I had a big lunch."

Dana sighed. "Sylvie, I know you want a man, but you really don't have to starve yourself to get him."

Sylvie reddened. "I just don't have a big appetite. I never have."

Dana was about to pursue the matter but she didn't really have the energy. Anyway, there was no point in trying to talk sense to Sylvie, she never listened.

An intelligent and pretty girl, Sylvie's only real flaw was that she was intent on finding a rich husband and seemed to think being incredibly skinny was the only way to reach her goal. Dana, who had never run after a man in her life, couldn't begin to understand it. She had dated lots of guys before Gus came along, men from all walks of life, but always on her terms. She'd had to be more discerning, of course, when she became rich as there were a lot of fortune-hunters around. She watched as Sylvie scanned the room with a calculating eye. Sadly, her PA might well be one of them.

Dana snuck a look at her watch. She was finding this evening hard going. Keeping a radiant smile on her face at all times was exhausting. A few acquaintances had already stopped by their table, some of them asking after Gus. "Aren't I allowed to have a girls' night out?" she'd trilled and changed the subject.

She forced a last piece of the delicious monkfish into her mouth and put down her knife and fork. "Shall we go?" she asked Sylvie, as it was clear that the girl wasn't planning to eat her meal and there was no point in even suggesting dessert.

"Sure —"

"Good evening, ladies, hope I'm not interrupting anything."

"Wally, what on earth are you doing in Dublin?" Dana smiled as her agent bent to kiss both her cheeks and then sat down beside her. Walter always let her know when he was coming to Dublin so it made her feel slightly uneasy that he'd just dropped in like this. Anyway, how the hell did he know she'd be here?

"Go and powder your nose, Sylvie, there's a good girl," he said sweetly, before telling a hovering waiter to bring him a gin and tonic. He waited until the PA had flounced off before turning back to his author. "Well, you don't look too bad, considering," he commented.

"Thanks a million," she said drily. "Please tell me you didn't come all the way from London just to check up on me."

"No, darling." He winked as the waiter set his drink down in front of him. "I've come to see my latest Irish author. He's suffering a little writer's block and so I decided to jump on a plane and come over and hold his hand." He grinned. "Not that it's a hardship; he's very easy on the eye. I'm taking him to dinner in some Japanese place in town."

"How did you know I'd be here?"

"Ian called me, of course."

She scowled. "I wish you wouldn't spy on me; there's no need."

"If you took my calls I wouldn't have to," he retorted.

"Sorry."

He patted her hand. "That's okay, darling. I understand this is a difficult time. Has Gus been in touch?"

Dana shook her head and reached for her wine glass. She was feeling dangerously close to tears.

"Bastard. I don't know how he could do this to you."

"That makes two of us," she said with a weak smile.

"You know work is the best medicine for a broken heart."

"Really? I find Chablis works quite well."

"Yes, but it also ruins your looks and addles the brain. Come on now, my darling, don't be defeated by this. Gus is gorgeous, it's true, but you have to move on. Trust me, I know all about it."

Dana squeezed his hand sympathetically. It was almost two years now since Wally had broken up with his partner. They had been together for an astounding twelve years when he discovered that Giles had been unfaithful at least twice. Even then, Walter was ready to forgive the love of his life but Giles decided to leave anyway. The agent hadn't dated since, and although he pretended interest in every gorgeous young man he met, Dana knew that it would be a long time before he trusted anyone again.

She could relate to that now as she never could before. "Oh, Wally, I'm not sure I want to go on without him."

"Balls," he retorted, then ignored the outraged look from the woman at the next table. "You can and you will. You were a star long before Gus Johnson came along and you'll still be one long after he's gone. No one can bring Dana De Lacey down."

"Thanks for the vote of confidence," she said, swallowing back her tears, "I just wish I could believe it."

He sat forward and took both her hands in his. "You know you must put all your feelings into this book. It will be hugely cathartic, make a damn good read, and," he added thoughtfully, "the whole ordeal may turn out to be an excellent way to promote the book."

"Wally!"

"Sorry, but I am your agent after all." He glanced at his watch, drained his glass and stood up. "Must fly. Try to enjoy yourself tonight, Dana. When Ian told me you were going out on the town I was so proud. I thought, 'That's my girl!' So go and show the world *and* your silly misguided husband exactly what you're made of. Understood?"

Dana nodded, clinging to him when he embraced her. "Thanks, Wally."

Sylvie slipped back into her chair and eyed Dana warily. "Is everything okay?"

Dana dabbed her eyes with a tissue. "Yeah, fine. Wally was in Dublin to see another author and he just dropped by to check up on me."

"Well, I hope it gets him off my back for a while," Sylvie said with feeling. "I take it you've told him all about Gus."

Dana smiled ruefully. "I hadn't intended to but he phoned rather late one night when I was halfway through my second bottle of wine. You can guess the rest. I must remember to put the answering machine on the next time I plan to get plastered."

Sylvie grinned. "Well, at least it was only Wally and he's your friend as well as your agent."

Dana sighed. "Yes, but he's also a businessman. I told him I wasn't writing and now he's going to be calling me on a daily basis to make sure I'm back working." Dana groaned. "Just like Gretta."

"To be honest, I think that's the mistake you've been making. It's because you wouldn't talk to them that they started to panic."

"That and the fact that this is the first time that, literally, I've been stuck for words."

"It's been a really difficult time." Sylvie's smile was sympathetic. "No one in your position would be able to work, never mind at something that requires creativity."

"Thanks, Sylvie, and I'm sorry I've made life so difficult for you these last few weeks."

"Don't worry about it, and don't worry about your writing either. Everything will be okay once you get back into a routine. I'm sure you'll fly through the book."

Dana said nothing. Once she would have agreed but the thought of getting back to work scared the hell out of her. Writing romantic novels had been easy when she was single and dating and then married to a man as gorgeous as Gus. But what would inspire her now? She felt as wrung-out as an old dishcloth and couldn't work up any enthusiasm for writing about passionate embraces or smouldering looks. How the hell was she going to finish The Mile-High Club?

"Dana?"

"Sorry." She snapped out of her reverie and realized that Sylvie was talking to her.

"I said shall we get the bill and head on to Lobo?"

"You know, I'm not sure that it's such a good idea after all."

Sylvie's eyes widened in horror. "Oh, no, you can't chicken out on me now. Ian will kill me!"

Dana stood up, suddenly feeling a hundred years old. "Okay, then, let's go and get this over with."

CHAPTER
THREE

The office of Johnson and Cleary Architects stood in a leafy laneway in Donnybrook, on the edge of Dublin city centre. It was a Victorian red-brick townhouse that looked exactly like its neighbours, but that's where the similarity ended. Gus and his partner, Tom, had designed an extension to the rear that was a masterpiece of glass and steel. It allowed light to flood into every corner of the house, giving it an airy and sophisticated feel that, strangely, worked with the older features of the building. It had cost them enormously in terms of time and money but it had won the men their first award and was an instant advertisement for their talent at mixing old with new, maximizing space and creating individualistic and unique spaces.

The boardroom Gus and Tom now sat in was equally impressive, with panelling in pale oak, a matching table that easily sat twelve, and chairs upholstered in soft, black leather. There was a small sofa and coffee table at the end of the room and a tall vase of lilies in one corner. Some pencil drawings of Johnson and Cleary's most impressive designs were the room's only adornment.

Tom Cleary called the meeting to an end and stood up. "I need to run; I'm having lunch with a client. Carla, can you type up those letters and get them out in this afternoon's post?"

"Sure." The girl stood too and looked down at Gus Johnson from under her long, sooty lashes. "What about you, Gus, are you going out to lunch or shall I get you something?"

He smiled absently. "No thanks, Carla. I have to go into town so I'll pick something up while I'm out."

"Oh, lord, she's got her sights set on you," Tom groaned when the young girl had sashayed out of the room. He pointed his finger at his business partner. "And don't even think about it."

Gus raised an eyebrow. "Why not? She's free, I'm free and she's got a great —"

"Future in this office," Tom cut in. "She's the best PA we've ever had and you're not free — not properly."

The smile faded from his partner's face. "Don't worry, I've had enough of women to last me a lifetime. Anyway, she's a bit young."

"That obviously doesn't bother her." Tom's eyes slid to the newspapers spread out on the coffee table at the other end of the room. "Did you see the photo?"

Gus's eyes followed his and his expression sobered. "Yeah."

"She looks well," Tom remarked lightly. "Not too devastated, thankfully."

Gus drummed his fingers on the table and stared straight ahead. "No."

"Well, that's good, isn't it?" Tom said, slightly impatient. "You wouldn't want her to be miserable."

Gus got to his feet, still not looking at his partner. "Of course not."

Tom glanced at his watch, and cursing under his breath he picked up his briefcase and headed for the door. "By the way, Ashling wants to know if you want to spend the weekend with us. She has this image of you living on crisps and chocolate and drinking too much."

Gus laughed. "Tell her thanks but I won't be in Dublin this weekend."

Tom paused, his eyes narrowing. "Oh? Where are you off to?"

"I've just got a few things to take care of," Gus said vaguely.

"Oh?" Tom was looking at him worriedly.

"It's nothing to do with work," Gus promised.

"I didn't think it was." When Gus didn't offer any more explanation, Tom sighed and turned to leave. "Gotta go, see you later."

Left in the conference room alone, Gus picked up the phone and dialled. "Hello? May I speak to Walter Grimes, please?"

Judy Higgins was sitting in Hannah's Hair & Beauty Salon in Wexford getting her highlights done when one of the girls handed her a selection of newspapers and magazines. "Thanks very much." She smiled at the girl and started to flick through one of the tabloids. She paused on the Social & Personal page to study the images of Ireland's rich and famous, and laughed when she saw a familiar face. "Oh, Hannah, look! That's my friend, Dana O'Carroll; we went to school together."

The hairdresser leaned over her shoulder to take a closer look. "She looks vaguely familiar. Is she in one of the soaps?"

"No, she's a novelist. Her pen name is Dana De Lacey."

"Is she the one who's married to that hunky architect?"

"That's right. Gus Johnson. He's gorgeous, isn't he?"

The hairdresser looked back at the picture. "She's quite well preserved but I suppose that's what money does for you."

Judy made a face. "Yes, you wouldn't think we were the same age, would you?" She glanced at her reflection which showed a friendly-looking, mumsy kind of figure — someone you'd trust to mind your kids or run the cake stall at the school fair.

"Looks aren't everything," Hannah said wisely. "She doesn't seem to be so lucky in love."

Judy frowned when she read the caption above the photo: LOVE ON THE ROCKS. "What on earth —"

She quickly read the short paragraph beneath.

Romance author Dana De Lacey was out on the town last night but without handsome husband, renowned architect Gus Johnson. When pressed, Dana admitted that they were taking some time apart, but would say no more.

"This is just terrible," Judy murmured. She'd always thought that her friend was very happily married and when they'd last talked, only a few weeks ago, everything had seemed to be fine.

"So, are you two close?" Hannah asked.

Judy sighed and shook her head. "Not really. Well, you know how it is; life takes you in different directions. Dana went to university in Dublin after school and never came back. I used to visit her a lot in the early days but then I got married and the kids came along and we sort of drifted apart. Now we just talk on the phone from time to time."

The hairdresser's eyes met hers in the mirror. "Maybe now would be a good time to call."

Judy nodded slowly. "Yes, I think you're right."

Iris McCarthy went to 9 a.m. Mass and, as she did every morning, she lit a candle for her late mother, father and brother before making her way briskly to the Johnsons' house in Ranelagh. Collecting the post and newspapers from the letterbox, Iris let herself in and went straight through to the kitchen. As she took off her coat and hung it on the hook, she noted that the room was immaculate. A sure sign that Mrs Johnson probably hadn't eaten — yet again. Iris decided that once she'd finished the dusting and cleaned the four bathrooms, she'd make some breakfast and take it up. Mrs Johnson would pretend to be annoyed but she'd probably eat a little of it, which was something.

An hour later she took a tray with a plate of fluffy scrambled eggs, toast and a pot of coffee upstairs, the newspapers clamped tightly under one arm. Outside the master suite, Iris shifted the tray slightly so she could knock on the door. Going in, she nodded in the direction of the bed but kept her eyes discreetly averted. "Good morning, Mrs Johnson. I've brought you some breakfast."

"Iris, you know I only ever take coffee," Dana protested mildly, emerging from under the covers and stretching.

"But you've hardly eaten a thing in days and you can't possibly work on an empty stomach," Iris pointed out.

Dana frowned. "Did Walter tell you that?"

Iris sniffed. "I'm sure I don't take orders from the likes of him."

Dana grinned as Iris set the food down. The eggs did look delicious, just the way her mother used to make them. "Believe it or not, I went out to dinner last night," she informed the housekeeper. "Sylvie and I went to l'Ecrivain and then on to a club. If Ian Wilson has done his job properly, we should be in one of those papers."

"That's nice," Iris said, not convinced that it was.

Dana quickly flicked through the papers until she came to the photo and then, with a snort, she handed it to Iris. "It's not the best of photos."

"You look lovely," Iris said truthfully and then frowned as she read the piece under the photo. "But why are they making such personal comments? What has your marriage got to do with your work?"

"Ah, good question! Apparently any publicity is good publicity."

Iris gave a sniff of disapproval. "You and Mr Johnson should be allowed to sort out your problems in private."

"What makes you think we're going to?" Dana challenged. She knew the woman had a soft spot for Gus and probably thought that he had left for good reason.

Iris smiled as she hung up Dana's clothes from the night before. "You belong together," she said simply.

"He doesn't seem to think so," Dana said miserably.

"I'm sure he'll come round. Now, Mrs Johnson, if there's nothing else I'll get back to work."

"There is one thing."

"Yes?"

"Please stop calling me Mrs Johnson. It's Dana from now on, okay?"

The housekeeper smiled sadly. "If that's what you'd prefer."

When she was gone, Dana tossed the paper on to the floor and reached for the plate of eggs. They tasted as good as they looked and with a pang of guilt she realized she hadn't even thanked Iris. She'd better apologize later for her grumpiness. As she munched on the lightly buttered toast her eyes were drawn back to the newspaper. She had to admit that Ian Wilson had done a good job. She looked quite good and reasonably happy. It would be great if Gus saw it. He probably thought she was devastated that he'd left, but this picture told a different story. Okay, it wasn't true, but he didn't know that.

Feeling slightly less humiliated and miserable than she had since Gus had gone, Dana decided that she'd try to write a few pages after her shower.

Before all of this madness started, *The Mile High Club* had been going really well. She remembered how caught up she'd been in the novel that night Gus had dropped his bombshell, and yet she hadn't written a single word since. Ridiculous, she decided, sipping her coffee thoughtfully. She couldn't turn into the kind of pathetic creature that fell to pieces over a man. "You already have," she said aloud, thinking of how she'd been locking herself away from the world. Well, no more. Last night hadn't been easy, but it would get better. The more she smiled and partied, the less people would pity her. And Gus would realize that she could manage just fine without him.

An hour later, dressed in loose cotton trousers and a vest top, she went down to her office, threw open the french windows that led into her beloved garden, and sat down at her desk. She was glad that Sylvie was at the dentist today; she didn't need an audience. She felt nervous enough as it was. Switching on her laptop, she searched for the *The Mile High Club* file and decided to print off what she'd written so far. While the printer was shooting out pages, she went into the kitchen in search of more coffee, and found Iris cleaning out the cupboards.

"Oh, Mrs John — er, can I get you something?"

"That's okay, Iris," she said, nodding towards the coffee pot, "I just need a refill." She quickly filled a mug and headed for the door. "And, Iris? Thanks for the brekkie, it was lovely."

Iris smiled. "I'm glad you liked it."

Armed with her coffee and sunglasses, Dana took the manuscript out to the garden and settled herself in a comfy sun chair. After taking a few moments to appreciate the warm summer sun on her face and the scent of roses in the air, she put on her glasses and started to read. Her confidence and excitement built with each page she read; this was even better than she remembered. When she finished — almost an hour later — she almost ran back inside, sat down at her desk and pulled her laptop towards her. She stared at the screen, her fingers hovering over the keys.

Bobbi couldn't wait any longer and taking out her mobile phone, she called Victor. His answering service answered and she frowned in irritation. "Hi, it's just me, Bobbi. Give me a call when you get a chance"

"Crap," Dana muttered and deleted the line. This was a cosmopolitan woman not some sad, silly girl whose whole life revolved around a man.

Victor hadn't called in three days, Bobbi realized, but then she wasn't that easy to contact given she spent most of the day in the air. Having said that, he could have left a message.

"No! What's wrong with you?" she chided herself in frustration. Bobbi Blackwell, the dynamic, sexy pilot, had turned into a paranoid wimp; how had that happened? As if she didn't know. Dana pressed delete again and stared at the screen, willing inspiration to come. After a few more pathetic attempts she cursed, stood up and walked over to the window. Maybe it was just the warm weather that was making it hard for her to settle down to work, she reasoned. It was a beautiful, balmy day and her garden looked luscious and tempting. Apart from the noise of a distant lawn mower there was only the buzz of insects flying among the roses and carnations and the many other more exotic blooms that she couldn't name. Creating a vibrant, colourful garden had always been one of her top priorities when she and Gus had bought this property. Sadly her fingers were far from green and her husband's were even worse so she had hired someone else to do the work and create her dream.

Dana turned back to her desk but couldn't bring herself to sit down. Perhaps a swim would help, she thought, brightening at the prospect. She quickly made her way down through the garden, and skirting the pool she went into the small, single-storey building behind it. Here was housed a bathroom, Gus's exercise equipment and a wardrobe with swimming costumes and towels.

Dana changed into a black one-piece and then turned to the mirror to pin up her hair. She stopped in her tracks at the sight of Gus's old trainers by the door. He'd obviously forgotten to check the pool-house when he was clearing out his stuff. She opened his drawer and, right enough, it was full of his things. An old razor, some eye drops, a comb, a few crumpled business cards, some loose change and a burgundy silk tie that he'd been complaining Iris had misplaced.

She smiled as she remembered the evening he'd joked that maybe Iris had nicked it to give to a boyfriend.

"One of the blokes from the church choir, I'll bet," he'd said, making Dana laugh, "or perhaps it's the parish priest himself."

"Priests don't wear ties," Dana had pointed out.

"Ah." He'd tapped the side of his nose. "Not when they're working they don't, but who knows what they get up to on their days off?"

She folded the tie carefully and put it back in the drawer. Then, taking a large fluffy towel from the cupboard she went out to the pool and dived in, gasping in shock at how cold it was. As she treaded water, allowing her body to become accustomed to the temperature, she looked up at the windows of her home. Her eyes were automatically drawn to Gus's office and she felt a pang of physical pain. He'd often worked from home and although he would be locked in his office and she in hers, she'd liked knowing he was there. She'd kept out of that room since he'd left. Somehow it felt like she'd be invading his privacy even though it was now empty of all his belongings. But, in truth, the whole house felt empty and slightly alien without him. Dana often found herself creeping around it like an unwelcome stranger.

Feeling the dark cloud of depression threatening to descend on her once more, Dana began to swim as if her life depended on it. She swam up and down the pool until her limbs trembled with the effort. When she finally stopped for a rest it was to find Iris standing by the pool, a towel in her hands. "There's a call for you, Mrs — I mean, Dana."

Dana's face lit up as she climbed out, took the towel and wrapped it around her. "Is it Gus?"

The housekeeper's eyes filled with pity. "I'm sorry, no."

"Then who?" Dana demanded crossly trying to mask her disappointment.

"Hi, Dana."

"Judy?"

"I just read about you and Gus in the paper and I had to call to make sure you were okay."

Dana sighed as she sank into a chair, her body still damp. "I'm fine."

"Are you sure? I just couldn't believe it. I thought you two were happy."

"Me too," Dana admitted, tears pricking her eyes.

"But what happened?" Judy persisted.

"He said he wasn't happy any more; that our marriage hadn't turned out the way he'd expected."

"That's it?" Judy's voice went up an octave.

"Pretty much," Dana said tightly. She didn't want to talk about what Gus had said that night to anyone, particularly not Judy Higgins. "Look, Judy, I can't really talk right now; I have someone with me. I'll call you back, okay?"

Judy was not so easily put off. "Soon, Dana, okay?"

"Yeah, Judy, soon. Thanks for calling. Bye." After she hung up, Dana stood up and, wrapping the towel tightly around her, went into the house. She was halfway across the hall when Iris appeared.

"I'm so sorry, Dana, I didn't mean . . ." she trailed off.

Dana smiled faintly. "To get my hopes up? Don't worry about it, Iris. He's not going to ring and it's about time I got used to the idea."

CHAPTER
FOUR

"You know, you were the last person I expected to be having a drink with on a Saturday night," Walter said. They were sitting in a quiet corner of the Donovan bar in Brown's Hotel in Mayfair and though it was busy, the conversation was muted and the privacy absolute.

Gus smiled slightly. "Thank you for agreeing to see me, Wally."

Walter frowned at him over his glass. "Only my friends call me Wally."

"I'm sorry you no longer consider me one."

"Are you surprised? I mean, what on earth were you thinking of, Gus? Walking out on Dana, after all this time! What's all that about? Is it another woman?" His lips twitched. "Or man?"

Gus shook his head. "Neither."

"Well, come on, then. You didn't come all the way to London just to sit looking at me."

"I wanted to ask you about Dana. About what she was like before I came along. What she was like when you first met."

Walter shook his head. "You answer my questions and then, maybe, I'll answer yours."

Gus shifted uncomfortably and pulled at his collar. His drink had sat untouched in front of him but now he picked it up and turned it round and round in his hands. "Recently I found out something about Dana's past that, quite frankly, came as a shock."

Walter leaned closer. "What?"

Gus shook his head. "I'm sorry, I can't tell you that."

"Did you tell her?"

"No. I gave her several opportunities to tell me but she said nothing."

"Why didn't you just come straight out and ask her?" Walter asked.

"Maybe I should have," Gus admitted. "But to be honest I was angry. How could she keep this from me? We've been together more than six years and she's never said a word."

"Well, you said it's from her past." Walter shrugged. "We all have skeletons that we like to keep in the cupboard."

Gus said nothing for a moment and then he looked up and met Walter's eyes. "Not all of it was in her past."

Walter sighed impatiently. "I understand your reluctance to talk about what are, obviously, very private matters, Gus, but I don't see how we can have a two-way conversation if I haven't the slightest idea what you are talking about."

"Okay, okay." Gus drained his glass and set it back on the table between them. "Did you know that Dana had a child?"

Walter's eyes widened. "No, that's impossible."

"It's true. I've read a letter that Dana wrote to him. There's absolutely no doubt it was to her son."

"I can't believe it," Walter said faintly.

"It's true," Gus said grimly and then signalled the passing waiter to bring them both refills. "I thought you might have known about it."

"I didn't, honestly."

"I believe you. In a way I suppose it would have annoyed me more if she had told you and not me. But, like I said, you knew her for, what, thirteen years or more before I came along?"

Walter nodded. "But there was never any mention of a child."

"Maybe he lived with her parents."

Walter shrugged. "It's possible, I suppose. I only ever met Dana in Dublin and rarely at her flat, and she hardly ever talked about her family."

"She must have said something," Gus pressed.

Walter smiled at the young waiter who'd brought their drinks and then sank back in his chair. "The very first time I met her she told me she wanted to write under the name De Lacey. I didn't really question her decision; O'Carroll was quite an ordinary name and Dana De Lacey sounded more glamorous and would look better on a front cover."

"So she never even told you who her father was?" Gus said incredulously.

"No. I only found out when her first contract with Peyton Publishing was announced. One of the Irish papers picked up on the fact that she was Irish and made the connection. I was a bit annoyed at first, to be honest. I might have been able to use it when I was negotiating the advance or, at the very least, used it to publicize her debut in the States. If there's one thing Americans love it's Irish literary figures."

"So you confronted her?"

"I asked her about it and she just said that she was estranged from her father and had no wish to ever have her name linked with his."

"There's no way she could have prevented that."

"No and when this book is published in Ireland, it will probably get worse."

"Did you tell her that?" Gus asked.

"I tried, but you know what she's like. She just clams up any time I mention the man."

"And Gretta is definitely going to use *The Mile High Club* to launch the Passion imprint?"

"She'd be mad not to. Your wife is talented, beautiful and she'll be an excellent ambassador for the brand." He sighed. "And now, it seems, she has a few skeletons in the cupboard. She's a chat-show host's dream."

Gus was silent for a moment, staring moodily into his drink.

"Do you know when she had this child or have any idea what age he is?"

Gus shook his head. "You've known her for twenty years, so I suppose he's more than that."

"She probably got into trouble when she was a schoolgirl, poor kid. Daddy wouldn't have been too pleased with that; it's probably why she left."

"Did you know Dana when her mother died?" Gus asked.

Walter screwed up his face as he tried to remember. "No," he said at last. "We had talked on the phone a few times but her mother died before I had secured the Peyton contract."

"So you weren't at the funeral," Gus said, deflated.

"Had it happened a few months later, no doubt I would have been. Sorry, I'm not much help, am I? What will you do now?"

"Forget about it and her," Gus said grimly, taking a long drink. "And get on with my life."

"Why don't you just talk to Dana?"

"I've been trying to talk to her for months," Gus snapped. "No, make that years."

Walter looked at him thoughtfully. "Then maybe you should talk to her brother."

Gus lowered his glass and stared at the agent. "Ed? I wouldn't even know where to find him."

Walter's eyes twinkled. "Now that I *can* tell you. He lives in their family home in Wexford."

Ian Wilson sat in his office looking at the long list of calls and emails he had to return. He should get stuck in but he couldn't get Dana De Lacey out of his head — or her beautiful, blonde assistant, for that matter. Walter Grimes was nagging him to organize some publicity for the author but it was next to impossible while the woman remained holed up in her room. He'd thought the night she'd gone to Lobo with Sylvie had marked the end of her reclusion but it seemed the woman was now worse than ever.

He picked up the phone and called Sylvie, hoping for some news. Even if there wasn't, it would be nice to hear her voice.

"Hello?"

"Hello, Sylvie. It's Ian Wilson."

"Oh, hi, Ian."

From the despondent tone of Sylvie's voice, it was clear that things hadn't improved. He could imagine her sitting at her desk, full lips pouting as she brushed her fringe out of her troubled blue eyes and stretched those long, lovely legs in front of her. He sighed.

"Ian?"

"Oh, sorry, Sylvie. I was just wondering if Dana was available for a quick chat."

Sylvie gave a short laugh. "No, sorry, she's not."

"Tell me, is it just me she won't talk to or is she like this with everyone?"

"Don't take it personally, it's everyone, and I'm the one who has to deal with the fallout."

"Poor you," he said sympathetically. "So I take it there's no sign of her and the husband getting back together."

"He's the one person who hasn't called," Sylvie confided.

"Is she writing at all?"

"Are you kidding?"

Ian closed his eyes and massaged the bridge of his nose. "That's not good."

"Tell me about it."

"Perhaps if you and I put our heads together we could think of some way of getting her out of this rut. We could meet up later and discuss it over a drink."

"If this is your roundabout way of asking me out, Ian Wilson, you can forget it."

He laughed. "Oh, well, it was worth a try."

"Goodbye, Ian."

She might have turned him down but he could hear the smile in her voice. He'd wear her down. It was only a matter of time. "Bye, gorgeous."

Sylvie hummed to herself as she took the bus home later that day. There was no reason for her good humour. Her day had been as boring as all the others lately and Dana's house was not a pleasant place to work at the moment, given it was as silent as the grave. The only highlight had been the call from Ian Wilson. He was a cocky, big-headed guy but at the same time he made her smile and he was quite attractive in an obvious, all-American sort of way. Pity he was broke. Not that you'd know that from the way he went on, but his car gave him away. Ian wasn't the successful businessman he presented himself as.

"Hi, Mum, I'm home," she called as she put the key in the door and let herself into the modest but pretty little house in Ringsend.

"Hello, love, I'm in here."

Sylvie followed the voice and found her mother in the kitchen, ironing and watching *Richard and Judy*.

"You're just in time for the book club slot," her mother told her with a smile.

"How's Dad?" Sylvie asked as she threw her jacket on the back of a chair and put on the kettle.

"Not bad at all today. Dana?"

Sylvie rolled her eyes. "The same."

"The poor girl."

"I'm sorry but I'm finding it harder and harder to be sympathetic."

"That's a bit hard, love," Maureen Parker said, one eye on the television. "It can't be easy for her."

"Oh, come on, Mum, give me a break. She has a fabulous house in Dublin, a farm in Cork, a wonderful career and — if she got her act together — she'd be published in Ireland and the UK too. Have you any idea how long she's dreamed of that? And now," she threw up her hands, "now she's just throwing it all away."

Maureen set down the iron and looked at her daughter. "You sound a little bit jealous."

"I'm not." Sylvie threw herself down on the small sofa and stared sullenly at the TV.

"She may have money, love, but she's approaching middle age and she's just lost the love of her life. Money is no fun if you've no one to share it with. And," she shook a finger at her daughter, "you just remember that your health is your wealth."

"Yeah, I'm sorry, Mum."

"I know, love." Maureen turned to the kettle and made a pot of tea. "Take your dad in a cuppa and have a chat; that will cheer you up."

Sylvie smiled. "Okay. Where's Billy?"

"Down on the green playing football."

"Shouldn't he be studying?"

It was her mother's turn to roll her eyes. "He's been at it all afternoon; I threw him out in the end."

"He has to study hard, Mum. It's important that he does well in his exams or he won't get a good job."

Maureen poured the tea, shaking her head sadly. "You have got to stop worrying about money, love; we'll manage."

"Will we? If Dana doesn't start writing again soon, I could be out of a job. How on earth will we be able to afford to pay the mortgage, the insurance and all the other bills and be ready for the next brick wall that's around the corner?"

Maureen handed her two mugs. "We'll cope."

Sylvie took the mugs and crossed the hall to their living room that now served as her father's bedroom. He had been only forty-two when he was diagnosed with rheumatoid arthritis and though it had progressed slowly in the first ten years, the last ten had been a lot harder. As it became more difficult for him to walk, William was forced to retire and when the stairs became too challenging, Maureen had moved their bed downstairs.

"Hey, Dad."

William Parker opened his eyes and smiled. "Hello, love, have you had a good day?"

"Not bad." Sylvie set down the mugs on the bedside table and bent to hug him. "How are you feeling?"

"Grand, grand."

"You always say that," Sylvie complained, taking her mug and curling up at the end of the bed.

He chuckled. "Do I?"

"Is the new medication working any better?" she persisted.

"Aye, I think so. My stomach doesn't feel as sick as it did on those other yokes."

"Good. Did Amy come today?" Amy was the physiotherapist who came in once a week to help her father exercise his swollen limbs.

"She did and, Lord, that girl's a slave-driver."

"You're mad about her."

He smiled. "She's a good kid."

"And your knees?" Sylvie asked. Her father's knee joints had proved to be the most swollen and painful of all in the last couple of months and the GP was talking about joint replacements.

"Forget about my bloody knees and tell me about your day," he said impatiently.

"Not much to tell," she said, ignoring the flash of temper. He was a saint, really, putting up with all this pain and she knew that the confines of these four walls got him down a lot. He had been a very active man in his youth but now it was an achievement for him to make it as far as the car for his hospital visits. "Dana's still spending most of the day in her room," she told him. "And I'm still getting my ear blasted off because she won't take any calls. Apart from opening the post and answering emails, I just file my nails or play solitaire all day."

"What was the man thinking of?" William shook his head in wonder. "She's such a pretty little thing."

Sylvie laughed. "Don't let Mum hear you talk like that or she'll kick you in your bad ankle."

He glanced down at his wasted body. "It's not as though I could ever get up to anything, is it?"

"Dana wouldn't look twice at you anyway," Sylvie said, swallowing back tears. "She's into the tall, fair and handsome type."

William put a hand up to touch his bald head. "Oh, well, two out of three . . ."

Sylvie finished her tea and stood up. "I'd better go and change."

"Going out tonight, then?"

She shook her head, laughing. "No, I need to clean the car, inside and out. Mind you, it's probably the dirt that's holding it together."

His face darkened. "I know it's an awful heap. I wish we could afford to replace it."

"It's not so bad," Sylvie said cheerfully. "It gets us around."

He stretched out a swollen hand to her. "You're a good girl, Sylvie."

She dropped a quick kiss on his thickened knuckles. "Call if you need anything."

CHAPTER
FIVE

"I'm not going this year," Gus announced when Tom reminded him that the charity fashion show they were sponsoring was on in the Shelbourne the following weekend.

"You don't have a choice," Tom retorted. They were having Sunday lunch in Tom and Ashling's kitchen and Tom swallowed his irritation with a mouthful of roast chicken, washing it down with some chilled Chardonnay.

"I went to the Architects' Dinner," Gus reminded him. "It's your turn."

"That's not fair, you know I only missed it because Ashling wasn't well."

"Yeah, sorry." Gus shot Ashling an apologetic smile.

"I know you're not really in the mood for socializing," Ashling said gently and pushed the dish of garlic and cream potatoes towards him, "but it is for a good cause and you don't have to stay for the whole evening."

Tom opened his mouth to protest but shut it again when his wife shot him a look.

Gus capitulated. "Okay, then, if you think it's important."

Tom reached over to take back the dish of potatoes. "People are paying five hundred euros a plate, Gus. I think the least we can do is show up."

"I just hate the fact that there are going to be reporters there," Gus admitted. "Now that Dana's made it public that we've separated, they're bound to want to talk to me."

"I'll stay by your side all night and kick them in the shins if they get too close," Ashling promised.

"And what about me?" her husband protested.

"You can go off and chat up the clients."

Tom reached over to kiss his wife and pat her bump. "Don't you worry about him. You just look after our son and heir."

"Or daughter," she pointed out.

"I don't care which," Tom said happily.

"Ah, now, if you two are going to get all sloppy, I'm off," Gus warned.

"I will not apologize for being a happy family man just because you've decided to become a bachelor again," Tom told him.

"Leave it, Tom. You know Gus doesn't want to talk about it."

Tom topped up his glass and, after a nudge from Ashling, topped up Gus's too. "Yeah, sure, I mean why would he want to tell his best friend what the hell he's playing at?"

"Let's just finish lunch and decide what movie we're going to see," Ashling suggested.

Gus wiped his mouth on a napkin and stood up. "You know, I don't think I'll join you after all. I've a lot of paperwork to catch up on."

"Oh, Gus, please don't go. I hate it when you two fight."

Gus came around the table to kiss Ashling. "We don't fight, do we, Tom?"

"Course not."

"Thanks for a wonderful lunch, Ashling. Take care of yourself and Buster."

"You can't keep calling it Buster; it could be a girl!" she protested, laughing.

Gus winked back. "It could be twins."

She shuddered. "Please. I still haven't got my head around delivering one, never mind two."

Tom stood up and led the way out to the hall. "I'll walk you out."

They ambled out towards the low-slung sports car.

"Are you sure everything's okay?" he asked.

"Fine."

Tom turned to face him. "I wish you'd trust me a bit more. How many years have we known each other? Ten?"

"Twelve," Gus told him.

"Yeah, and you're like a brother to me." Tom shifted from one foot to the other. "We'd like you to be godfather."

Gus stared at him. "Really?"

Tom nodded. "Of course, who else would we ask?"

"I'm honoured, really I am." Gus patted his friend's shoulder awkwardly. "Don't worry about me, mate. I promise that if I need to talk, you'll be the first one I call." He grinned. "Well, you or your wife."

Tom pushed him towards the car and turned to go back inside. "See you tomorrow."

Gus felt fed up as he drove back to his new home. He'd always loved his time with Tom and Ashling but now it was proving hard to be with them. Their happiness was painful to witness and made him ache for Dana.

He turned into the car park of the small, city centre hotel that was currently his home. Though he had a large suite with every facility he could ask for, he was already tired of living in such impersonal surroundings. He needed to find somewhere more permanent but it seemed such a huge step and he baulked at taking it. He knew that his life with Dana was over; that though he loved her as much as ever, he could never trust her again. But he couldn't move on, he realized, until he talked to her brother. Though Walter had been able to tell him where Ed was, Gus hadn't managed to talk to him yet. It seemed Ed was a photographer who travelled a lot and would be out of the country for several weeks.

In the privacy of his suite, Gus threw his jacket over the back of a chair and walked to the floor-to-ceiling window that gave him a panoramic view of Dublin. He stared out at the vibrant city, its streets awash with people in summer clothes and sunglasses enjoying a relaxed Sunday afternoon. The Liffey sparkled in the distance but the beautiful view somehow served only to make him feel even more isolated.

He had lived alone for nine years — well, most of the time — before meeting Dana and he'd liked it that way. But within two months of meeting her, he'd moved into her house in Rathgar and the following year they'd bought their first home together in Ranelagh.

Dana had loved the house the minute she'd set eyes on it whereas Gus approved of it in a more objective way. With his professional hat on, he knew it was a good investment and, more important, in an excellent location. It was a lovely old house that had been built in the late nineteenth century. The previous owners had restored all its original features with taste and sensitivity, and yet he couldn't quite manage to fall in love with it. It was too big and too grand to feel like a family home, but their farmhouse in west Cork was a different matter altogether.

A city boy through and through, Gus had nevertheless been completely blown away by the wild beauty of Cork. As the taxi drove him from the airport out to Bantry, he had become more bewitched with every passing mile. Given it was a miserable winter's day, that said a lot. When the driver had finally turned into the lane and he caught his first glimpse of the plain stone building with the stunning view of Bantry Bay in the background, Gus decided to beg Dana De Lacey to sell him the property. Before he even put pencil to paper, ideas were crowding his head of how it could be restored and embellished to maximize the views and create an idyll that would inspire creativity. It quickly became a labour of love when he fell for the owner as hard as he had for her house.

It still stunned Gus when he thought about how quickly they'd clicked. They could discuss politics, have a laugh and talk avidly about every issue under the sun. At the same time, there was an unmistakable frisson between them; their attraction to each other was almost palpable. Gus had just turned thirty-four when they met and had been in enough relationships to realize that this was the real thing. He had proposed within weeks, seeing no point in wasting time, and, happily, Dana had agreed.

Gus had hoped that they would spend most of their time in Bantry; it was the perfect place for Dana to write and he could easily commute to work in Dublin a couple of days a week. But Dana had other ideas. She loved the farmhouse, he didn't doubt that, but there was something about the solitude that seemed to unnerve her. After a couple of days there she would start to get restless and edgy and finally find some excuse to return to Dublin. He had accepted this without giving it much thought, but lately it had occurred to him that perhaps it was being alone with him that was the problem.

In hindsight, though, he wondered if the rural location just reminded her too much of home and her unhappy childhood. He didn't know much about Dana's family and she'd never told him the reason they were estranged. He had broached the subject several times in the early days but Dana made it clear that she found it too painful to talk about. He was aware that she'd visited a psychiatrist and had taken antidepressants for a time so he left it at that. Rightly or wrongly he'd allowed her to pull a veil over her previous life in Wexford, and he put his efforts into making her life with him as happy as was humanly possible.

He'd thought he'd succeeded but he'd been fooling himself, or, rather, she'd made a fool of him. When they made love, Gus was sure that she cared as much about him as he did about her. He felt her give herself totally to him in those intimate moments and he would forget everyone and everything when she was in his arms. It had been that way right up until the end. He remembered vividly the last night he'd held her in his arms. It had been the day he'd found the letters; the day when everything had changed.

They had gone to a party later and he had watched her move easily through the room, like a beautiful butterfly flitting from flower to flower. There had been little opportunity for them to talk and he'd been glad of that. He'd had so much information to process, his head was reeling. He'd watched her all night, wondering how he could have lived with her all these years and not really known her.

When they got home late that night, she had turned to him in bed and he had taken her quickly, almost violently. At first she'd been surprised by his roughness, then she responded with passion. How could she possibly fake this? But how could she possibly love him and be so duplicitous at the same time?

As they'd lain together he'd held her body close to his and wished he'd never seen the bloody letters.

He'd been in the garage hunting for the old jacket he wore when he washed the cars, and had come across a large box; it must have been sitting there since they'd moved in. It was probably just old manuscripts — Dana, superstitiously, liked to keep hard copies. He was about to dump it in the bin but then realized he should check it first, in case there were any personal papers that needed shredding.

When he tore the box open it was to find that it was full of press cuttings and old publicity shots of Dana, with a variety of hairstyles dating back to long before he'd met her. Chuckling, he flicked through them, wondering which would be the best one to produce at a dinner party to embarrass her. As he reached the bottom of the box, his fingers closed around a thick envelope. Pulling it out he frowned when he saw that it was sealed. Hesitating for only a moment — it wasn't addressed to anyone and was probably just more photos — he opened it and pulled out several smaller envelopes. None of them were addressed and they were all sealed. He stared at them, wondering what he had stumbled on. These hadn't got here by accident. They had been deliberately hidden and they must have been hidden by his wife.

He tried to push away the feeling of unease that was gripping him; there was sure to be an innocent explanation. Perhaps they were love letters from an old boyfriend. If they were, Dana obviously hadn't been interested in this rather old-fashioned suitor or she would have opened them. Of course they didn't necessarily have to be from her past. Dana was a very attractive woman and Gus had seen plenty of men eyeing her up. But just because someone fancied her, didn't mean she returned the feelings; it didn't mean she was guilty of anything.

Curiosity mixed with jealousy got the better of him and he opened one of the envelopes, taking care to ease up the flap without tearing it. There were two sheets of heavy, cream paper inside and he slid them out, hesitating before unfolding them. It would be an invasion of privacy to read the contents but there was no way he could stop himself now. He smoothed out the pages and read quickly. The first thing that surprised him was the date; the second, the signature. "What the hell . . ."

"Do you think they'll get back together?" Ashling asked sleepily. She was stretched out on their bed beside Tom, who was going over some papers for the next day.

"What?" he asked absently.

"Gus and Dana, do you think they'll get back together?"

"Probably."

She propped herself up on one arm so she could look at him properly. "Why?"

He took off his reading glasses and shrugged. "He's obviously miserable without her."

"But then why did he leave?"

"God knows."

"She must have done something really bad to make him walk out like that. Either that or he's found out something about her; something she's kept secret from him."

Tom grinned at his wife's intentness. "If you say so, Miss Marple."

"I'm right, you just wait and see," she told him, wriggling down in the bed and snuggling up against him. "Gus isn't the sort of man to leave without a reason."

"There could be someone else," Tom mused.

"You know there isn't," Ashling protested. "Gus might have been a bit of a playboy in the past, but he's never so much as looked at another woman since he met Dana."

"And you know this how?" he teased.

She pulled a face. "I just know."

"Of course you do."

"You know I'm right."

"Yes," he agreed. "I would be surprised if he'd found someone else. For a start, I don't think he'd be underhand about it. But why is he being so secretive?"

Ashling shrugged. "Chivalry? Pride? Embarrassment? Who knows?"

"Not me, that's for sure."

"He'll tell you when he's good and ready, Tom, and I bet it will make sense to you when he does."

"What do you mean?"

She shook her head. "I'm not sure. I just feel there's something not quite right about Dana. Even after six years I don't really feel that I know her that well."

"She's a private person; there's nothing wrong with that."

"She's also a very isolated one. Do you remember their wedding? She didn't have one member of her family there."

"Not all families are like yours," Tom teased. He'd often joked that when he married Ashling, he'd also

66

married her three sisters as they seemed to spend as much time in his house as he did.

"Yes, but where were her friends?"

"She had friends there," he protested. "What about her bridesmaid and flower girl? And then there was the guy who gave her away."

Ashling shook her head in exasperation. "You have a lousy memory. Her bridesmaid was that girl Judy, her old schoolfriend. The flower girl was some relation of Gus's and it was her agent who gave her away."

"Oh, yeah."

"It was all very weird," Ashling murmured.

"What's even more weird, Mrs Cleary, is that we're still talking about her," Tom said, pulling her as close as her bump would allow.

Ashling smiled as she wound her arms around his neck. "So what are you going to do about it, Mr Cleary?"

CHAPTER
SIX

Dana sat in her office, staring out into the garden. She had drunk pot after pot of coffee, finally switching to wine at two. When Iris had insisted on making her a chicken salad, her whole body bristling with disapproval, Dana had suppressed a smile. Iris had never let a drop of alcohol pass her lips and didn't begin to understand why anyone would. She saw drink as the road to ruin, and Dana knew she was finding it hard to sit back and say nothing as the empties started to build up in the bottle bin outside the back door.

Dana was past caring. She found it hard to get through the day and wine made it slightly easier. When Sylvie was here, Dana kept to her bedroom, unable to cope with the PA's nervous chatter and worried looks. The rest of the time she sat in her office with the door firmly shut and stared at her blank screen. Occasionally she had spurts of creativity and would write a page or two, but when she read it back she always felt it had no vibrancy or pace. It was as if her whole way of looking at things was skewed. She couldn't see the point in carrying on and neither, so it seemed, could her characters.

She had managed to continue dodging calls from Gretta and Wally, although it wasn't fair to Sylvie. Her PA was looking increasingly stressed and frustrated. It did make Dana feel guilty; just not guilty enough to do anything about it. She didn't worry too much about Gretta. She didn't owe the woman anything. But Wally was different. She knew he must be climbing the walls. She just couldn't deal with his disappointment right now, though. She felt apathetic and jaded and nothing — not even the fact that she was probably throwing away her chance to finally make it big in Ireland and the UK — seemed important any more.

Dana had never seen herself as the kind of woman that would fall apart over a man. In the past, she had always been the one to leave, and her romances had never lasted longer than a few months. But it was different with Gus. She had found something unique behind those twinkling eyes, and her hard shell had softened in the heat of his charm and passion.

Dana glanced at the clock. Nearly three o'clock; time for another drink.

Iris was sitting at the kitchen table polishing cutlery when she walked in.

"Mrs Johnson — sorry — I mean Dana, can I help you?"

"No thanks." Dana went to the fridge to fetch the wine. She was on her way back to the office when she heard the buzzer announcing that there was someone at the gate.

Iris came out to answer it.

"I'm not here," Dana said quickly.

Iris nodded briefly and took up the handset. "Hello?"

"Hello, is Dana there? It's Ashling."

"No, I'm afraid —"

"No!" Dana had stopped and turned around. "You can let her in. Show her into the sitting room. I'll be there in a minute."

"I'm sorry, Mrs Cleary, I was mistaken, she is here. I'll open the gates for you."

Dana hurried upstairs and changed out of her pyjamas into jeans and a white shirt. Her hair was greasy so the only thing she could really do was pull it into a knot on top of her head. She sighed when she looked in the mirror at the result. Her skin was pale, and without the miracle of make-up you could see lines around her eyes and mouth. No doubt stress and alcohol had taken their toll. But she didn't really care. Still, she didn't want Ashling to pity her or, worse, tell Gus she was letting herself go. Quickly she slapped on some tinted moisturizer, rubbed some cream blusher into her cheeks and lined her eyes with kohl. She stood back and examined her handiwork. It was only marginally better but it would have to do. She couldn't keep Ashling waiting any longer.

She took a deep breath before pushing open the door of the sitting room and going to greet her guest. "Ashling, how lovely to see you." They hugged briefly and then Dana stepped back to look at the other girl. She was hugely pregnant and it suited her. Ashling's eyes were bright and clear, her hair shone in the afternoon sunlight and she oozed happiness. She was only two years younger than Dana but she could easily pass for thirty. "My goodness, look at you!"

"I know, I look like an elephant," Ashling said but her smile was radiant.

"You look absolutely wonderful." Dana gestured to the sofa and looked up to see Iris standing in the doorway. "Tea?" she asked Ashling.

"That would be lovely."

"And coffee for me, thanks, Iris." Dana turned back to Ashling. "How have you been?"

"Fine, absolutely fine. And you?"

"I'm fine too." Dana smiled brightly. She was full of questions: where is he, what's he doing, is he seeing anyone? But she was damned if she was going to ask. "How's Tom?" she asked instead.

"Fine, though I think he's a bit nervous about becoming a parent."

"He'll be great at it, you both will," Dana said and she meant it. Tom and Ashling were a lovely couple and she missed them.

"Thanks."

There was an awkward silence, then they both started talking at once.

"I'm sorry about —"

"I hope you don't mind —"

They laughed.

"You first," Dana said.

"I was just going to say I'm so sorry about you and Gus."

Dana looked down at her hands. "Me too."

"It came as a complete shock to us," Ashling told her. "We had no idea that you were having any problems."

"We weren't. Did Gus say we were?" she asked sharply.

"He hasn't told us anything." Ashling stopped as Iris entered with a tray. "Thanks so much, you're very kind," she said to the housekeeper.

Iris nodded. "You're very welcome, Mrs Cleary."

"She's so old-fashioned, isn't she?" Ashling said when they were alone again.

"I couldn't handle being called Mrs Johnson any more and I told her to call me Dana. She almost chokes every time she tries to say it."

"You're still Mrs Johnson," Ashling said softly. "Don't write him off just yet."

Dana couldn't keep quiet any longer. "Has he said anything to you or Tom?" she asked anxiously.

Ashling shook her head. "Not a word. It's been driving me mad, to be honest. I've always been a nosy cow."

Dana was torn between relief that Gus wasn't discussing their marriage with everyone and frustration because it meant she was still none the wiser.

"We've hardly seen him," Ashling continued, "socially, that is. When we have he clams up if we even mention your name."

Dana flinched. "Where's he staying?"

"Some hotel in town — I don't remember the name. But that in itself is a good sign, don't you think? If it

72

was definitely over he'd have bought a house or flat by now. Has he asked you for an official separation?"

"I haven't heard from him since the night he walked out," Dana said, feeling close to tears. "It's so unfair, Ashling. It's bad enough that he's gone but why can't he tell me why?"

Ashling frowned. "Didn't he give you any reasons at all?"

Dana looked away. "He went on about our marriage not turning out the way he'd expected, but he wasn't making a lot of sense. I thought it must be a midlife crisis or —" Dana met the other woman's eyes — "he'd found someone else. Be honest with me, Ashling. Has he?"

"Definitely not. He is not at all happy, Dana. I have no idea why he's left you, but it's obviously tearing him apart."

"If only I could get him to talk to me. How can we resolve anything if we don't at least meet?"

Ashling looked at her thoughtfully. "We could arrange for you to meet, accidentally on purpose, at our place."

Dana shook her head. "He'd probably just walk out. He'd feel that he was being press-ganged into a situation and he'd resent you and Tom for interfering."

"You're right. It was a dumb idea."

"No, it wasn't. You're just being a good friend and I really appreciate it. But I don't think there's anything you or I can do. Gus will come back if and when he's ready. I'm just not sure I'm prepared to wait." Lies, all lies, but Dana had her pride. Let Ashling go back and tell him that.

She felt the tears welling up inside and decided to bring this meeting to a close before she made a show of herself. She glanced at her watch and shot the other girl an apologetic smile. "Oh, Lord, I'd no idea it was that time! I'm so sorry but I'm expecting an important call from my editor any minute."

Ashling stood up immediately. "No, that's fine. I have to go anyway. How's the book going?"

"Really well." Dana smiled widely. "I'm almost finished."

Ashling shook her head in wonder. "I don't know how you do it, you're amazing."

Dana walked her to the door. "Thanks for coming, Ashling, it was kind of you."

"No problem. Call me any time if you want to talk."

Dana laughed. "I think you're going to have enough on your plate, don't you?"

"Yes," she agreed, "but the offer is still there."

Dana's eyes filled up as they hugged. "Thanks, Ashling, I appreciate it."

As she closed the door, Iris emerged from the kitchen.

"She's a nice girl, isn't she?" the woman commented, going into the sitting room to collect the tray.

Dana trailed after her. "Yes."

"You need your friends at times like this," Iris continued.

"Yes," Dana said again, thinking maybe it was time she called Judy.

"Dana, I'd almost given up on you!"

"Sorry, Judy."

"That's okay, I'm just happy you called. I've been so worried about you."

Dana smiled. How could this woman — who never saw her from one end of the year to the other — care so much? "How are things with you?"

"Too unbelievably boring to talk about," Judy said breezily. "Now, tell me about you."

"Nothing to tell."

"If there was nothing to tell you wouldn't be calling me," Judy retorted.

Dana smiled although she felt close to tears. "Okay, then, I'm falling apart. Will that do?"

"Oh, Dana! Would you like me to come up?"

"No, of course not, silly! You've got the kids to look after."

"Phil could manage for a few days."

"No, really, it's okay. I just need to pull myself together and get back to work."

"You're not writing?"

Dana sighed. "No. I've tried but I just can't seem to produce anything other than gibberish."

"Wow. That's a first," Judy breathed.

Dana closed her eyes and gripped the phone tightly. "Yes, it is."

"You know what I think? I think you need to go and see Gus and find out exactly where you stand."

"I'm not going crawling after him."

"I'm not suggesting you do anything of the sort. Just ask him to clarify things. If it's definitely over then you need to know. You need to make it official."

"But I don't want to," Dana wailed. "I just want him to come home."

"And you really don't know why he left?"

Dana stiffened at the incredulity in Judy's voice. "Not really."

"Talk to me, Dana," Judy said firmly.

Dana sighed. "He said I didn't confide in him. He asked if I'd trusted him with my deepest, darkest secrets."

"Which of course you hadn't."

"Judy!"

"Well, it's true." Her friend was unabashed. "Did you ever even take him down to Wexford?"

"Of course I haven't. You know that."

"It's your home!"

"Was," Dana corrected. "But that was a very long time ago."

"Have you really told him nothing?" Judy's voice was barely a whisper.

"Nothing."

For a moment there was a stunned silence at the other end of the phone. "But you love him and he loved you."

Dana closed her eyes briefly at Judy's use of the past tense. "Judy, you know what it was like at home; can't you understand why I wouldn't want to talk about it?"

"You know I do, but Gus is your husband! He loves you, Dana. Can you imagine how hurt he would be if he heard the truth from anyone else?"

Dana shivered. "That could never happen."

"You don't know that." When Dana didn't reply, Judy continued more gently. "Go and see him, Dana. Make him talk to you. Even if your marriage is over, you won't be able to move on until you do."

Dana relented, realizing the truth of Judy's words. "I suppose that's true."

"Call him," Judy instructed.

"Maybe in a few days —"

"No, right now," Judy insisted. "Before you get cold feet."

Dana swallowed hard and nodded even though her friend couldn't see her. "Okay, then, I will."

"And let me know what happens, won't you?"

"Promise. And Judy? Sorry I didn't call sooner."

"Hey, you never have to say sorry to me."

"Johnson and Cleary, can I help you?"

"Hi, Ann, it's Dana here. Is Gus in?"

"Oh, hi, Dana," the receptionist said brightly. "No, I'm sorry, he isn't here today."

"Oh, okay, I'll try his mobile."

"You may not get him," the girl warned. "He's in meetings all day at a customer's offices and he said he would probably have his mobile switched off. If you like I can put you through to his office and you can leave a message."

"No, that's okay, I'll get him again." Dana put down the phone, disappointed. She decided against phoning his mobile; it wouldn't be possible to talk if he was with a customer. It could wait, she decided. In fact, she'd leave it until Monday and spend the weekend making herself look reasonably presentable. If he did agree to meet she didn't want to look like some washed-out mess. Picking up the phone again she called her beauty salon. "This is Dana De Lacey. Could I make an appointment, please?"

CHAPTER
SEVEN

"Wow, are we the only normal people here?" Ashling murmured as she looked around enviously at the tall, willowy beauties who filled the room. Every year this fashion show seemed to get more glamorous. "I feel enormous among all these double zeros."

Tom squeezed her hand. "You look fabulous."

Ashling had thought she looked quite well too, in her sleeveless silver dress — until she'd walked into the ballroom of the Shelbourne hotel. Everyone here seemed to be famous, rich, gorgeous or, in some cases, all three. "Where are we sitting?" she asked. Standing for more than fifteen minutes at a time was proving a challenge these days.

"The top table, of course," Tom said, putting a hand in the small of her back and steering her through the crowds. "Can you see Gus anywhere?"

Ashling scanned the room. Gus was head and shoulders above most people and usually easy to spot, but he was nowhere in sight. "No."

Tom sighed as he pulled out a chair for his wife. "I'll go and look for him."

"Don't argue," Ashling warned.

Tom held up his hands. "I won't."

He made slow progress back across the room, stopping to shake hands, exchange hugs and kisses and give the occasional instruction to one of the hotel staff. As he neared the door he spotted Carla in the corridor and made a beeline for her. "Have you seen Gus?" he asked, without preamble.

Carla shook her head. "Do you want me to go and look for him?"

"No, I think I can guess where he is," Tom said grimly. "If you do see him, though, tell him to get his butt in there."

As he'd suspected, Gus was sitting at the bar with a whiskey in front of him. With his wife's words ringing in his ears, he made his way to his partner's side and caught the barman's eye. "Jameson, please."

Gus looked up at him and grinned. "Yo, partner, how the hell are ya?"

Tom's eyes widened as he took in Gus's red eyes, his undone tie, and the distinct smell of alcohol on his breath. The barman returned with his drink. "And a pot of black coffee," Tom said stiffly. "Make it strong." He steered his partner to a quiet table in a far corner of the room and glared at him. "What the fuck do you think you're playing at?"

"Relax, Tom. I'm just having a quick drink."

"You've had several by the look of it. How could you, Gus? This place is crawling with our clients, not to mention the press."

"I'm fine," Gus told him.

The coffee arrived and Tom poured some, tugged the glass from his partner's hand and replaced it with the cup. "Drink," he instructed.

With a sigh Gus obediently raised the cup to his lips. "I'm fine," he repeated.

"You look like shit." Tom looked around nervously. "The show starts in ten minutes so keep drinking that coffee. And don't even dream of touching another drop of alcohol tonight."

When Gus didn't reply, Tom shook his head in frustration. "Why are you behaving like this, Gus? Is it Dana?"

Gus stared sullenly into his coffee.

Tom was about to press the matter when Carla appeared at his side.

"Oh, good, you found him. It's time to take our seats."

"Damn." Tom stood up. "Carla, you stay here and get at least two more cups of coffee into him before you bring him inside."

Carla's eyes widened as Gus gave her a drunken grin. "Sure, yeah, you go on."

"Not another drop tonight," Tom repeated, before disappearing into the crowd.

"Are you okay?" Carla asked, taking Tom's seat.

"My esteemed partner says not. What do you think?"

Carla smiled apologetically. "You do look a little the worse for wear. Here, let me fix your tie." Stretching across the table the girl bit her lip in concentration, then sat back to appraise her handiwork. "There, you're gorgeous!"

"So are you," Gus murmured, smiling into her eyes.

Carla's smile faltered and she looked away. "Drink your coffee."

"If I drink any more of this stuff I'll throw up."

"How about some water?" she suggested.

"How about we get out of here and go for a real drink?"

"If we do that Tom will kill you, and fire me," she said lightly. "Now come on, let's go." She pulled him to his feet and led him out into reception. "I know you're not in the mood, Gus, but a couple of hours and you're out of here."

He sighed. "Okay, okay, I'll do it for you," and stopping, he turned, smiled and bent his head to kiss her lightly on the lips. "Thanks, Carla."

Blushing, she took his hand and led him into the function room.

"Is he okay?" Ashling murmured to her husband once the lights had gone down.

"He's had a few too many but he should be able to hold it together. Just keep the wine bottle away from him."

Ashling nodded slightly, turning as Gus slipped into the seat on her other side.

"Don't have a go at me," he warned. "I'm not going to make a show of you."

She smiled. "I didn't think you were."

"Sorry."

"That's okay." She reached out a hand to squeeze his, then turned her attention back to the show.

Gus looked up at the models strutting their stuff in front of him and let his mind wander. He was glad of the darkness, and the fact that he didn't have to make mind-numbingly boring conversation with the wife of his latest client. Since he'd left Dana, he'd found it harder and harder to put on a show for people he didn't care about. He was able to do his job easily enough. Once he started drawing he got completely lost in his work and managed to forget his troubles. Dana was the same. There were times when he had watched her tapping away on her laptop, completely oblivious to his presence. How much had she used her work to blot out the real world, he wondered. How much did she use her writing as an excuse not to communicate? How much did he really know her at all?

Gus reached for his glass and, realizing it was empty, looked around for a bottle. Ashling passed him the water jug instead. Smiling, he obediently poured himself a glass. She and Tom were being great about all this, he admitted to himself. He might be still able to draw, but Tom was shouldering the lion's share of their responsibilities at the moment.

Gus had always been the one to chat up the clients and convince them that they should be more daring and adventurous in their designs. Now, though, he kept his contact with them to the bare minimum. Tom, who had always been happy to take a back seat, had been forced to step in.

It couldn't continue, of course. Tom would be taking a few weeks off as soon as the baby was born and Gus would have to step up to the plate.

The lights came up again as the presenter announced a break. Immediately Gus was on his feet, drawing a questioning look from his partner. "I'm just going to the loo, okay?" he murmured as he passed Tom's chair.

"Just make sure you don't go via the bar," Tom warned.

Gus wove his way between the tables, nodding and smiling as he went. As he pushed open the door, he felt some resistance, and pushed harder.

"Ow!"

Stumbling into the corridor, Gus almost fell over a girl lying in a heap on the floor. "Oh my God, I'm so sorry! Did I hurt you?"

"Yes, you did," she mumbled, easing her sandal off to reveal a bloody toe.

"I am so sorry," he said again. "Here, let me help you. Sit down over here and I'll go and see if I can find you a bandage."

"There's no need," the girl said, but her eyes were scrunched up in pain and a tear was sliding down her cheek.

"Stop arguing," Gus told her and was turning to leave when a waitress approached him.

"Can I help you, sir?"

"Yes, please. Do you have a first-aid kit? This lady has cut her foot."

"Of course, I'll go and get it."

The waitress disappeared and Gus crouched down to take a closer look at the injury. The wound wasn't deep but the skin had been dragged back where her foot had got caught under the door. He looked up into the girl's face. "I am really terribly sorry."

"I wish you'd stop apologizing," she said faintly, trying to smile. "It was an accident."

"I'm Gus, Gus Johnson."

"Yes, I know. I'm Terry Andrews, I work for the *Daily Journal*."

He winced slightly. Trust him to injure a member of the press. "Are you here to cover the show?"

She nodded. "Yes, although I don't know how I'm going to do it now. I'm supposed to get at least four interviews and I've got nothing yet. My photographer said to stand near the door, that I was sure to nab someone."

Gus grinned. "Well, I suppose he got that right."

The waitress reappeared with a damp towel, some antiseptic cream and a large plaster.

"Thank you." Gus nodded at the girl, then gently dabbed the cut before applying the cream and carefully sticking on the plaster. "How's that?"

"Fine, thank you, Dr Johnson." Terry smiled as she slipped her sandal back on and went to stand up. "Ouch!" She grimaced in pain as she put weight on her foot.

He lowered her back into the chair. "I think you'd better stay here for a while."

"But I have a job to do," she wailed. "My boss will kill me if I go back with nothing."

Gus thought for a moment. She seemed genuinely upset; much too nice to be employed by a rag like the *Daily Journal*. "Tell you what, why don't I arrange for a few people to come out to you to be interviewed and then we'll get you into a taxi home?"

She brightened. "Could you do that?"

"It's my show," he reminded her with a wink.

Terry laughed. "Great."

"So who would you like to interview?"

Immediately Terry rattled off four names and, with a sly smile, added his on the end.

He grimaced. "I suppose I can hardly refuse."

"I'll be gentle," she promised with a delighted grin.

"I'm sure," he said drily, before nodding towards the waitress still hovering in the background. "Would you like a cup of tea or coffee, or maybe something stronger?"

"Coffee would be great, thanks."

Gus gave the order and asked the waitress to add it to his bill. "Right, I'll go and see who I can find. The second half will be starting in a few minutes, so you might have to wait until the show is over."

Terry settled back in her chair. "No problem, I'm used to hanging around. It comes with the job."

After having a word with the producer of the show, Gus made his way back to his table, stopping off to murmur in the ears of some of the people Terry wanted to interview.

"Where on earth have you been?" Ashling hissed, when he eventually returned to his seat. "Tom's hopping mad."

Gus leaned forward to look at his furious partner and winked. "Talking to the press."

Ashling's eyes widened. "You're kidding."

"No, but you don't have to worry. Everything's under control." Gus settled down to watch the show, his mind still on Terry Andrews. Who'd have thought he would ever look forward to a press interview?

The *Daily Journal* photographer crossed the reception to Terry's side, a broad grin on his face. "Well, you're some player, I'll give you that."

"What do you mean?" Terry frowned.

"Gus Johnson." He tapped his camera. "I got the whole thing. I can see the caption now. AUTHOR'S HUBBY FINDS NEW HEROINE. Nice work."

"You can't use any of those shots," she warned him. "He's off now arranging interviews for me and he's even agreed to talk to me himself."

Stan's eyes widened. "About his marriage breakdown?"

Terry smiled. "Well, I hadn't planned on discussing the weather."

CHAPTER
EIGHT

"Oh, Ian, I just can't believe it!"

The PR man had phoned Sylvie first thing and when Iris told him the PA wouldn't be in until lunchtime, he'd begged the housekeeper to get in touch with Sylvie and ask her to call him ASAP. After a brief conversation, Sylvie had charged down to the nearest newsagent and now sat with the *Daily Journal* spread out in front of her. "I can't believe it," she said again. "I never thought he'd do something like this."

"You don't know he did anything," Ian told her. "It's just a photograph. It may be totally innocent."

"But it says that they were together all evening."

"As my father always says, 'Paper never refuses ink.'"

"Pardon?"

"It could be all lies," Ian translated.

"Oh. Still, it doesn't matter. Dana will still be devastated if she sees it."

"Which is why I've called. You must make sure she does."

"What?" Sylvie shrieked. "Are you mad?"

"No, just trying to do my job. Look, Sylvie, if Dana doesn't pull out of this stupor soon you could be out of a job. You must realize that."

"So?" Sylvie said, reluctantly.

"So, perhaps this photo is the kick-start she needs," he said gently. "I know it might hurt her initially, Sylvie, but maybe it will make her come to her senses."

"Are you saying we should be cruel to be kind?"

"She's going to hear about this sooner or later. It would be best if she heard it from you."

"What?" Sylvie shrieked again.

"Call her," he urged. "If you don't, I will and I know which she'd prefer."

Iris was halfway up the stairs with Dana's coffee when the phone rang. She paused, wondering if she should retrace her steps and answer it, and then realized that Dana already had. When she knocked and went into the bedroom, Dana was sitting in the armchair by the window with the phone in her hand.

"Good morning, Dana, how are you today?" Iris did a double take. "What is it? Has something happened."

"Have you got the *Daily Journal* there?"

Iris pulled the papers from under her arm and looked through them. "Yes, here it is."

Dana snatched it from her and flicked through it until she came to a two-page spread of coloured photographs. They were all of the fashion show in the Shelbourne the previous evening.

Iris, who was looking over her shoulder, smiled. "Look, it's Mr and Mrs Cleary!"

Dana nodded dumbly. It was a nice photo of Ashling but Tom looked slightly stern at her side.

"And Mr Johnson — Oh!" Iris pulled up short.

Dana froze as she, too, saw the photographs — three of them. They showed Gus in a variety of poses with an attractive young blonde. In one of them, his arm was around her. In the next, her hand was on his arm and she was looking up into his face. In the last photo, they were walking away from the camera, arm in arm. Dana's heart beat wildly in her chest as she stared at the photos and then ran her eye down through the text until she spotted her husband's name.

Gus Johnson, who's been lying low since his split from his wife, prolific author Dana De Lacey, seems to have found someone to help him through this difficult time. Friends reported that he spent most of the evening with the beautiful young blonde and had eyes only for her.

"I'm sure it was completely innocent," Iris said with conviction.

"I'd like to be alone," Dana said quietly.

Iris put a hand out to her. "Mrs Johnson —"

"Don't call me that!" Dana cried, tearfully.

"I'm sorry, but I'm sure —"

"Please! Please, Iris, just leave me."

When the door had closed after the housekeeper, Dana threw down the paper and stared at the phone. Was there any point in calling Gus now? It seemed he had moved on. Of course, it could be completely innocent. Women always flocked to Gus on social occasions like this. Everyone kissed and hugged these days. Her eyes were drawn to the photo where she could clearly see his hand on the small of the girl's back. It was a gentle — almost intimate — gesture. Coupled with the warm expression in his eyes — which was clear even in this fuzzy photo — it was enough to worry Dana. "Bastard didn't wait long," she muttered bitterly, wondering whether he'd only just met her or whether she was the reason he'd left. Was she, in fact, his date last night? No. Ashling had said he wasn't seeing anyone. Still, it was always possible that Gus had brought her along and not bothered to warn his business partner.

Dana picked up the paper again and studied the picture of Tom and Ashling. Yes, Tom definitely looked pissed off about something. Dana stared at the phone and considered her options. She could phone Gus and pretend that she hadn't seen the paper. She could phone Ashling and ask what exactly had happened last night. Or, she sighed, flopping back in the chair, she could do nothing. Her eyes filled up as the familiar feeling of depression started to engulf her. Gus had a new woman. Her career was going down the tubes. What was the point in going on?

She could almost hear Judy's voice in her head. Fight! She dashed the tears from her cheeks and took a deep breath. It was up to her if she fell apart. It was up to her to show Gus that she didn't care. It was up to her to get up off her arse and get on with life. Going to the mirror, she studied herself critically. Since her visit to the beauty salon on Saturday she was looking a lot better. Her hair was cut in a shorter, blunt bob. Her skin had a glow that had been lacking for some time.

Her eyebrows were plucked into a perfect arch. But the eyes they framed were troubled and sad. They gave everything away. Still, Dana managed a wry smile, that's why God had invented sunglasses.

Striding into her dressing room, Dana rummaged through her clothes until she found her white linen trouser suit. Next she called Sylvie back, taking deep breaths as she waited for her PA to answer.

"Hello?"

Dana forced herself to sound bright and breezy. "Hi, Sylvie. Fancy going shopping?"

"I can't believe it! Thank you, God! Where is she now?"

Sylvie laughed at Ian's delight. "We're having lunch in Les Fréres Jacques and washing it down with Möet. She's just nipped out to the loo."

"So she saw the photos?"

"I rang her, like you said — I have to tell you that wasn't easy — but she hasn't mentioned the photos since we met up." Sylvie shot an anxious look at the door. "But I'm sure she has. She's done up to the nines and obviously putting on a show."

"You see? Didn't I tell you it would work?"

"Well, let's hope it stays working this time."

"You need to play along, make it a great day and boost her confidence and ego as much as you can," he urged. "Don't let her drink too much, though, or she'll get depressed and end up back in that bloody bedroom again."

"I'm not a childminder, Ian."

Ian laughed. "Oh, like you're having such a miserable time."

"I suppose I can just about cope." Sylvie smiled as she took a sip of her champagne.

"You need to keep her on the go all day," Ian continued. "Don't give her time to think. Take her to an uber-trendy bar later. Let me know where first and I'll make sure someone's there to snap you. Be her best buddy, Sylvie, do whatever it takes to get her back on the straight and narrow. Tell her that being seen out socializing is the best way to let Gus and everyone else know that she's over him. The only way to save face."

"This could backfire on us," Sylvie pointed out. "If she starts going out every night, she might be too tired and hung-over to write."

"We'll worry about that next week. For now, let's just concentrate on keeping her out of that bedroom."

The door opened and Dana strode back into the restaurant, receiving several appreciative stares from men and envious ones from women.

"Gotta go, she's coming," Sylvie whispered.

"Everything okay?" Dana asked.

Sylvie grinned. "Oh, yes."

"What?"

"Everyone in the place is watching you."

Dana frowned. "Do they recognize me, do you think?"

"Maybe, but I think it's just the fact that you're looking gorgeous today. I love your hair like that."

Dana put up a self-conscious hand to her bob. "I went to the beauty salon on Saturday."

"Well, you look great."

"Thanks." Dana nodded towards the phone in Sylvie's hand. "Problems?"

Sylvie shrugged. "I just checked the answering machine and Gretta is looking for you again."

Dana sighed. "Wouldn't you think after eighteen books I'd be entitled to take a break?"

"She's worried because you won't take her calls," Sylvie said gently. "If you talked to her and Walter, they'd back off. You're scaring them because you've never behaved like this before."

"I've never been dumped by my husband before," Dana reminded her.

"I know it's hard, Dana, but try not to shut us all out. We're really worried about you."

"Worried that the gravy train's about to stop, you mean."

Sylvie reddened. "That's not fair."

Dana grasped her PA's hand. "Oh, Sylvie, I'm sorry! You know I didn't mean you. But Gretta is as tough as nails, and while Wally is a great friend, he's still a businessman with a job to do."

"Tell me about it," Sylvie murmured, having been on the end of several lengthy phone calls.

Dana smiled. "But they can all wait for another week or so. I've had a lousy time and I plan to make up for it. My husband obviously isn't sitting home, crying into his pillow."

"You saw the photos, then?"

Dana nodded. "Do you know who she is?"

Sylvie shook her head.

"See if Ian knows, will you?" Dana asked, looking suddenly very vulnerable. "I need to know if it's real or not."

"I'll talk to him," Sylvie promised.

"Don't tell him I asked," Dana said hurriedly.

"No, of course not."

"Right. Good. Okay, then, let's go." Dana drained her glass and put on her sunglasses. "Time to hit the shops again."

CHAPTER
NINE

Gus slumped at his desk and stared miserably out of the window. He'd only been in the office an hour and already it was promising to be a really shitty day.

It had started almost as soon as he'd walked through the door. Carla's face had lit up as she wished him a bright good morning, her eyes all hopeful and her smile shy as she brought him his coffee. He had groaned inwardly as he remembered — through the fog of his hangover — how he'd flirted with her. Tom would throttle him if he knew. What he couldn't understand was why a lovely young girl like Carla would be interested in a separated man so much older than herself.

He'd been rooting in his desk for some painkillers when the girl had returned, flung the papers down in front of him and left again without a word.

As Gus had sipped his coffee and waited for the tablets to take effect, he'd flicked quickly through the papers, almost choking when he reached the double-page spread in the *Daily Journal*.

"For fuck's sake." Gus studied the pictures of himself and Terry Andrews before turning his eyes to the copy. He'd scanned through all the drivel about the party but could find no details of the interview he'd given her. Just a ridiculous piece about him and Terry that implied she was his girlfriend. "The bitch set me up," he'd muttered, feeling stupid and furious in equal measure.

Grabbing the paper he'd marched into Tom's office and flung it down in front of him. "Have you seen this shit?" he'd said, dropping into the chair opposite Tom and drumming his fingers on the arm.

"And good morning to you too," Tom had said calmly.

"Is that all you've got to say?" Gus had been incredulous.

Tom had shrugged. "It's no big deal."

"You are kidding? You do realize that girl is the reporter for the *Daily Journal*. I bandaged her foot, I organized interviews for her. I even let her interview me. And all they've printed are lies. I should sue."

"You'd be better off ignoring it. It's not as if you'll be seeing her again, is it?" Tom's eyes had held his.

"No, of course I bloody won't!"

"Well, then, the story is as good as dead."

"Maybe," Gus had admitted grudgingly. "I just hate being stitched up like this."

"Especially by a good-looking woman". Tom had grinned.

"I'm glad you find it so funny, Tom," Gus'd snapped. "What will Dana think if she sees this?"

"Does that really matter?"

"Well, of course it matters! Just because we've split up doesn't mean I want to hurt her."

"She was in the papers first," Tom had pointed out.

"Yes, but not with a man on her arm."

Tom had picked up the paper and looked at the photographs. "She is a gorgeous-looking woman, and you do look more than a little interested."

Gus had rolled his eyes. "What man wouldn't? And you know the state I was in last night."

"Yes, so I hope you've learned your lesson. You may not have been plastered, but you were still too jarred to realize you were being taken for a ride." He had grinned. "You weren't, were you? Taken for a ride, I mean."

Gus had smiled ruefully. "No such luck. No, she just got what she came for and disappeared."

"Good." Tom had tossed the newspaper back to his partner and bent his head over the file in front of him. "Then forget about it and let's get on with some work. Don't you have a new client coming in at ten?"

Gus had groaned as he glanced at his watch. "God, yes, I had totally forgotten. And don't —" he'd held up a hand as Tom had opened his mouth — "say another word about drinking too much."

"Wouldn't dream of it."

Gus had retired to his office, picking up more coffee en route and studiously avoiding Carla's reproachful gaze as he passed her desk. The new client was a middle-aged lady who wanted to turn her three-bedroom semi-detached house in suburbia into a country cottage, complete with flagstones and inglenook fireplace. Gus had tried to be both patient and persuasive but the woman wasn't interested in his views, only in how soon he could achieve her dream and how cheaply he could do it. Fed up and irritated — his head still ached a bit — Gus had deliberately inflated his estimates simply to get rid of her.

She had just left when Ann had phoned to tell him that Terry Andrews was on hold. He had momentarily considered taking the call and giving the girl an earful but common sense prevailed, so instead he had told Ann to say he was unavailable. Altogether Terry had left three messages asking him to call — two with Carla — but Gus had balled up the yellow Post-its and tossed them in the bin.

At four-thirty, Gus decided to call it a day. He was achieving nothing here and maybe after a strenuous workout in the gym he'd be in a better frame of mind to work.

He found that the evening sunshine that poured through his hotel window, and the lively scene below, inspired him. Most evenings he would sit at the table in front of it, sketching furiously until the dusk forced him to abandon his pad, and then he'd go out for something to eat.

With a tight, polite smile at Carla, Gus wished her goodnight and swung out of the office. As the day progressed she had thawed slightly when he didn't return any of Terry's calls. Still, he was terrified of even looking the girl in the eye in case he gave her the wrong idea.

"Wimp," he muttered to himself as he tossed his briefcase into the car and climbed in after it.

"Mr Johnson?"

He jumped as someone tapped on the window and he frowned with irritation when he saw it was Terry Andrews. He lowered the window and made a great show of looking around. "Where's the photographer, behind a tree? Or perhaps you've one in your bag."

"Look, I can understand that you're angry —" she began.

"You've got that right."

"Yes, I was too. I did all those damn interviews and they didn't print one of them."

"Are you trying to tell me you knew nothing about this?" he said, his mouth twisting into a contemptuous smile.

She looked horrified. "Of course not! Why on earth would I do something like that?"

"To get a story? To impress your editor?"

"Look, I'm training to be a serious journalist and I would never get involved in that sort of thing —"

"Yeah, sure." Gus fired up the engine.

"I am really sorry, Mr Johnson, but please believe me, I had nothing to do with it. I'm gutted that they didn't use any of my stuff and as embarrassed as you are. How do you think I feel, being portrayed as some kind of bimbo?"

She turned away slightly and he saw her surreptitiously wipe her eyes.

"So ask them to print a correction in tomorrow's newspaper."

"I did, but —"

"Yeah, I know, lies sell more papers. If you really want to become a journalist, you should find yourself a job with a more reputable publication."

She nodded miserably. "I agree. That's why I handed in my notice."

"What?" He stared at her.

"I can't work for them now, not after this."

"There's no need to be hasty," he backtracked. God, this was the last thing he needed. "Why don't you find yourself another job first?"

"Too late."

Gus studied her, wondering if he could believe this girl or if this was just another ruse. Still, the slump of her shoulders and the desolate look in her red-rimmed eyes persuaded him she was telling the truth. "Go back and grovel," he told her. "Tell them you changed your mind. They won't want to lose someone with so much potential."

She looked surprised. "You think I've got potential?"

He grinned. "Well, you managed to wangle a fair bit of information from the people you interviewed last night."

"That was just because you persuaded them and they'd all had a few drinks. *You* didn't give much away."

"I never do. I'd better go." Gus glanced back at the office. The last thing he needed was for Tom or Carla to appear.

"Yeah, sure, sorry for delaying you. But please tell me that you believe me. I promise you, I had nothing to do with those photos."

"I believe you."

"Thanks." She looked up as big drops of rain started to fall.

"Where's your car?" he asked.

"I don't have one. Don't worry, the bus stop's not far."

Gus hesitated for a moment. This really wasn't a good idea. He should say goodbye and drive away. It was the only sensible thing to do. He leaned over and opened the passenger door. "Get in."

"Oh, no, I couldn't ask you to —"

Gus looked around nervously. "You didn't. Now please get in before someone sees us, puts two and two together and comes up with five."

Terry hurried around to the passenger side and climbed in beside him. "This is very kind of you."

"It is, isn't it?" He looked at her and couldn't help smiling. She was very pretty in a messy, bohemian sort of way. She had a cheeky grin and a way of looking at you that seemed both direct and honest. How could he have thought she was behind those photographs? "So, where to?"

She shrugged. "Drop me anywhere in the city centre."

"Where do you live?"

"Oh, town's fine, thanks all the same," she said quickly. "I have some shopping to do."

He shot her an amused look. "I wasn't hitting on you."

"Oh, God, no, I know —"

"Calm down, I'm kidding."

She smiled shakily. "Yeah, sorry, it's just I'm still feeling a bit raw. I'm not used to being in the newspapers."

"It's not nice, is it?"

"No," she agreed. "I definitely prefer being behind the camera."

"What got you into journalism — and I use that word loosely."

"That's not fair —"

"I'm kidding again."

"Oh, sorry."

"If you want to be a serious reporter, you're going to have to stop apologizing or no one will give you an interview."

"You did," she reminded him with a grin.

He laughed. "True. You must be good. Please go and beg for your job back, Terry," he added as he pulled into the kerb.

"I will, but I am going to start looking for another job."

"Glad to hear it."

"Thanks for the lift."

"Nice to meet you, Terry, despite the circumstances."

She leaned back in the car and smiled. "You too."

He watched for a moment as she walked away, hips swinging and head held high. If things were different . . . He sighed and pulled back into the traffic, feeling guilty at his attraction to the girl. He was still married, he was still in love with his wife — despite everything. He had no business looking at another woman, especially a bloody reporter.

Putting Terry out of his mind, Gus headed for the gym. He focused his energy on exhausting himself to the point where he was too tired to think or worry about anyone or anything. On the way back to the hotel, he picked up a Chinese takeaway — there was only so much hotel food he could stomach.

Later, sprawled in front of the television, a beer in his hand and his dinner congealing in cartons on the table in front of him, Gus decided that maybe it was time he talked to Dana. Maybe it was even time he told her exactly why he had left. It would be better if he had talked to Ed first but he felt he couldn't afford to wait any longer. It was over a month now since he'd seen her and it appeared she was getting on with her life. Perhaps, though, she was the victim of press fabrications just as he had been. Feeling better now that he'd reached a decision, he switched off the TV and decided to have an early night. Tomorrow morning, bright and early, he would pay Dana a visit. And he wouldn't leave until he got some answers.

CHAPTER
TEN

Dana sat in the VIP section of the hottest new Dublin club, smiling politely as the conversation buzzed around her. She was bored out of her mind and would have left long ago if it wasn't for her PA. Sylvie was in her element. She looked stunning in one of Dana's cast-offs and was obviously enjoying herself immensely. A rich, portly man stood close by, leering at her in a way that made Dana feel slightly sick.

The whole scene sickened her really. Dana had fully enjoyed socializing in the past but now it all seemed fake and faintly ridiculous. The champagne flowed, the men wore silk suits, the ladies clutched designer bags and they were all playing the same game. The single women were after rich men, and the ones who were already married just wanted to flaunt the fact that they'd made it. Made what exactly? she wondered, taking a sip of champagne and nodding her thanks when her glass was immediately topped up.

The man at her side, who did something in theatre, was talking — in fact he hadn't stopped since they'd been introduced — but he seemed satisfied if she nodded occasionally, which suited her just fine; it had been a long and busy day.

While it had served its purpose, distracting her from the photos of Gus and that woman, her husband was never far from her mind. When they'd finished shopping, Sylvie had persuaded her that they should stop off at the beauty salon and she could have a relaxing head and neck massage. It had been a good idea really; Dana had felt tense and a little sleepy after the wine at lunch. Rather than leave the girl waiting, Dana had treated Sylvie to a pedicure and manicure and she had been thrilled. After their beauty treatments, they'd taken a taxi home. As Dana arranged her new clothes in the wardrobe, she'd tossed several of her old ones on to the bed, inviting Sylvie to help herself to anything she wanted. Sylvie hadn't needed to be asked twice. She'd pounced on the clothes, inspecting labels, feeling fabric and muttering happily to herself. Dana had sent her off to the guest suite to try the clothes on and prepare for the night out while she took a long, hot bath.

Dana tuned back into the drone of the man at her side and then stood up abruptly. There was only so much a body could take. "I must go to the bathroom," she said sweetly, and with her bag tucked under her arm she pushed her way through the crowd. Instead of going to the Ladies, though, she slipped out on to a balcony that the smokers used. Thankfully, she had it to herself. She closed her eyes and took a deep breath of crisp night air. It was a little chilly and she pulled her wrap closer around her bare shoulders. Her eyes still shut, she imagined herself at home in the privacy and solitude of her own garden, wishing she'd never come out in the first place.

"Are you okay?"

Dana's eyes flew open and she sighed as a tall man emerged from the shadows. God, couldn't you go anywhere in this place without someone trying to chat you up? "Yeah," she replied, turning her back on him and gazing out across the rooftops, hoping he'd get the message.

"You must be married and, or, successful," he observed, undeterred.

"Why do you say that?"

"If you weren't, you'd be in there looking for someone who was going to either marry you or make you famous."

Dana chuckled. It was a pretty accurate description of most of the women in there. "That's a bit harsh. What about the men? Most of them are married and just looking for a night's entertainment."

"Touché." He came forward into the light and Dana found herself looking up into twinkling dark eyes. She looked away again. The last thing she needed right now was another twinkly-eyed charmer.

"I'm not, by the way," he said. "Married or looking for a night's entertainment."

"So why are you here?"

He sighed as he stubbed out his cigarette. "Babysitting. I have some clients visiting from Japan. I'm showing them the sights."

"And you brought them here? We have wonderful architecture, museums, Trinity College and the Book of

Kells," she reminded him. "Would they not be more appropriate 'sights'?"

He laughed. "Oh, believe me, they've done all that too. But they like their drink and they love their women, so here we are."

"And you don't?" she asked.

He grinned. "Yes to both, but I prefer quieter venues and less obvious women."

"Then I'd say you're in the wrong place."

"You too," he said softly.

"I must go." She smiled at him and went back inside. After a quick visit to the loo she returned to her seat and was relieved to see that the theatre bore had found some other ear to bend. Sylvie was nowhere in sight. Dana hunted in her bag for her phone and was about to call Sylvie's number when she saw there was a message waiting. It was from Sylvie.

Sorry, Dana, couldn't find you and was feeling tired so gone home. See you tomorrow. Tnx for a great day.

Home indeed, thought Dana crossly. Sylvie had probably gone on to another club or, worse, a hotel room with that awful man. Despite her annoyance, Dana was worried. They didn't know anything about the guy; Sylvie really shouldn't take such chances. Dana felt more like her mother than her employer. She also felt more than a little responsible, given that she had brought her PA here in the first place.

Dana gathered up her bag and wrap. There was no reason to stay now. As she got ready to leave, the man from the balcony appeared and sank on to the sofa beside her.

"I thought we should get to know each other better."

"I'm leaving," she said curtly.

"Sounds great, where shall we go?"

She couldn't help smiling. He was attractive, in a reserved kind of way. But though his suit and tie were sober, there was an air of quiet confidence about him that she liked. "You're very presumptuous."

He shrugged. "Maybe, but it's not often I meet someone like you."

She sighed. "You really need to work on your chat-up lines."

"Let's go somewhere quiet," he suggested, "and you can give me some tips."

Over the next couple of hours, they talked and flirted and Dana had the most fun she'd had in months. This man was exactly what her bruised ego needed. He was sexy, intelligent and had made it very clear that he fancied her. His name was Ryan Vaughan and he was a director of some Japanese electronics firm based in the north of the city. When questioned, it turned out he too had just emerged from a long-term relationship.

"Why?" Dana asked, as they sat in a small, cosy bar drinking brandies.

"She wanted us to settle down and start a family."

"And you don't want kids?"

"Oh, I do. I just realized I didn't want to have them with her."

"Ah."

He sighed. "Yes. She wasn't impressed, to put it mildly."

"So you left."

"No, she did. I would have been happy to go on as we were but her body clock was ticking, as they say, and she didn't want to waste any more time on me."

"Hard luck."

He shrugged. "So how about you?"

"My husband left me because he says I didn't talk to him."

He raised an eyebrow. "Not a complaint you'd hear from most men."

She laughed. "True."

"So why didn't you talk to him?"

"I did." She looked away. "I don't understand what he meant and he didn't hang around long enough to explain."

He nodded wisely. "I see."

Her eyes narrowed. "What do you see?"

"Well, there's obviously a breakdown in communication."

"Oh, please! I'm too pissed for anything heavy."

"So he's right, you don't talk." He grinned innocently.

She drained her glass and stood up, slightly unsteadily. "I've had enough psychoanalysis, thank you. I'm going home to bed."

He stood up and folded her wrap around her shoulders. "What a good idea."

110

She raised an eyebrow. "I suppose you want me to invite you back for coffee?"

He shook his head solemnly. "No, but I wouldn't say no to a night of unbridled passion."

Dana gazed up at him. "Let's go, then."

The next morning when she woke, she felt as if there was a freight train going through her brain. Cocktails and champagne were a lethal combination. Then, of course, there was the brandy — Oh shit! She opened one eye. Sure enough, there he was, lying beside her. Lying where Gus should be. "Oh, God," she groaned. Moving as gingerly as she could, Dana slipped out of the bed and made a run for the bathroom. Inside, she pulled on a bathrobe and stared at herself in the mirror. She looked very slightly green; her eye make-up was halfway down her face and her mouth — swollen from fairly intensive kissing — hung open in shock. She swallowed hard as a wave of nausea engulfed her. She wasn't sure if that was down to the drink or the realization of what she had done. She had, for the first time ever, been unfaithful to Gus. Not that it really counted. Gus was gone. She didn't owe him any kind of loyalty. Strangely, that didn't make her feel any better. She sank down on to the edge of the bath and wondered how the hell she was going to get that man — Ryan? — out of her bed and out of the house before Iris or Sylvie arrived. "Fuck," she muttered, hearing the unmistakable sound of the front door opening and closing. Going to the sink she quickly washed her face, combed her hair and tightened the belt of her robe,

111

then took a deep breath and went back into the bedroom.

Ryan sat up and stretched, exposing a tanned, smooth chest. He smiled lazily. "Good morning."

"You've got to get out of here now," she said urgently, gathering up his clothes and tossing them at him.

"I thought you were separated," he replied, throwing back the duvet.

Dana averted her eyes. "I am, but my housekeeper is downstairs and I don't want her to see you."

He grinned as there was a gentle tap on the door. "I think it's a bit late for that."

"Just a minute, Iris," Dana called. "Get into the bathroom and stay there until I call you," she hissed frantically.

"Oh, come on!"

"Bathroom — please?"

Shaking his head he sauntered across the room, his clothes over his arm.

Dana waited until he'd closed the bathroom door before opening the bedroom door a couple of inches. "Sorry, Iris, I was in the bathroom."

"I'm sorry to interrupt you." Iris's eyes twinkled excitedly. "It's just that I thought you'd want to know, Mr Johnson is outside."

"Gus!" Dana gasped.

Iris nodded, smiling. "He's sitting in his car talking on his phone, so I'm sure he'll be in any minute."

"Oh, God, you can't let him in."

Iris frowned. "But —"

"No, of course, you *must* let him in." Dana thought quickly. "Just tell him I'm in a meeting and he'll have to wait."

Iris nodded. "I'll show him into the front sitting room."

"No!" Dana smiled weakly. "Why don't you take him into the kitchen and make him some breakfast? He'd love that."

Iris beamed. "Very well. And don't you worry; I'll keep him talking while you —"

"What?" Dana snapped.

Iris frowned in confusion. "Get dressed?"

"Ah, yes, great, thank you. I'll do that."

Dana hurriedly closed the door and crossed to the bathroom. "You can come out now," she whispered.

Ryan emerged grinning and thankfully fully dressed. "I feel like a teenager again."

"I'm so sorry but —"

He held up a hand. "No need for explanations, I need to head off anyway. I have a meeting and I need to go home first and change."

"But you can't." She blocked his way.

"I'm sorry?"

She sighed. "My husband's here, and I really don't want him to see you."

He frowned. "I thought you were separated."

"We are," she assured him. "I haven't set eyes on him since the day he walked out. I have no idea why he's here now. But if he saw you here it would really complicate things."

"You've got the moral high ground and you want to keep it that way?"

"Something like that," she admitted.

He glanced impatiently at his watch. "I appreciate your position but I really have to go."

She thought for a moment. "Okay, just let me get dressed."

With a sigh of resignation, Ryan nodded and walked to the window.

Dana grabbed trousers and a shirt and fled to the bathroom. She'd sneak him down to her office, she decided, and then very loudly escort him to the door as if they had been in there all along. Of course, the fact that he was wearing a casual jacket over chinos and didn't have a briefcase was a problem. Still, she could give him a couple of files to carry, and that would have to do. Anyway, what business was it of Gus's who he was or why he was here? After over a month of silence he didn't deserve any explanations.

She dressed quickly, closing all the buttons of her white shirt. She left it loose over the trousers and quickly dabbed some concealer under her eyes and applied gloss to her lips.

"Very proper," Ryan teased as she hurried out and slipped her feet into a pair of white pumps.

"Okay, here's the plan. I'll take you down to my office and then I'll walk you to the door —"

"At which stage you'd like me to talk loudly and call you Ms De Lacey."

"Exactly!" Her smile faltered. "You know who I am."

"It clicked when you brought me back to this place," he admitted.

She frowned; still, what difference did it make now? "Wait here," she said and crept out on to the landing. All was quiet so she hurried back to Ryan. "Okay, let's go but, please, be as quiet as you can."

Dana led the way down the stairs, checked the kitchen door was still closed then quickly led Ryan the opposite way towards her office. At the door she turned and smiled at him. "Let me just get you a file to carry. Sorry," she added, seeing the flash of irritation cross his face. "I'm really sorry about this, and very embarrassed."

He sighed. "Forget it, just get me the damn file and let's get this over with."

As Dana turned away from him there was the sound of a flush from across the hall and the door of the loo opened. "Gus!"

Her husband stood there, his eyes going from her to the man at her side. "Hello, Dana. Sorry, I seem to have got you at a bad time."

"No! No, it's okay. We just finished our meeting, isn't that right?" She flashed a desperate smile at Ryan.

He nodded lazily, his arms hanging loosely at his sides. "That's right."

"Why don't you go and have a cup of tea, Gus, while I show Ry — Mr Ryan out?"

Dana held her breath as Gus looked from Ryan back to her. "No, I'll go."

"But why did you come?" she blurted out, as he turned to leave.

He looked back at her, and shook his head slightly. "I really don't know."

"Fuck, fuck, fuck," Dana muttered, tears coursing down her cheeks as she stood alone in the doorway. Gus had left abruptly with a screech of brakes and Ryan had made his escape shortly after, mumbling something about picking up a taxi on the main road. Dana hardly even heard him. She felt sick to her stomach and it had nothing to do with alcohol. Gus had come back and she had blown it.

Closing the door she went in search of Iris.

Dana found the housekeeper setting the table with the best cutlery and crockery.

"Breakfast is almost ready and the kettle is on," she said with a smile.

"I'm sorry you've gone to so much trouble, Iris, but I'm afraid he's gone."

"Gone?" Iris looked at her, confused.

Dana nodded. "Did he say anything, Iris? How did he seem to you?"

"Well, I couldn't really say —"

"Please, think — it's important," Dana begged.

"Well, I told him you were in a meeting, like you asked me to. I asked him would he like some breakfast while he waited. He said yes, that he hadn't had a decent cooked breakfast since he'd left." She paused, allowing herself a small, proud smile.

"Go on," Dana urged.

Iris thought. "Well, he asked me how I'd been, how my rheumatism was and how Jules was . . ."

"Jules?"

"My cat," Iris explained. "He got caught in some barbed wire the week before Mr Johnson left."

"Did he?" Dana said faintly. She hadn't even known Iris had a cat. How come Gus knew?

"And then he said he'd have a look around the garden while I was cooking."

Dana froze. "He went outside?"

"Well, yes. That's okay, isn't it?" Iris said, a tad defensively.

Dana thought of Ryan standing in the window of her bedroom while she went to get dressed. "And then?" she whispered.

Iris shrugged. "He came back in quite quickly, excused himself to go to the bathroom, and that was the last I saw of him."

"Shit."

Iris's mouth tightened with disapproval but she said nothing. Dana turned to leave. "What about this breakfast, Dana? Won't you, at least, have some?"

"No, I'm sorry, Iris," Dana said dully. "I don't feel very well."

CHAPTER
ELEVEN

Gus was livid, and more than a little shocked as he drove away. How could she? How the fuck could she? And in their bed too.

The sound of Prince's "Kiss" began to play loudly, interrupting his furious thoughts. He looked blankly at the silent radio. Then he realized the music was coming from under the passenger seat. Pulling into the kerb, he reached down and fumbled about until his hand closed around a mobile phone. "What the hell?" he muttered as it continued to ring in his hand. After a moment's hesitation he answered it. "Hello?"

"Is that Gus Johnson?"

"Yes, who is this?"

"It's Terry Andrews and you're holding my phone."

"I am?"

"Sorry, it must have fallen out of my pocket last night."

"Oh, right," he said vaguely. He was still seeing Dana's guilty face, and the smug grin of that bastard she was with.

"Could I drop by your office and pick it up?" Terry was saying.

"No," he said shortly.

"Look, I'm very sorry to inconvenience an important and busy man such as yourself," she said angrily, "but I need my phone."

"Fine. But I'm not in the office."

"Oh. Sorry."

"Where are you now?"

"Er, sitting in a café on Baggot Street."

"Right, if you tell me which one, I'll be with you in ten minutes."

As he drove, Gus forced himself to calm down. He tried to persuade himself that Dana really had been having an early morning meeting, but he knew it wasn't true. He'd seen that bastard standing at their bedroom window; Dana had been casually dressed — she never dressed down for meetings. As for this Ryan character, he didn't have a car, never mind a briefcase.

Gus banged his fist down on the steering wheel and cursed loudly. They'd spent the night together; it was obvious! How could she do it to him? He sighed and closed his eyes briefly as the traffic slowed to a stop. But then, why shouldn't she? He'd been pictured in the papers with his arm around a strange woman. He'd made no effort to get in touch with her or explain why he'd left. "Stupid pillock," he muttered as the traffic started to move again.

She had looked lovely too. He always loved it when she abandoned the cool, sophisticated, successful woman look in favour of the softer one. He adored seeing her engrossed in her work, a pencil through a knot in her hair, her brow knitted in concentration as she padded absently around the house and garden between frantic sessions on her laptop.

God, he missed her.

When he got to the café, Terry was sitting at a table in the window, biting on a pen and frowning at a pad on the table in front of her. He was stunned at how much she resembled Dana when she was engrossed in her work. He pushed his wife out of his mind and strode over to the table, a polite smile in place. "Sorry I took so long, the traffic's crap."

She looked up and nodded politely. "No problem."

Gus handed over her phone. "You're very popular, it's rung three times since I talked to you."

"Sorry."

He sighed. "It was an observation not a complaint."

"Sorry," she said again and then grinned. "We seem to say that a lot to each other. Can I buy you a coffee to make up for the hassle of delivering this?"

He sank into the seat opposite. "It was no hassle, but yeah, I could murder a black coffee."

She went to the counter and returned moments later with two large mugs of black coffee.

"I thought all you girls drank skinny lattes and mochas and all those other fake drinks."

"That's very sexist," she told him. "No, I need at least three of these in the morning to get me started."

Gus stared into his cup. "I think I need something a lot stronger to get me started today."

"Oh?"

He looked up into her curious face and remembered it was a journalist he was talking to. "Don't mind me, I just got out of the wrong side of the bed. So, tell me, did you get your job back?"

"Yeah."

"And what have you got lined up for today? Planning any interviews, or are you just going to sit at your desk and make it all up?"

"That's not fair," Terry protested, colour flooding her cheeks.

He raised an eyebrow. "Isn't it?"

"I already told you I had nothing to do with those photos being published. You said you believed me."

"And I do. But I still think that if you're serious about journalism you should look for a new job. How can you bear to have your name linked with a rag like that?"

"I have to start somewhere and I also have to eat. Anyway, for all you know I might be rubbish. Have you ever even read anything I've written?"

"Probably not," he admitted with a grin. "But you're a very good interviewer."

"Am I?"

He noticed how her eyes lit up at the compliment. "Yes. You're not too intrusive, you make friends with the interviewee without being too forward and, as a result, they open up to you."

"Thanks, that's a lovely thing to say." She sighed. "I wish my editor felt that way."

"Why, what's his problem?"

"Her," Terry corrected him. "Basically she thinks I'm not pushy enough."

He held out his hands. "I told you it was a rag."

Terry pushed her cup aside, shoved her notebook into her bag and stood up. "Yeah, well, thanks a bunch for the career advice, but I've got to go."

He put a hand on her arm. "Hey, don't be like that. I'm not having a go at you. I just hate what you do."

Terry sighed dramatically. "Yeah, well, I suppose I'm just going to have to live with that."

He laughed. "That puts me in my place. Please, sit down," he added quickly, knowing he shouldn't. "You haven't even finished your second coffee, never mind had your third."

Her expression softened. "If I do, will you quit having a go at me?"

Gus nodded solemnly. "I promise." She sat back down and he smiled. He should dislike this girl. He certainly shouldn't trust her. But there was something about her that he admired. She was a tough nut and, despite the nature of her work, he suspected she was basically honest. With those mischievous eyes and the ash-blonde hair that hung in soft waves around her shoulders, she was also very pretty.

"But I can't stay long," Terry said, taking a sip of coffee. "I have to interview a woman whose cat has psychic powers."

He opened his mouth to comment and then thought better of it.

"I know it's pathetic but someone's got to do it," she said glumly.

122

"Then do it to the best of your ability, no matter how dumb the subject. That's what will get you noticed. Oops, sorry, I promised no more advice."

"No, that kind of advice is acceptable." She smiled.

"So maybe we could meet again and you could benefit some more from my words of wisdom," Gus said recklessly.

Terry stared. "Are you asking me out, Mr Johnson?"

He saw the glint of humour in her eyes and the full, pink lips that were completely bare of make-up. "I suppose I am. Does that horrify you?"

She shook her head slowly. "No, but I am a bit surprised. Aren't you afraid I'll say yes just to pump you for information about your private life?"

Gus shrugged. "Strangely, no. Why? Is that the kind of thing you would do?"

She held his gaze. "No. No, it isn't."

"So?"

She nodded. "Okay, then, on one condition."

He let out a breath that he hadn't even realized he was holding. "I should have known there'd be a condition."

"I pick the venue."

"Fair enough," he murmured, wondering what he was letting himself in for.

"Can you meet me tomorrow at seven-thirty at the Grand Canal Dock train station?"

Gus frowned as he pulled out his Notepad and checked. "Yes, I'm free that evening. But there's no need to take the train; I can pick you up."

"No, that's fine, we won't need transport."

He looked at her curiously. "I don't know of any restaurants down there."

She grinned. "Who said we were going to a restaurant?"

As he walked back to his car Gus couldn't stop smiling at how his mood had lightened. Less than two hours ago he'd been devastated at his wife's infidelity; now he was grinning like an idiot because he had a date with another woman. It was probably the whole rebound thing, he realized as he drove to the office. Terry was young, pretty and available, that's all it was. She was also a journalist, he reminded himself. The first sign of her showing too much interest in his private life and he'd drop her like a hot potato. But it was no big deal. It was only one date. It didn't have to go any further than that. He could stop it any time he liked. If there was one thing Gus was sure of, it was that he had no interest in any kind of permanent relationship. Not any more.

"Where the hell have you been?" Tom marched into Gus's office seconds after Gus sat down.

"Sorry, I had some stuff to take care of."

Tom scowled. "I don't suppose that 'stuff' had anything to do with our company?"

"No. No, it didn't. Listen, Tom, I really don't need this —"

"Well, tough. We're supposed to be partners but you seem to have forgotten that —"

"I went to see Dana."

Tom dropped into the chair on the other side of Gus's desk and stared at him. "How did it go?"

Gus shook his head. "It didn't."

"She wouldn't see you?"

"Oh, yes, she agreed to see me all right. The only problem was she had to get rid of her lover first. Sadly for her, she wasn't quite quick enough."

"She had a man there?"

Gus sighed. "I suppose I shouldn't be surprised. We knew she was getting on with life. Then, of course, she may have seen the photos of me and Terry."

Tom frowned. "Terry?"

Gus felt his face redden. "The reporter from the other night."

"Oh, right. Still, even so. Are you sure you haven't got your wires crossed?"

"Pretty sure. I wandered out into the garden while I was waiting for her to come down and this bastard was standing at the bedroom window. *My* bedroom window," he added, the anger starting to surface again.

"Shit," Tom murmured.

"I went there this morning to talk to her; something I should have done weeks ago. But I've left it too late."

"What is it all about anyway, Gus?" Tom asked, unable to hold his silence any longer. "Why did you leave her in the first place?"

Gus raised his eyes to meet Tom's. "Because our whole marriage has been a lie."

"What?" Tom looked baffled.

"It's complicated."

"Do you want to talk about it?"

"No. Thanks, but I'd just like to get down to work, and forget about it for a while."

With a sigh, Tom stood up and walked to the door. "No problem. If you change your mind —"

"Sure."

Tom hesitated in the doorway. "Why don't you head down to Cork for a few days? You could bring some work with you."

"That's *her* house," Gus said bitterly.

"Rubbish! You've invested money, not to mention blood, sweat and tears into that place. And she's never loved it the way you have."

Gus nodded thoughtfully. "Maybe it's time we put things on a more official footing. Dana could keep the house here — she's welcome to it — but I would love to hold on to the farmhouse. I'll have to find a flat in Dublin too. I'm going nuts in that bloody hotel."

"You know you're welcome to our spare room —"

"No," Gus said quickly. He couldn't imagine anything worse than living with his happily married, pregnant friends. It would be torture. "Thanks for the offer but I need some space at the moment."

Tom nodded. "You're probably right. It would be only a matter of time before Ashling roped you into decorating the nursery."

The phone rang and Gus put his hand out to get it. "Sorry, Tom, but I'd better get on."

"Yeah. You know where I am if you need me."

After sitting in a stupor in her office for several hours, Dana picked up the phone.

"Hello?"

"Judy, it's me."

"Dana? Dana, are you all right?"

"Not really. Is there any chance you could come up?"

"You're scaring me now. What is it? Are you sick?"

"No, nothing like that. Sorry, don't mind me. I'm being stupid. Forget I called."

"No! Don't hang up," Judy yelled. "If you need me, I'll come. I can be with you by six, will that do?"

"But the girls —"

"Mum will mind them, don't worry. See you then."

Dana put down the phone and smiled through her tears. Judy was something else. She really didn't deserve a friend like her. She wasn't even sure why she wanted to talk now, but somehow she felt that she was losing her grip on life. She needed someone sensible to help her figure out what to do next. Who better than Judy?

Dana had sent Sylvie home. The girl had skipped into the office this morning full of chat about the previous night and was stunned to see her boss looking miserable. Dana had no intention of explaining herself so she said she was sick and told Sylvie to take the day off.

She fetched wine from the fridge and headed out to the garden. She was settling down to wait for Judy when she decided a cigarette would be nice. She didn't often indulge, but if there was a day she deserved a smoke, this had to be it. She was jumpy and she didn't think the wine would be enough to calm her.

Going back inside she rooted in drawers and coat pockets but, apart from an empty Silk Cut packet, there wasn't a sniff of tobacco in the house. "Damn," she muttered, the craving growing as she searched. She'd have to either nip down to the filling station at the corner or do without. The latter was suddenly inconceivable so she grabbed her coat, slung her bag over her shoulder and set off down the road. She bought twenty Marlboro Light and was out of the shop and back up the road within a couple of minutes. As she neared the house, she groped in her pocket for the remote control for the gate. As it slowly opened, a car drew up alongside her.

"Hey, Dana, how's it going?"

She looked around, smiling automatically. "Hi."

"Good night, last night?"

She frowned. The sun was in her eyes and she couldn't see the man's face clearly.

"Who are you?"

"I'm a reporter on the *Daily Journal*. Would you like to tell us about this new man in your life?"

She stared at him. "What?"

"Go on, Dana, give us a quote. Can you imagine your husband's face when he sees the photos?"

"Photos?" she said faintly.

"Yeah, we took a few at the club, then a couple of you when you got back here." His grin widened. "You make a very attractive couple."

"I have nothing to say," Dana said with as much dignity as she could muster, and she hurried inside. "Damn, damn, damn," she groaned when she was in the safety of her kitchen. This day was getting steadily worse. With trembling fingers she opened the packet of cigarettes.

CHAPTER
TWELVE

"Sylvie! What a nice surprise." Ian waved the PA into his office.

"Hi, Ian."

"Sit down, sit down. I'm dying to hear all about last night. How did it go?"

Sylvie sat down on the small, lumpy couch and crossed one long leg over the other. "I'm not quite sure."

"What do you mean?"

"We had a pretty good day and her mood was good. Then we went to the club and we kind of got separated. I kept an eye on her," she said hurriedly, when she saw his expression darken. "She was talking to this guy for a while, and then she was gone. I asked the guy and he said she'd gone to the loo, but when I checked she wasn't there."

"And then?" he prompted.

"I left."

He blinked. "You left?"

"Well, yeah. You see I was invited to this really cool party and Westlife were going to be there —"

"So you deserted Dana."

"No, of course not. I'd looked for her and when I couldn't find her I just assumed she'd gone home."

"Didn't you try phoning her?"

"My phone died," Sylvie said, unable to meet his eye. "Sorry." Of course, the truth was that when Dana had disappeared, she'd grabbed the opportunity and left with the man who'd been chatting her up all evening. She hadn't planned to but as soon as he told her he drove a Jag, that he was separated and had a villa in Spain, she had stopped noticing his thick lips, receding hairline and clammy hands. She'd convinced herself that he was probably a very nice person and it was just a matter of getting to know him better. The fact that he turned out to be incredibly boring, had a slightly affected laugh and was lousy in bed had changed her mind. Yes, she'd slept with him. She wondered if Ian would still fancy her if he knew she was capable of something like that.

But he didn't know what her life was like. She wasn't prostituting herself in order to live a celebrity lifestyle — although that would be nice too. She just wanted security for her family. This episode with Dana had made her realize how uncertain her future was, and she lay awake at night wondering how they would manage if she lost her job.

"Are you cold?" Ian asked.

Sylvie hadn't even realized she'd shivered. "Someone walked over my grave," she said with a weak smile.

He studied her closely. "Why do I get the feeling that you're not telling me everything?"

131

She sighed. "When I went in this morning she sent me home. She was obviously very upset but she wouldn't tell me why."

Ian dropped his head in his hands and groaned. "Oh, for the love of God, what is wrong with the woman now? Give me a male author any day. They just get pissed and feel up the shop staff."

Sylvie giggled. "Maybe she just has a hangover. We did have a lot to drink."

"I warned you that I didn't want her making a fool of herself," he said sharply.

"She didn't, honest! She was fine all evening. She didn't get loud or messy or anything."

He sighed. "I'd better go over there and see what the story is."

"I doubt she's in the mood for visitors."

"Then at least let me phone her."

Sylvie shrugged nonchalantly. "You'll just get the answering machine."

Ian opened his mouth to reply but the phone rang. "Ian Wilson?" He grinned widely at Sylvie. "Dana, I was just going to call you." He listened, frowning. "No, no reason, just wanted to check in. What?" He started to scribble on a pad in front of him. "Yes, well, I can understand why you might feel that way. It might be better if we just waited to see what they actually publish —" He listened again for a moment, pulling a face at Sylvie. "Look, let me see what I can find out."

Sylvie could hear Dana's raised voice at the other end of the phone.

"Fine, fine," Ian soothed. "Leave it with me. Yes. Yes, I promise I'll get straight back to you as soon as I've got any news."

He flung down the phone and threw his hands up in the air. "Bloody hell! I have got to get out of this business."

"What is it?" Sylvie asked, watching him nervously.

"Apparently she got lucky last night but was photographed with the guy. Some reporter's just turned up on her doorstep, looking for a quote. He says he has pictures of the two of them, outside the club and the house."

Sylvie had a vague recollection of the man that Dana had spent the evening with and she'd been sure he was gay. "But what's the problem? Isn't that what she wanted? I thought the whole idea was to make Gus jealous."

"It was, until Gus dropped by the house this morning and when he saw the guy there he left. Dana's worried that if the photos are published it will ruin any chance of them getting back together."

"I would have thought it was ruined the moment he realized she'd slept with this other guy."

"Yes, well, she thinks they could get past that. But he's a proud man and if it's in the papers he won't give her a second chance."

"But what can you do about it?" Sylvie asked.

He sighed. "I'm not sure. I can find out what photos they have but I can't stop them being published. Not unless they actually got into her garden and invaded her privacy in some way. But if the photos are of them kissing outside the club, or of them getting into a taxi together . . ." He shook his head. "I need to talk to a lawyer."

"You know, this could put us right back to square one." Sylvie chewed a nail nervously. "She'll probably be locked away in that bedroom for months now."

"I hope you're wrong." "What the hell am I going to tell Walter? He'll go mad."

"I don't blame him."

Ian picked up the phone.

"Are you going to call him?" Sylvie asked.

"Lord, no. Not until I've tried everything else first."

Dana poured Judy some wine and handed it to her.

Judy eyed the size of the glass. "It's just as well I'm staying the night."

"Are you sure that's okay?" Dana asked. "Will Phil and the girls be all right?"

"Jess and Janey," Judy reminded her.

"I knew that," Dana protested.

"I know," Judy said gently, pulling her jacket tighter around her. "So, tell me what's wrong."

Dana took another drink and lit a cigarette with shaky hands before answering. They were sitting in the garden watching the sun sink low in the sky, and though there was a slight chill in the air, Dana was past caring. "I slept with someone last night."

Judy choked on her wine. "Well, I suppose it was only a matter of time," she said when she'd caught her breath. She mopped at her face and chest with a tissue and grinned. "Was he any good?"

Dana smiled, relieved that her friend was being non-judgemental. "Yeah, from what I remember." It was the first time she'd had a chance to think about it but, despite the amount of alcohol they'd consumed, she remembered that the sex had been brilliant.

"So what's the problem?"

Dana sighed. "He stayed over and Gus chose today, of all days, to show up."

"Oh, dear."

"Yes."

Judy patted her hand. "Well, it was unfortunate, but it's been weeks now. What can Gus expect? Anyway, what was he doing, turning up unannounced? That was completely out of order."

"Maybe he was coming to tell me he wanted to move back in," Dana said sadly.

"Maybe he was coming to ask you for a divorce," Judy shot back, but immediately covered her mouth with her hand when she saw the look of shock on her friend's face. "Oh, Dana, I'm sorry, I didn't think. I'm sure I'm wrong."

Dana looked back at her, her eyes huge in her white face. "I'm not."

"Did you try calling him?" Judy asked.

Dana shook her head. "What's the point?"

"You could lie. Tell him he jumped to the wrong conclusion. That it was all completely innocent."

"I can't. The *Daily Journal* has photos of Ryan and me together. It will probably be in the paper tomorrow."

"But they couldn't have any photos of you actually doing anything." Judy's eyes widened. "Could they?"

"No, but if there's a photo of Ryan and me leaving a club and Gus recognizes him as the same man who was here this morning . . ." She shrugged.

"Lie," Judy said glibly. "If you want Gus back, lie through your teeth. Tell him Ryan was an absolute gentleman, he escorted you home and then he passed out on the sofa. Gus will believe you, because he'll want to believe you."

"I didn't know you could be so devious," Dana remarked.

Judy laughed. "Tell me, if Ryan hadn't been here and Gus had come to ask you if he could come back, what would you have said?"

"Are you crazy? I'd have said yes, of course."

"So you still love him."

"Yes!"

"Then why did you sleep with this other guy?"

Dana groaned. "I was drunk, he was there, he made me feel wanted, all the usual pathetic reasons."

"They're not pathetic," Judy said gently. "They're human. I tell you, if I got chatted up by a man even remotely attractive, I'd jump on him."

"Judy!" Dana looked at her friend in astonishment.

"Why are you so surprised? I may be a wife and mother but I'm still a woman. A very bored woman who gets fed up being taken for granted all the time."

"But Phil's great," Dana protested.

"How do you know?" Judy retorted. Her friend and her husband had met only a handful of times. Even

136

then, they'd exchanged nothing more than the usual polite pleasantries.

"You've told me he is," Dana reminded her.

Judy sighed. "He is, most of the time. It's just, well, sometimes I wish he'd treat me more like a lover and less like the live-in housekeeper. You know, he hardly ever calls me Judy any more. It's always 'Mum' or 'your mother'."

"But that's when the girls are there," Dana reasoned. "What about when you are alone?"

"I watch telly and he messes about on his laptop."

"You must talk," Dana insisted.

"Oh, we do — about the girls, about what bills need paying, about who's going to take the car to the garage for a service. It's all just so fucking boring, Dana."

"Judy, you don't curse." Dana stared at her.

Her friend scowled. "Yeah, well, maybe I should start. Maybe if I stopped being good old reliable Judy, he might notice me more."

"You need a break," Dana announced, sloshing more wine into their glasses. "We both do."

"How can I take a break? A night off is one thing. But anything more would be impossible."

"Surely Phil could take a week off work?"

"The way he talks, the business would fold if it wasn't for him. You'd think he was the head of the Central Bank instead of an insurance broker."

Dana laughed. "That's men for you; they need to feel indispensable."

"Anyway, forget about him. I'm here to talk about your problems."

"I don't think I want to any more. Let's go out."

"Out?" Judy blinked.

"Yes, why the hell not? We could go for a nice dinner and then on to a club."

"But after what happened last night, shouldn't you lie low for a while?"

"That's what everyone will expect me to do," Dana pointed out. "If I'm out with my best friend instead and we keep away from men —"

"Oh, great!" Judy made a face.

Dana laughed. "Okay, then, we don't have to keep away from them. Just don't leave me alone with any."

Judy looked doubtful. "But if they have photos of you with this man they're still going to print them."

"Let them," Dana said defiantly. "I'm going to have to pretend it just doesn't matter."

"You're right." Judy nodded enthusiastically. "I think that's a great idea."

"So let's go and get ready."

"But I've nothing to wear," Judy reminded her.

Dana waved away her protests. "I've plenty of stuff that will fit you. Go on up and have a look while I phone Ian."

"Ian?"

"He's the guy that looks after my PR. We need to make sure that we get photographed tonight."

"What on earth will Phil will say if he sees his wife in the papers?"

"You said you wanted to shake things up a bit, didn't you?" Dana grinned.

Judy smiled slowly. "I did, didn't I?"

CHAPTER
THIRTEEN

"Sylvie, we're going out."

Clutching the phone to her ear, Sylvie slipped out of the kitchen where the telly was blaring and sat on the stairs. "Ian, I've told you, I'm not interested. Anyway, it's nearly ten o'clock."

"Dana's going to the Pod tonight."

"What?"

"Yeah. Great, isn't it?"

"She's going on her own, or with this guy she picked up last night?"

"Neither. She's going with some old school friend, which is just perfect."

Sylvie felt a bit miffed and more than a little disappointed that Dana had found someone else to socialize with.

"So we're going too," Ian was saying. "To make sure everything goes according to plan this time."

"How do we do that?" Sylvie asked sulkily.

"A word in the right ear, spread the odd rumour — you know the sort of thing."

"I'm PA to an author not a PR specialist. Anyway what's all this about? I thought Dana was in the depths of depression again."

"She was, but then she decided to persuade Gus and the rest of the world that the guy she slept with — I mean brought back for coffee — just passed out on her sofa and it was all completely innocent."

"Yeah, right! Who's going to believe that?"

"Everyone, my dear. Because you are going to tell them that you were there the whole time."

"Me?" Sylvie squeaked. "But I went to a party, remember?"

"You still could have gone back to Dana's place afterwards."

Sylvie had crept out of Larry's place at about five, so it was possible. As it was, she'd told her mother that she stayed at Dana's. "I suppose," she agreed.

"Come on, Sylvie. It means another night out in a top club absolutely gratis."

"True." Sylvie smiled in anticipation. "Where will we meet?"

"I could pick you up —"

"No, that's okay," she said hurriedly.

"Always so mysterious, Ms Parker. No wonder I'm mad about you. Meet me at eleven in the Horseshoe bar."

"This place is crawling with celebrities," Judy murmured, as she sipped her champagne cocktail. "Do you know all of them?"

"Hardly any," Dana said, looking around. "We all nod and smile at each other but for the most part, I only know their faces from the papers."

"Are there any press here?"

"God knows. I saw a gossip columnist on the way in. Patti Monk."

"Yes, I saw her. She's great."

"You think? The photographers aren't allowed in but as everyone has camera phones now, you're never safe."

"It's a different world," Judy marvelled.

"But not a better one," Dana assured her. "Don't be blinded by the glitz, Judy, it's not real."

"But you always seemed to enjoy it so much. You were always full of chat about the celebrity gossip."

Dana cringed inwardly. She had boasted to her friend about her glamorous life, exaggerating much of it. "I suppose it just made me feel important."

Judy stared at her. "But, Dana, you're a famous author. Why do you need them to make you feel important?"

"I just get the feeling I always have to apologize for my books," Dana admitted. "In the US, they think what I do is great. In Ireland, I'm a producer of raunchy drivel. Oh, and Conall O'Carroll's daughter."

"That's not true," Judy said staunchly. "You're a great writer."

"I write trash," Dana said sadly.

"Stop that," Judy hissed, her face worried. "You give enjoyment to a lot of women."

"Maybe for an hour or so but most of them won't even be able to remember the title of the book a week later."

"I never remember book titles," Judy said blithely. "Except the really good ones . . ." she trailed off.

"Exactly."

"Sorry. Can you just wait while I take my big foot out of my mouth?"

Dana hugged her. "Don't worry about it."

"I'm sure you could write more serious books if you wanted to. You just decided to write this type of stuff instead."

"I didn't decide anything, Judy," Dana told her. "I was broke and I wrote what they told me to write and that's what I've been doing ever since."

"Then change," Judy said simply. "Try something new, something completely different."

The music cranked up, saving Dana from having to reply. She raised a hand to attract a passing waitress and ordered more champagne. As she did, Ian and Sylvie appeared. "You'd better make that two bottles," she told the girl. "Judy, this is my PA, Sylvie Parker, and PR consultant, Ian Wilson."

"Nice to meet you," Judy said.

"What are you two doing here?" Dana asked.

"Moral support." Ian smiled broadly and shook Judy's hand.

Judy opened her mouth to say something but Ian and Sylvie had already turned away.

"They're working," Dana explained when she saw Judy's face. "Ian's checking the room for important people that I should be seen with, or press that he wants to lick up to. And Sylvie is looking for a husband."

"She's very pretty," Judy said without envy. "Although a little on the thin side. I wouldn't have thought she'd have any problem finding a man."

142

"Oh, she's no problem pulling," Dana agreed. "They're just usually not rich enough for her."

"I see," Judy murmured.

"I am here." Sylvie turned around and shot her boss a reproachful look.

Dana smiled. "Now don't get touchy, you know it's true." She paused as the waitress returned with the champagne. "So, Ian, what's the plan?" she asked when the girl had left.

Ian took his glass and stood up. "I'll work the room and then come back for you. Remember, if anyone mentions last night, you laugh it off and tell them you're going to have to build an extension for all the partygoers who end up crashing at your place."

"Good line." Judy nodded approvingly.

"That's what I'm here for," he said with a small bow and was gone.

"So good-looking, and charming too," Judy mused, wishing she was a few years younger and a few pounds lighter. "Don't you think, Sylvie?"

The girl shrugged silently.

Judy and Dana exchanged glances. "They would make a nice couple," Dana agreed, "if she'd only give him a chance."

Sylvie took her glass and stood up. "I think I'll have a look around. See you later."

"Strange girl," Judy observed.

"She's fine when you get to know her. Just a little preoccupied with money. But then, look around you — she's not alone. How many people do you see engrossed in conversation? None. They're all busy looking over each other's shoulders to see who's who, who's *with* who, and whether they could be talking to someone richer or more important."

Judy laughed. "You're funny. Actually, that's what you should do: write something funny."

Dana pulled a face. "Comedy isn't really me, especially the mood I've been in lately."

"Do you know that most of the most brilliant comedians are manic depressives? Robin Williams, Stephen Fry —"

"I thought he was bi-polar?"

"Same thing, I think. Anyway, don't split hairs. You know what I mean."

"What? Because I'm miserable maybe I can write something brilliantly funny?"

Judy shrugged. "It's worth a shot."

"So you do think the stuff I'm producing at the moment is rubbish," Dana accused.

"I never said that!" Judy glared at her. "I'm going to the loo. Cheer up before I get back or I'll be looking for someone more interesting to talk to as well."

Dana sank back in her chair with a sigh as she mulled over Judy's words. She wasn't sure she could write anything any more. Occasionally she felt the creative urge, but as soon as her fingers touched the keys her mind went blank. She'd scanned the chapters of *The Mile High Club* and felt slightly sick. It was as good as if not better than her other books, but it just didn't do it for her any more. It seemed so meaningless, empty and trivial. Maybe she should try her hand at non-fiction. Her mouth twisted into a bitter smile.

Maybe she should write her father's life story. How cathartic would that be?

"At least you're smiling." Judy sat back down beside her.

"I was just thinking that I should write Dad's biography."

Judy stared. "You wouldn't!"

"Why not?"

Judy shot her a worried look. "Come on, Dana, don't go down that road."

"Why not?"

"There might be an initial feeling of triumph," Judy said gently, reading her mind, "but once you let that particular cat out of the bag, you can't take it back."

"You're right," Dana whispered.

Judy took her hand and held it tightly. "It's over, darling. Don't start brooding about it again."

Dana smiled wanly. "I suppose I do have enough to brood about at the moment."

Ian took the seat across from them looking like the cat that had got the cream. "I am so good at this job," he murmured, rubbing his hands together. "What would you do without me?"

Dana raised an eyebrow. "No idea. So, tell me?"

He leaned closer. "As we speak, Sylvie is talking to Jack Dawson about how Ryan not only conked out on your sofa but threw up on your cream Kashmir rug first."

"Who's Jack Dawson?" Judy asked.

"He works for Patti Monk," Ian explained.

"Ooh, this is all so exciting and glam." Judy giggled.

"I hope she hasn't told him Ryan's name," Dana said worriedly.

Ian looked affronted. "Of course not. Actually, our Sylvie's quite a good actress. She's looking reluctant to be gossiping about her boss, but enjoying the attention of the press at the same time. Trust me, Dana, this is working out perfectly."

"Good." Dana relaxed slightly. "So can we go now?"

"But I thought we were out for the night," Judy protested.

"We are," Dana assured her, "but let's go somewhere a little less false."

The karaoke bar Dana took her to was both busy and loud. A woman with a shock of blonde hair and an enormous bust was belting out "Stand by Your Man".

"Bloody hell, she's going to pop out of that dress any moment." Judy watched transfixed.

"That's what they're hoping." Dana nodded at the line of men standing at the bar. She ordered two beers and two packets of crisps, and led Judy towards a small table at the back of the room. "It's slightly quieter here."

"Is it? I can't believe you're drinking beer."

"You wouldn't want to drink the wine served in a place like this." Dana clinked her bottle against her friend's. "Cheers."

"How on earth did you find this place? It's not really your sort of thing now, is it?"

"Sylvie's been to a few hen parties here and she always seemed to have a good time."

"Does she get up and perform?"

Dana laughed again. "If she has she's never admitted it. At least we're highly unlikely to meet any press here, unless it's their night off."

The blonde finished her song to tumultuous applause and was immediately replaced by a couple, rather the worse for wear, performing a tuneless version of "Hopelessly Devoted to You".

The crowd booed and laughed and the couple were hustled off stage.

"This is fun." Judy took a slug of beer and grinned at her friend. "We need to get together more often."

"I'd like that." Dana too was enjoying herself, her earlier blues forgotten. She realized that she felt more relaxed in Judy's company than in anyone else's. Perhaps that was because she could be herself.

Judy stood up and wolf-whistled as a young guy climbed on to the stage, opened his shirt to the waist, and started to do an Elvis number, his gyrations challenging those of the King himself. She signalled a waiter for two more beers. "I like it here. Although it's not exactly the kind of place you come to if you want to have a quiet conversation," she yelled.

Dana grinned. "No, it isn't, is it?"

Judy shrugged good-naturedly. "I came up here because you needed me. Whether you want to talk or not, that's up to you."

"Thanks, Judy."

"What?" Judy cupped her hand to her ear.

"I said thanks!"

"Any time, pet. Any time."

"Where's Dana?" Sylvie asked, slipping into the seat beside Ian.

"Gone."

"I've been working my butt off trying to get her off the hook, and she leaves without even saying goodbye or thank you. Charming."

"But she did buy us another bottle of champagne before she left." Ian indicated the ice bucket and two glasses on the table in front of them.

Sylvie grinned. "Oh, well, then, I suppose I'll forgive her."

"So, how did it go?"

"No problem. I'm pretty sure he swallowed it hook, line and sinker. But I could do with a shower after the way he was mauling me."

"You're some woman," he murmured, pouring the wine and edging closer. "We make quite a team."

Sylvie took the glass he proffered. "A good working team," she corrected.

"Nothing wrong with mixing business with pleasure occasionally," he said, running his fingers along her bare arm.

Sylvie shivered slightly. "Stop that."

"Come on, let's dance."

"Why on earth would I want to dance with you?"

"Because Jack Dawson is on the way over and he has a lecherous look in his eye."

Sylvie put her hand in his. "Lead the way."

CHAPTER
FOURTEEN

On Wednesday evening Gus stood outside the train station wishing he was somewhere else. He would have cancelled the date if he could, but his only way of contacting Terry was by ringing that bloody newspaper, and there was no way he was going to do that. Not knowing where she was taking him, he'd opted for black jeans, a black T-shirt and a leather jacket.

"Hey there."

He turned to see Terry standing across the road, smiling. She was also wearing jeans and had a denim jacket slung over her shoulder. Immediately he felt better. "Hi. Where did you come from?"

She nodded to a distant apartment block. "I live down there. Did you take the train?"

He shook his head. "No, it was such a nice evening I decided to walk. So, are you going to tell me where we're going?"

"No," she grinned. "But don't worry, it's not far."

"Greyhound racing!" he exclaimed as they turned into the entrance of Shelbourne Park racetrack.

She shot him a nervous look. "Are you disgusted?"

He laughed delightedly. "Not at all, it's a lovely surprise. I haven't been here since I was a kid."

Terry insisted on paying and buying programmes for both of them and then led him upstairs to the sitting room. While Gus fetched them a couple of beers, Terry nabbed two stools near the window looking down on the course.

"You're going to have to help me out here," he said, as he sat down beside her and bent his head over the programme. "The last time I did this I wasn't allowed to gamble."

She explained how to read the form of the dogs and the different kinds of bets. "I usually just do a reverse dual forecast. That's where you pick two dogs and once they come in first and second in any order, you win. You can put on a bet up here." She pointed to a wall of kiosks at the end of the corridor. "Or if you're a real gambler, you go down there." He looked down at the line of bookies standing on boxes along the edge of the course, scribbling odds on blackboards.

Gus nodded. "It's all coming back now. I remember the last few seconds before a race there would be a big scramble to put on a bet to get better odds."

"That still happens and you see some very large notes change hands. I usually stay up here and place fifty-cent bets but don't let me stop a high-flyer like you from blowing your fortune."

He laughed. "I think I'll stick with you for the moment."

In the first race, she put a bet on five and six and Gus put a euro on number four. Hers romped home in first and second place. Four was last.

150

"Oh, come on," Gus yelled at the dog. "What kind of a performance is that?"

"Waste of time and money betting on a dog like that," the man next to him said. "He's only ever won in track six."

"I told him that," Terry agreed. "But he's more money than sense."

He made a face. "So how much have you won?"

Terry looked up at the TV screen in the corner. "Seven euros and fifty cent!"

He raised an eyebrow. "I see. So are you going to put it all on the next race?"

"Are you mad?" Terry looked scandalized and leaned across him to talk to their neighbour. "I told you he'd more money than sense. No, I'm going to put fifty cent on Runaway Lad and Ballydun."

Gus looked at his programme. "Five and six again, eh? So that's your strategy." He nudged the man beside him. "Any tips?"

The man tapped his nose. "Number one."

Gus stood up. "Right, so. Number one it is. Would you like me to collect your winnings and put on your bet?" he asked Terry.

"You won't do a runner with my winnings, will you?" she asked, suspiciously.

"As if!"

"Go on, then."

Terry won the next two races and in the third, Gus finally had a winner. "Yes!" He punched the air.

His neighbour shook his head. "Ah, lad, sure he was the favourite. You'll be lucky to get your money back."

"What?" Gus pretended outrage.

Terry laughed. "You're not very good at this, are you?"

"No, but you are. Now I know why you brought me here. You just wanted to feel superior."

"I don't need to bring you racing to do that," she retorted.

Gus sighed. "True."

That was his only win for the night and when the last race finished, he tore up his tickets with an exaggerated sigh. "Well, I'm glad that's over. I'd be broke otherwise."

"You got greedy. Let me go and collect my winnings and then we can go." Minutes later Terry was back, brandishing another eight euros. "Dinner's on me," she told him. "There's a good chipper just down the road."

He shook his head solemnly. "I wouldn't dream of eating into your winnings. Dinner's on me. There's a nice place about a ten-minute walk from here if you're up for it."

Her eyes met his. "I'm up for it."

Fifteen minutes later they were sitting in a crowded Filipino restaurant called Bahay Kubo, studying menus. "I recommend the curry," Gus said.

"Me too."

He looked up to see that she was laughing at him. "Sorry, am I being very pretentious?"

"Just a little."

"I forgot you were a local. Do you come here often?"

"Now there's an original question."

He groaned. "Do you have a smart answer for everything?"

She shook her head. "I'm sorry. It's just you're such good company I keep forgetting that I hardly know you. I'm not watching my every word like I usually do on a first date."

"I'm not either," he admitted, surprised. "And I was determined to be guarded, given your line of work."

"That's understandable, but then, we haven't had a chance to talk much about ourselves at all; we've been too busy gambling."

"And having fun," he said quietly.

She smiled. "That too."

"Is that what this is, by the way?" he asked later, as they strolled back to her apartment. "A first date?"

She stopped and turned to face him. "You tell me. Are you in a position to be dating?"

"I'm separated, and that doesn't look like it's about to change. So, yes, I suppose I am."

Terry raised her eyebrows. "You're such a romantic."

"Sorry." He looked shamefaced. "I just want to be straight with you."

"Good."

"So, to that end, can I say that I would very much like to kiss you?"

Terry's eyes twinkled as she moved closer. "Well, get on with it, then."

Gus whistled as he walked back into town. He felt like a completely different man to the one who'd left the hotel earlier, happier than he had been in a long time.

Terry hadn't invited him in for coffee or anything else and he was glad of that. Although that last kiss had left him wanting more. He should feel guilty, but he didn't. Dana had found someone new, why shouldn't he? Still, he reminded himself, he was vulnerable and he should take things slowly. His ego and heart had taken quite a battering. Terry had happened along at just the right time and the fact that she was a lot younger — he guessed her to be in her mid-twenties — was flattering.

It helped him deal with the fact that Dana was sleeping with another man — or men. For all he knew she was bringing home a different one every night. She had left two phone messages for him since he'd slammed out of the house yesterday morning but he'd ignored them; he wasn't ready to listen to her lies. Tom had shown him the piece in the paper. There was a photo of Dana with *that* man getting out of a taxi. The piece underneath it read:

Author Dana De Lacey is getting on with her life but, a close friend confided, she is not looking for a replacement for handsome architect Gus Johnson. "Dana has lots of friends and they have been helping her get over her marital breakdown. But there is no one special at the moment." Dana is photographed with a friend, coming home after a night's clubbing.

But Gus hadn't believed it for an instant. He had no doubt that she'd slept with that bastard; he had seen the look of panic and guilt in her eyes and the distinct challenge in the eyes of the other man. It hurt, of course it did. Tonight, though, the pain wasn't as bad. For the first time he was able to imagine a future without Dana. Tomorrow, he decided, he would start looking for a flat. He'd also call Terry and thank her for tonight. And then — well, then he'd just wait and see.

"I know that voice, I'm sure I do," Walter Grimes drawled.

Dana covered the mouthpiece with her hand. "This could take a while," she told Judy.

"I'll go and shower, so."

"Wally —" Dana started.

"No, really don't tell me. I'm very good with voices. I'm sure it will come to me — eventually."

"Wally, I'm sorry, okay? I just wasn't ready to talk to people."

"People!" he said, his voice filled with disgust. "I'm not people!"

She sighed. "No, of course you're not. But though you're a friend — and a good one — you're also my agent."

"The same guy who's been fighting to keep you employed," he pointed out.

"I know that and I'm grateful," she said humbly. "Am I forgiven?"

"Of course you are, darling! So, tell me all."

"Sorry?"

"I believe there's a new man in your life."

"No there isn't. I just had a very drunken one-night stand."

"Oh, well, that's good too. Tell me about him."

"I'm sure you already know everything there is to know," Dana said shrewdly.

He chuckled. "Ian may have mentioned something."

"And sent you the press cuttings?"

"Them too. Good-looking guy, although not quite as handsome as your husband."

"Ian did a great job — I don't know how. Even I'm beginning to think I'm innocent. Gus, however, doesn't appear to be fooled."

"Haven't you heard from him?"

"Not a word," she said glumly. She'd tried to contact him but there had been no response. He obviously believed the evidence of his own eyes rather than the story printed in the newspaper, but then, he was an intelligent man. She felt a sense of pride and admiration that he wasn't taken in so easily but sad that it looked like she's totally screwed up any chance of getting him back.

"He's a proud man," Wally said, echoing her thoughts.

"He is," Dana agreed. "And I'm devastated that I've lost him. But I need to get on with my life now. I'm going to forget about men for a while and get stuck into my writing."

"Oh, Dana, I'm so proud of you." Walter's voice wavered with emotion. "This book will be your best yet, I just know it."

156

Dana didn't share her agent's optimism but he didn't need to hear that right now. "I've got to go now. But, I promise, from now on, I'll keep in touch."

"Make sure you do. Goodbye, my darling. Write well."

When she'd hung up, Dana went in search of Judy. Her friend had ended up staying another three days, much to her husband's surprise. Judy had rather enjoyed his reaction.

"He won't be taking me for granted for a while," she'd said with satisfaction.

"Ready to go?" Dana asked now, as Judy came down the stairs.

"All set."

"You could stay on for the weekend," Dana wheedled. "We could do some more clubbing."

"No, darling, sorry. If it was just Phil, I'd stay like a shot. But I'm missing the girls."

"I understand. Just come back again soon." Dana enveloped her in a tight hug. "Thank you so much for everything."

"Thank you for a very exciting three days!" Judy laughed. "Are you going to be okay?"

"I'm going to be writing so much that there'll be smoke coming from my laptop," Dana promised.

"Good for you." Judy hugged her again.

After Judy had left, Dana went straight into her office and sat down at the desk. She switched on her laptop and opened the *The Mile High Club* file. After staring at it for a moment, she closed it again and opened a new file. Then she began to write.

It was probably the day of my twelfth birthday when I first realized that Daddy didn't treat my mother very well. I had just come downstairs, dressed in the red velvet dress that we had bought the previous weekend on our trip to Dublin, and his face lit up when he saw me. "Look at you! You must be a princess, for only a little princess could look so pretty and carry herself so well."

I remember blushing even though I was used to Daddy's elaborate and lavish compliments. I ran into his open arms feeling treasured and special.

"Is that what you're wearing?" he said over my shoulder, his tone now clipped and cold.

"I can change, if you don't think it's suitable," my mother responded quietly.

I remember she was wearing a simple navy linen suit and I thought she looked pretty but sad.

"There's no time for that now," my father snapped. "We're due at the restaurant in fifteen minutes. Where the hell is Edmund?"

My brother, looking awkward and uncomfortable in a jacket and tie, dragged his gawky, teenage body down the stairs.

My father's sigh was eloquent. "I suppose you'll have to do." He turned to me and held out his arm. "Come, my princess. Your carriage awaits."

We went out to his large, old Mercedes and he held the front passenger door open for me before walking around and getting into the driver's seat. Mother locked the front door before scrambling into the back seat beside Edmund.

"Would you like to sit here, Mother?" I asked, for the first time struck that it seemed wrong and slightly subservient that she should always be expected to sit in the back.

"She's fine where she is," my father said curtly as he guided the old car down the long driveway.

"I'm fine, Dana." My mother's hand was on my shoulder in a gesture of gratitude. But I felt that it was also a warning. Don't make trouble, she was telling me. Don't make him cross.

Dana flopped back in her seat, feeling drained and emotional. This was so different to her usual work but maybe that's what was needed to get her back into the saddle. She'd just write a few more pages and then she'd get stuck into *The Mile High Club*. First, she needed a drink. In the kitchen, however, she discovered she and Judy had finished the white wine. She went to the drinks cupboard — there was sure to be a bottle of red somewhere — but no, nothing. The only thing she could find that held any attraction was a bottle of cognac. She smiled slightly as she poured a large measure into a crystal balloon. The last time she'd had this stuff, was the night she spent with Ryan.

Back in her office, she opened the doors to the darkened garden and let in the cool night air. Settling back in her chair she cradled the glass in her hands and sighed. She felt guilty about her adulterous behaviour — she had never even looked at another man before.

But, under the circumstances, was it any surprise that she had fallen for Ryan's charm? He had got her at a weak moment. And because he was a stranger, she'd talked to him in a way that she normally never would. It had been a case of right time, right place. Had it been like that for Gus and that girl?

Turning back to her laptop, Dana set down her drink and got back to work.

It was a birthday much like the others. We always went to the poshest restaurant in Wexford town and Father ordered for all of us. His only concession to the fact that it was a birthday celebration and that we were just children was to allow us chips, or pommes frites as he would say, instead of the usual mashed potatoes. He had always insisted that we eat "proper" food and when we were small he'd even objected to our mother cutting up our meat for us.

The concept of inviting my friends over for a birthday tea with cake and ice cream was inconceivable to him. The O'Carrolls were above such juvenile behaviour. The less his children were exposed to their school friends, the happier he was.

As the waiters gathered around to sing "Happy Birthday" to me and I blew out the candles on the chocolate gateau, Father produced my present with a flourish. I smiled politely and took it, knowing that it would be yet another book. Thankfully my mother had already presented me with her own offering — a delicate silver bracelet that had been her mother's. I fingered it now as the waiter cut and served the cake.

"Well, come on, then. Open it!" my father said, his eyes full of excitement.

Smiling at him, I carefully unwrapped the expensively shop-wrapped book. Inside was a leather-bound copy of *Wuthering Heights*.

"I know it's a bit advanced for your age," he said hurriedly. "But you're such an avid reader and way ahead of your class. I think you'll be well able for it."

"Thank you, Daddy. It's great." I stood up so that I could reach over and kiss his cheek.

He flushed, waving away my affection. "Oh, it's nothing, princess, nothing. Although," his eyes slid to the bracelet on my wrist, "slightly more useful than that little trinket."

I bristled at his criticism of my pretty bracelet and, as I suddenly realized, of my mother. "I love it," I told him coldly, resuming my seat.

His shrug was indulgent. "Well, you're a girl. Now —" he clicked his fingers for a waiter — "a cognac and a cigar for me, and some tea for my wife."

"Maybe she wou — wou — would li — li — like a cognac too," Ed said, a mutinous look in his eye.

"What's that, Edmund? Sorry?" My father cupped a hand to his ear in an exaggerated manner. "Could you say that again, didn't quite catch it. The English language is a beautiful thing, try not to abuse it."

"Conall!" my mother hissed, her eyes flashing with uncharacteristic anger.

Ed slunk down in his chair and studied his plate.

Father eyed my mother coldly. "Did you want to say something, my dear?"

She looked into his eyes for a moment, then shook her head and looked down.

My father smiled but I could see the irritation in his eyes. "Now, where's that damn cognac?"

After that I was suddenly conscious of an atmosphere in my family that I hadn't noticed before. Ed's stammer, I realized, was at its worst when Daddy was in the room. Mother was happier and more fun when her husband wasn't around. I asked Ed about it a few weeks later. We were in the sitting room. Daddy was safely in his study and my mother was working in the kitchen.

"On my birthday, Ed. Why did you say that to Daddy about Mummy having a cognac?"

He shrugged, his eyes on the Rubik's cube that was usually in his hands.

"Ed, please tell me," I said impatiently.

"Because he — he — he never asks her what she wants. He just tells her."

I was silent. Several examples of what he was saying sprang to mind. He was right. Why hadn't I noticed it? "That's wrong, and I'll tell him so," I stated, with all the bravery and innocence of the favourite child on the edge of puberty.

Ed's fingers stilled and he looked up. "Stay out of it."

"But, Ed, it's wrong," I insisted.

"Dana, you're just a kid. Keep out of it. If you say anything you'll just make it worse for Mum."

I opened my mouth to protest, but at that moment my mother called us to tea. Ed shot me a warning glance.

"Leave it, Dana."

162

I nodded and obediently followed him out to the kitchen.

"You're very quiet," my mother remarked as we sat at the table eating jam sandwiches. "Is everything okay?"

I glanced briefly at Ed and then nodded. "Fine, Mum."

Dana saved the file and closed her laptop. The room was freezing now and she shut the windows. Glancing at her watch she was startled to find it was almost midnight. She was tired but she knew she was also too wound up to sleep. Going to the kitchen, she topped up her glass and then, pulling a warm jacket around her shoulders, she went into the moonlit conservatory, curled up in a chair and let the silence and darkness envelop her.

CHAPTER
FIFTEEN

Dana had just walked out through the door when the phone rang. Sylvie picked it up. "Hello?"

"Sylvie?"

"Oh, hi. If you're looking for Dana, I'm afraid she's gone out for a couple of hours."

"No problem, it's nothing urgent. How are things?"

"I'm not sure," Sylvie told him. "Dana's behaving a bit oddly."

"She's writing, though, isn't she?"

"Yes. Only . . ."

"What?"

"She seems to have changed her whole routine. She used to write in the mornings and give me pages to proofread as she produced them. Now, she sleeps in and works very late. And she doesn't want me around when she's working. So I'm working mainly mornings. When she gets up I brief her, and then I go home. It's very odd."

"Well, her life has changed," he pointed out. "She's lonely and has nothing else to do at night now her husband has gone."

"I suppose." Sylvie wasn't convinced. "But it still doesn't explain why she hasn't given me any chapters to proofread. She's been working since Friday, and yet not a sausage."

"She's probably nervous of letting you see her first efforts. Remember, she hasn't written for weeks. She may be finding it hard to pick up where she left off."

"You're right," Sylvie agreed. "And she does seem to be on edge."

"She's bound to be. I'm sure there's nothing to worry about, Sylvie. Last Tuesday night was a huge success and the press coverage the next day and at the weekend was fantastic. Everyone empathizes with Dana now. Things couldn't be better. We had quite a good night ourselves too," he added, a smile in his voice.

"Yes, it was good fun."

"Maybe we should do it again," Ian suggested.

"I don't think so."

"Oh, come on, you know you're crazy about me."

Sylvie laughed. "The word crazy does come to mind when I think of you."

"Ah, so you do think of me?"

"Ian, go away. I have work to do."

"Sylvie Parker, you're a cruel and heartless woman."

"You've got that right. Go and find yourself a nice girl."

"Nice girls are boring."

"I'm hanging up now. Goodbye, Ian."

"Bye, Sylvie."

"So, Dana, how are you today?"

She laughed. "You'd think I'd seen you only last week, the way you said that."

The psychiatrist peered at his notes. "No, it's been about seven years."

Dana sighed. "Yes. Just before I met my husband."

"It's never wise to stop treatment without consulting your doctor," he said gravely. "Especially when you're coming off antidepressants."

"I'm sorry, but I followed your instructions to the letter," she promised. "And, quite frankly, I didn't feel the need of another session."

"So marriage cured you?" The doctor smiled.

"Yes, something like that. You'd have liked my husband. He was great."

He frowned. "Was?"

"Still is, I'm sure. Only we're not together any more."

"I'm sorry. Was it a joint decision or . . ."

She shook her head. "No, he left me. Which is why I'm here."

"So what went wrong?"

"I wish I knew. One evening he said wasn't happy and that he was leaving."

Dr Corcoran made notes. "And did he tell you why?"

Dana crossed and recrossed her legs. "He said we hadn't grown as close as he'd hoped; that I didn't talk to him. I don't understand any of it. I loved him. He was my best friend. And, as far as I was concerned, we were blissfully happy."

The doctor looked at her over his half-moon glasses and waited for her to continue.

"Yes. So, it's been quite difficult. And I haven't been able to sleep or to write. And I've been feeling very down. I think I need to go back on the antidepressants."

"Why do you think he left, Dana?"

"I have no idea. Maybe he got fed up with me. Maybe he fancies someone else. Maybe he's having a midlife crisis." She shrugged.

"You don't sound like you believe any of those reasons."

She rested her chin in her hand and sighed. "I don't know what to believe."

"And you've been feeling down."

"Down, sad, hopeless — the usual things you'd expect of a woman who's just been dumped." Dana laughed weakly.

Dr Corcoran nodded thoughtfully. "You know, I remember you telling me that you never suffered from writer's block. You told me that, no matter what happened, you could always write. Until now."

"Gus was the love of my life. His leaving has knocked me for six."

"I'm sure, but you've suffered more traumatic experiences in your life and they didn't affect your writing."

She said nothing.

"And you're having problems sleeping?"

"Yes. I feel exhausted when I go to bed but then I just lie there thinking. So now I get up again and work."

He looked up from his notes. "But I thought you couldn't write?"

Dana felt the colour rise in her cheeks. "I can't write fiction," she explained. "Instead I've been working on something else."

He put down his pen and looked at her. "Are you writing about your own experiences, by any chance?"

She nodded. "How did you know?"

He smiled. "Just a guess. So why do you think you felt the need to write about your life?"

"Isn't it obvious? My husband has left me. I'm at a turning point. I'm depressed."

"So you're writing about your marriage?"

She sighed. "No."

"I see." He picked up his pen again and wrote something down.

"What do you see?" she said irritably. "The only reason I'm here is because my marriage has broken up and I need some help to get over it. Just write me a prescription, and I'll let you get on with your work."

He sat back, folding his hands in his lap. "I have plenty of time."

Dana stared at him. If he thought she was going to spill her guts, he had another think coming.

Dr Corcoran smiled, as if she'd spoken the words aloud. "Did you tell your husband about what happened to you when you were young?"

Dana stiffened. Maybe coming here hadn't been such a good idea after all. "Why would I?"

"You said you loved him."

"I did." She sighed. "I do."

"And didn't you want to tell him everything that happened?"

She looked away. "I talked to you about my problems. That's why I came to you. Why bother him with something that was part of my past? It was all over, finished."

"Some people cannot understand the point of therapists," the doctor told her. "They think that's what a family is for. It's a good point."

"Yes, well, I haven't had much experience of that," Dana muttered.

"And what about your husband? Is he close to his family?"

"His parents are dead and he has one sister. They're close but she lives abroad. They don't see that much of each other."

"So you became his family and he yours," Dr Corcoran mused.

"What's your point?"

"I was just thinking that maybe when he married you, he thought he was getting a family. But in your head, you've really stayed single."

"No, I haven't!"

"Dana, husbands and wives are supposed to share. Granted, we don't tell our partners everything about our past but it is rather unusual to be as mysterious as you've been."

"It hasn't been an issue." She was adamant. "He knows I had a problem with my father. He knows my brother left home at a young age. He knows about Mum. And he knows about you and the fact that I suffered from depression. So I don't think you can say I was mysterious." She shook her head and smiled.

"So you told him exactly what everyone else already knows about Conal O'Carroll and his daughter. And he accepted that?"

Dana studied her hands. He made it sound so bad. "He pushed it a little," she admitted. "But I told him that I needed to put the past behind me."

"And he left it at that?"

"He's asked questions from time to time."

"And did you avoid answering or tell him that you didn't want to talk about it?"

"I usually distracted him or changed the subject." She sighed. "It's all so long ago. And the longer I left it, the harder it was to say something. Anyway, if he wanted answers he should have just asked the questions outright," she said angrily and dropped her head in her hands.

He frowned. "Dana, I think we should resume our monthly sessions."

She shook her head. "No, there's no need for that. I just need the tablets."

"I'm sorry, Dana, but I'm not happy to prescribe medicine unless you continue with the therapy."

"But this is just a temporary glitch. I'll be fine."

"When did your husband leave you?" he asked suddenly.

"A few weeks ago. Why?"

"Why has it taken you so long to come and see me?"

"Well, I don't know . . ."

"You're not here because your husband left, Dana. You're here because you've started to write your story. And it's difficult."

She looked at him, tears in her eyes. "It's so difficult. It drains and upsets me — and I've only just started. I wish I could stop."

"I know it's hard, Dana, but it will help. Do you remember what I asked you to do when you first came to see me?"

She nodded slowly. "You said I should write my father a letter. You said I should write down everything that I'd ever wanted to say to him. You said I didn't have to send it to him — just writing it all down would be cathartic enough."

"And did you do it?"

She nodded.

"And did it help?"

She nodded again.

"Maybe you should write to your husband too. But this time, maybe you should post the letter."

CHAPTER
SIXTEEN

Walter Grimes fixed his tie and combed his hair, so that the thin patch in the centre wasn't as obvious. He eyed himself sternly in the small mirror. "Okay, Wally, show time." A final spray of cologne and he went back into his office to collect his Paul Smith jacket.

He was meeting Gretta Knight for lunch at one, and he felt uncharacteristically nervous. When she had called to invite him, he had been immediately suspicious. Usually the editor's trips to Britain were planned weeks, if not months, in advance. The first he'd heard of this visit was last Friday. The fact that she was bringing along her opposite number at Peyton UK made him more uncomfortable. Of course it might be just a courtesy. Angela Wiseman would be responsible for the Passion imprint, and maybe she just wanted to discuss the launch of *The Mile High Club*. Given the events of the last few weeks, though, it seemed unlikely. Gretta's calls had become more frequent and more abrasive as time passed and still Dana wouldn't talk to her. He had done his best to placate the editor, but Gretta had a nose for trouble.

Walter would be happier dealing with anyone other than Gretta Knight. She was a hard-nosed, thick-skinned businesswoman who parked her heart outside when she went into negotiations. She and Dana had always had a good relationship, but Walter knew that meant nothing. If Dana didn't come up with the goods, he knew Gretta would drop the author, without a second thought.

Dana's recent behaviour could affect her whole future with Peyton, but she didn't seem to realize that. Or, if she did, she didn't care. It didn't help that there were a couple of new authors on the block snapping at Dana's heels. Walter had tried a couple of times to explain this to Dana, in the gentlest possible terms, but he doubted she'd even heard him. And now that she had started writing again, he didn't want to do or say anything that might send her off the rails.

Walter checked he had his wallet and phone, and hurried out into the busy London streets. Dining at the Ivy usually filled him with delightful anticipation. He loved the food, he loved people-watching, but most of all he loved to be seen. Not because he had a huge ego, but because it was important in this business. He was one of the top agents in the country and he'd worked long and hard to achieve that. But it wasn't enough to be at the top. You had to be *seen* to be at the top. It was all part of the game. He sighed as he crossed the road, zigzagging his way between cars. But he wasn't in the mood for games today. He had to convince Gretta that everything was okay. Dana might be a client but she was also his friend. He couldn't let her down.

He paused for a moment outside the door of the famous restaurant and took a few deep breaths. Sadly, his nerves were directly linked to his stomach. The thought of eating as much as a lettuce leaf made him feel nauseous. A large drink, however, would be most welcome.

The two women were already seated when he was shown to the table. His heart sank at the sight of the large bottle of sparkling water they were sharing. Bloody Americans, he thought miserably. Alcohol-free lunches were so uncivilized.

He smiled widely as Gretta stood to greet him. She was a small, round woman who could be mistaken for someone's beloved mother — until she opened her mouth. She had a distinct and sharp nasal twang that grated on Walter's nerves. Her personality didn't redeem her. Gretta was abrupt and tactless and didn't believe in wasting time on pleasantries when there was business to do, and money to make.

"Gretta, you look marvellous," he gushed, as he held out his arms to embrace her. Gretta wasn't the demonstrative sort and she endured the hug with obvious discomfort. He kissed her cheek for good measure.

Gretta pulled away as soon as politeness allowed and gestured to the other woman. "Walter, this is Angela Wiseman. Angela, meet Walter Grimes."

Walter shook the other woman's hand. "Delighted."

Angela nodded, her smile friendly and her hand firm in his. He took to her instantly. She was everything Gretta was not. Tall and slender, she wore a beautifully tailored dark-green trouser suit that suited her fair colouring and brought out the green in her eyes. Her

174

jewellery was as tasteful as Gretta's was loud, and she held herself with grace and poise. If I were straight, Walter thought, this is the kind of woman I'd fancy.

"Drink?" Gretta asked, as they all sat down.

"Feel free to have a real one," Angela added. "Gretta and I have a rather full afternoon so we have to behave ourselves."

Walter smiled gratefully. "A G & T would be greatly appreciated. I've had a long and difficult morning."

Angela gave the order and they chatted casually as they studied their menus.

"I don't fancy a starter." Gretta snapped her menu closed and shot Walter a challenging look.

Obviously on yet another weird diet, Walter surmised.

The waiter hovered at Gretta's shoulder.

"I'll have the Dover sole, no spinach, with the dressing on the side," she told him. "Have you got any pasta to go with that?"

"It comes with baby new potatoes," the waiter said quietly.

Gretta eyeballed him. "I can see that, but I'd like pasta."

"Some penne, perhaps?" he suggested.

"That will do."

"I'll have the same," Angela said with a smile, "but exactly as it comes."

"And the Thai sea bass for me," Walter added.

"Would you like some wine, Walter?" Angela asked as Walter swallowed half his gin in one gulp.

"That would be lovely."

Angela went up further in his estimation by ordering a half-bottle of Chablis rather than a glass. Or, he worried, perhaps was she just trying to loosen him up so he'd spill the beans about Dana.

Gretta got straight to the point as soon as the waiter had left. "So, Walter. Fill me in. What's happening with Dana?"

"I'm happy to report that we're back on track." He smiled at each woman in turn. "As you know, poor Dana has been through a terrible time. She was devoted to Gus and devastated when he left. I think what she finds hardest is that she doesn't even know why."

"Because he's a man," Gretta snarled. "They're all selfish, insensitive bastards."

"Present company excepted, of course," Angela added.

Walter sighed. "Sadly, I have to agree with Gretta. Most men seem to have a cad gene. I know, I've been there."

Gretta rolled her eyes. "Let's talk about Dana. Is the book finished yet?"

"No, but she seems to be working around the clock." Walter forced an enthusiasm into his voice that he didn't feel. "I think going through this trauma has given her a new focus, and I think *The Mile High Club* will be a better book for it."

"Have you read any of it?" Gretta asked, unmoved by his optimism.

"Oh, no, I only ever read the finished product. It's the way Dana and I work," he explained to Angela.

"Well, it's not the way Dana and I work," Gretta retorted. "The first fifteen chapters, she was hardly off the phone. Then nothing. I haven't a fucking clue what's going on. How do we know she's really working on it at all, Walter? Do I need to remind you that there's a lot riding on this book?"

"You do not."

"Will she meet her deadline?" For the first time Angela joined the conversation.

"If she doesn't, she won't be far off. And given her punctuality in the past, I think we have to make allowances. There are extenuating circumstances, after all." Walter drained his glass and shot a desperate look at the waiter, who was uncorking the wine.

"I think I've been very patient, given that she's ignored all my calls for weeks." Gretta scowled as their food was set down in front of them.

"She did call you yesterday, but of course you were on a plane."

"Yeah, I got the message," Gretta admitted.

"She feels terrible about the way she's behaved," Walter assured her. "She's never done it before and, I know she never will again. I think it's important that we remember what a consummate professional she has always been." He turned his gaze on Angela. "Eighteen books in as many years; it's quite an achievement."

"It certainly is," the other editor agreed.

Gretta nodded. "I hear what you're saying, Walter, but I'd like it from the horse's mouth." She turned thoughtful eyes on Angela. "Maybe I should go and see her. Hey, I've got a great idea. Why don't you come with me, Angela?"

"When?"

Gretta shrugged. "Tomorrow?"

"I'd need to double-check my diary, but I think it's possible."

Walter swallowed hard. "It's really not necessary. I'm sure you're far too busy —"

"No, really," Angela said, shaking her head, "I think it's a wonderful idea. It would be lovely to meet Dana."

The agent forced a smile. "Wonderful. She'll be so thrilled."

"Have you visited Ireland before, Gretta?" Angela asked.

"Yeah, once, about five years ago. I must pick up some of that Waterford glass. And an Aran sweater for JJ. He's originally Irish, did I mention that?" The editor softened visibly as she thought of her new boyfriend.

"Really?" Walter said politely.

"Yeah. His great-grandfather was born in Drogeeda."

"I think it's pronounced Dro-ha-da," Walter told her.

Gretta shrugged. "Whatever."

Walter gave up and turned his attention back to the English editor. "So, Angela, you must be excited about introducing the Passion imprint to Britain."

"Very. Gretta and I have been talking about it for some time, but we've had to deal with a lot of negativity. Some of our directors took a lot of convincing that this genre would work in the UK."

"Haven't they heard of Mills & Boon?" Walter said, incredulously.

Angela laughed. "Well, exactly! It's a snobbery of sorts, really. But, thankfully, we've overcome it."

"I believe that choosing Dana De Lacey to launch it is a master stroke. She is such a pro and she understands the subtle differences between the two markets. The fact that she's Irish and the daughter of a famous poet —" Walter splayed his hands and smiled — "it's the icing on the cake."

Angela inclined her head. "Yes, but, as I'm sure you know, Walter, what works in the US doesn't always work over here. We've found that out to our cost. We need to read *The Mile High Club* before we can come to a final decision."

Walter felt slightly sick. "I'm confident that you will be more than happy with it."

Gretta set down her fork and looked at him, her eyes as hard as flint. "Walter, let's cut the bull. The fact that Dana was punctual, reliable and humorous got her where she is today. But there are now a lot of female authors snapping at her heels. They're gutsy, they're greedy and, frankly, they're cheaper. I don't want to lose Dana — Angela will tell you that."

"Absolutely not." Angela nodded sincerely. "We love Dana."

Gretta sighed. "But business is business."

"I'm sure *The Mile High Club* will be wonderful," Angela enthused. "And we'll be able to forget we even had this conversation."

Walter drained his glass. "I'm sure."

Out on the street, Walter blinked in the sunshine and felt horribly sober. Taking out his phone, he phoned his secretary. "Get me on a flight to Dublin first thing tomorrow."

Less than thirty minutes later, Sylvie put down the phone. She looked out of the window at Dana, who was wandering around her garden, obviously lost in thought. If Gretta or Walter saw the author in this pose, they'd be delighted. But Sylvie knew the reality.

When Dana went out yesterday, Sylvie had had a sneaky peek at the *The Mile High Club* file on Dana's laptop. As she'd suspected, no work had been done on it for weeks. But the author was definitely working on something. Sylvie knew the signs. Dana was agitated and distracted, a sure sign that she had embarked on a new project. The PA had scanned the directory for files that had been accessed most recently. There was just one and it had been updated only yesterday. Sylvie had sat and stared at it for a moment. It would be wrong to open it. Still, if she knew what was in it she might know whether or not she'd have a job in six months. Sylvie hadn't been able to resist any longer. She'd opened the file and started to read. She hadn't had long and she'd only got through two chapters when she'd heard the front door open. She'd quickly closed the file and retreated behind her own desk. She'd felt bad. She'd felt as if she'd just read Dana's diary. But then, she'd realized, that was exactly what she'd done.

Now, with a sigh, Sylvie went out into the garden. She had to break the bad news to her boss that she was going to have visitors the next day. Dana's reaction was fairly predictable.

"Holy fuck," she muttered, her eyes round with shock. "When is Walter coming? He will be here, won't he?"

"His secretary is trying to get him on a morning flight but she hasn't confirmed yet."

"And Gretta?"

"She gets in around four, but she wants to do some shopping so Walter said to meet here about seven."

"How the hell did he let this happen?" Dana wailed. "What was he thinking of, arranging this behind my back?"

Sylvie handed her the phone. "You can ask him yourself. He's waiting for your call."

Dana dialled her agent's mobile and he picked up immediately.

"Dana, darling, I'm so sorry."

"What's going on, Wally? Why the hell is Gretta coming to Ireland?" She flopped into a garden chair.

"She was in London for a meeting with Angela Wiseman — Peyton UK's editor."

"Oh, okay. But why are they coming to see me?"

"They're nervous, Dana. They want to see the whites of your eyes, as it were."

"I'm not sure I'm up to this, Wally."

"You have to be," he said urgently. "And you have to do your best to deliver this book on time, or as soon after as humanly possible."

"It's not going to happen."

There was silence for a second and then a strangled cough. "Okay, then. I'm sure I can wheedle an extra couple of weeks out of Gretta if necessary —"

"I'd need at least six weeks and even then . . ."

"Even then what?" he prompted.

She sighed. "That would only be enough if I was actually able to write something."

"Dana?"

"I'm sorry, Wally, but I just can't do it." Her voice wavered.

"No, darling, please don't get upset."

"But I've let you down," she wailed. "I've let everyone down."

"We haven't lost the war yet."

"But, Wally —"

"No buts," he said firmly. "We'll figure something out. You get a good night's sleep and I'll see you first thing."

"But Sylvie said you were having a problem getting a flight." Dana's voice rose in panic.

"My darling girl, I will be with you tomorrow morning, even if I have to stick a feather up my arse to get there!"

She laughed through her tears. "Oh, Wally. You're the best."

CHAPTER
SEVENTEEN

Iris knocked gently and stuck her head around Dana's bedroom door. "Mr Grimes has arrived and I've shown him into the conservatory."

"Thank goodness. Has the food arrived?" Realizing preparing a dinner for four at short notice was asking a lot of her housekeeper, Dana had ordered food from a nearby restaurant. There was a lobster bisque to start — Iris just needed to heat that. For the main course there was cold, poached salmon that would be served with asparagus and baby new potatoes, and there was a lemon tart for dessert. And as Wally was arriving early, Dana had ordered some lunch. She'd also given Sylvie the day off. She didn't want her PA to see how nervous she was, or to witness Walter's reaction when he realized how behind she was on the book.

"Yes, and the wine too."

"Put some white in the fridge, would you, Iris?"

"Already done."

"What would I do without you?" Dana smiled gratefully.

"Shall I serve lunch now?" Iris asked as they went downstairs.

"No, you've enough to do. We'll help ourselves when we get hungry."

Iris nodded. "Good luck, then — Dana."

"Thank you, Iris." Dana gave her a quick hug. She paused in the hall and studied herself in the large mirror. She had dressed in a simple brown linen dress. A single string of topaz beads adorned her throat and on her feet she wore flat, flimsy sandals of the same colour. Her short bob shone and a pale peach lipstick was her only make-up.

When she walked in, Wally was perched on the arm of a chair, staring into the garden, an empty glass between his manicured fingers. He looked tired and drawn and she felt a pang of guilt because she knew that she was probably the reason.

"Hi, Walter."

He stood immediately and, putting down his glass, came to embrace her. "My darling!"

Dana felt her eyes fill as he held her at arm's length to study her.

"You are as gorgeous as ever," he pronounced, "but you look worried."

"I am worried! Gretta's coming." She went to the table in the corner, where Iris had set out drinks. "Can I get you another?"

"I shouldn't, but I will." He handed over his empty glass. "Your housekeeper makes T & G rather than G & T."

Dana smiled. "She's never touched a drop in her life and doesn't really approve of anyone else drinking either."

"She'd soon change her mind if she worked in publishing," Walter retorted.

Dana poured his drink and a glass of wine for herself and led the way out into the garden. "Can you believe how lovely the weather is?" she marvelled, holding her face up to the sun.

"Wonderful." Wally dusted off a garden chair, before sitting down. "Talk to me, darling."

Dana put on dark glasses. "I'm sorry, Walter. I've tried, but I just cannot finish *The Mile High Club*."

His eyes widened in horror. "But, Dana, you must! We're at a very important crossroads in your career — probably the most important since you were first published."

"I realize that, Wally." She shrugged. "But there's nothing I can do about it."

"Of course there is!" Walter flushed angrily. "You can't just give up, Dana."

Her eyes filled with tears. "But what else can I do?"

"But you told me you were writing." His eyes narrowed. "Were you lying to me?"

She shook her head, glad that he couldn't see her eyes. "No. I've been working on something else. It's just an exercise that I thought would help get me back into writing again. But any time I go back to *The Mile High Club* . . ." She sighed. "Nothing."

He patted her hand. "Perhaps if you went away for a few weeks; sometimes a different environment helps."

"Perhaps," she said, knowing it wouldn't.

"Or maybe you need someone to work with you. I'm sure I could find someone who'd be interested."

"Are you talking about a ghostwriter?" Dana said incredulously.

Walter shrugged. "We have to do whatever it takes to finish this book. If we don't . . ."

"What?" Dana looked at him.

He sighed. "It's not just about the book being published over here. If you don't come up with the goods, I don't believe Gretta will offer you a new contract in the US either."

Dana gaped at him, her glass halfway to her lips. "But she can't do that to me — can she?"

He shrugged, lighting a cigarette and inhaling deeply. "Once you're out of contract, Dana, she can do whatever she wants."

"The bitch! Well, she can go to hell. There are other publishers who will be only too happy to have me. It's time I moved on anyway."

Walter shot her a pitying look. "You still have to finish this book, Dana. If you don't, Peyton could sue. And, quite frankly, darling, if you leave them on bad terms, no one will touch you with a bargepole."

Dana reached for one of Walter's cigarettes and lit it. "So what on earth am I going to do?"

"First, I think we should eat," Wally said half-heartedly. "We need to have our wits about us this evening."

"I'll go and get us something," Dana murmured but didn't stand up.

"You stay here. I'll go."

Dana couldn't even summon up the energy to reply. How had it come to this? In a matter of hours her career could be at an end. This was what Gus Johnson had done to her. Single-handedly he had destroyed everything she had worked for. Well, if she ended up with nothing she'd make damn sure he paid. She'd file for divorce and she'd take everything. And, if she had her way, he'd never see his beloved house in Cork again.

"Your housekeeper is full of surprises," Walter commented as he arrived with a tray of food.

"It's courtesy of the local deli. If I'd left it to Iris you'd be eating a big fry-up or corned beef and cabbage."

He laughed. "I quite like fry-ups. They remind me of my childhood. My mother used to cook one every Saturday night for supper. It was a real treat. I don't think we got any meat the rest of the week."

Dana was momentarily distracted. "I always thought you were posh."

Walter smiled, showing off his perfect, even teeth. "That's what you're supposed to think."

He put some food on a plate and pushed it towards her. "Now. Eat."

Like a child, Dana let him feed her: slices of ciabatta spread with rich pesto, baguette smothered in runny Brie, and bruschetta with Parma ham. She ate more in an hour than she'd eaten in the time since Gus had left. Finally, Walter presented her with a strong espresso and a glass of port.

"That's your last drink till dinner," he warned. "And even then, limit yourself."

She leaned across and stole another one of his cigarettes. "What would I do without you, Walter?"

"Go broke," he said smartly. "And you shouldn't be smoking; you gave up years ago, didn't you?"

She nodded. "But can you blame me, after all that's happened?"

"I know how tough it's been, Dana. Believe me, I've been there. For months after Giles left, I didn't want to go outside the door. There didn't seem to be any point to anything. Money, food, even wine — nothing's enjoyable when you do it alone."

"Exactly!"

"Except you're not alone, Dana. That's what you haven't realized yet. Life may not be the same, but it does go on." He nudged her playfully. "And it didn't take you long to climb back on the horse, did it?"

Dana flushed. "It was just one night. I was on the rebound."

"Hey, I'm not knocking it. I wish I could be more like you."

Dana looked at him and saw the sadness in his eyes.

"One day someone will fall madly in love with you, and you with him. I can't believe it hasn't happened before. You're such a lovely man."

Wally's eyes filled with tears. "Bless you, darling. And, you'll find someone too. And, in the meantime, you've got your friends; you've got me. Please don't forget that. Don't make me grill Sylvie to find out what's going on in your life, Dana. I'm your agent and your friend. We have to work as a team. If you don't tell me what's going on, how can I possibly help?"

"Sorry," Dana said meekly.

He beamed at her. "It's forgotten. Now, let's get to work. We have to persuade Gretta that you've almost finished the book, and that it's your best, juiciest work yet."

Dana stared at him. "How in hell are we going to do that?"

"If my memory serves me right, darling, you're in the habit of scribbling in notebooks, *n'est-ce pas?*"

Dana nodded. "Yes. If I'm out without my laptop and get an idea I write it down."

"So perhaps we can get some inspiration from there."

"I doubt it. We're talking disjointed paragraphs, random ideas, that sort of thing."

"No, darling," he said firmly, "we're talking desperate. Now, tell me, how many thousand words have you written? And," he waggled a finger at her, "I want the truth."

"I'll have to check my laptop to give you an exact figure," Dana prevaricated.

"Well, go get it and I'll take this back to the kitchen." Walter began to pile all the dishes and glasses back on to the tray and led the way into the house.

"I had no idea you were so domesticated," she teased.

"I am all things to all men." He winked.

Dana went into her office and sat down at her desk. She flipped open her laptop and went into the *The Mile High Club* file. Her heart sank as she checked the word count. It was even worse than she had remembered. Setting it aside, she went in search of her notebooks. It took some time. She had one in each of her larger hand-bags, one in her bedside table and one in the car. She realized as she carried them back to her office that there was also one in the glove compartment of Gus's car.

When she returned, Walter was sitting at her desk, staring at the screen of her laptop. His face was decidedly pale. "Thirty-five thousand words?" he croaked. "Remind me, how many words are there usually in your novels?"

Dana swallowed hard. "Eighty-five thousand."

Walter nodded slowly, his eyes still on the screen. "And you normally write about two to three thousand words a day, yes?"

"On a good day," she hedged. "And then, of course, I go back over it and edit . . ."

"So if you were to start tomorrow, you could easily have finished this book in less than three weeks, couldn't you?" His face lit up and he sprang to his feet to kiss her. "We're saved."

"Aren't you forgetting something?" she said wearily. "I told you, I can't do it."

"Sure you can, you just need some help." He sat down at her desk again, rolled up his sleeves and took a sip of his coffee. "Now, print off a copy of what you've written so far, and I'll get reading. While I'm doing that, you can go through those," he nodded towards the notebooks, "and see if there's anything we can use."

Moments later, the printer was spewing out sheets of paper. Dana watched nervously as the pages of her book flipped out into Walter's greedy hands but he chased her away.

"You get started on the notebooks," he urged, his voice brooking no argument. "We don't have much time."

Resignedly, Dana lit yet another cigarette, took the pads and a pencil and went out to the garden. She knew she owed it to Wally to make an effort, but in her heart she also knew that it was a waste of time. Still, if they could come up with enough copy to buy them some time, it would keep everybody happy for a while. The problem was: what then?

Dana opened the first notebook and began to read. It took her a while to get into it. As she'd told her agent, there were many disjointed ideas — not just for *The Mile High Club* but for other books too. She winced at some of the sloppy rubbish she'd written and raised her eyebrows at the more raunchy pieces. She flushed as she remembered how she had sometimes sat up in bed writing this kind of stuff after some energetic love-making, Gus out cold beside her.

As Iris put together the simple but elegant dinner, Walter and Dana worked, she in the conservatory and he in the office. Occasionally he came in to ask a question, but for the most part they worked alone. At five-thirty, Walter called Dana. "Okay, my darling, tell me what you've got."

He listened and made notes. Finally, at six-thirty, he laid down his pen. "Right, I think we have enough to go on."

"You do?" she said, doubtfully.

"I do. Now, Ms De Lacey, go and make yourself beautiful. And wear lots of make-up — you're far too pale."

So much for the natural look, Dana thought.

"And," he warned, "leave the talking to me."

"Gretta won't have that," Dana assured him.

"Trust me, I'll handle her. You talk to Angela. Quiz her about the UK operation and the plans they have for promoting the Passion label. Put her on the back foot. That way, you'll look in control and we'll avoid discussing the real issue."

"Which is that I've stopped writing."

"That's not technically correct," he pointed out, smiling. "So you don't even have to lie." He stood up and stretched. "Now, darling, may I use one of your luxurious bathrooms? I badly need a shower."

Wally looked as fresh as he had when he'd walked through the door, but Dana knew he must be as drained as she was. "Would you like a reviving drink to take up with you?"

"Excellent idea. Then, as the Yanks say, we'll blow their socks off!"

192

CHAPTER
EIGHTEEN

Dana changed into a white lace skirt and a sleeveless white T-shirt that showed off her tanned and reasonably toned arms and legs. Her face took a bit more work. Sleep deprivation showed in her eyes and belied her otherwise relaxed, carefree image. She rummaged in her make-up drawer for drops that promised to make her eyes sparkle; a white pencil that would make the whites appear whiter; and some miracle cream that would disguise the bags underneath. She wasn't convinced.

She applied some delicate-pink eye shadow, grey eyeliner and pink lipstick, then brushed her hair until it shone, pulling down a few wisps to cover the frown lines on her forehead. Adding gold hoop earrings and a thick bangle, she slipped her feet into gold wedge sandals and went downstairs.

Walter was relaxing in the conservatory and nursing a G & T when she walked in. He came to kiss her on both cheeks. "Perfect, darling, just perfect. We'll get through this, you'll see. Just keep your cool. What we need them to see tonight is an author who is so caught up in her work she's blotted everything and everyone out. As far as Gus is concerned, I suggest that you appear sad and contemplative but not distraught. They must not think you've gone over the edge."

"Even though I have," she said with a sad smile.

"You have not! Don't talk like that. You're just a little stressed."

She sighed. "I know what you're saying, Wally, and I'll do my best, I promise. Only —"

Dana never got to finish her sentence as the buzzer at the gate interrupted her. She went out into the hall and buzzed in the taxi, then stuck her head into the kitchen to let Iris know that their guests had arrived. When she came back into the hall, Walter was waiting for her.

"Ready?" He watched her anxiously.

She smiled. "Sure."

The car pulled up and Walter threw open the door. As Angela paid the driver, the agent opened Gretta's door with a flourish. "We meet again!"

"Walter, what a surprise," Gretta said drily, standing stiff as a board as he embraced her.

"Hello, Gretta," Dana said softly from behind her agent.

Gretta almost shoved Walter to one side. "Dana, honey!" She kissed her on both cheeks and then stepped back to stare into her face. "You look great."

"You too, Gretta, it's wonderful to see you. I couldn't believe it when Wally told me you were coming."

"Yes, me too. It was just a mad impulse I had at lunch yesterday. I wasn't expecting your agent to join us, though," Gretta murmured.

"That was my idea," Dana said quickly. "I thought it would be nice for us to have an evening together.

194

Telephones and emails are all very well, but it is nice to talk face to face. Maybe it's my lonely occupation that makes me feel that way." She stopped suddenly, realizing that Walter was shooting her a warning look. She was babbling.

"Dana, let me introduce Angela Wiseman," he said.

The elegant woman who'd been standing silently in the background now came forward to shake Dana's hand. "It's wonderful to finally meet you."

"And you. Please, come in."

"You have a lovely home," Angela remarked, following her inside.

"Isn't it wonderful?" Walter agreed. "Wait till you see the garden — it's to die for."

"Dinner will be ready soon," Dana told them. "Let's have a drink in the conservatory first." She and Walter had discussed having some champagne on ice but, given Gretta's mercurial moods, they decided against it. Instead the drinks cabinet was filled with every kind of soft drink, water, a range of spirits and a very expensive dry burgundy. "Wally, would you do the honours?" Dana asked, as she sat down on one of the large sofas next to Gretta.

He clicked his heels and bowed. "I'd be delighted. What will it be, ladies? Can I tempt you with a cocktail, perhaps?"

Gretta fanned herself wearily. "I'd kill for a Bloody Mary. Those damn airports exhaust me. Why does everything have to take so damn long?"

"Bloody Mary it is. Angela?"

"Yes, why not?"

Dana and Wally exchanged a look of pure relief.

"I think I'll have one too," Dana said.

"We all will," Walter announced.

"I'm sure all the ingredients are there, Walter, but you'll have to go out to the kitchen for the tomato juice."

"No problem." Walter skipped off to do her bidding.

"So, tell me, Dana. How are you?" Gretta asked when he had gone.

She was attempting to look sincere and empathetic, though it didn't come easy. Dana suppressed a smile and played along. "I'm okay, Gretta. It was difficult at first. When Gus walked out I was knocked for six."

"I can imagine." Gretta patted her hand awkwardly.

"But now that I've had time to get used to being on my own again, well —" she paused and smiled — "I'm quite enjoying it."

"Really?" Gretta didn't look convinced.

"Yeah. Though in a way I've turned into a bit of a recluse. I'm just living to write and writing to live." She laughed. "A publisher's dream, eh?"

"Indeed." Gretta was trying to hide her surprise. "But a little bird tells me that you haven't been home alone every night."

Dana put her hands to her face to cover a guilty smile — who knew she could be such an actress? — and simpered, "I admit it, I've had a few nights out, but then, you've got to wash that man right out of your hair, right?" Okay, now where did *that* come from?

"You are absolutely right," Angela said emphatically. "No man is worth pining over. You just have to move on." The normally cool editor was suddenly flushed and quite fierce.

"Angela recently divorced," Gretta explained.

"I'm so sorry," Dana said.

Angela waved away her sympathies. "Don't be, I'm better off without him."

"Here we are, ladies." Walter arrived back, brandishing a carton of tomato juice, and within minutes he had mixed four potent cocktails. After he'd served the three women, he raised his glass. "To *The Mile High Club*!"

Dana winced. That was pushing it a bit. She smiled faintly as she realized both women were looking at her and raising their glasses expectantly. "*The Mile High Club*," she echoed.

Angela walked to the conservatory doors and looked out into the garden. "Aren't you lucky having such a large garden? It's beautiful."

"It was one of the main reasons we bought the place," Dana said, standing up. "Let me show you around."

"You do that." Walter took her place on the sofa. "It will give Gretta and me a chance to chat."

Gretta opened her mouth to protest but Dana hurried Angela outside before she could say a word. The editor frowned at Walter. "I came here to talk to Dana."

"We have plenty of time," he assured her. "I just wanted to have a quick word *entre nous*. As you know, Dana hasn't let anyone see this manuscript —"

"Don't I know it?" Gretta grumbled.

"— but this afternoon I had a sneak preview." He clapped his hands excitedly and thought of the pathetic things he had to do in this job. "I really think it might be her best yet!"

Gretta's painted-on eyebrows disappeared into her lacquered hair. "Yeah?"

Walter nodded emphatically. "It's got it all. Suspense, mystery, humour and —" he rolled his eyes in ecstasy — "it is really hot. And, Gretta, I know there are a lot of new kids on the block. But not many authors can do sex with taste." He allowed a respectful silence so that they could both take a moment to appreciate Dana's genius.

"Can I have a look?" the editor whispered, hooked.

Walter shook his head and looked nervously towards the garden. "She'd kill me."

Gretta's eyes narrowed suspiciously. "Why? I'm her editor. I'm always the first to read her manuscripts."

Walter sighed. "Well, I'm embarrassed to admit this, Gretta, but . . ."

She stared at him. "She doesn't know you've read it, does she?"

He looked shamefaced. "It was just a couple of chapters. I couldn't help myself. She left me in her office alone while she went to talk to her housekeeper and . . ." He sighed again. "I'm only human."

Gretta nodded in a rare moment of solidarity. "I wouldn't have been able to resist either."

"Really? Oh, thank you. That makes me feel much better."

"Now I really can't wait to read it," Gretta said, taking a long slug of her drink.

"I hope I've put your mind at rest," Walter said. "And that you will bear with us and give Dana just a little more time."

Gretta's eyes narrowed. "How much more?"

"Six weeks?" he ventured.

Her eyes widened. "Oh, you cannot be serious!"

"If you want *The Mile High Club* to be THE book, the one to launch both Passion and Dana De Lacey with a bang, isn't it worth it?"

A look of uncertainty crossed Gretta's face. "I'll have to talk to Angela."

"I'm sure you can persuade her."

"Six weeks, no more," Gretta warned.

"You won't be disappointed, Gretta," Walter said, desperately hoping he was right. If Dana didn't deliver, it would leave his reputation in shreds.

There was a knock on the door and Iris announced that dinner was served.

"I'll go and find Dana and Angela," Walter said, glad of the opportunity to escape. When he got outside, he paused to catch his breath. He really was getting too old for this game.

The mood around the dinner table was light and relaxed and Dana shot Walter a quizzical look. He smiled back and topped up their glasses. "Not too much for the author," he teased Dana. "We want you tap-tap-tapping away first thing in the morning."

"Do you prefer to work in the mornings?" Angela asked, as she speared a piece of asparagus with her fork.

"I used to, but recently I've taken to working in the evenings." Dana smiled sadly. "It passes the time."

An awkward silence followed but Walter jumped in to fill it. "Vary it," he suggested. "It's not healthy to stay in every night and there's no reason why you shouldn't be out there socializing, you're a free woman."

"Technically I'm not," she pointed out with a frown. "Maybe I should do something about that."

Walter smiled though he was gritting his teeth. "I think you should wait, Dana. You don't want to rush into anything. You have enough on your plate just getting the book finished."

"Yes, and we are under pressure," Gretta added. Dana opened her mouth to explain, but Gretta's smile was tolerant. "It's okay, Walter has explained everything."

"He has?"

She nodded. "Angela and I will need to talk, but I'm sure we can work something out."

Dana looked blank. "Oh, that's great. Marvellous."

Dana lapsed into silence as the conversation turned from her to more general gossip. Wally was at his best, enthralling the two women with tales about other people in the industry.

"I can't believe that," Angela gasped, when he told her of one agent's antics at a dinner the previous week.

He pointed to his own eyes. "My sources are very reliable."

Dana smiled absently, glad that she didn't have to contribute. She was conscious, though, that the shrewd UK editor was shooting her speculative looks. She looked at the almost untouched plate of delicious food in front of her and felt like throwing up. How was she going to get through the remainder of this evening? She forced herself to eat, knowing that she'd get an earful from Wally later if she didn't play her part. Not long now, at least. Gretta always went to bed early and it was after nine now. She was grateful for that. She hated all of this lying and subterfuge. In any case, Peyton Publishing had made a lot of money off her back. It wouldn't kill them if, for once, she delivered late. But would she be able to deliver at all? And though she'd explained this to Wally, he hadn't listened. He had cobbled together a range of notes and suggestions this afternoon and he thought that was that. But that wasn't the way she worked. Either the story — and yes, it wasn't just sex and romance, there was always a story too — was in her head or it wasn't. At the moment, she knew that it wasn't. If she finished this book, the first third would be vibrant and pacy while the rest was wooden and lifeless. Gretta would be furious when she finally read it.

"It will be fine," Walter had said, overriding her protests.

Who was he trying to convince, she wondered, watching him now as he entertained the two women. He was a force to be reckoned with when he pulled out all the stops. He'd certainly done that today. If her contract with Peyton wasn't renewed, of course, it would mean a large hole in his income over the next couple of years. But she knew that he was just as worried about her as he was about his income. He was a kind man and a good friend. It wasn't fair that he would suffer because of her. She reached for her glass at the thought of this extra pressure. How wonderful it would be if she could just disappear. Get away from the job, her life — all of it.

"Dana?" Angela was obviously waiting for a response to a question that Dana hadn't even heard.

Walter whooped delightedly. "She's gone again! You were off in you own little fictional world again, weren't you?"

"Yes," Dana lied. "I'm so sorry. How rude of me."

"Honey, don't apologize," Gretta said warmly. "You're making three people very happy."

"It's so exciting to think that you're creating as we sit here eating dinner," Angela marvelled. "Does that happen often?"

Dana shrugged. "Sometimes. When I really get my teeth into something, I find it hard to concentrate on anything else."

"And long may that continue," Wally said, slurring slightly.

"We should get going." Angela looked at Gretta, who was drooping in her chair. "We have an early start tomorrow."

Dana looked around the table at the remains of their desserts and coffees, and realized just how long her mind had been wandering. "Where are you staying?" Dana asked as Wally helped Gretta to her feet.

"That new uber-modern hotel out at the airport," Angela replied.

"Me too," Wally said, punching a number into his phone. "I'll call a cab and we can share."

"Thank you so much for coming to see me," Dana told the two editors as he went outside to make the call. "I'm sorry for not being very good company."

"Don't apologize." Angela kissed her on both cheeks. "I've really enjoyed my evening."

Gretta grinned drunkenly. "I knew you wouldn't let me down," she said, hugging the author as if they were bosom buddies.

Dana patted her back distractedly and cursed Wally. What had he told Gretta? Why had she let him talk her into this ridiculous subterfuge? It could only end in tears.

The man in question tripped back into the room, his eyes bright and his face flushed. That was due in part to wine but mostly, Dana knew, to the exhilaration of pulling the wool over Gretta's eyes. He gathered Dana into his arms.

"Now, darling, don't work too hard," he said loudly. "I'll call you tomorrow," he added softly, looking intently into her eyes. "And remember, I'm with you all the way." He hugged her to him again, to hide her look of despair from the other women. "Keep smiling," he whispered. "A few more minutes and it will all be over."

"So will you go to bed now or to work?" Angela asked.

Dana drew away from her agent and smiled. "Do you know, I think I will write a few lines."

"That's my girl." Gretta beamed.

The buzzer in the hall sounded and Dana almost fainted with relief. "That will be the taxi," she said, trying to look suitably sorry to see them go. "Thanks again for coming."

Gretta laughed throatily. "Yeah, but I bet you can't wait to see the back of us."

Dana opened her mouth to protest.

"So you can get to work," Gretta clarified and patted her cheek. "Well done, honey. I'm sure this is going to be your best book yet."

As the women climbed into the taxi, Wally turned to give her the thumbs-up.

Dana sighed and shook her head.

His smile faltered slightly. But he had started this show, and he was going to finish it. "Goodbye, my darling. Talk soon."

CHAPTER
NINETEEN

Dana went into her office, sat down at her desk, and started to write.

I soon realized that life was a lot better in the O'Carroll household when my father was working. While he was writing, he kept to his study for most of the day, even eating at his desk — when he remembered to eat. Mother prepared his meals as usual but wouldn't dare disturb him. If he came looking, the food was there waiting. A fact, I realized, he took completely for granted.

When he occasionally took a break, he went for long solitary walks along the seafront. Sometimes, if he needed distraction, he would venture into town for lunch or a drink at one of the better hotels. He always made a point of taking a book or newspaper to discourage anyone from joining him. My father was not there for the company.

Paradoxically, he was a pious and religious man, who made a point of never working on Sundays. He was happy, however, for my mother to cook breakfast. Then we would dress in our best clothes, attend twelve-thirty Mass and go on into town for lunch.

In this environment, he was in his element. He would talk loudly, regaling us with stories of his childhood or comment — always negatively — on the TV programmes my mother watched, or the books my brother read. I was oblivious in the early days to the tension at these lunches, but I never enjoyed them either.

When Father was in one of his moods, though, Sunday lunches were miserable, fraught occasions. These were the days when my mother and brother were on the receiving end of his attentions. Little things would irritate him. Ed slouching in his chair. Mother coughing delicately into her lace handkerchief. Even I would receive a glare of disapproval for trimming every ounce of fat from my roast beef.

He was an attractive man, in an austere sort of way. But when he was angry, his face would flush, a blue vein would throb in his temple, and he looked ugly and menacing. I was terrified of him on these occasions, yet he had never so much as raised a hand to me. Ed wasn't always so lucky. The atmosphere on the drive home would be charged, and we rarely made it to the house without my father exploding over something.

My mother tried her best to protect us when he was like this and would send us to play in the garden, or up to our rooms to do our homework. When I was smaller and didn't know any better I sometimes protested. But as I reached my teens, I realized what my mother was doing and silently obeyed.

Sometimes it worked. She would go to the kitchen and bake; Father would retire to his study to sleep off his brandy; Ed and I would play battleships or chess in my room.

Other times we weren't so lucky. Father would prowl the house like a caged animal waiting to strike. It would be something small that would set him off. Ed playing his radio too loud, or Mother forgetting to switch off the immersion heater.

"Do you think I'm made of money?" he'd roar.

Money was a constant theme, now I come to think of it. You would think we were poverty-stricken the way he went on about turning off lights and pulling out plugs. He even complained once that Ed was using too much toothpaste. Yet I realized from looking at how my friends lived that we were relatively rich. None of the other kids were ever brought to a hotel for lunch or dinner — let alone every week. They went to the Wimpy bar in Wexford for beans and chips — Ed and I were green with envy.

Once my father got started on one of his rants, he lost all control. Not with me, of course. The worst he ever did with his little princess was to roar, "Get up to your room!"

But my poor brother took the full brunt of our father's anger. He would demand to see Ed's homework and systematically denigrate it. The handwriting was spidery, the maths weak, the spelling atrocious — "You're an embarrassment," he would say in disgust.

I remember him firing questions at my brother about history and geography. Then he'd switch from English to Irish, until Ed was so nervous and confused that his stammer would render him almost incoherent. If Ed was lucky, my mother would intervene at this stage, and send Ed to bed. If he wasn't, my father would take off his belt and order Ed into his study. Mother and I would hold each other as we heard his cries, but we knew better than to interfere.

If Mother managed to distract Father, Ed and I would be sent up to bed. Then he would start on her. Ed and I would perch on the top stair, him biting his nails and me silently sobbing. Father would taunt and belittle her and it was usually about Ed. It was her fault that Ed was such a useless specimen. She had mollycoddled him, made him too soft and taught him no discipline. Thank God, Dana, at least, took after his side of the family. Already showing a creative flair, she was pretty too; it was an excellent combination in a young woman. But Ed, my father would sigh dramatically, was good for nothing. I would slip my hand into my brother's as we listened. I could see he was upset but he would fight back the tears and just mutter, "I'll show him."

Mother would try a number of different tactics to calm him. Sometimes she'd agree with Father and apologize, telling him she'd try to do better. The first time I overheard this, I was incensed. But Ed just smiled and squeezed my hand. "It's okay, Dana. Mother doesn't mean it. She's ju — ju — just saying it to shu — shu — shut him up."

Other times, Mother would open a bottle of wine and pour a glass for them both. Daddy would continue to rant for a while, but by the second glass his voice would quieten and he would finally sit down. He was always at his most dangerous when he was on the move. So once he was ensconced in his armchair, we knew the worst was over. These sessions usually culminated in my parents going to bed early. I used to worry about the noises coming from their room, afraid that maybe my father was hurting Mother in some way. But Ed would grin knowingly and tell me that's how grown-ups made up. I was a naive little thing, and though I didn't understand, neither did I question.

On reflection, I didn't question many things in those days. I was becoming a typical teenager: engrossed in my own world and oblivious to anything or anyone outside it. I spent my days fantasizing about Liam O'Herlihy, with his dreamy eyes and long curly hair. When my parents thought I was doing my homework, I was usually doodling "Dana O'Herlihy" or "Liam loves Dana" in the margins of my text books. I progressed to love poems — I was, after all, a poet's daughter, and knew that I had some talent. The nuns fawned over me and my natural ability when it came to writing essays or poems, but they wouldn't have approved of the stuff that went into my diary each night.

I was fourteen when Ed left. It was a beautiful Saturday morning in July. I was lying on the grass in the back garden, reading Jane Austen and working on my tan. Maybe Liam would finally notice me and ask me to dance at the disco that evening.

When the shouting first started, I ignored it. Father was always shouting about something these days, and once I wasn't in the firing line I tended to keep my head down until it was all over. And then I realized that it wasn't Father's voice but Ed's that was raised, and it was terrifying in its anger.

My mother's scream had me on my feet and running for the back door.

I will never, to my dying day, forget the sight that greeted me when I burst through the kitchen door. My brother had my father pinned to the wall, a carving knife to his throat. Mother was begging Ed to stop but he didn't seem to be even aware of her. He was staring into my father's face; his own was twisted with hate and anger.

My father smiled at him. "Don't worry, Rosemary," he told my mother. "He's not going to hurt me; he doesn't have the balls."

I couldn't believe the way he was taunting my brother. Even then, face to face with his own mortality. There wasn't a trace of fear, hurt or even shock in his expression. It was almost as if he were enjoying the little drama. He broke eye contact with Ed and looked past him to me. "I'm sorry if we disturbed your study, princess," he said politely. "Edmund's just having a little tantrum. Why don't you and your mother go into the garden while I take care of this?"

I stared at him, not knowing whether I should be impressed by his bravery or dumbfounded at his blasé attitude.

My mother pushed me towards the door. "Go and get help," she urged.

"No!" Ed and Father bellowed in unison.

"Well, at least we agree on one thing," my father said drily.

"Why do you want to save him, Mother?" Ed asked, incredulously. "Why would you want to save a man who has made our lives mi — mi — miserable for years?"

My mother gave a nervous laugh. "Don't be silly, Edmund."

Ed turned to stare at her, and in that instant of inattention my father moved like lightning. He twisted Ed's arm around behind his back and shoved his face into the wall. The knife fell with a clatter on to the slate tiles.

"Well, big man, what are you going to do now?" Father hissed in his ear. "Call for your mammy to save you?"

"Leave it now, Conall," my mother said, edging closer.

"Stay where you are," he barked. "You too, Dana," he added, when he saw me staring at the knife at his feet. "My God, it's a sad day when a man can't get respect in his own home." His lips were against Ed's ear, his voice low. "After all I've done for you this is the thanks I get."

"All you've ever do — do — done for me, is make me wi — wi — wish I'd nev — nev — never been bo — bo — born!"

"Edmund!" My mother gasped and put a hand to her mouth in horror.

"And tha — tha — that's what you wish too," Ed said, turning his eyes on his father.

My father was silent for a moment. Then he shrugged slightly, releasing his hold on Ed and bending to pick up the knife. "And who could blame me? What man would want a son like you?"

"Conall!"

"Daddy!"

Mother and I both stared at him. It seemed impossible that he could be this cruel.

Father ignored us both. He carefully replaced the knife in the drawer and walked to the door.

"I'm lea — lea — leaving," Ed flung after him. "I'm leaving and you can't ma — ma — make me stay."

Father calmly took his sports jacket from the hook in the hall and put it on. He checked his image in the mirror by the door, and smoothed down his thinning hair. He looked back at the three of us, his expression remote and dispassionate. "I wouldn't want to."

For the next hour, Mother and I beseeched Ed not to go, but to no avail. Tears streamed down his face as he loaded up an old suitcase with clothes and books, and when he could fit no more in he went into the garage in search of a sack.

"But where will you go?" my mother asked, wringing her hands together in anguish.

"I have friends," he said vaguely.

"What will you do?" I asked.

"I don't know but anything is better than this."

"Your exam results will be out in August," Mother reminded him. "You'll have to come back then, or at least let me know where you are so I can send them on."

"I'll be in touch," he promised. He pulled Mother into his arms and held her tightly. Then, turning to me, he smiled and patted my cheek. "Cheer up, princess. It will be much easier for you and Mum this way."

"Don't call me that," I said in disgust and threw myself into his arms. "Please don't go."

"I have to." Gently, but firmly, he pushed me away, picked up his bags and went to the door. "If I don't it's only a matter of time before I ki — ki — kill him or he ki — ki — kills me. This is for the best."

"Wait." Mother rushed into the kitchen, returning moments later with her sewing box. Opening it, she pulled out a roll of fifty-pound notes from a pocket secreted at the back behind her bobbins and buttons. "Here."

His eyes widened. "Where did you get this?" He flicked through the notes. Even I could see that there were at least twenty.

She smiled though tears rolled down her cheeks. "It's my rainy-day fund. And today looks like it might get pretty wet."

He hugged her tightly and then it was she who pushed him away. "Go on now, before he gets back, or there'll only be more trouble."

"I love you, Mummy," he said, walking backwards down the drive.

The childish endearment unleashed a fresh flood of tears. "I love you too, son."

I was not so easy to shake off. All the way down to the gate, I begged and pleaded with him not to go, or, at least, to come back after a couple of weeks. "Father will have calmed down by then and everything will be okay."

He stopped at the gate and looked at me, his expression a mixture of pity and bewilderment. "It can never be okay, Dana. Even you must realize that. Now, promise me you'll look after Mother. You're nearly fi — fi — fifteen and well able to st — st — stand up to him. Better than I ever could. Don't let him bully her any more."

"But what can I do?" I felt tears fill my eyes. He was asking too much. I was just a kid, despite my posturing in front of the bedroom mirror and dreams of romance.

"He lo — lo — loves you, Dana. He'll do anything for you."

"I hate him," I said with all the fierceness of youth.

"Maybe, maybe not," he said mildly. "But ju — ju — just remember you — you — you're the only one that he cares about. That ma — ma — makes you very powerful."

Then he was gone.

CHAPTER
TWENTY

Dana was woken at ten by the sound of Iris cleaning up after the night before. Pulling on her dressing gown, she went downstairs. "Morning, Iris."

The housekeeper switched off the hoover and smiled. "I'm sorry if I woke you."

"No, I was awake," Dana lied. She'd only got to bed at four and felt exhausted. As she poured coffee into a large mug, she debated whether she should shower or just crawl back under the covers. "It's very good of you to come in on a Saturday."

"It's no trouble. Did everything go all right last night?" Iris asked.

"It seemed to, though I've no idea why. I have a feeling my agent was telling more than a few fibs on my behalf."

Iris frowned. "Was that wise?"

Dana sighed. "Good question. He believes so."

"Shall I make you some breakfast?"

"No, coffee is fine for the moment. I think I'll go and have a shower before I start work."

Iris smiled. "You're going to write?"

"I have to try. I'll be letting a lot of people down if I don't."

214

Iris opened her mouth to reply but was interrupted by the sound of the intercom buzzer. "Who could that be?"

"I'll get it on my way up." With her mug in one hand, Dana went out and picked up the handset. "Yes?"

"I've brought you breakfast."

"Who is this?"

"Charming. I know it was a brief encounter, but I had hoped it was at least memorable."

She smiled. "Ryan?"

"Glad I'm not completely forgettable."

"What are you doing here?"

"I thought I'd give you an opportunity to explain how I ended up in the newspaper."

"I'm so sorry, Ryan, but I had no way of contacting you —"

"Are we going to conduct this whole conversation via intercom? Only, I brought breakfast . . ."

She laughed. "Sorry. Come on in. But you'll have to give me five minutes. I need to dress."

"Not on my account."

"Wait in the sitting room, Ryan. I'll be as quick as I can." Dana went into the kitchen to ask Iris to let him in. Ignoring the look of disapproval on the woman's face, she hurried upstairs. This was the last thing she needed, after the night's work she'd put in. But she couldn't help feeling pleased that he had dropped by. She'd felt bad that he'd ended up in a tabloid newspaper because of her, but that couldn't be helped. She didn't have his phone number and so had no way of warning him.

Dressing quickly in jeans and a T-shirt, Dana tucked her hair back behind her ears, put on some lip gloss and went down to join him.

He stood up and smiled when she walked in. "You look wonderful."

She made a face. "I'm wearing no make-up. I have a slight hangover. And got about five hours' sleep — I don't think so!"

He came over and kissed her cheek. "I think you look beautiful."

She stepped back, embarrassed and very conscious of how small she felt next him. "Let's go into the conservatory and eat there. I hate missing out on any of this sunshine."

He followed her through to the other room. "It is incredible weather." He carefully lifted two large cups of latte out of a bag and then took croissants and pains au chocolat out of another.

"You're into healthy eating, then," she teased as he spread the food out on the coffee table in front of them.

He lifted a finger and then pulled out two small plastic containers of mixed fruit and two brown scones. "I'm ready for anything."

Dana laughed at the double entendre. "I'm not. I'm completely exhausted, so don't get any funny ideas."

"Out clubbing again, eh?" he said casually.

Lord, he was jealous, Dana thought delightedly. "No, my publisher and agent were here for dinner. Drinking was the only way to get through it. Then, when they were gone, I started writing and lost track of time." She took a sip of coffee. "Thanks for this."

"I wasn't sure what way you liked your coffee. I hope this is okay."

"Perfect. I'm sorry about the papers."

He shrugged. "It gave my colleagues great pleasure. They photocopied it and pinned it up all over the office."

"Oh, that's awful," she groaned.

He smiled. "It wasn't so bad. Some of the other guys were quite impressed."

She shook her head. "Anyway, a journalist showed up looking for a comment. Of course, I didn't give him one," she said hurriedly. "He told me he also had photos of us outside the house. Well, then I panicked. I knew that once Gus saw them, he'd know for sure that you had stayed the night. I phoned the guy who handles my publicity and he came up with the story."

"Quite plausible, but if I were Gus I wouldn't have swallowed it. He pretty much caught us red-handed."

"What do you mean?"

He shrugged apologetically. "He saw me standing at your bedroom window."

"You knew he'd seen you? Why didn't you say so at the time?" she said incredulously.

"What was the point? It wouldn't have helped anything."

"I suppose not. And you're right, he didn't swallow it. I've tried to talk to him, but he won't take or return my calls."

"The man's an idiot." Ryan helped himself to a croissant.

"He is not," she said crossly. "He's just hurt."

Ryan nodded thoughtfully. "Remind me — it was he who left you, wasn't it?"

She nodded reluctantly.

"And he didn't get in touch for weeks until he arrived that morning unannounced. Oh, and I'm forgetting that he'd already been snapped by the press with another woman."

"How did you know that?" Her eyes narrowed suspiciously. "You said you didn't even know who I was until you brought me home."

"Ah, yes, but I have a sister who follows the tabloids with pathetic devotion and she was able to fill me in on all the gory details."

Dana shuddered. "You told your sister about me?"

"I tell my sister everything," he admitted.

Her eyes widened. "Everything?"

He grinned. "Well, no, I don't go into any sort of intimate detail and neither does she. God, I couldn't handle that. I do not want to know about what men might get up to with my kid sister." It was his turn to shudder.

"It must be nice to be that close to your family. Are there just the two of you?" Dana curled up on the sofa with her coffee. She'd forgotten what good company Ryan was. He also looked pretty good in daylight. His eyes were darker than she remembered and she loved how they crinkled round the edges when he smiled. Her eyes were drawn to his mouth. He had been a great kisser too —

"Dana?"

She felt her cheeks flush. "Sorry?"

He smiled knowingly. "I was asking if you had any brothers or sisters?"

"One brother."

"Are you close?"

Dana hesitated. "We were when we were young, although he is three years older than me. I don't think he ever confided in me, though. I was just his kid sister."

"And now?"

"We don't see that much of each other."

"That's a pity."

She shrugged. "It's life."

"Don't you miss him?"

"I've lived longer without him than I did with him. Anyway my life is here, in Dublin. I have lots of friends here."

He studied her over the rim of his cup.

"What?" she asked.

"Nothing."

"Go on. Say what you were thinking."

He shook his head. "You won't like it."

"Try me," she challenged, enjoying the banter.

"I was just going to make an observation. You'd probably think it was presumptuous."

"Really, say it. I'm fascinated that in the short time we've known each other and from the snippets you've learned from your sister, you figure that you know me."

"I didn't say that."

She waved away his correction. "Oh, stop prevaricating and just spit it out."

"Okay," he said slowly. "I don't think you were as happy with your husband as you pretend. I think you miss your brother, and I doubt that you have lots of friends."

"Well! Thanks for the honesty." She stared at him in silence for a moment, then stood up. "I think you'd better go now."

He looked up at her and smiled. "See, I knew you didn't really want to hear the truth."

"It's not the truth," she protested. "It's total bullshit. You don't have a clue what you're talking about. You know nothing about me."

Ryan took her hand and pulled her down beside him. "No, but I'd like to," he said gently.

She looked into his eyes and saw humour there but kindness too. "It's really not a good time to start a relationship —"

"Is there ever a good time?"

"I'm not ready," Dana whispered.

"Then we'll just be friends."

"Oh, right, sure." She rolled her eyes. They were sitting so close she could feel the warmth of him and smell his spicy cologne.

"No, I mean it," he told her, smiling straight into her eyes. "At least until you get to the point where you can't resist my charm any longer. We can do lunch, visit the zoo, go and watch a football match —"

"I hate football."

"You'll learn to love it," he promised. "I'll even teach you the offside rule."

She shook her head, smiling. "Why?"

"It's essential if you want to understand the game," he said, straight-faced.

"You know what I mean." She slapped his thigh, laughing.

He caught her hand in his and stroked her palm with his finger. "I feel we really clicked that night. I haven't stopped thinking about you since. That hasn't happened to me in a long time."

She stared at him, thinking that if she leaned forward just a fraction, she could kiss him. The temptation to do just that and then drag him up to bed was enormous. But there was Iris to think of. And, anyway, it would be wrong. She couldn't commit to Ryan. Her head was all over the place at the moment; it wouldn't be fair to him. But, God, he was sexy and the fact that he fancied her too was a huge turn-on.

"Okay, you've weighed up the options," he said quietly. "What's the verdict?"

She put her head on one side and pretended to consider the question. "No to the zoo. I hate the smell. Yes to lunches. As for football: I'm sorry but the intricacies of the offside rule hold no appeal. How about rugby instead?"

He grinned. "I was the hooker on my school team."

"Now, why doesn't that surprise me?"

She stood up and pulled him with her. "Thank you for breakfast, and for being so understanding about the piece in the newspaper."

He lifted her hand to his lips and kissed it. "No problem."

"Friends don't do that," she told him.

He shook his head. "No, friends don't do this either." And bending his head, he kissed her.

Dana felt herself go weak at the light, but firm pressure of his lips on hers. Just as she was about to wrap her arms around his neck, he pulled away and smiled. "But it would be nice if they did."

"I can take it or leave it," she said casually, turning him towards the door.

"I don't believe you." He whistled as he strolled back into the hall. "Should I go and say goodbye to your housekeeper?"

"Not if you want to get out of the house in one piece," she murmured, nudging him on towards the door.

"She'll grow to love me," he assured her. "I have that effect. Don't I?"

She laughed. "Don't ask me. I'm just your friend."

CHAPTER
TWENTY-ONE

Gus was signing some letters before leaving the office for the day to meet Terry, when his phone rang. "What is it, Carla?"

"There's a call for you from a Mr O'Carroll. He said you were expecting his call. I asked him what it was in connection with but he wouldn't say."

Gus stared at the phone.

"Gus? Will I put him through?"

"Yes, Carla, thank you." Gus held his breath as he waited to hear Dana's brother's voice for the first time.

"Hello? Ed?"

"Yes."

"This is Gus Johnson."

"Nice to finally talk to you," Ed replied. "It's only taken us, what, six years?"

"Almost seven."

"I must say, I was surprised when I got your message."

"Why's that?"

"I thought if we ever did get to meet or talk, it would be with Dana present. But given that you asked me to call you at work, I assume that she doesn't know anything about this."

"No, she doesn't."

"Oh, well. I suppose that was too much to hope for."

"Why?" Gus asked.

"Why did you want to talk to me, Gus?" Ed asked, ignoring the question.

"Dana has never talked about her family. She's always said it was too painful and she didn't want to think about that time of her life, never mind talk about it." Ed said nothing so Gus ploughed on. "Recently I found out some things about Dana, and, well, I felt shocked and hurt that she never confided in me."

Again Ed was silent for a moment. "Did you ask her about these 'things'?"

"No, I left."

"You've left her?" Ed sounded incredulous.

"Yes." Gus began to feel defensive.

"I see." Ed's tone was cool.

"No. No, you don't. You don't know anything about it. You don't know me; and I'm beginning to wonder, do you even know Dana?"

"I knew Dana the little girl. But no, I don't know Dana the woman."

Gus sighed. "I'm sorry. It's just so bloody frustrating."

"I know." Ed finally sounded sympathetic. "If you like, we could meet up. But I don't have all the answers. I can't even promise I'll tell you everything you want to know."

"I'd appreciate any help you can give me at this point. It's probably a waste of time but . . ."

224

"You're hoping that I'm going to tell you something that will allow you to forgive her?"

Gus sighed. "Yes, maybe I am."

Sylvie knocked on Dana's bedroom door and stuck her head in. "Is there anything else you want me to do before I head off?"

Dana groaned. "A new brain?"

Sylvie came in and sat down. "Still not going well, then?"

"You could say that. God, I could kill Wally for telling Gretta I could do this."

"But you can," Sylvie assured her. "You just need to get your *mojo* back."

"My *mojo* is a distant memory," Dana told her with a weak smile. "I don't suppose you fancy going out tonight?"

"Yeah, great. What did you have in mind?"

"Some dinner and then maybe we could go to the pub you were telling me about; the one that has those live jazz sessions."

"Cassidy's, in Temple Bar. Yeah, okay. Where will we meet?"

"I could pick you up."

"Oh, no, that's okay. I'll meet you in town."

"Are you sure?"

"Yeah, really."

"Okay. How about Nico's at eight?"

Sylvie nodded. "Fine."

Dana handed her PA the latest pages of *The Mile High Club*. "My latest pathetic offering. You get off home; it can wait till morning. I'm off for a bath. See you later."

"Yeah, see ya." Left alone, Sylvie went back to the office and sat down at her own desk. She couldn't wait until morning to read Dana's latest work. She hoped it was better than the last chapter. She bent her head and started to read.

"Are you staying the night?" Bobbi tried to sound casual but she saw from Victor's irritable expression that she just sounded needy.

"No, I can't tonight."

"That's fine." She moved closer to him and stroked his cheek. "But you don't have to go straight away, do you?"

He flung back the covers and stood up. "Yes. I'll go shower."

"Want me to help?" she murmured, with a suggestive smile.

His smile was forced. "Sorry, darling. I really have to hurry."

"Go on, then," she said, petulantly. "Hurry back to the little wife."

Victor paused for a moment and then went into the bathroom, shutting the door behind him.

Bobbi flopped back on the pillow, tears in her eyes. She was his mistress, for God's sake. He wasn't supposed to tire of her. Still, she wasn't supposed to nag either. When had she turned into such a sad specimen of womanhood? What had Victor Gaston done to her?

He showered and dressed, and less than ten minutes later he had bade a hasty goodnight and left. He had dropped a kiss on the tip of her nose and quickly moved away as she'd put up her arms to embrace him. He'd call, he'd said. Bobbi wondered, as she always did lately, if he would.

Sylvie skipped forward to the next page, and then the next. There was just more of the same. Dana's heroine didn't seem to do anything other than wonder about her lover and her life. Not unlike the author. Nothing seemed to be happening in the book — hadn't been for the last couple of chapters. Bobbi spent all her time navel-gazing, phoning her lover or waiting by the phone for his call. Sylvie wasn't surprised Victor had lost interest. The heroine had become a pathetic and irritating woman. Even the love scenes were pedestrian and lacklustre.

This was nowhere near what Dana was capable of. It certainly wouldn't be good enough to launch the Passion imprint. Gretta would be furious. Sylvie felt sorry for Dana but she couldn't help thinking how it would affect her life too. Dana wouldn't need a PA if she didn't have a contract. And how could Sylvie help to support her family if she lost this job? Her only real skill was typing, and she had a limited knowledge but no flair when it came to looking after Dana's website. She had been very lucky the day Dana had employed her. The flexible working hours allowed her to help out with her father. And the money and perks were great. She wasn't sure she would be so lucky the next time. Still, having Dana's name on her CV had to count for something.

Feeling frustrated and helpless, Sylvie put on her coat, grabbed her bag and left the house. As she hurried to catch the bus that would bring her the short distance to her home in Ringsend, Sylvie wondered what to do. Going out tonight no longer appealed to her. She prayed Dana wouldn't ask her what she thought of her work; she didn't want to have to tell her. But maybe a night out was exactly what Dana needed. Maybe it would inspire her.

"Hello, love. Good day?" Her mother was sitting at the kitchen table, watching the news on the small television on the dresser.

"Quiet."

"She's still not working, then?" Maureen said, a frown creasing her brow.

"She is. Just not very well." Sylvie put on the kettle and, fetching a mug, spooned coffee into it. "Want one?" she asked her mother.

Maureen shook her head. "I just had some tea. So what will happen, do you think?"

"I'm not sure. If she carries on like this, though, I don't think they'll publish the book at all."

"That's terrible."

"Yeah." Sylvie made the coffee and sat down opposite her mother. "And what's worse is that both her agent and editor think she's back to normal and that the book will be finished by the end of next month." She shook her head, sadly. "But even if she makes that deadline, they're going to be so disappointed in the book."

228

"And where will that leave you?"

Sylvie looked her straight in the eye. "I really don't know, Mum."

"Why does everything have to happen together?" her mother groaned. "The doctor was here today and he thinks your father might need another operation."

"Oh, no." Sylvie reached out to grasp her mother's hand. If only it were possible to take the worry from her eyes.

"And your brother needs a new jacket."

"But he just got one," Sylvie protested.

Maureen nodded. "I know. He left it on the bus apparently."

"He'd lose his head if it wasn't screwed on," Sylvie complained. "Where is he?"

"Gone to study at Alec's house."

Sylvie checked her watch. "I'm going out with Dana later."

Maureen's eyes widened. "Again?"

"Yeah. Maybe it will cheer her up; it's worth a shot."

"Is she going to end up in the newspaper again?"

Sylvie laughed. "No. Tonight we're just going for dinner and a quiet drink. Is there anything you want me to do before I go and get ready?"

"No, love, you go on. There's plenty of water if you want a bath."

"Lovely. I'll just nip in and say hi to Dad first."

"Don't mention the operation," Maureen warned. "I'm not telling him until we're sure one way or the other."

"Okay."

Sylvie left her and went in to see her father. He was lying on his side, reading. She was struck by how small he looked; this cursed disease seemed to be making him shrink. He was barely half the size he'd been ten years ago. "Hi, Dad."

He turned his head to look at her and smiled. "Hello, love. How was work?"

"Fine. I'm off out with Dana again."

"Somewhere swanky, I suppose."

She smiled. "Maybe. I'd better go and get ready. Can I get you anything?"

He shook his head. "Just come in and see me before you go; I love seeing my little girl all dolled up."

"Okay, Dad."

"Where's your brother?"

"Down at Alec's, studying."

"I hope he is. He needs to work hard if he's going to do well in those exams. I worry about the maths; he's never been good with figures."

"I'll go over it with him at the weekend, Dad, don't worry."

"You're a good girl, Sylvie. I don't know what we'd do without you."

Later, as she applied her make-up, Sylvie's thoughts returned to her plight. How much longer, she wondered, would she be employed by Dana De Lacey? Maybe she should just ask the author outright. Tonight. She might as well. It wasn't as if she had a lot to lose.

Sylvie took a last look at her reflection, slipped on her highest sandals and carefully made her way back downstairs. She went into her dad's room and twirled in front of the bed.

"You look gorgeous," he told her. "But that skirt's too short and you'll break your neck in those heels."

Sylvie laughed and bent to touch her lips to his forehead. "Night, Dad."

CHAPTER
TWENTY-TWO

After she'd said goodbye to her mother, Sylvie hurried — as fast as her shoes would allow — to the restaurant in Temple Bar. It was a fifteen-minute walk but she didn't want to waste money on a bus fare and walking kept her slim. As she walked, she wondered how to raise the subject of *The Mile High Club*. Dana knew that Sylvie read the chapters as she wrote them but they never discussed them unless Sylvie offered a compliment. She hadn't said anything since Dana had resumed work on the novel. She was as good as the next person when it came to flattery and ego-massaging, but she just couldn't bring herself to lie to Dana. Not when the outcome was so important to so many people.

When she pushed open the door of the restaurant, Dana was already seated at a table in the centre of the room, studying the menu. A champagne bucket sat next to the table and a foaming glass was at Dana's elbow.

"Hi!" The author smiled up at her, gesturing to the waiter to pour her PA some champagne, and to top up her own glass. "I thought we should start as we mean to go on," Dana said, raising her glass in a toast. "Cheers."

"Don't go too mad," Sylvie teased, taking a sip. "You've so much to do tomorrow."

Dana's smile faded. "Thanks. Can't I just forget about the bloody book for a couple of hours?"

"Sorry."

"It's okay," Dana said, but she still looked annoyed.

Sylvie took another sip of champagne and stuck her head into the menu. As usual, she couldn't understand most of it and didn't know what to order. "I'm not sure what to have," she said. "Any suggestions?"

Dana rolled off a number of options and Sylvie dived in when she eventually mentioned something simple. "The prawns with garlic sound good."

"Yes. I'll have the same," Dana said without interest, and closed her menu.

The waiter took their order. Avoiding Dana's eye, Sylvie asked for a large bottle of sparkling water.

Dana raised her eyebrows. "Feeling thirsty?"

"I'm just trying to help," Sylvie protested. "I know you're finding it hard to write at the moment. And a hangover isn't going to help, is it?"

"Anything else you want to get off your chest?"

This was the perfect time to say something but Sylvie felt her mouth dry up as she searched for the right words.

Dana pushed back her chair. "In that case, I'm going to the loo."

Sylvie watched her leave. She'd missed her chance. Maybe it was for the best. It wasn't her job to counsel her boss or offer advice. In fact, the more she thought about it, the more foolhardy such a course seemed.

Dana would shoot the messenger and that would leave Sylvie exactly where she didn't want to be: out on her ear. No, all she could do was try to cheer Dana up. And maybe, if Dana relaxed a bit, Sylvie could drop some subtle hints about jazzing up the storyline. Sylvie took another sip of her bubbly. Better enjoy it while she could.

Dana reapplied her lipstick and mascara and prepared to go back into the restaurant, but her earlier good humour had dissolved. She didn't want to sit through dinner trying to make conversation with her glum PA. Sylvie's disapproval was obvious. Dana should have stayed home, or called Ryan and gone for a quiet drink with him instead. But calling him so soon would give him the wrong idea — he'd expect the evening to end in her bed. And, it probably would. This whole friends thing was a joke. Dana knew she would never be able to resist him if he turned on the charm. And she didn't want to appear desperate either. Lord, it wasn't easy being single again. It certainly wasn't as much fun at thirty-seven as it had been when she was in her twenties. For a start, men treated her completely differently now that she was no longer accompanied by Gus. Then, she'd received compliments and respect. Now, she was fair game.

She didn't know how Sylvie could stand it. True, the girl was only twenty-eight. But because she was looking for a rich man, she frequented the older clubs and subjected herself to the leers and mauls from some real creeps.

With a weary sigh, Dana closed her handbag and went back inside. She managed to summon up a smile as she sat down. "Hope you haven't drunk all the bubbly."

"I'm sorry, Dana. I didn't mean to preach to you," Sylvie said. "It's just I've been worried about you."

"Worried about me? Why on earth would you be worried about me?" Even Dana realized that she sounded more than a little defensive.

Sylvie shrugged, nervously. "You're not yourself."

"Then who am I?" Dana quipped.

Sylvie pulled a face and said nothing.

"I'm sorry. Go on."

"Are you sure?"

Dana nodded. "Sure."

"Well, you haven't done that much work on the book. Yet you promised Walter you'd finish it —"

"And I will."

They fell silent as their food was served. Dana looked at her plate, pushed it away and topped up her glass instead.

Sylvie watched, her large eyes full of concern. "Maybe. But do you think Gretta will be happy with it?"

Dana lowered her glass and stared. "Are you trying to say something?"

Sylvie looked down at her plate. "I'm sorry, Dana. I just don't think that it's your best work."

Dana sat in stunned silence. She knew that *The Mile High Club* was far from her best novel. Hell, it was crap. But for Sylvie to say so . . .

"I'm sorry. I'd never normally say anything — there's never been reason to before —" Sylvie's words tumbled out in a rush. "But when I read those pages today . . ."

"Go on," Dana said quietly.

Sylvie raised her eyes to meet Dana's. "I just thought it was a bit . . . tame."

"Tame?" Dana swallowed hard.

Sylvie nodded.

Dana forced a tight smile. "Well, don't stop now. You've started, so you may as well finish."

Sylvie took a drink. "Okay, then. But please understand, Dana, I'm not trying to tell you how to do your job. I've no idea how you turn out book after book. I think you're amazing —"

"Oh, please —"

"But I mean it," Sylvie protested, distressed. "I've always loved your books, and it's really exciting for me that I'm the first one who gets to read them. That makes me feel very special."

"Sylvie, really! My books are not exactly literary masterpieces," Dana retorted.

"No, they're pure entertainment."

Dana's lips twitched. "I'm not sure I'd use the word 'pure'."

Sylvie laughed, relief flooding her face. She continued, braver now. "Women read your books to escape. They read your books because they're fed up with fat, balding husbands or drunken, cheating boyfriends. They want heroes who are sexy, who are handsome and who, above all, put what the woman wants first."

"It is total fiction, isn't it?" Dana said sadly. She had thought Gus was such a hero. But it had turned out he was just an ordinary man. He didn't notice when she'd got her hair done, or lost a few pounds. When he was sick he was a difficult and grumpy patient. Though he was handsome enough to be a model, he still left the toilet seat up. And, on occasion, he even snored loudly in bed.

"You are great at what you do, Dana," Sylvie was saying quietly and seriously. "And you have so many fans. They love you because you let them have a glimpse of a life that they will never know."

Dana shook her head. "So I'm showing them something that they'll never have? Surely that should make them suicidal."

"No, it's not like that. People aren't like that. I mean, I watch all those programmes about stars in Hollywood and their fabulous homes and huge cars, and I love it. It's so glamorous and the women are all stunning." She shrugged. "They fascinate me. It's like a fairy tale. Do I think I'm ever going to have a life like that? No, of course not, but that's okay."

"Oh, come on, Sylvie, you're doing your damnedest to secure a life like that," Dana couldn't help teasing. "As soon as you're introduced to a man you want to know what he does for a living, what he drives and where he lives."

Sylvie reddened. "That's not fair."

"Then tell me something, Sylvie. Which would you choose — a poor man you were in love with, or a rich man you only liked?"

Sylvie stiffened. "Some of us can't afford love."

"What does that mean?"

"Nothing." Sylvie looked away. "Sorry, my turn to go to the loo." She stood up and hurried out of the room.

Alone, Dana picked half-heartedly at her food and finished off the champagne. Maybe they should call it a night. The atmosphere had gone from bad to worse and now Sylvie had obviously taken offence. Which was ironic. Dana should be the one feeling hurt and insulted after what the girl had said about *The Mile High Club*. Except it was all true. Dana even agreed with the word Sylvie had used. "Tame" was exactly what her work had become. Tame, boring and predictable.

Walter had done his best to help and inspire her. He sent encouraging little emails each day, but she just couldn't come up with the goods. What's more, when she'd searched through her old books for ideas, she'd found herself criticizing and even ridiculing her own work. She seemed to have lost all of her confidence. It didn't help that she couldn't stop thinking about her own story. Dr Corcoran would be proud of her. He said write it all down, and that's exactly what she was doing. And once she started, it was as if she couldn't stop. Deep into the night, she'd sit there, her fingers flying over the keys. The compulsion to write everything down was intense. Dana felt she had no control over it. The story seemed to come from the dark recesses of her brain straight to her fingertips. Some nights she would actually find herself sweating by the end of a session.

Some nights, crying. She always felt drained by the time she switched off the machine yet, still, sleep evaded her. Invariably she'd end up in the conservatory staring out into the darkness, dragging herself to bed in the early hours or falling asleep in the chair.

Iris had found her like this a couple of mornings, and huffed and puffed that it was an unhealthy way to live.

"Don't fuss, I'm fine, Iris," Dana told her before traipsing upstairs to sleep for a couple of hours. Then she showered and returned to her desk, to tap desultorily at the keyboard.

Sylvie returned from the loo.

"I'm sorry for being a bitch," Dana said.

Sylvie shook her head. "I shouldn't have said anything. It's my fault."

"No! I can't say it's nice to hear, but I appreciate your honesty, Sylvie."

"Really?" Sylvie eyed her warily.

"Really." Dana looked at her PA's face and realized there was more. "What? Come on, Sylvie. Don't stop now."

Sylvie's eyes met hers. "I read some of the other book you've been writing," she admitted.

Dana froze. "What?"

"I didn't mean to pry. I just came across it and, well, I couldn't resist."

"I don't believe this."

"It's brilliant, Dana." Sylvie hurried on. "I've never read anything so moving. If Walter saw it, he wouldn't care about *The Mile High Club*. You're so talented."

Dana shook her head. "You went into my computer? You looked through my files and then read something that was very obviously private?"

"I — I — didn't mean to pry." Sylvie baulked at her boss's furious expression.

"How dare you! You have abused my trust and your position."

"I just wanted to help," Sylvie cried, drawing looks from the surrounding tables.

Dana looked around for a waiter. "Where the fuck is everyone?"

"The manager's at the front desk. Will I go and ask him for the bill?"

Dana glared at her. "No, I don't need your help, thank you very much. Not tonight. Not tomorrow. Not ever."

Sylvie stared at her, white-faced. "But Dana —"

Ignoring her, Dana stood up and strode through the restaurant to the front desk. She was rooting angrily in her bag for her wallet when the front door of the restaurant opened, letting in a gust of cold air. A pretty blonde girl came in, laughing up into the face of her partner. Dana gasped as her eyes met his.

"Come on," Gus said to the girl at his side. "Let's go somewhere else." And with an apologetic look at Dana, he guided the other woman back out on to the street.

Sylvie was at her side in an instant. "Are you okay?"

"It was her, did you see?" she whispered.

Sylvie nodded. "Yes. I'm sorry, Dana."

Dana looked at her. "Are you? Are you really, Sylvie?"

"Yes." Sylvie was close to tears.

Dana gave the manager a curt nod as he handed back her card. She pushed open the door and stepped out on to the pavement, Sylvie on her heels.

"I'm so sorry." Sylvie was crying openly now. "I just wanted to help."

Dana watched her, unmoved. "Well, you can help. Come in first thing tomorrow and clear your desk."

"No!" Sylvie shook her head. "Please, Dana. I know you're angry. But I'm sorry. I'll never do anything like that again."

"You're right about that. You won't get the chance."

Sylvie, tears pouring down her cheeks, opened her mouth to say something, but seeing the look on Dana's face she turned and stumbled away.

Dana stood watching as Sylvie tottered away in her ridiculous heels. Whereas moments earlier she'd been close to tears too, now Dana just felt numb. Reaching into her coat pocket she pulled out her phone and sent a text.

I NEED A DRINK AND I'D LIKE SOME COMPANY. INTERESTED?

Within seconds, Ryan responded.

TELL ME WHERE.

CHAPTER
TWENTY-THREE

"I need juice." Ryan groaned as he rolled over. "My mouth is like the Sahara and my head feels like it's about to explode. You are very bad for my health, Dana De Lacey."

"I didn't pour it down your throat," she retorted, pulling the covers over her head.

"So, do you have any?"

"What?"

"Juice."

"No idea. Check the fridge."

And so it was that Ryan was padding across the hall in his boxers, carrying two glasses of juice when Iris walked in. "Morning," he said, as she looked at him, horrified. It was just as well he wasn't naked, the old dear would probably have keeled over.

"Your housekeeper's in," he said, climbing back into bed.

Dana sat up, rubbing her eyes. "Iris? Great, that's all I need."

He chuckled. "She's not your mother."

"No, she's worse." Dana glanced at the clock. "Don't you have a job to go to?"

He raised an eyebrow. "You just want me for sex, don't you?"

Dana smiled and took his hand. "You gave me a lot more than that last night, Ryan."

He leaned over and kissed her on the lips. "Any time. And you're right, I do have to go. But are you going to be okay? If you want, I could always phone in and tell them I've been delayed."

"No, really. I'll be fine."

He'd listened patiently while she'd ranted and raved about Sylvie — though she didn't go into any details. It was bad enough that Sylvie had discovered she was writing her autobiography; she didn't want anyone else to know. She had, however, admitted to him that *The Mile High Club* was a disaster. He'd grinned when he'd heard the name and offered to help her with the research.

"So, what are you going to do?" he asked now.

"Sleep," she told him, snuggling back down under the covers. "I'm exhausted."

He shook his head sadly. "And that should be down to me. But, sadly, it's because we talked so much and you've had less than three hours' sleep."

"We didn't *just* talk," she reminded him. "Do you think you'll get any work done at all today?"

"I'll manage." He swung himself out of bed and headed for the shower. "Why don't you come over to my place tonight? Chelsea are playing Liverpool."

"Do I have to?" she groaned, pulling a pillow over her head. "We agreed no soccer."

"Oh, come on. It will be fun."

"You think?"

It was after twelve when Dana made her way downstairs, confident that Sylvie would have been and gone by now. She peeked into the office and saw that Sylvie's desk was indeed bare save for an envelope propped up on the keyboard. Dana opened it and read.

Dana,
I can't tell you how sorry I am for reading your story. Please believe that I never meant to pry. I only wanted to help. Yes I was worried about my job too. But that was because my parents and brother depend on my income and I didn't want to let them down.
    Best of luck with the book. I'll miss working for you,
        Sylvie

Dana swallowed hard. As notes went, it was gracious and moving. But what was this about her parents and brother? Dana had imagined Sylvie lived alone in one of those cool new city apartments, spending all of her money on make-up and clothes. The girl had never mentioned family before. Perhaps she was just trying to make Dana feel guilty. Maybe she thought a sad story would win her back her job. Well, she was wrong. Dana couldn't forgive her for what she'd done. Sylvie had always had access to Dana's files and computer. This might not be the first time the girl had looked at something she shouldn't have. How could Dana possibly trust her again?

Feeling very fed up and more than a little sorry for herself, Dana went out to the kitchen to get a strong cup of coffee. It was odd, now she thought about it, that Iris hadn't brought her one earlier. She must have heard Ryan leaving. Dana pushed open the door and stopped at the sight of Iris sitting at the table, wearing her hat and coat, her handbag in front of her. "Iris, is everything okay?"

The woman looked up and met Dana's eyes, her face grim. "No, Ms De Lacey." She pushed an envelope across the table. "I'm afraid I must tender my resignation."

"What?" Dana looked from the envelope back to Iris. This really couldn't be happening. Not today. "But why?"

Iris reddened. "You're a grown woman. What you do in your private life is your own business —"

"Yes, Iris, it is," Dana said firmly, realizing that this was all about Ryan.

"But it's my decision as to whether or not I want to witness it," Iris said quietly. "And I don't."

"Look, Iris, I had no intention of embarrassing you. I'm sorry. Please don't resign; it won't happen again."

Iris shook her head sadly. "I'm sorry, but I've made up my mind."

"Is this because I slept with another man? Because I was unfaithful to your beloved Mr Johnson?" Dana laughed bitterly. "You might be interested to know that he was out on the town last night with a very young blonde. What do you think of that?"

"It's not for me to say," Iris murmured but Dana saw the look of shock that crossed the housekeeper's face.

"But you're happy to condemn me."

"I have not condemned you and, I assure you, I feel anything but happy."

Dana smiled sadly. "Then we have one thing in common."

Doubt flooded the housekeeper's face. "If you like, I could work my notice —"

"Don't bother. I'm sure I'll have no problem finding a replacement."

Iris looked hurt but she just nodded politely. "I'll say goodbye, then, Ms De Lacey. And good luck."

"I make my own luck," Dana retorted to the woman's retreating back. "And I don't need your help, or my beloved husband's, or my dishonest PA's either. I'll do just fine on my own. Do you hear me?"

Iris didn't reply, just closed the door after her with a gentle but firm click.

Dana sank into a chair and put her head in her hands.

She was still sitting there some time later when the phone rang. It kept ringing and she suddenly realized that there was no one to answer it. It stopped and then started again. With a heavy sigh, she decided she'd better go and answer it.

"Hello?"

"Dana? How is my gorgeous girl?"

"Hi, Wally," Dana said and immediately started to cry.

"Dana? Dana, my darling, what is it?"

246

It took her a moment to answer. "Oh, Wally, why does everyone hate me?" she hiccupped.

"No one hates you! Who's been upsetting you like this?"

"I had a row with Sylvie and sacked her. And then Iris walked out."

"Your housekeeper?"

"Yes. She came in this morning and Ryan was here. So she handed in her notice and left."

"Silly old bag. So, you and Ryan are an item?"

"No. We're just friends."

He laughed. "Oh, right."

"Stop it, Wally. I'm not in the mood."

"I'm sorry, darling. But why did you sack Sylvie?"

Dana hesitated a second. "She accessed some of my private files without my permission."

"No!"

"Yes. I don't think she was going to actually do anything," she added hurriedly, "but I couldn't possibly trust her after that."

"No, I understand. We're going to have to find a replacement though, and quickly," he said worriedly. "You'll need help to finish the book."

Dana heard the note of panic in her agent's voice. "Don't worry, Wally. I'll finish it."

"I know you will, Dana. I just want to make it as pain free as possible. What can I do to help? Shall I get on to Ian and ask him to find you a new cleaner?"

"I doubt he'll want to help. He's going to be disgusted when he hears I've fired Sylvie."

"Oh? Is there something going on there?"

"No, but it's obvious he fancies her."

"Well, no matter. Business is business. He must keep his private life to himself and I shall tell him so."

"Don't worry, Wally. Ian's the least of my worries." Dana sniffed. "I saw Gus last night. He was with that girl — the one he was photographed with. I saw them with my own eyes. They were so obviously together. She's young and pretty —" Dana broke off with a sob.

"My poor, poor darling. I wish I was there to look after you."

Dana found a tissue and dabbed at her eyes and nose. "Me too."

"Forget about him, Dana. You have a new love in your life too, remember."

"Yes, you're right. And he's a nice man."

"There you go, then."

"He's funny, sexy, kind —"

Walter groaned. "I sense a 'but' coming."

Dana sighed.

"He's not Gus?" Wally suggested.

"No," Dana agreed, tears welling up again. "He's not."

Walter talked to Dana for a little longer. He did his best to bolster the author's mood but he was still worried after he'd hung up. He asked his secretary to get Ian on the phone and he paced his office while he waited.

"Ian Wilson on line two, Walter."

"Thanks. Ian?"

"Hi, Walter, how are you?"

"I've been better, Ian. I just hung up the phone on Dana. There's a problem."

"Not another one," Ian groaned. "What's she done now?"

"Her housekeeper's walked out and Dana's had to fire her PA."

"What? Why on earth would she fire Sylvie?"

Walter smiled at the anger in Ian's voice. Dana was right. The man must be in love. "Never mind, but I assure you, she had good reason. Anyway, I'm more concerned about Dana. She's at a very low ebb and all alone in that house. We need to get someone in there, and fast. I'm afraid she may become reclusive again and that would be a disaster on a professional and personal level."

"So you want me to hire a cleaner and a PA?"

"Not your job, I know, Ian. But I would appreciate it if you could help."

"Of course. Leave it with me," Ian had replied, and hung up.

But Walter still wasn't happy. Even if Ian did find new staff for Dana, it wouldn't be the same as having someone around that she could trust or confide in. He thought for a moment, and after checking his personal diary he picked up the phone again and dialled. It rang only once.

"Walter?"

"Hello, Gus."

"Is something wrong?"

"I think you know the answer to that. It was a bit of a blow for Dana running into you like that. But there's more."

"Oh?"

Walter quickly went on to fill Gus in.

"This is awful, Walter, but what can I do about it?"

"I was wondering. Have you found her brother?"

"Yes. We're actually meeting up tomorrow."

"That's great. Maybe you could fill him in."

"I can, Walter, but I don't see that it will make any difference. She won't want to see him any more than she'd want to see me. They haven't talked in years."

"It's worth a try," Walter said desperately. "I have to do something."

"Why not call Judy?"

"I thought about that, but she lives in Wexford and has two kids. She can't do much more than be at the end of a phone."

"True. Look, I'll talk to Ed," Gus promised. "But I can't promise anything."

"I know that. One more thing?"

"What's that, Walter?"

"Please go and see her."

"There's no point —"

"There's every point. And you owe it to her."

CHAPTER
TWENTY-FOUR

Gus was feeling more than a little nervous as he walked into O'Dwyer's pub. It had been Ed's idea to meet here and he'd agreed immediately. It was late afternoon and there weren't many people about. After scanning the room, Gus figured Ed hadn't arrived yet. Going to the bar, he ordered himself a pint of Guinness.

"Make that two."

Gus swung around. "Ed?"

The other man smiled and held out his hand. "Hello, Gus."

"How did you know me?"

"I've seen your photograph," Ed said straight-faced.

Gus sighed. "Of course. Shall we get a table?" He watched Dana's brother as he led the way. He was dark and slim, like Dana, but there the similarity ended. Ed's eyes were greyish blue. His hair was cut tight, his arms were muscled and he was almost as tall as Gus. He had a healthy, outdoors glow about him. He must be forty now but he could easily pass for thirty-five. "I can't believe I'm sitting here with you after all this time," he marvelled when they'd found a table.

"I can't quite believe it myself," Ed replied. "So how's my sister? Have you seen her?"

"Sadly, yes," Gus said and explained how he and Terry had bumped into Dana. Then he went on to tell Ed about Walter's phone call. "She's had a tough time. Walter — that's Dana's agent — thought maybe you could help?"

Ed laughed. "Me? What could I do?"

"Just be there for her," Gus suggested.

"She wouldn't want me anywhere near her!"

"Why? What happened between you? I know she had problems with your father and . . . other things. But why did you two fall out?"

"I'm not entirely sure," Ed said sadly. "She never hung around long enough to tell me."

"Not very good at talking, your sister, is she?" Gus remarked. "That's why I left. We were so close — at least I thought we were. And then I discover that I hardly know her at all. Tell me about your nephew."

"Nephew?" Ed shook his in confusion. "I don't have a nephew."

"Look, Ed, I know Dana has a son. I read a letter she wrote to him."

"No. No, she doesn't."

"But the letter —"

"I don't know anything about that. What I do know is there is no child." Ed closed his eyes briefly. "Dana had an abortion when she was sixteen."

"What?" Gus stared at him in shock. "What happened? Was she attacked? God, it wasn't your father —"

"No! Of course not. He wasn't the best father in the world, but he'd never harm a hair on Dana's head." Ed's smile was sad. "She was his princess."

252

"So, what happened?"

"It was a couple of years after I'd left home and Dana and I have never discussed it, so I can only tell you what I've heard second-hand."

"Go on."

"Dana was seeing a boy secretly, a local kid. I don't think it was serious — my mother didn't seem to think so. My father didn't let her go out often, he was very strict. But she'd pretend to be at a friend's studying, and then sneak off to meet him. Then she went on a school trip to London. My father didn't want her to go but my mother begged him to let her. She said it was educational and all the other girls in her class were going. He eventually agreed and off they went. They got a phone call a couple of days later to say that Dana had gone missing. My father immediately made arrangements to go over and look for her. By the time he got there, Dana had turned up. She told him that she'd just had an abortion."

"What? But how could she have? She was only a child herself and where did she get the money?"

"She was sixteen, so it was completely legal. As for the money — my mother had a 'rainy day' fund. Dana helped herself."

"Your father must have been upset," Gus said.

"That's putting it mildly. That his princess had got pregnant was bad. But the fact that she had an abortion was ten times worse."

"Surely he wouldn't have expected her to go through with the pregnancy? She was still so young."

"You know what it was like back then. No one had abortions or, if they did, they certainly didn't admit it. My father was very proud but he was also a very religious man. He'd have been mortified that Dana got herself into such a predicament. But he'd have expected — no, demanded — that Dana have the child, no matter what. And she knew that."

Gus looked at him. "What do you mean?"

"Apparently the main reason Dana had the abortion was to punish him."

"That's ridiculous!"

"Is it? As far as Dana was concerned, my father was responsible for me leaving and for making our mother's life a misery. But he adored his only daughter. She knew how much this would hurt him."

"Are you saying that she got pregnant on purpose?"

Ed shook his head. "She would never have been that calculating. But once she found herself in that situation, why not make the most of it?"

"So, what happened then?"

"Father brought her home, forbade her to talk of it ever again. Then he packed her off to a boarding school for her last year."

"But that's awful. How did your mother agree to that?"

Ed shook his head. "My mother didn't have a say about anything in that house. Anyway Dana was probably better off. Life wouldn't have been easy for her if she'd stayed at home."

"So how do you know so much?" Gus asked, suddenly remembering that Ed had been absent while all of this transpired,

Ed said nothing for a moment and then stood up. "I pieced it together when my mother died. I'm sorry, would you excuse me for a moment? I just remembered I have to make a phone call. Back in a sec."

Gus watched him walk away and wondered what he'd said to prompt Ed's sudden discomfort. Today's revelations had been a shock, but Gus knew they were just the tip of the iceberg. He was relieved that Dana hadn't had a baby. Somehow it was easier to accept that she had concealed a teenage pregnancy rather than a child. It made sense too. The O'Carrolls wouldn't be the first Catholic family to cover up a scandal like that, and the fact that Conall was a celebrity of sorts made everything make even more sense. And Dana had kept the secret for so long, he could almost understand why she hadn't thought it necessary to confide in her husband. Almost. But there were more secrets, of that he was sure. He wondered if Ed could or would reveal them. He didn't have to wait long to find out.

Dana's brother returned, brandishing his phone. "I have to go."

"Oh! Is there something wrong?"

"No. No, it's just work. I'm sorry about this, truly I am. I'll call you and we'll get together again soon."

"What about Dana?" Gus raised his voice as Ed turned to go.

The other man hesitated.

"Will you contact her?" Gus urged.

Ed smiled and then nodded. "Of course. Will you?"

Gus had arranged to meet Terry later, but he sent her a text message saying he had to work. It was the second time he'd avoided her that week. She was a lovely girl and she turned him on too. But since he'd slept with her, it just felt wrong. It didn't help that their first time had been just before they'd bumped into Dana.

His phone beeped and he read Terry's reply.

NO PROB. CALL ME WHEN UR DONE. X

He sighed. He didn't want to call her or see her. He didn't know what he wanted. On impulse he phoned Ashling. "Any chance I could drop in for a coffee?"

"So?" Ashling settled back in a chair and crossed her arms over her bump.

"I was just passing," Gus said, staring into his mug.

"Of course you were."

He sighed. "It's such a mess."

"Tell me."

"I met Dana the other night."

"Oh, yeah?" Ashling grinned.

"It wasn't planned. I was with Terry."

"Who?"

Gus looked away. "The journalist from the photo."

Her eyes widened. "But you said that was totally innocent."

"It was! But she came to see me afterwards to apologize and —" He closed his eyes. "It's a long story but the fact is that we're together now. Sort of."

"Sort of?"

He looked at her. "It just doesn't feel right."

"You still love Dana."

"I don't know. I suppose so. You can't just turn it off, you know? No matter how angry or hurt you are."

"So, you were hurt and angry with Dana. That's why you left." He said nothing. Ashling sighed. "I'm delighted you came to talk to me, Gus. Only, I feel a little bit in the dark."

He nodded. "Yeah, sorry." He was silent for a moment. "I left Dana because I found out that she'd been keeping secrets from me. They didn't concern me or our relationship. But I felt, as her husband, she should have told me. If she trusted me, she'd have told me." He looked at her, his eyes narrowed. "Do you have secrets from Tom?"

"Sure," she said easily. "I don't tell him when I spend a fortune on a handbag and I never tell him my real weight."

He shot her a reproachful look. "Ashling."

She looked into his eyes and shook her head. "No, Gus. If there's anything in my past that I haven't told him, it's because it wasn't important enough to mention. Maybe it was the same for Dana."

He laughed. "No. No, it doesn't fall into that category at all."

"You know you're driving me mad with curiosity, don't you?"

"I'm sorry, Ashling." He stood up. "Maybe I'll be able to tell you one day, but not today. Thanks for everything."

"I didn't do anything," she said, standing up more slowly.

He bent to kiss her cheek. "Thanks for trying."

CHAPTER
TWENTY-FIVE

After my brother left, life was indeed quieter. But that wasn't just down to my father's improved temperament. My mother and I distanced ourselves from him and left him to his writing and his books. We lived in the same house but that was all, really. While I missed Ed hugely, I loved having my mother all to myself. We had never been so close. In the evenings, I'd curl up on the sofa beside her and listen to her talk. It was a novel experience. Mother had always been the doer and Father did enough talking for both of them. Now I found, though, that my mother had much to say.

She would regale me with stories of her own childhood and her love for her mother and father. They sounded as gentle and loving as she. She'd tell tales of Ed and me as young babies, with a tenderness in her smile that made me reach out to her. She even talked about Father and their courtship. The man she described bore little resemblance to the one I knew. I wondered whether she was rewriting history or he had just changed. If it was the latter, I wondered why. I did ask but Mother's answers were always vague. She did, however, try to explain my father's erratic behaviour, which she put down to his upbringing.

I was shocked to learn that his father — my grandfather — had been a drunkard and a petty criminal. Now I knew why the man was never mentioned! His wife, my grand-mother, had been a weak, frail woman who lived in the shadow of her husband. Between my grandfather's bad example and his wife's lack of control, my father turned into a wayward, troublesome boy. Finally, after some pressure from the local parish priest, he was sent off to a strict boarding school where he learned obedience the hard way. It was drilled into him that he would rot in hell if he followed in his father's footsteps. My father emerged chastened, law-abiding and devout.

"Isn't that even more reason for him to be a better person?" I argued when Mother told me this story. "After going through so much himself, how could he be so cruel and unkind to his own son?"

"Your father was afraid Ed would inherit his grand-father's bad blood," she explained. "That's why he was always so hard on him. He may have been misguided, but he meant well."

I found this a little hard to swallow. Why was he only tough on Ed? Were bad genes only passed on to male offspring? But my mother either couldn't or wouldn't expand further. It didn't matter anyway. There was nothing she could tell me about my father that would change my feelings for him. He'd driven my brother away and I hated him for that.

It was at the boarding school that my father's love affair with his native language began. It was down to his Irish teacher, who was one of the kinder and gentler priests. He soon spotted Conall's talent and cultivated it. My father took comfort in his writing and the words of praise from his teacher. He went on to become a primary school teacher himself, although in his heart he was always a poet. He was in his late thirties, however, before his talents were recognized. Finally, eight years later, he gave up teaching and devoted himself to his art. I could imagine his students cheering when they heard the news.

Ed leaving had another effect on my life. My parents grew more lenient. My mother, because she was trying to compensate for the loss of my brother; my father, in an effort to ingratiate himself. He appeared defeated by my new, hostile attitude and tried everything to win back my love. I revelled in his misery and triumphed in the fact that the shackles were off and I could live and behave like a normal teenager.

As a result, I had a whole new freedom I hadn't enjoyed before. I was allowed to spend more time with Judy, to join the basketball team and even to attend the monthly school disco.

And so began my love life. When my parents thought I was at Judy's studying, or at choir practice, or playing basketball, I was often receiving lessons of a different sort. Liam O'Herlihy had finally succumbed to my charms and I was in seventh heaven. I should have played it cool, of course. I should have kept him at arm's length. I didn't. When I lost my virginity it was on our fourth date — my father would have been apoplectic. It was not a romantic or memorable experience. I lay on the floor of Liam's father's barn while he fumbled and panted. Predictably, I felt dirty and ashamed afterwards. Not enough, however, to say no the next time, or the time after that.

I realized very quickly that I must be pregnant. As a convent girl, my sex education had been limited to say the least. But I had always suffered badly with heavy, painful periods and when I was pain free for eight weeks, I figured out that I had a problem. Strangely I didn't panic, nor did I go rushing to tell Liam. Instead I bought a couple of magazines and combed the problem pages and the small ads. Once I had a plan, I confided in my best friend, Judy. She was shocked and terrified on my behalf.

"Your dad will kill you," were her first words.

She was even more aghast when I told her what I was going to do. "Aren't you scared?" she asked me, wide-eyed.

Of course I was terrified, and racked with guilt. But I had been taken over by a strange compulsion. This was a way of punishing my father on every level and, in a weird way, it felt right. I look back now on these words and feel physically sick. What was I thinking? How did I behave in such a way? Where did I find the strength to do what I did? Even today I don't have the answers.

After much begging on my part, Judy covered for me while I visited a clinic in Wexford and made the necessary arrangements. It was a stroke of luck that the school trip to London was planned for later that month. So I didn't have to worry about travel or accommodation. All I had to do was finance the procedure. I knew, thanks to my mother's sewing box, that wouldn't be a problem.

It was easy enough to slip away from the group during our visit to the Tower of London. It didn't take me long to find the clinic either. Walking through the door was more difficult. But dealing with the guilt afterwards — that was the really hard part. It was all over so quickly. I was in a daze as a kind woman led me to a small room and fed me tea and biscuits. She gave me a leaflet with a phone number and made me promise to attend the clinic in Wexford the following week for a counselling session. I walked back to the hostel in a state of shock. I had been missing for seven hours and everyone was in a flap. The two teachers had called my father, who was now on his way over. While we waited for him to arrive they quizzed me as to where I'd gone and what I'd been doing. I maintained I'd got separated from the group and then had difficulty finding my way back to the hostel. They didn't swallow that for a minute. Why hadn't I phoned someone? I shrugged and said nothing. They would have their answers soon enough. But if what I had just done was to make any sense, my father had to be the first to know. I needed to see the look of shock register in his eyes. I needed to stick the knife in the wound. And then — well, then I didn't care what happened to me. Before the procedure I had thought I would go back to living a normal life. As I waited for my father to arrive though, I realized that nothing would ever be the same again.

It was late when my father got in. All the other students had been sent to bed and I sat at the kitchen table while the teachers whispered nervously in a corner. There was a look of pure relief on his face when he walked through the door and saw that I was okay. At that moment, I felt a pang of guilt. The teachers started to fill him in. They were at first apologetic and then defensive under his accusing glare. Finally he turned to me and asked me where I'd been. And so I told him. At any other time I'd have fallen about laughing at the shock on my teachers' faces. But I didn't feel much like laughing now. I watched a variety of emotions cross my father's face. Anger, disgust, shock, sorrow and, then, confusion.

"Why?" he cried. "We would have helped you. We would have taken care of the baby. Why didn't you come to me? Don't you realize you've broken the fifth commandment? You've murdered your baby — your own flesh and blood!" Tears rolled down his cheeks as he held out his hands in supplication. "For the love of God, why?"

"Because I wanted to hurt you the way you hurt Ed. The way you hurt Mother and the way you've hurt me."

"I never hurt you," he protested. "I loved you!"

"You took my brother away." And I turned from him to my teachers, tears filling my eyes. "Can I go to bed now, please?"

With uncharacteristic tenderness, the older woman took me up to her own room and put me to bed. She stroked my hair as I cried, and then sat with me until I fell asleep.

The next morning, my father and I left for the airport. He didn't talk to me in the taxi, or in the airport. He said nothing on the plane or in the car home. When my mother opened the door, he pushed past her, went into his office and closed the door. She looked at me, her eyes full of pain, but she still held out her arms to me. I fell into them and cried like the child I still was. "I'm so sorry, Mum. I'm so sorry." I said it over and over again like a mantra.

"Hush," she said, holding me tightly to her. "You're home now. Everything will be okay."

* * *

Realizing that her tears were falling on the keyboard, Dana closed the file and switched off her laptop. She stumbled from her office, feeling distressed and disoriented. Night was turning to day; it was bright enough for her to make her way to the kitchen without turning on a light. She shivered violently. The mornings were colder now, and she was vaguely aware that the heating didn't seem to be working, but she'd no idea of how to fix it.

She put on the kettle, and as she waited for it to boil she looked around her. Iris had only been gone a week, and already the place was a tip. The floor tiles were stained and grubby, and the granite worktop — what you could see of it — was covered with rings from coffee mugs, wine glasses and bottles. The bin was full to overflowing and there were an embarrassing number of empty bottles by the back door. It was a disgrace and Dana decided that once she'd had a hot cup of coffee, she'd give the place a good clean.

After that, she'd get stuck into *The Mile High Club*. She hadn't done much this week — too busy feeling sorry for herself. But no more. It was time to get back to work. It was hard going, though. She'd had to rewrite the last three chapters; they were boring and flat, and Gretta would be horrified if she handed them in as they were.

In that, her PA had been right. Dana sighed at the thought of Sylvie. She was starting to regret firing the girl. What she had done was probably down to normal curiosity, and Dana felt maybe she herself had over-reacted. The note was also playing on her mind.

She'd asked Ian about Sylvie's family but despite the fact that the two had obviously grown close, he knew nothing.

Dana took her drink and went upstairs. She should climb straight into a shower and then go down and tackle the kitchen, but her eyes were heavy with sleep. She decided that a short nap was in order first. She wouldn't be able to write if she was exhausted. She crawled into bed and pulled the covers up around her ears. Just an hour would be enough. Forty winks and she'd be ready for anything.

After ringing on the door for a good five minutes, a slightly worried Gus let himself into the house. "Dana?" He stood in the hall, nervous of going any further. Dana would probably freak that he'd even had the audacity to use his key. He called her name again but there was still no reply. But it wasn't unusual for Dana to become deaf to the world when she was working. "Dana?" he called again, heading towards the office. It was lunch time so she should be at her desk by now.

He knocked tentatively and stuck his head in, but the room was empty. He sighed and went back into the hall. She must be up in bed but he was loath to go up. After being away for so long he felt like he would be invading her private territory. Instead he crossed to the kitchen. He paused in the doorway, taken aback at the state of the room. Iris had always kept it immaculate but now the place was a mess and there was a row of bottles by the door. He sighed as he counted them; five wine, one gin and one brandy, and an empty plastic tonic bottle too. He hoped that meant that Walter or even her new boyfriend had been to visit, and that Dana hadn't drunk all this on her own. Going to the fridge he opened it and stared at the contents. Half a carton of milk that was past its best-by date, a rotting lemon, three bottles of wine and, stuffed in the bottom drawer, some cartons of soup and smoothies. That was something at least.

"Seen enough?"

He whirled around to see Dana standing at the door watching him. "Dana!"

"Who were you expecting?" she said drily, coming into the room.

"I knocked for ages," he protested. "I came in because I was worried."

"And you thought you might find me in the fridge?"

He smiled. "Okay, you've got me there. Wally phoned me. He's worried about you. He says you're on your own."

"Iris walked out on me," Dana retorted.

"Why?" As he waited for her answer he took in her dishevelled appearance — she must have just got out of bed even though it was lunchtime. Her arms were clasped around her as she watched him. Her hair was lank, her eyes wary and her face pale. He felt like reaching out to hug her . . .

"It's not important," she said.

"Aren't you going to offer me a coffee?"

Her eyes widened in disbelief. "I don't think so!"

"We have things to talk about, Dana," he said gently. "So much has happened and I think there have been a lot of misunderstandings —"

"I've called you and I've left messages. You're the one who wouldn't talk, Gus. Let's be clear on that."

He nodded. "You're right. I was wrong and I'm sorry. I did come over to talk to you that morning, but when that guy was here —"

She levelled him with a scathing look. "You're one to talk."

"What's that supposed to mean?" He wasn't ready to talk about Terry, not yet.

"Stones, glasshouses . . ." She shrugged. "You get the drift."

"Fair enough. But I'm here now. Let me stay. Let's talk."

She sighed. "Okay."

He smiled. "Look, why don't you make some coffee and I'll load the dishwasher?" He took off his jacket and started to roll up his sleeves.

"I don't need your help," she muttered, although she had picked up the kettle.

"I know that, but I may as well help as I'm here. You're obviously working flat out; how's it going?"

She shot him a suspicious look. "Why do you ask?"

"It was just a simple question, Dana. There was no hidden agenda behind it."

"Sorry."

"I hear you fired Sylvie. What happened?"

"What's it to you?"

He paused in his work. "There's no point in me staying if you're going to be like this."

"Sylvie invaded my privacy. She knew I was writing but suspected it wasn't on *The Mile High Club*. So she went nosing through my private documents, trying to find out what I was working on."

Gus paused again. "I can see that she overstepped the mark, but isn't firing her a bit of an overreaction?"

"Maybe," she admitted. "Did you know that Sylvie's father is disabled?"

He nodded. "He's suffered from rheumatoid arthritis for years. I think he may be bed-bound now."

"How do you know all of this?"

He shrugged. "No idea. She must have just mentioned it in passing."

"She never mentioned it to me." Dana stared into space for a moment and then turned to pour the hot water into two mugs.

"If you think you could forgive her," he said gently, "I'm sure she'd learn from her mistake. Whatever she did, Dana, she's always worshipped the ground you walk on."

"Yeah, sure." Dana set the mugs on the table and he came to sit opposite her.

"It's true. She also needs the money and the flexible hours suit her perfectly. When she's not here, she looks after her father."

"I didn't know any of this," Dana murmured. "Why didn't you tell me?"

"It just never came up. I suppose I assumed that you knew. So, will you give her another chance?"

She sighed. "I'll think about it."

He watched her over his coffee mug. "You must be lonely, rattling around this place all on your own."

"Who says I'm alone?" she taunted.

He couldn't resist letting his eyes run from her tousled hair to her pink woolly socks. "It's just a wild guess."

"Bastard," she mumbled.

Gus shook his head. "I'm sorry, forgive me. I'm really not here for a slanging match."

She drew a packet of cigarettes from her pocket and took one out.

"Do you have to?" he murmured trying to keep a rein on his irritation. Dana knew he hated cigarette smoke.

"I really do." Dana lit one, inhaled and then blew the smoke in his face. "So, what do you want to talk about?"

"I just wanted to know what's wrong."

"Er, my husband left me, didn't you know?"

"This isn't all about me. Aren't you ready to admit that yet?"

"I'm under a lot of pressure about the book," she said, not meeting his gaze.

"From Gretta?"

She laughed mirthlessly. "From everyone. I stopped writing after you left and they're all scared shitless that I'm not going to deliver."

He sighed. "I'm sorry. I didn't think anything or anyone could stop you writing. You've always kept going in the past, no matter what."

She smiled bitterly. "Well, my husband never walked out on me with no explanation before."

"I did explain," he protested.

"You did not!"

"I did," he insisted, "you just weren't listening."

"That is complete bullshit! We were happy, everything was fine."

He shook his head. "How can you say that? It hasn't been fine for a long time. I'd tried to talk to you but you just retreated every time I got close."

"That's not true."

"It is! I gave you so many chances to talk to me, but you wouldn't. Then I knew I had to leave."

Dana shook her head but she still wouldn't meet his eyes. "What exactly is it you wanted me to say?"

"I wanted you to tell me about your family, Dana. I wanted you to tell me what happened in Wexford all those years ago."

"I don't know what you mean," she said, her voice barely a whisper.

"You do," he told her firmly. "You *do* know, Dana. And even now you won't talk to me about it. What kind of marriage have we got, Dana, if you don't trust me?"

"There's nothing to say," she murmured, not looking at him. "It's all in the past."

Gus looked at her, his eyes sad. "You can't bury Dana O'Carroll no matter how much you might want to."

She put a hand to her mouth and he noticed her fingers were trembling and her face was positively grey. Gus knew he'd have to back off. He wasn't at all sure if she was emotionally up to any of this. He stood up. "I wish you'd talk to me, Dana," he repeated, putting a hand on her shoulder. Turning away he walked, frustrated, to the door.

"Gus?"

He looked back, hopeful. "Yes?"

"The central heating isn't working properly. Could you take a look at it before you go?"

CHAPTER
TWENTY-SIX

Ian was amazed when he got Dana's call. He'd been trying to get new staff for her but so far had just found a cleaner who could do two hours a week. Dana would have to do her own shopping and cooking for a while. He'd had no luck in replacing Sylvie, either. But then he hadn't tried that hard. He had met her once since she'd lost her job, and had been shocked at how upset she was.

"You'll easily pick up another job," he'd assured her. "A smart girl like you? It will be no problem."

And then she'd explained about her circumstances.

So when Dana rang to say Sylvie could have her job back, he was delighted.

There were conditions, though, Dana had told him. The job was only on offer if Sylvie worked from home and they communicated via email and phone. "She can't come back here," Dana had said. "I can't trust her."

Ian wasn't about to tell Sylvie that last bit.

Rather than just phone with the good news, he got her address from Dana and hurried around there. Sylvie would be so thrilled.

He was more than a little baffled, then, when she burst into tears.

"But I thought you wanted your job back," he said, bemused.

"Of course I do! But I can't work from home, Ian. We don't have a computer, never mind access to the internet."

"I've an old machine I could lend you," Ian said. "You could set up in a corner of your living room —"

Sylvie shook her head. "Would you like to see my living room, Ian?"

He shrugged. "Sure."

Sylvie led Ian into the kitchen where her mother was baking. "Mum, this is Ian."

Maureen's eyes widened as she hurriedly cleaned her hands. "Hello, Ian, nice to meet you. Sylvie doesn't often bring her friends home."

Ian took her hand and smiled. "Lovely to meet you too, Mrs Parker."

"Would you like a cup of tea?"

"Lovely, thanks —"

"He doesn't have time for tea," Sylvie said shortly. "Is Dad awake?"

Maureen shot her daughter a look. "Yes, why?"

"I just wanted to introduce him to Ian."

Maureen smiled. "He'd like that. Tell him I'll be in with his tea when I've finished this."

"Come on." Sylvie turned Ian around and pushed him across the hall. She tapped gently on the door before sticking her head in. "Daddy? I've brought someone to meet you, is that okay?"

"It's not another doctor, is it?" Ian heard the gruff reply.

"No, it's a guy I work with."

"Oh." The voice brightened considerably. "Grand."

Sylvie opened the door and led Ian into a small room. It was crammed with furniture, the main piece being a bed, in the centre of the room, on which a frail old man was lying. Ian slipped into professional mode and, crossing the room, held out his hand and smiled. "Hi, Mr Parker, I'm Ian Wilson." The hand that took his felt like it might snap if Ian squeezed too hard. But it was large too and it was obvious that this man had once been a lot more imposing.

"It's not often Sylvie brings boyfriends home," the man said, shooting his daughter a sly look. "Have you come to ask for her hand?"

Sylvie laughed as she perched on the edge of the bed. "Sorry, Dad, you're not getting rid of me yet. Ian was asking me about doing some work from home and I was just showing him that it might be a problem."

William Parker shook his head sadly. "As you can see, lad, we're a bit stuck for space. I keep telling them that if they slipped something into my tea they'd be a lot better off. I know I certainly would."

"Dad, don't talk like that!" Sylvie admonished.

"Sorry, love. Do you like football, Ian?"

"I do."

"Who do you support?"

"Liverpool, of course."

William grinned. "Good man."

Sylvie leaned over to kiss him. "We've got to go."

"Nice to meet you, Mr Parker."

"And you, lad. And if you do need anyone to work for you, you won't get better than our Sylvie. She's a real grafter. You'd want to see the day she puts in before she goes to work, and then when she comes home."

"Dad, shut up," Sylvie mumbled, steering Ian towards the door.

"No harm in telling people your good points, love," he called after her. "Goodbye, Ian, nice to meet you."

"And you."

They said goodbye to Sylvie's mother, and then Ian drove them to a coffee bar nearby. When they were sitting at a Formica-covered table drinking coffee out of cartons, Sylvie finally spoke. "Well?" she said, her expression defiant.

"Nice people, your parents," Ian said, deliberately misunderstanding her. "But I can see why working from home is not an option. I do, however, have a solution."

"You do?" she said doubtfully.

"You can work from my office."

"But —" she started.

"No buts, it makes perfect sense. It's not exactly a palace and if you want a cuppa you have to go to the café at the corner, but it's home." He hurried on, as already he could see the doubt in her eyes. "We'd need to get you a desk and a chair —"

"And a computer and a phone line." Sylvie shook her head. "It's hopeless."

"I told you, I have an old PC, and it will take no time to get an extra phone line — Dana has to pay for that."

"I can't let you do all this for me."

"Who says I'm doing it for you?" he said, with a scornful look, designed to stop her feeling like a charity case. "It would be good for me too. You could answer my phone and take messages for me when I'm not around. I help you, you help me and, hopefully, between us we can help Dana finish this book."

"I wouldn't bet on it," Sylvie said grimly. "But I'd be happy to hang on to this job for as long as possible."

"So, do we have a deal?"

She smiled. "Yeah. Yeah, we do."

"Good." The urge to kiss her was immense, but Ian knew she'd be horrified. Instead he stood up and held out his hand. "Come on, let's go and sort out your office."

Within a few hours, Ian had hooked up the old PC and added Sylvie as a user to his email account. "You can use this while you're waiting for your own account to be set up," he explained.

"Ian?"

He looked up from where he was fixing the old swivel chair that he'd charmed out of the solicitor from upstairs. "Yeah?"

She smiled. "Thanks for your help."

He grinned, wondering if she realized that he'd scale Mount Everest in his underwear for a smile like that. "Don't worry, you'll earn it."

Dana had written fifteen hundred words of *The Mile High Club* and sent them off to Sylvie. She'd earned the right to a drink, a smoke and maybe even a few paragraphs of her autobiography. It was a chilly day and she had pulled on an ancient cashmere sweater, a pair of faded denims, and woolly socks. She'd better start paying more attention to her appearance, she thought as she caught a glimpse of herself in the hall mirror, or Ryan would soon lose interest. And, she realized, she didn't want that to happen. He cheered her up. He was easy to be with. And she found herself opening up to him in a way that was completely alien to her.

That could be down to him, or to the fact that she was feeling so vulnerable after Gus walked out. Or maybe it was down to the autobiography. Writing her story was having the strangest effect on her. Without it, she might have given up altogether and been discovered, sodden, at the bottom of a bottle by now. Gus had wanted her to talk to someone. Maybe this was the next best thing.

On an impulse, she sent a text to Ryan asking him over for dinner the following evening. The reply was immediate.

YEAH, SURE; BET YOU STAND ME UP AGAIN!

She smiled. He kept going on about that night that she was supposed to go to his place to watch the football. That had been the day Sylvie and Iris had left. She had been so upset that she had forgotten even to call him.

She typed a message quickly into her phone.

I WON'T. PROMISE.

She sent the message and waited. When he sent his reply she laughed.

YEAH, YEAH, BELIEVE IT WHEN I SEE IT. C U AT 8. X

She would phone the bistro around the corner and arrange for a main course and dessert to be delivered. That would leave her time to give the house a good clean. Well, her bedroom, the bathrooms and the kitchen anyway. Phew, she was exhausted just thinking about it. And the house wasn't the only thing getting a makeover. She picked up the phone again and called the beauty salon to make an appointment. When she hung up, she poured a large glass of wine and carried it back into her office. She took a deep breath before opening the file on her laptop and starting to write.

I was right when I thought that life would never be the same again. Father kept me home from school for a full week after we returned from London. Then one morning as we sat at the table, eating breakfast, he announced that I was to start in a new school on Monday. It was thirty miles away and too far to commute so he said I was to become a boarder.

"I won't go," I said immediately.

He didn't even look up. "You'll do what you're told."

"Conall, I don't think it's a good idea to send Dana away after . . . everything."

He shot her a cold look. "What? After fornicating with a pimply youth, getting pregnant and then killing her own child?"

278

"Conall!"

"It's okay, Mum. Maybe it would be better if I went."

"You've no choice," he retorted. "The convent won't have you back; you're a bad example to the other girls. Go and pack. I'll take you there on Sunday afternoon."

My new school was a grey prison, and a narrow cell was to be my home for the next year.

"Then you can come back to me," my mother said, hugging me tightly before they left.

All through that year, I kept to myself, I wrote long letters to Judy and my mother, and I studied hard. I needed to win a place at university in Dublin. I had to make sure that I would never have to depend on my father again. And maybe I could even liberate my mother.

In my daydreams, I saw myself arriving at the house in Wexford in a flash car and whisking my mother off to live with me in my Dublin mansion. In my nightmares, I saw my father dragging my baby from my arms and walking away. I would scream and cry and beg him to bring it back, but he'd just keep walking. I would wake up with a jolt, my pillow soaked with tears.

When I wasn't studying, I was writing or walking. It struck me that I was behaving like my father. The realization made me nauseous. Once a week I'd phone my mother and we'd talk non-stop over each other, trying to make the most of our precious few minutes. Afterwards I'd lie on my bed and try to recapture the sound of her voice and hold it in my head and heart. I missed her so much, even more than I missed my brother. I lived for the Christmas holidays when I would see her again, but my father landed a bombshell. He'd arranged for me to stay on through the holiday and take extra maths lessons. Mother protested but I assured her it was what I wanted to do. It was all lies, of course. But she was alone in the house with my father now, and I didn't want her to do anything to antagonize him. Not now I wasn't there to watch over her.

I sailed through my exams in June and was confident that I'd won my place at university. I pre-empted my father's plans for my final break by securing a job helping out in my school's summer camp. My mother was disappointed that I wasn't coming home, but I knew that if I'd tried, he'd have found some way to stop me.

I only ever saw my mother once more. She took me up to Dublin before I started university, and we had three wonderful weeks together. She helped me find a reasonably clean bedsit that was only ten minutes' walk from Trinity College. She bought me a colourful duvet cover and curtains to liven up the drab room, and an electric fire to warm me in the winter nights ahead. We visited the cinema and shopped for clothes and even spent a day at the zoo. I had never seen my mother so gay and carefree. At least, not since Ed had left.

"Do you ever think of him?" I asked, the night before she went home. We were lying in our twin beds in the hotel room, turned towards each other.

"Every day," she said.

"I wish he'd come home."

"He can't," she said simply.

"Why don't you leave Dad, Mum?" I sat up. "You could come to Dublin. We could set up house together."

"I can't do that, love."

"Why not, Mum? Why would you want to stay with him after everything he's done?"

"It's where I belong."

"And what about me?" I said like an angry child. "Where do I belong? Where does Ed belong?"

"You must make your own life, Dana. You must put everything behind you. This is your big chance, my darling. Take it with both hands."

And I suppose, to a certain extent, that's what I'd done. I reinvented myself in Dublin. I was, on the face of it, a normal, happy arts student, and no one knew anything about me. And while I lived it up a little, I studied hard too. When I wasn't attending lectures or studying, I was scribbling — I couldn't believe how easily stories came to me. I filled notebooks with the words that tumbled from my mind.

I was flicking through a discarded magazine in the canteen one day when I realized that I could turn my talent into cash. Readers were invited to send in stories — both fiction and non-fiction — and if your piece was printed, you got fifty quid. I read two of the winning entries and knew I could do better. I went out and bought half a dozen more magazines and found they all made similar offers. This had the potential to be a nice little earner.

I got stuck in straight away, confident that I could do it. The money started to roll in almost immediately. Depending on my mood, I would write seriously about controversial subjects or, in contrast, churn out a romantic and slushy short story. I took a perverse pleasure in writing anything that I thought would upset my father. When I wrote non-fiction, I would take the opposing view to his.

When I wrote fiction, it was the light, fluffy material he abhorred. The results were lapped up by the magazines and my bank balance grew. And while I was doing it merely to amuse myself, I felt proud of my prowess. I was able to look at a magazine, size up the type of reader it attracted, and produce a piece of bespoke fiction to match. I took an enormous amount of pleasure in watching some of my fellow students devour my stories, completely unaware that I was the author. I used a variety of pen names and told no one what I was up to.

And then one day, along with the cheque in the post, came a note from one of the editors telling me that I had "some" talent and should think about writing a novel. I discounted the idea at first — I didn't have time to produce such a large piece of work — but it planted the seed. My romantic stories were well received and were easy to write. Also, in this genre, novels were usually shorter than the average paperback. Over a weekend, I came up with a synopsis and two main characters and wrote the first pages of my debut novel.

At the end of eight months, I'd produced what I felt was a marketable seventy-thousand-word manuscript. I carefully chose six agents — two in Dublin and four in London — and sent it off to them. I heard nothing for weeks and grew quite disheartened. But then I got a letter from an agent in London that I had never even heard of. He wrote that my manuscript had been passed on to him by a colleague, and he was impressed by it. He didn't believe that it was suited to the UK market, but he thought a publisher in the US might be interested. The US! I almost fainted with happiness. Immediately I went to pick up the phone to call my mother. But no, it was premature. The agent could be useless; it might all come to nothing.

Determined not to get my hopes up, I threw myself back into my studies, and even went to some parties. And then the second, fatter envelope arrived. It was from the same agent but this time it included a letter and two contracts. He explained that I had received an offer from the US publisher and that the contract was enclosed. He asked me to call him as soon as possible so that we could discuss the matter further. It was signed Walter Grimes, literary agent.

I couldn't believe my eyes as I read the contract. Happy? I was bloody ecstatic. Wait till I told my mother. I jumped up and down on my flimsy bed, squealing with delight. I was laughing so hard I didn't hear the phone ring in the hall below. Finally, my neighbour came up and banged loudly on the door. "Phone!" he yelled.

"Coming." I hurried down the stairs after him. "Who is it?"

"Your old man."

I froze on the spot and just stared at the dangling receiver that was banging against the wall. Slowly I went over and picked it up. "Hello?"

"Dana?"

"Yes, Father, it's me."

"Dana, you must come home."

"What? But it's the middle of term. What is it? What's wrong?"

He didn't reply at first, and then when he spoke his voice was fainter. "I'm sorry, Dana, but your mother has passed away."

Her eyes full of tears, Dana pushed away her laptop and stood up. She was too emotional and drained to keep working; it was time for a break. She decided to take a bath, then have a healthy supper followed by an early night. She didn't want any bags under her eyes, not with Ryan coming. She smiled, her mood lightening at the thought. She was about to go upstairs when she remembered she hadn't checked the post box. Yet another thing Iris did that she had taken for granted. Going outside, she fetched her post and newspapers, tucking her empty glass under her arm as she flicked through the letters. Distracted, she didn't pay attention to where she was walking and stumbled over the kerb. She went down like a ton of bricks, the glass splintering into thousands of pieces around her. The last thing she remembered was a sharp pain in her arm, and then everything went black.

CHAPTER
TWENTY-SEVEN

"Dana?"

She opened her eyes and blinked.

"Dana, are you okay?"

She opened her mouth to reply but at that moment the world started to spin around her and once again she was falling.

When she came to a second time, she was lying on the sofa in the sitting room, a cold cloth on her forehead and a ferocious pain in her arm. She stared at the man leaning over her. "Ed?"

He smiled tenderly. "No, you're not dead or dreaming. It is me. Hello, sis."

"What are you doing here?"

"Just be glad I am," he retorted. "What happened?"

"I tripped and fell. I think I've hurt my wrist."

"I'd say it's broken."

"No it can't be," she groaned. "I've a book to finish."

He shrugged and helped her sit up. "I'm no doctor, but it looks broken to me. I'll take you to hospital and we'll soon find out."

It was almost ten o'clock when they got home from the hospital and Dana was exhausted. The casualty doctor had confirmed she had a mild concussion and a broken wrist. Ed offered to help Dana undress for bed but she refused. However, after several unsuccessful attempts at pulling on her pyjamas, Dana called him back. When he had settled her in bed, Ed went downstairs, and returned minutes later with a mug of tea.

"I'd prefer a glass of wine," she grumbled.

"If you hadn't been drinking, you wouldn't be where you are now," her brother said mildly, as he tidied away her clothes.

"I'd only had one glass of wine," Dana protested. "I just wasn't looking where I was going and tripped. It was an accident."

"Right."

"It's true."

He shrugged and sat down on the edge of her dressing table. "None of my business. If you want to drink yourself into an early grave and live in total squalor, that's your business."

"I'm not and I was planning a major clean-up tomorrow."

He raised an eyebrow. "Of course you were."

Dana scowled at him. "I think you should go now." Handing him back her mug, she tried to wriggle down under the covers.

"Go?"

She nodded. "Thanks for your help, but I'll be fine now."

286

Ed's lips twitched in amusement. "Oh, okay, and how are you going to look after yourself?"

"I'll manage."

"How will you wash your hair?" he demanded.

"I'll do it in the shower."

"You can't take showers; you'll get your cast wet."

"I'll take baths," she said triumphantly.

He laughed. "I'd love to see you climb in and out of a bath one-handed. And what about buttons? And zips? Cooking? Driving?"

Dana's eyes filled up. "Oh, I can't believe this has happened to me now. I was just getting my act together."

"Were you?"

"Yes!" she cried in frustration, tears spilling out onto her cheeks. "And now this happens." She raised her left arm and let it fall again, then howled in agony.

Ed sat down on the bed beside her and wiped her tears away with his thumb. "It's going to be okay, Dana. I'll look after you."

"Don't you have a job?"

"I'm a freelance photographer. I can work from anywhere."

Dana looked up at him, her eyes suspicious. "Why did you come here today?"

"I was in Dublin, and I thought it was about time I came to visit my little sister."

"I've lived in Dublin nearly twenty years and you've never felt the need before."

"Would I have been welcome?" Ed challenged.

"No. No, you wouldn't," she agreed.

"I didn't think so. Now, would you like me to help you out to the bathroom before you settle down for the night?"

"I don't need help." But as Dana tried to get up from the softness of the pillows, she realized that between the weight of the cast and the pain in her wrist, she was rendered almost helpless. "I'm sure I'll be fine in the morning," she said, allowing him to slide his arm around her waist to lift her.

"Of course you will."

"You can stay in one of the guestrooms, but there are no beds made up —"

"Don't worry, I'll cope." He sat her on the loo and discreetly left the room. When she flushed he came back in, to find her standing staring at her reflection in the mirror. Her brow had gone a strange shade of purple, there were enormous bags under her eyes and she was ghostly white. "I had an appointment in the beauty salon tomorrow," she said, sadly.

"I could take you," he offered.

She shook her head and turned to go back to bed.

"You'll feel so much better in the morning. I could help you wash and dry your hair, if you like." He settled her into bed and turned to leave.

"Ed?"

He paused in the doorway and looked back.

"Thanks."

He smiled. "You're welcome."

Dana sat in the conservatory, her injured arm resting on a cushion. She couldn't believe how weak and fragile she felt, and that a broken wrist and a bad headache could incapacitate her to such a degree.

As promised, Ed had washed and dried her hair, and helped her dress. She'd hated that. And then realized that there was no way she could close her bra, never mind manage buttons. While she'd dithered, her brother had come to her rescue.

"I don't suppose you have anything as naff as a tracksuit, do you? Stretch pants and zip-up top, that sort of thing?"

"I do actually." Dana had directed him to where he'd find the clothes and he brought them over to the bed.

"Underwear?" he'd asked.

She had winced. "Get out. I'll manage that if it kills me." And she had. Only it had taken ages to pull on some pants. She'd abandoned the idea of trying to do battle with a bra and instead put on a loose vest top. But even that had been a challenge. She had made her way slowly downstairs and silently handed her brother her tracksuit top. He had helped her into it and zipped it up with a smile, but had the good sense to say nothing.

It was then that Dana had noticed the gleaming kitchen. "You didn't have to do this," she'd told him.

Ed had just shrugged. "It had to be done."

"And I was going to do it today," she'd insisted.

"Well, you can't do it now," he'd pointed out. "And it's going to be quite some time before you'll be able to."

"I don't have to. I've a new cleaner starting on Monday. She's going to come in two hours a week."

"That's good. Now why don't you go and sit down? I'll bring you some coffee and toast when I've finished here."

Dana spent most of the day in the conservatory, reading, while Ed polished and scrubbed. When he went upstairs to change her bed, Dana sneaked into the kitchen for a glass of wine. But there was no bottle open and she was no match for the corkscrew. Almost crying in frustration, she abandoned the wine and had a whiskey instead. She'd have preferred brandy but she couldn't get the stopper out of the bottle.

She was feeling very sorry for herself when her phone beeped on the table in front of her. It was Ryan.

STILL FEEDING ME?

Lord, she had completely forgotten their date! She smiled slowly. This had worked out perfectly. Her house would be lovely and clean, she could still order in some delicious food, and Ryan would be on hand to open the wine. Of course, a night of passion was out of the question but it was probably no harm; it would keep him keen. It was also an excellent way to get rid of her brother.

She could pretend that Ryan was a permanent fixture in her life. That he would look after her. And so there was no reason for Ed to stay. She didn't want her brother around. It was way too late for reconciliation. He still hadn't given her a straight answer as to why he

290

was here or why now. She was determined to find out, then he could go.

She quickly sent Ryan a text.

YES. C U AT 8.

Next she went out to the address book in the hall, got the number of the bistro and phoned in an order for two.

Ed walked in as she was draining her glass. He sniffed. "Whiskey?"

"Can't stand the stuff, but I couldn't manage the corkscrew."

He frowned. "And you're so desperate for alcohol, you'd drink something you don't like?"

"Oh, shut up, Ed. I'm in pain here."

"Judging by the number of empty bottles outside, you appear to be in constant pain."

"It's none of your business," she snapped.

"Nope, it isn't. Would you like me to open a bottle of wine for you?"

"Why not? Bring two glasses. Then you can tell me exactly why you're here."

Dana sat up straighter in her chair, and moved the cushion under her arm to a more comfortable position. The effort made her wince.

"Do you want me to get you some paracetamol or something?"

She shook her head. "The wine will do the trick."

He poured it and put hers on the table next to her right hand.

"Thanks. So. Tell me, Ed, why are you really here?"

He sat down and made himself comfortable before replying. "Gus asked me to come."

Dana stared at him dumbstruck. Gus had never even met her brother — what was he doing calling him now?

"He's worried about you," Ed told her, as if she'd asked the question.

"He called you?" She could barely get the words out. How did Gus even know where to find Ed?

Her brother nodded. "After he'd been to see you he rang to tell me he was concerned about you living alone. He wanted someone to stay with you until you were . . . feeling better."

"Oh my God. He thought I was going to top myself, didn't he? The big-headed bastard! He thinks he's so great, that I'm going to end it all just because he left. What an asshole. What did I ever see in him?" Dana knew the wobble in her voice probably gave away her true feelings, so she took refuge in her drink.

"He just thought you were a bit down and had been through a rough time — what with your housekeeper and PA leaving."

"My PA didn't leave, I threw her out," Dana corrected. "And I've since re-hired her. And the only reason Iris left is because she's a narrow-minded old prude who thinks the sun shines out of Gus's arse."

Ed threw back his head and laughed.

"How did Gus find you?" Dana asked.

"Your agent told him where I lived."

292

She nodded. Of course Walter knew that. Though she was surprised he'd remembered.

"There are lots of people who obviously care about you," Ed said with a smile.

Dana sighed. "I think they're more concerned about the book."

"I'm sure that's not true."

"You don't understand. This book is supposed to launch a new label in Ireland and the UK. It needs to be good or else they'll choose a different author. And the publisher probably won't even renew my contract in the US."

"I'm sure it will be fine."

"I don't think so."

"The break is going to slow you down," he agreed, "but you can still use your right hand."

She shook her head. "It's not that. I just can't seem to produce those sort of books any more. At least, not good ones."

"You've been through a rough patch. It will come back. You've written eighteen bestsellers — that wasn't exactly a fluke."

"How do you know that?" she asked, surprised.

He looked at her as if she was mad. "You're my sister! I've followed your career every step of the way. And boasted about you on occasion!"

"Really?"

"Really."

"Well, number nineteen definitely won't be a bestseller," she said, her face sad.

"Because of Gus leaving?"

She nodded, swallowing back her tears. This wasn't supposed to be happening. She didn't want to spill her guts, and certainly not to Ed.

"Well, you were together a long time. But I'm sure it's just a temporary problem."

"How are you sure?" she scoffed. "You don't know anything about me."

Ed inclined his head in acknowledgement. "I meant that going through a break-up would probably have the same effect on anyone."

Dana sipped her drink in silence.

"That won't help." He nodded at the glass in her hand.

"On the contrary, I find it helps enormously." Dana winced as she reached for the bottle.

"Let me."

"Maybe I will take something."

Immediately he was on his feet. "What?"

"The doctor gave me some painkillers; they're on the bedside table upstairs."

"Is it okay to take them with alcohol?"

"Just get them, Ed," she said, tired. When he had gone she sank back into the cushions, cradling her arm. She couldn't believe that Gus had contacted Ed. Did that mean he still cared, or just that he had a guilty conscience? Probably the latter.

Ed returned with the capsules and a glass of water. She swallowed them with a mouthful of wine. "Okay, okay, I get the message," he said, and topped up his own glass.

"So what else did my darling husband have to say for himself?"

"Not much."

"Did he tell you about my replacement?"

Ed's face changed. "No, he didn't. Are you sure there is one?"

"Not only has their photograph been in the paper, I saw them together with my own eyes — bumped into them in a restaurant."

"I'm sorry," he said.

She shrugged and smiled. "That's okay, I have a replacement of my own. He's coming over later."

"I suppose I'd better make myself scarce, then."

"Yes, please. But thanks for coming. It was very good of you."

His eyes twinkled in amusement. "I said I'd make myself scarce, Dana, not that I was leaving."

"But I don't need you."

"How will you manage alone?"

Dana widened her eyes and smiled. "Who says I'll be alone?"

"You were when I found you yesterday," he reminded her. "Does this guy work for a living?"

"Yes, but —"

"Then you'll still be alone all day."

"There's the cleaner —"

"Who'll be here for two hours a week. How will you make a sandwich, open the coffee jar, get your shopping or —" his eyes widened in mock horror — "open a bottle of wine?"

She scowled at him. He made it sound awfully difficult, and her wrist did hurt like hell. But she could pay someone to come in and look after her. Still, the thought of a stranger helping her wasn't very appealing.

Ed stood up. "I'm going to take a shower. As soon as your company arrives, I'll make myself scarce. But," he added, adopting a bad Arnold Schwarzenegger accent and shaking his finger at her, "I'll be back."

When Ryan buzzed to be let in, he was taken aback to hear a male voice. "Hello, I'm Ryan Vaughan. Dana is expecting me."

"Come in."

When he got out of the car, there was a man standing at the door waiting for him. "I'm Ed, Dana's brother."

Ryan put out his hand. "Nice to meet you."

Ed ignored it. "My sister's been through a tough time. She doesn't need to be messed around."

Ryan smiled. "No, she doesn't."

"What exactly are your plans?"

"Well, I was hoping to have some dinner and wash it down," Ryan held up a bottle, "with a rather nice Burgundy."

Ed didn't smile. "I'll be watching you."

CHAPTER
TWENTY-EIGHT

"Are you okay?" Ryan asked.

"Yes. Sorry. I haven't been great company, have I? This wasn't quite the evening I had in mind." Dana smiled apologetically.

"You've been lovely as always," he said gallantly. "But I'd better go. You need to rest. And I don't want your brother beating me up."

She frowned. "Why, did he say something?"

Ryan shrugged off the question. "He's just being a protective brother, and who can blame him?"

"Considering he hasn't been in my life for twenty years, I can. Ignore him, Ryan. I'm going to send him packing as soon as I can find someone to babysit me."

"Surely you could tolerate him until the cast comes off. He seems okay."

"It's not that simple. We have history, as they say."

He stood up and stretched. "Maybe this will be an opportunity for you to deal with that."

"Don't hold your breath."

He bent to kiss her tenderly. "I'll call you."

"Will you?"

"Sure, why not?" He looked surprised.

She gestured to her arm. "I'm not going to be much fun for a while. And now I've a bodyguard trying to scare you off."

Ryan traced a finger down the side of her face and bent to kiss her lips again. "It would take an awful lot to get rid of me. Now, would you like me to escort you up to bed before I go? I'd be happy to help you undress."

She laughed. "Well, thanks for the offer, but I think I might do some work before I turn in."

"Are you sure you're up to it?"

"Sometimes it's like I don't have a choice," she admitted. "It just sort of takes me over."

"I find that fascinating," he said as they walked together into the hall. "So you must have nearly finished the book by now."

Dana pulled a face. "Ah. But it's not *that* book that I want to work on."

"Oh, you have a new project?"

"Um, sort of."

"I'd love to read it."

"Really?"

"Absolutely."

"We'll see."

He kissed her. "Don't stay up too late, okay?"

"I won't. Goodnight, Ryan. Drive carefully."

It was a couple of hours later when Ed returned. After a few minutes there was a knock on the door and he stuck his head in. "Lover boy gone?"

Dana didn't look up. "Yes."

"I thought you couldn't write?" He came in and sat down in Sylvie's old chair.

"It's not the novel. Look, I don't like being watched when I'm working."

"But you're not working."

She looked up at him. "Where have you been?"

Ed stood up. "I met some friends. Fancy a nightcap?"

"Yeah, okay. Let's have it in the sitting room."

He went off to get the drinks and she saved her work, closed down her machine and went into the other room. It was colder in here and she shivered.

"Will I put on the fire?" Ed said, coming in and setting the drinks down on the coffee table.

Dana picked up a remote and flicked on the fire. "No need."

"Very fancy." He sat down in the armchair. "Did you have a nice evening?"

"Lovely."

"Where did you meet this guy?"

"I picked him up at a club," Dana said, deliberately baiting him.

"Very classy. And is it love?"

"No, but it's a lot of fun."

"Gus really hurt you, didn't he?" It was a statement rather than a question. "And yet he seems like a nice enough bloke."

"As I've learned over the years, people aren't always what they seem."

"You're so touchy, Dana. Why is that?"

"You're great with the questions, aren't you, Ed? But not so good with the answers."

He looked her in the eye. "Try me."

"Why did you do it?"

"You know why. I thought you and Mum would be better off if I left. Dad only got angry because of me. If I wasn't around, I knew he'd calm down."

She shook her head. "That's not what I meant."

"Then what?"

"Mum's funeral," she said.

"What about it?"

"What about it?" She sat forward, jolting her arm in the process. "Ow!"

"Look, let's not talk any more tonight. You're tired and in pain —"

"I'm fine."

"You're not."

"I don't want to go to bed yet."

He drained his glass and stood up. "If you want my help, you'll have to."

"If there was any way I could do this without you, believe me I would."

"But you can't," he said smugly, "so just put up and shut up."

"Is there anything else you need?" Ed asked, when she was tucked in.

Dana realized that she had already started to drift off, and opened her eyes in surprise to see him standing over her.

"I've left your painkillers right here and a glass of water with a straw; I thought that would be easier for you to manage."

"Thank you," Dana said, touched by his thoughtfulness.

"Is there anything else you need?" he asked again.

"Could you bring up my laptop and charger?" she asked. "If I can't sleep I may as well write."

"Sure." Ed returned a few minutes later with the laptop and set it up beside her on Gus's pillow.

"Thanks."

"No problem. Sleep well, Dana."

Ian rolled his eyes at Sylvie and held the phone away from his ear.

"I'm sorry, Dana, but I haven't had much luck so far. It's impossible to get a housekeeper/nurse. One agency could supply you with a part-time nurse, but she wouldn't be willing to take on any domestic duties. Also, it would probably be a different nurse each week."

"Dear God, what's the point of running an agency if you can't meet people's needs?"

"Yes, disgraceful, isn't it?" Ian sympathized. "I'll keep trying, Dana."

"Thanks, Ian. Call me if you come up with anything."

"So did she tell you how she broke her wrist?" Sylvie asked as Ian hung up.

"Tripped and fell."

Sylvie sighed. "She was probably drunk."

"Probably."

"At least she's still able to write."

"But is she?"

"Absolutely. We're nearly there now, really." Sylvie turned back and looked at the writing on her screen.

"Let me read it," Ian said, pushing his chair over beside hers.

She blocked his line of sight. "Not a chance."

"Ah, come on."

"No, go away."

"Then at least give me an ETA."

"A what?"

"Estimated Time of Arrival," Ian explained.

"Three weeks tops," she said confidently.

"Even with her dodgy wrist?"

Sylvie frowned. "I think so. Though it would help if you found someone to look after her."

"It's a sad state of affairs, isn't it? All that money and yet there's no one she can call on to help."

Sylvie looked at him to see if he was being sarcastic, but he seemed sincere. She patted his hand and smiled.

"Goodness, you're a right little ray of sunshine today, aren't you?"

Ed went to the supermarket, leaving Dana in her office surrounded by everything she might need. As soon as she'd put down the phone to Ian, she called Judy.

"You poor thing," her friend cried when Dana filled her in on the latest drama. "How on earth are you going to manage? I wish I could come and stay, Dana, but I'd have to bring the girls with me and then you'd get no work done at all."

"Don't be silly, Judy. You've got your hands more than full already."

"You could come here," Judy suggested. "The spare room isn't very big but —"

"You're a sweetheart. But you know there's no way I'd set foot in Wexford again. Which brings me to my other bit of news: Ed is here."

"Ed? Your brother Ed?"

Dana smiled at Judy's astonishment. "I know, I can't believe it either. It appears that Gus called him and said he was worried about me."

"Well, well, well. That's interesting, isn't it?"

"Is it?"

"Yes. It shows that Gus must still care about you."

"Or he's feeling guilty. Or worse — sorry for me."

"No, I think it's a very good sign." Judy was determinedly optimistic. "But tell me all about Ed."

Dana sighed. "He hasn't changed much. Although, no, that's not true. He's more confident, more sure of himself than he used to be. Still, he should be. He's forty now, a middle-aged man."

"Have you talked?"

Dana gave a short laugh. "We've squabbled. Or rather, I have. He just nods and listens and tries to tell me that he did what he did for my mother and me. I wish he'd just leave, Judy, I don't want him here."

"You mean he's staying with you?"

"Yes, he insisted. But as soon as I can find someone to help, I'm throwing him out."

"Don't be too hasty, Dana," Judy cautioned. "I know it must be hard having him there. But surely it's better than having a stranger in your home."

"He is a stranger!"

"But this could be fate. Maybe it's time you confronted him. Surely a part of you must want to know why he behaved the way he did?"

"I've already tried asking, but he's not exactly forth-coming."

"Keep asking," Judy urged. "He's your brother, Dana, and you two used to be so close. I'm sure he still loves you. He came as soon as Gus called, didn't he? Why don't you give it a few days? It can't hurt."

Dana sighed. "I'm not so sure of that."

"Try it. If it gets too tough, call me and I'll come and boot him out personally."

Dana laughed. "Oh, Judy, what would I do without you? I wish you lived around the corner. Then you could pop in and out for a coffee all the time."

"Sort out your problems with your brother. Then maybe you can come and live around the corner from me," Judy replied.

"I doubt it."

"Stranger things have happened."

Dana moved the chicken around her plate like a reluctant toddler.

"Try some, It's quite good," Ed said cheerfully, clearing his plate at an alarming rate.

"I didn't know you could cook," she said. There were a lot of things she didn't know about her brother. He was, in essence, a complete stranger now. She felt bereft at the thought.

"I used to work in a restaurant," he told her. "It was a basic sort of place but the chef did a great curry. This is his recipe."

"You said you were a photographer," Dana said suspiciously.

"I am. But I did a lot of different jobs before that. When I first left home I went to work in a supermarket in Cork city."

"We thought you'd left the country," she murmured. She didn't know why she and her mother had thought that. He hadn't told them where he was going.

"Peter, my best friend, had just emigrated to Canada. Mum probably assumed that I'd gone after him. But I had no real wish to travel; just to get away."

She hopped on him immediately. "So you admit it — you did do it for you and not for us."

He put down his fork and looked at her. "I did it for all of us, Dana. We were all miserable. Especially Mum. I knew if I left, things could only get better. And I was right, wasn't I?"

"You could have stayed in touch," she retorted, pushing the curry aside and reaching for her glass. "You didn't have to disappear into thin air."

"Maybe that was a mistake," he admitted. "But I thought if Father knew that you or Mum were in touch with me, he'd take it out on you."

Dana sat in silence for a moment while she digested this. He had a point. Hadn't she had similar thoughts when she left home?

He reached out to take her good hand. "Dana, I was little more than a child myself when I left, only seventeen. I thought I was doing the right thing, please believe that."

She studied him closely. He seemed to mean what he said but that didn't help. "What I can't handle is what you did when Mum died."

He looked at her. "What do you mean?"

"You forgave him, Ed," Dana cried. "You behaved as if none of it had happened. After everything he'd done to us — to you — you forgave him." She clicked her fingers. "Just like that."

"It wasn't like that."

"Then what was it like?"

He grabbed the empty bottle and stood up. "I think we need some more of this."

"Ed —" Dana started, but he was already out of the room and walking quickly towards the kitchen.

He was gone a long time. While she waited, Dana gazed out at the sodden, floodlit garden. Even with rain lashing down on it, it still looked pretty. She had a feeling that she was destined to spend the rest of her days like this. Staring into space, asking questions that no one seemed able to answer. She would have to get a cat. Then people could talk about the little old eccentric lady who lived alone and never left the house. Would it be so bad? she wondered. Did she really care any more?

"Here we are." Ed returned with a second bottle of wine and refilled their glasses. "If Mother saw us she'd be shocked. She always said anyone who had more than two drinks had a problem."

"Did she?" Dana scowled, raising her glass to her lips. He was stalling, evading her questions, and she'd had enough of it.

"Do you think you have a problem?" he asked casually.

She gazed at him coldly. "I have several, and I'm looking at one of them right now."

Ed smiled, seemingly unperturbed by her belligerent attitude. "It's like old times, the two of us bickering like this."

Dana shook her head in frustration. "No, Ed, it's not. Why won't you answer me? Why won't you explain? Why won't you tell me, at least, that you're sorry?"

He looked shocked. "Of course I'm sorry! I'm sorry I left you. I'm sorry I didn't realize how much it would affect you."

"And Dad?" she asked, tears running silently down her cheeks.

Ed's eyes filled up too. "Of course I'm sorry for Dad —"

"*For* Dad," she repeated, shaking her head. "What are you talking about?"

Ed shrugged. "I'm the reason he was the way he was."

"No! No, you're not. I can't believe you could even think that."

"It's true."

"No, no, no." She banged her sore arm on the edge of her chair in frustration, and then yelped with pain.

"Hey, be careful! You'll hurt yourself. Don't get so upset! It was all a long time ago."

"I don't understand you at all," she whispered. "You had it so much worse than me. What's happened? Have you become a born-again Christian or a Scientologist or something?"

"No. For some reason, religion never did it for me."

She smiled and swirled the wine around in her glass. "Do you remember those terrible Sunday lunches?"

He groaned. "How could I ever forget them?"

"What was all that about? I mean, why did he drag us along to those places every week?"

"He liked to see himself as the grand patriarch. The successful rich poet with the good-looking family. He lorded it over us and everyone else." Ed smiled at her. "And he loved to show off his little princess."

She shivered. "I don't know why you didn't hate me. I'd have hated you if our situations were reversed."

"I couldn't ever have hated you. You were such a sweet little thing. And you were always trying to protect me."

She shifted in her chair in an effort to ease the dull throbbing in her arm.

"Shall I get your pills?" he asked.

She shook her head. "No. I'm sorry, but I need to go to bed now."

"Of course. It's late." He stood up and stretched out a hand to her.

She ignored it. "I can manage. Just bring up my drink for me, and my laptop."

"Hey, say 'please'. As Mother used to say, it costs nothing to be polite."

"Shut up and get me upstairs."

CHAPTER
TWENTY-NINE

Gus and Terry sat in a restaurant near his office, eating lunch. Or rather, he was eating, she was just pushing salad around the plate.

"Don't you like your food?" he asked, noticing her lack of enthusiasm.

"It's fine, I'm just not hungry."

"You're very quiet."

Her eyes met his. "I'm not the only one."

He looked back down at his plate. "What does that mean?"

"You've been behaving a bit strangely since we bumped into Dana," she said quietly.

"Have I?"

"You know you have. Look, if you're having second thoughts about us, I'd prefer you to just come right out and say it."

"Us?" he echoed.

She reddened. "Oh, sorry, was that presumptuous? It's just that we've been seeing each other for a few weeks now and I thought — obviously wrongly — that it was going quite well."

"It was, it is," he assured her. "Look, I'm sorry if I've been a bit distracted lately, Terry, but it hasn't been an easy time. Dana has some problems and, well . . ." he trailed off. It was always at the back of his mind that Terry worked for a tabloid. He wasn't about to reveal any private information about his wife. "Let's talk about something else."

She pushed aside her plate and stood up. "No, let's not."

"Oh, come on, Terry," he said wearily. "Sit down."

"I thought you were separated, Gus."

"I am."

"Then why are you still so involved in her life?"

"It's complicated."

"So you said. I tell you what, when you've helped her sort out all of her problems, give me a call."

"Terry," he protested but she had turned on her heel and was making her way through the restaurant towards the door. By the time he'd paid for their meal and followed her outside, Terry had disappeared. "Shit," he muttered, and walked back to the office. He could call her and apologize. He could buy her dinner tonight and show her he was sorry. But would that be fair? She was right. He was preoccupied. Ed had sent him a text message to say that he'd moved in with Dana and would call him. Gus couldn't wait to hear from him. He'd have given anything to be a fly on the wall when brother and sister met again after all these years. It had to be going well. Otherwise Dana wouldn't have allowed him to stay. It was a good sign, he decided, as he turned in at the gate of his office.

"Gus!" He turned as his partner got out of his car and crossed the car park to join him. "I was going to phone you from the car."

"What is it?" Gus noticed Tom's anxious expression and the beads of sweat standing out on his forehead.

"Ashling's gone into labour."

"What? But it isn't due for a couple of weeks."

"Yes, well, apparently babies don't operate to a timetable," Tom said, pulling nervously at his tie.

"Well, don't just stand there, mate! Go and take her to the hospital."

"She's already on the way; her sister and mother are with her. Luckily they were there when her waters broke."

Gus shuddered. "Too much information. Tell me what I can do. Do you want me to drive you over there?"

Tom shook his head. "No, I'll need my car later but I have a new client arriving for a meeting. He's due any minute."

"I'll take care of him," Gus promised. "Anything else?"

Tom ran a hand frantically through his hair. "I'm not sure, I can't think straight. Ask Carla, she'll know."

"Will do. Now go." Gus pushed him gently towards his car. "I'll look after the shop."

"I'll call you when I know what's going on," Tom called over his shoulder.

"Wish her luck for me," Gus shouted. "And don't worry. Everything will be fine."

Carla was on her feet the moment he walked in.

"I know, I met him in the car park," he told her before she could say a word. "Can you get me the file on this client so that at least I look as if I know what I'm talking about?"

She handed it to him. "Right here."

"What would I do without you?" he said, heading for the meeting room. "Would you be a real darling now and organize some coffee?"

"There's a pot already on," she called after him.

"You're an angel," he said, disappearing inside.

"Gus?" Carla hurried after him. "There was a call for you while you were out. It was from Ed O'Carroll. He asked if you'd call him as soon as you got in."

"Thanks, Carla." Gus looked at his watch. There was no time to call Ed now. It would have to wait until after the meeting. Today the business had to come first.

Between Tom's work and his own, Gus never got time to phone Terry or return Ed's call. But he had rather enjoyed being so busy. He had been coasting for weeks now, and it was time that changed. Tom would be taking at least two weeks off once Ashling and the baby came home. And even when he came back to work, Tom wouldn't be up to par, given the sleepless nights that lay ahead of him.

Going to the door, he called to Carla, "Any word?"

She looked up from her desk. "Nothing."

"But it's been ages."

"This is nothing," Carla said with a laugh. "My sister was in labour for eighteen hours."

Gus winced. "Poor old Tom. It's going to be a long night."

Carla fired a pencil at him. "And what about poor Ashling? She's the one doing all the work."

"Just kidding. So what about you, Carla? Any maternal feelings surfacing yet?"

"No way!" she said, shaking her head. "I love being an aunty, but being tied down twenty-four-seven? I'm too selfish for that."

"Me too."

"So weren't you and Dana going to have children?" Carla ventured.

"No. We did argue a lot about having a dog, though. I wanted one, she didn't." Gus laughed. "I suppose that means I would have got custody."

"So you're definitely going to separate? Officially, I mean?"

For the first time Gus noticed the rapt look on the girl's face and the way she had turned her chair around to allow him an excellent view of her legs. Oh, fuck.

"Not sure." He edged back towards his office. "It's late, Carla. Why don't you go on home?"

Her face fell. "I don't mind hanging on. I haven't typed up the minutes of that last meeting yet."

"It can wait until tomorrow."

"Well, if you're sure." She looked reluctant.

He beamed. "I'm positive. 'Night." He closed the door on the confused girl and sat back down at his desk. "You'll never learn, Johnson," he muttered. He would have to be very careful how he handled Carla in Tom's absence. He closed his eyes briefly. Maybe "handle" wasn't the best word to use. Were all women this complicated, Gus wondered. Or just the ones he knew?

He picked up the phone and dialled Terry's mobile. She answered on the first ring.

"Hi, it's me."

"I know," she said coolly.

"Look, I'm sorry about earlier. It's just, like I said —"

"Complicated."

"It has nothing to do with us."

Terry gave a weary sigh. "But, Gus, if you've left her why are you running back there every five minutes to help her?"

"I've been back twice," he corrected her. "And you have to understand, Terry, you can't end a six-year relationship just like that."

She hopped on his words. "So you are ending it?"

He grinned. This was one of the drawbacks of dating a journalist. "Sure. Why don't I pick you up and we'll go out to dinner? It will make up for the lunch you didn't eat."

"I can't. I have a job on."

"Oh, okay. Do you want to meet for a drink when you finish?"

"No, I've an early start."

"Right."

"Why don't we leave it for a few days, Gus?"

He sighed. "If that's what you want."

"It is. Bye, Gus."

He hung up with a sigh. He couldn't blame Terry for being fed up with him. She was a clever girl and it wasn't surprising she'd picked up on his mood. Maybe it would be better if they didn't see each other for a while. He was going to be busy in work and he knew he'd be preoccupied until he found out all of Dana's secrets.

With that in mind, he dialled Ed's number. "It's Gus Johnson, Ed."

"Oh, hi. Hang on a minute."

As Gus waited, a message came in on his mobile. He smiled delightedly as he read it.

WANT TO COME OVER AND MEET MY DAUGHTER?

He immediately sent a message back.

SURE. THEN I'LL HELP YOU WET HER HEAD! CONGRATS. LUV 2 ASHLING.

"Gus, are you there?"

"I'm here."

"Sorry about that."

"That's okay."

"Listen, I just wondered if you wanted to meet up. I thought you might like an update."

"I'm sorry, Ed, but I can't meet you tonight. How about lunch tomorrow?"

"No, I'm taking Dana to the hospital."

"What?"

"It's okay, she's fine. She had an accident and broke her wrist. I have to take her back tomorrow for a check-up."

"What kind of accident? Was she driving?"

"No, nothing like that. She had a fall. Really, Gus, she's fine."

"A fall?"

"Yeah."

"She was drinking, wasn't she?"

Ed's sigh was audible. "She says not."

"Huh. So when did this happen?"

"Last week. I actually found her. She was out cold in the driveway."

"Jesus! She could have been there for days!"

"Calm down. It was a mild concussion. She came round very quickly. Honestly, Gus, I'd have called you straight away if there was anything to worry about."

"Okay. So, how's it going?"

Ed chuckled. "A little strained."

"Still, she let you stay. That's a good sign."

"She didn't have much choice! She's in plaster to her elbow and can't manage without help. I suppose I was just lucky she has no one else."

Gus said nothing. He had this image of Dana lying undiscovered in their driveway with no one knowing or caring.

"Hello? Gus, are you still there?"

"Yes. Sorry. You were saying?"

"There isn't much else to tell you at this stage. But it's early days. I just wanted to let you know about the accident."

"Thanks for that. Are you at the house now?" Gus asked.

"Yes. Why?"

"Maybe I could just say hello."

"I don't think that's a good idea. She wouldn't be impressed if she knew I'd been on the phone for the last ten minutes talking to you."

"No, that's true. I'll call her tomorrow evening. I'd like to know how she gets on at the hospital."

"Good idea. I'm sure she'd appreciate that."

"But —" Gus frowned. "How do I know about her accident?"

Ed laughed. "This is getting complicated, isn't it? Look, I'll answer the house phone when you call and I'll tell her that I filled you in on the accident."

"Good idea. Okay, then. Goodnight, Ed. And thank you. Thank you for everything."

"Goodnight, Gus."

Gus put down the phone and sank back in his chair. He took a moment to examine his feelings. When Ed had told him about Dana's accident, his gut had twisted in terror. Whatever had happened between them, he still loved her. He was in no doubt of that. But the more time he spent with Terry, the more he realized how strange his marriage had been. He'd only got to meet Dana's brother because he went hunting for him in Wexford. And he'd found out more about the O'Carroll family from him than he ever had from his wife.

By contrast, in the short time he'd known Terry, he already knew her mother was slightly agoraphobic. Her father was nuts about Gaelic football. And her younger sister was a constant worry to them all because she couldn't settle on a career.

Terry's openness made Gus realize how troubled Dana must be. She had always presented an image to the world of a confident, sophisticated and carefree woman. And though she had let her guard down with him to a certain extent, she still wouldn't discuss her past. She had mentioned Ed from time to time but never told him why they didn't keep in touch. He knew she had been close to her mother and that the woman had died while Dana was away at university. Gus knew that Conall O'Carroll was the crux of all Dana's problems, but Dana refused point-blank to discuss him. One night in the early days of their marriage, when they had been more than a little drunk, he had asked her about him.

"I don't have a father," she'd said bitterly.

"He's dead?" Gus had said.

"Happily, yes."

Gus had found that slightly shocking. He had always been quite close to his family. Both his parents were dead now and his sister lived in Auckland, New Zealand. But, though he didn't see Annie that often, they were still very close.

His sister hadn't liked Dana, he remembered now. Oh, she hadn't said as much, and she'd made an effort to get on with his fiancée when they met just before the wedding. But he could tell there was no meeting of minds there. It had saddened him at the time but not worried him greatly. Women were strange like that.

They made snap decisions about each other and that was that. He knew, had Annie lived in Ireland, she would have grown to love Dana as much as he did. Or was he kidding himself? He must call her and ask.

But not tonight. Gus stood up and put on his jacket. Tonight, he smiled at the prospect, he was going to meet his god-daughter. God-daughter! Who'd have thought!

CHAPTER
THIRTY

"I've brought the post and the papers. Fancy a coffee?" Ed stood looking down at his sister but she was obviously miles away. "Dana? Is there something wrong?"

She smiled. "Not at all. I just got an email from Gus. Ashling — that's his partner Tom's wife — had a baby girl. They've called her Holly."

"Pretty. Are you going to go and visit?"

Dana made a face. "I don't think so. I'll send one of those baby baskets — that should do."

"I'm sure she'd be pleased to see you."

"How would you know? You don't even know her."

"Doesn't every woman want to show off her baby?"

"Ed, go away. I've got work to do."

"So you do," he said mildly. "How's it going, by the way?"

"Fine." She sat rigid in front of the keyboard, waiting for him to leave.

"Good. So, coffee?"

She sighed. "Please." When he left she turned from the screen and gazed out into the garden. Perhaps Ashling *would* expect her to go and visit. She had, after all, come to see how Dana was doing. But what on earth would she say to her? Dana knew nothing about babies.

The phone rang, interrupting her thoughts. When Ed didn't pick up, Dana saved her file and answered. "Hello?"

"Hello, my darling, how are you?"

Dana smiled. "Hi, Wally. Still a bit sore, I'm afraid."

"Poor you. Is your brother taking good care of you?"

"He's doing okay."

"You must be having fun catching up."

"Stop fishing, Wally. You know I haven't seen the man in years. We're practically strangers."

"All the more to talk about," he said, unabashed. "You have a lot of catching up to do."

"And I have a lot of writing to do," Dana reminded him.

"Ah, so you do."

Dana smiled. That shut him up.

"Which brings me to why I'm phoning. Will you call Gretta?"

Dana groaned. "Why? What's wrong now?"

"Nothing at all," he reassured her. "I just called to tell her about your accident and she was a little suspicious. I want her to hear from you that we're still on schedule."

"Are we?"

"Dana —"

"It's okay, Walter, I'm just kidding. I'll phone her this evening."

"Good girl. Right, then, I'll leave you to it. Bye, darling."

"Bye."

★　★　★

"So are you going to visit her?" Ed asked, when they were in the car and on their way to the hospital.

Dana frowned. "Who?"

"The new baby."

"I don't think so. It would only be awkward. And I wouldn't know what to say."

"Ask her how she is, how the baby is; does she sleep through the night and is she feeding okay. That should take you through the entire visit," Ed told her.

Dana eyed him suspiciously. "How do you know so much about babies? God, you're not a father, are you?" She didn't know why the thought was so incongruous. Ed was almost forty after all.

He let out a belly laugh. "No. No, I'm not."

"Why is it so funny?" she asked.

"Oh, I don't know. I just can't imagine having kids."

"Me neither," Dana murmured. "What does that say about our upbringing?"

Ed shook his head. "You can't blame everything on Father. Some people just aren't cut out to be parents."

"He certainly wasn't."

Ed laughed.

"What about a relationship, Ed? You know all about me and you haven't told me anything about you. Has there ever been anyone special? Is there someone special at the moment?"

"First, I would contest the statement that I know everything about you. Has there been anyone special? Yes, but I screwed it up. Is there anyone now? No. I think I'm destined to be a bachelor."

"Doesn't that bother you?"

He shrugged. "What's to be will be."

"I don't want to end up alone," Dana said miserably.

"I'm sure you won't. Anyway, maybe you and Gus will sort things out."

"I don't think so."

"Don't be too quick to write him off," Ed told her. "And then there's always lover boy."

She smiled. "Ryan is nice."

"Nice? Poor guy. I'd hate anyone to call me nice."

"Okay, he's better than nice. But, it's not love."

"I'm glad he's around to cheer you up, Dana. But if you still have hopes of reconciliation with Gus, it might be wiser to give Ryan his marching orders."

"Gus is dating a beautiful young girl," she reminded him. "He's hardly in a position to complain."

Ed smiled. "Oh, Dana! You are so naive."

Dana remembered her brother's words when Gus phoned later. They talked politely for several minutes and he seemed genuinely concerned about her accident. He quizzed her in depth about her injuries and asked what the doctors had said. And then, when he seemed satisfied that she was going to be all right, he told her all about Holly. She was amazed at how awed he was.

"She's so beautiful, Dana. And did I tell you — they've asked me to be god-father."

"Wow. That's . . . lovely."

"Does that mean I have to hold her when the priest is pouring the water over her head?"

324

"No. I think you just stand there looking proud," Dana said, smiling.

"Oh, okay. What do you think I should buy her? I've no idea what the protocol is."

"Me neither. Why don't you ask your sister?"

"Good idea. I'll phone Annie later. So, how are you and Ed getting along?"

"Fine."

"He sounds nice."

"Yeah."

"You must have a lot to talk about."

"Yeah. Look, Gus, I have to go."

"Oh, okay, then."

"Thanks for the call."

Dana thought a lot about their conversation, and then over lunch a few days later, she announced to Ed that she'd decided to go and visit Ashling.

"Great idea," he pronounced. "I'll drive you, if you like. Or are you too embarrassed to be seen out with your big brother?"

She looked at him. "Why would you say that?"

He shrugged. "I'm part of your big secret, aren't I, Dana? You certainly haven't been going out of your way to introduce me to any of your friends."

"I don't have any," she pointed out, "except Judy and you already know her."

"Judy! There's a name from the past. You still keep in touch?"

"Yes. I don't know what I'd have done without her these last couple of months. I don't know why she bothers with me, though. I hardly know her husband and don't even ask me how old her girls are."

Ed raised an eyebrow. "Well, that's brutally honest."

She shrugged. "I'm not proud of myself. I just have so little in common with her now. But as soon as the news hit the papers that Gus had left, she was on the phone. She's a very good and kind person. She's my best friend. And I've no idea why she bothers with me." Tears welled in Dana's eyes and she swallowed them hastily. God, what was it about Ed? He always managed to turn the conversation to something that brought out emotions she hadn't even realized were there.

"Maybe you're not as big a bitch as you seem to think you are." He smiled and stood up to clear their dishes. "Now, why don't you go and put your face on and I'll drive you over to see Ashling and her beautiful baby?"

"How do you know she's beautiful?" Dana asked with a grin.

He rolled his eyes. "All babies are beautiful, Dana. Even when they're not."

"Shall I wait or call back for you?" Ed asked, as he pulled into Ashling and Tom's driveway.

She eyed his paisley shirt, beige chinos and shiny leather shoes. "Seeing as you've dressed up you may as well come in." Dana secretly hated the idea of going into Tom's house alone and was glad to have her brother by her side. She also felt more than a little proud of him. He looked handsome today and she knew that with his impeccable manners and kind nature they would take to him immediately.

She rang the doorbell and waited nervously, half hoping that there was no one home.

"It will be fine," Ed said, with a reassuring smile.

How did he do that? And why couldn't she read him as easily as he apparently read her?

"Dana, what a surprise!" Ashling had opened the door and was smiling uncertainly. "Oh, look at your poor arm! Gus told me what happened. Is it very sore?"

"It's fine, really. I feel a bit silly to be honest. I just fell over the kerb in my driveway. If it wasn't for Ed —" She stopped as she realized that Ed was standing behind her, waiting patiently to be introduced. "Oh, sorry, Ashling. This is my brother, Ed."

"Pleased to meet you, Ed." Ashling smiled.

"If it's a bad time, we'll go," Dana said. "I just wanted to drop this off." She indicated the gift in Ed's arms.

"How beautiful." Ashling looked at the basket lined with pink satin and stuffed full of newborn essentials and the cutest little pink teddy bear. "No, come in. It's lovely to see you." She led them through to the kitchen and moved some ironing and bags of nappies off two chairs so that they could sit down. "Sorry, the place is a mess. Holly is a darling but I can't believe how much she's turned our lives upside down. How about some tea?"

Dana pushed her gently into a chair and smiled. "I'll make the tea, you sit down."

Ed shot a pointed look at Dana's cast. "No, I don't want to end up in the burns unit, thank you very much. Why don't I make the tea while you two have a natter?"

Dana and Ashling laughed and then sat down facing each other.

"So, how are you?" Dana asked.

"Happy, tired and tearful, all at the same time," Ashling said honestly. "We're muddling along. And Holly seems amazingly contented, given her parents don't have a clue what they're doing."

"You'll get the hang of it," Dana told her. "And don't your sisters live nearby?"

Ashling looked upwards and clasped her hands together. "Yes, thank God! I don't know what I'd do without them. Rosie is doing all of our shopping, and Vanessa babysits a couple of hours a day so I can have a lie-down."

"It sounds like you have a great family," Ed remarked, as he filled the teapot and looked around for mugs.

"In the cupboard above your head," Ashling told him. "Speaking of families, it's lovely to finally meet you, Ed. Have you been living abroad?"

"All over the place," he said cheerfully. "And if you're wondering why Dana doesn't talk about me, it's because I'm the black sheep of the family."

Dana rolled her eyes at Ashling as she felt the colour rise in her cheeks. "Just ignore him."

Ed winked at Ashling. "See? I told you."

"So where is the little darling?" Dana asked.

"Asleep. And I'm sorry, you aren't getting anywhere near her until she wakes. She didn't get much sleep last night, so I didn't either!"

"Sit back and enjoy that," Ed said, handing Ashling a mug of tea.

"Thanks. There are biscuits somewhere," she said vaguely.

"That's okay, we've just had lunch. So did everything go okay? Are you and Holly both well?" Dana avoided her brother's amused gaze.

"Holly was a little jaundiced at first, but she's fine now. The labour went well — relatively speaking. Although I was sure Tom was going to pass out."

"Where is Tom?" Dana asked.

"He went into the office for a couple of hours. He wanted to run through some of the projects he was working on with Gus. The baby was two weeks early so she took us a bit by surprise. Everyone had warned us that first babies were usually late." She checked her watch. "He should be home soon." With that there was a thin wail from the next room. Ashling smiled. "It looks like she wants to meet you."

She disappeared into the darkened room leading off the kitchen, and returned seconds later with a lemon bundle. Dana and Ed stood up to admire the baby, as Ashling loosened the blanket to afford them a better look.

"What a beauty," Ed said with a tender smile.

Dana stood staring down at the little girl, lost for words. Then, aware that Ashling must be waiting for her to say something, she smiled at the other woman.

"She's gorgeous, Ashling. And look at all that hair!" Dana reached a tentative hand out to touch the dark curls that framed the small face. Holly stared back at her from enormous blue eyes.

"Gus says she certainly doesn't take after her father," Ashling laughed.

Dana's smile faltered at the mention of her husband's name. She could imagine Gus slagging off Tom's receding hairline. She could see him here, in this kitchen with them. The thought made her feel incredibly lonely and isolated. "She's really beautiful," she said softly.

"Would you like to hold her?"

"Oh, no! I mean, not with this." She indicated her cast. "I'd be afraid I'd drop her."

Holly had turned her face into her mother's breast and was nuzzling.

Ashling laughed again. "Well, it looks like she's decided it's lunchtime anyway."

"Would you excuse me, ladies? I have a call to make." Ed was closing the door behind him before either woman had a chance to reply.

"He's lovely." Ashling sat down in a rocking chair in the corner, opened her shirt and put the baby to her breast. "And discreet."

"Yes," Dana agreed.

"He wasn't at your wedding, was he?" Ashling asked, her eyes curious.

"No, he wasn't around."

"Still, he's here now, which is great. You must be thrilled."

Dana just smiled.

"So. You and Gus are talking again."

"Sort of."

"It's a start."

Dana shook her head. "I don't think there's any hope for us, not now he's found someone else. Have you met her?" she added softly.

Ashling looked down at her baby. "No."

"But you know about her?"

Ashling looked up at Dana and nodded. "But I don't think it's serious."

"Hey, you don't have to say that."

"No, I mean it," Ashling said urgently. "I know he's being a prat, Dana. But please don't give up on him."

Dana stood up. "I'd better go."

"Don't go. Tom will be here soon."

"I doubt he'll want to see me."

"Why would you say that, Dana? Tom is just as upset as I am that you and Gus have split up."

Dana looked into the other woman's face and saw nothing but sincerity and sympathy there. She reached out to stroke the baby's tiny hand, and smiled when her finger was grasped. "Thanks, Ashling, but I really have to go."

Gently, Ashling unlatched Holly from her breast so she could walk out with Dana. Ed was waiting in the hall.

"She is going to break hearts," he told Ashling with a smile.

"Tom says he's building a moat," Ashling said laughing. "I think she's going to be Daddy's little princess. Aren't you, darling?" She closed her eyes as she nuzzled her baby's neck, and missed the look that passed between Ed and Dana.

"It was lovely to meet you, Ashling," Ed said. "Please forgive us for calling in unannounced, but Dana was dying to meet Holly."

Ashling kissed his cheek. "I'm delighted you did. Take care of Dana for us, won't you?"

He saluted with a grin. "I am her obedient slave."

"More like a sergeant major," Dana retorted. She hugged Ashling, careful not to squeeze the baby, then dropped a kiss on the child's downy head. "Lovely to meet you, Holly. Welcome to the world."

Ashling beamed at her. "Thank you so much for the present. Come back and see us soon."

"We will," Ed said before Dana had a chance to answer. "She needs to get out more. Maybe when she gets the cast off she could even babysit."

Dana's eyes widened in alarm, but she smiled when she saw that the other woman was laughing.

"Bye, Ashling, give Tom my best and tell him congratulations," Dana said as Ed helped her into the car. "Go back inside now, it's cold."

"I will. Goodbye, Dana."

"She's nice," Ed said as they drove away.

"Yes."

"Beautiful baby," he added.

"Yes."

He grinned. "I mean it."

She smiled. "Yeah, me too."

CHAPTER
THIRTY-ONE

Dana saved *The Mile High Club* and sat back. "Thank God," she murmured. Going into her email, she wrote a message to Sylvie and attached the file. Then she phoned her PA.

"Hi, Sylvie."

"Oh, hi, Dana. How are you?"

"Relieved. I've just finished the book."

"That's great news, congratulations."

Dana smiled. "I think we both know that congratulations aren't really in order."

"Well, at least it's over and now you can move on."

Everyone talked about her moving on, Dana mused. To what?

"So shall I send it on to Gretta once I've checked it?" Sylvie asked.

"No, I think we'd better let Walter have a look at it first. It's only fair to prepare him. I'll call him now and tell him to expect it."

"I'll get it to him before close of business," Sylvie promised.

Dana called Walter's office but it turned out he was at meetings and wasn't expected back until the following day. Rather than leave a message, Dana sent her agent a short email.

Dear Wally,
By the time you read this, you should have the final manuscript — I thought you should read it before we sent it to Gretta. I'm sorry.
X
Dana

She swallowed back her tears as she pressed send. Poor Wally. Despite all his encouragement and help, *The Mile High Club* was still the worst book she'd ever written. There was no way that Gretta would publish it. Strangely Dana felt worse for her agent than she did for herself. She had known for weeks that it wasn't going to be good enough, but she had tried. And she felt awful that she'd let Wally down. Some day, she promised herself, she'd make it up to him. She had no idea when or how, but she would.

"Here we are." Ian came into his office, two beakers in his hand. "Have you read the final chapters yet?"

Sylvie shook her head and took a grateful sip of coffee. "I've printed it out but I'm putting off reading it. I know it's going to be bad."

Ian sighed. "And she really seemed to have got her act together. I don't understand."

"She just doesn't seem to enjoy it any more."

"Maybe she needs to hit rock bottom," he mused. "Maybe being out of contract will make her realize what she's thrown away."

"By which time, I'll be out of a job," Sylvie said glumly.

"You'll get another job, Sylvie, don't worry. Have a word with Walter, he knows everyone in the publishing industry and I'm sure he'd be happy to write you a reference."

"I'm not sure I even want to stay in the publishing industry. I'm not sure I know what I want, to be honest."

"You do."

"I don't," she protested.

"You do," Ian insisted. "Just make a list of all the things you like doing and all of your talents and see what job fits."

"That's going to be a very short list," Sylvie said, pulling a face.

He laughed. "Don't talk rubbish. I could make a list right now off the top of my head."

She sat up. "You could? Would you?"

"I'd love to, but I have to go out."

"Okay, then." Her face fell and she reached for the printed copy of Dana's final chapters.

"But," he said and smiled at her, "if you have dinner with me tonight, I'll be happy to discuss it."

Sylvie looked at him. "Are you asking me out on a date?"

Ian held her gaze. "Yes, Sylvie, I am."

"Okay, then." She smiled slowly. "Why not?"

He grinned. "Great. Now, get to work."

Sylvie sighed. "If I must."

It didn't take long to finish *The Mile High Club* and there were few errors. Sylvie quickly made the changes, saved the file and sent it to Walter. She was sitting staring into space, close to tears, when Ian arrived back from his meeting.

"Moving?" Ian asked hopefully, handing her a tissue.

"Crap," she sniffed.

"I'm sure Wally will be able to talk Dana into making a few changes."

"It would take a lot more than that," Sylvie assured him. "At the moment it reads as if the second half of the book was written by a different author."

His eyes widened. "You don't think —"

"No." She shook her head emphatically. "You can read in it all the heartache and trauma she's being going through. The heroine is as miserable as she is."

"Maybe we should get her to write her autobiography instead. Misery memoirs are big at the moment." Ian put an arm around her and gave her a quick hug. "Come on, cheer up. We'll go out tonight and celebrate."

Sylvie stared. "Celebrate what?"

"Your new career, of course! Whatever it may be."

"You look nice, love." Maureen smiled as her daughter came into the room, putting on her earrings. "Going anywhere special?"

Sylvie shook her head. "Just out with Ian."

"He's a nice lad. You could do worse."

"Now, Mum, don't start. And don't say anything to him or I'll murder you."

"Wouldn't dream of it, love."

The doorbell went. "That will be him. Not a word," Sylvie warned her mother.

"Take him in to see your da before you go, love. It will cheer him up."

And it did. Sylvie sat quietly on the end of the bed while Ian and her dad discussed Liverpool's performance the previous night. Her father was almost animated and looked younger and more vital than she'd seen him in years.

"We should go over to a game sometime," Ian said.

"Are you mad, son? Sure it would cost an arm and a leg."

"Ah, but I have contacts." Ian tapped the side of his nose.

"No, son. It's good of you to offer, but getting me there and back would be too much like hard work. It's not worth the hassle."

"Everywhere is wheelchair-friendly now, Dad," Sylvie pointed out.

Her father shook his head. "Leave it, Sylvie. You two go off and enjoy yourselves, I'm tired now."

"Would you like to be a copy editor?" Ian asked. They were sitting in a Chinese restaurant, drinking coffee and talking about the future.

"Are you crazy?" Sylvie laughed. "I barely scraped through school."

"Okay, then. But you like organizing people; you enjoy socializing; you deal with people sensitively and respectfully —"

Sylvie's eyes widened. "I do?"

"Yeah, you're great with your dad."

"But that's because he's my dad," she protested.

"And you've been great with Dana," he continued. "You never knew from one day to the next what mood you would find her in, and yet you coped with that and managed to be her friend when she needed it, too. I know, you could be a social worker!"

She shot him a dirty look. "I could be out of a job in a matter of hours, and you're making jokes."

"You are not going to be out of work for long. If all else fails, you can always work with me."

"What?"

"We make a good team, don't we? What?" he added, when she looked away.

"I don't know, Ian. You've been very good to me and I appreciate it, but . . ."

"You're afraid that I'll want you to do more than answer the phone."

She raised her eyes to meet his. "And won't you?"

He smiled. "I wouldn't mind. Is it such a scary thought?"

"It's too quick, we hardly know each other."

"I think we know each other very well. What's wrong, Sylvie? Aren't I rich enough for you?" he challenged.

"That's part of it," she said, looking him straight in the eye. "Don't blame me for wanting more. And stop trying to rush me. It's our first date! I'm trying to get

338

my head around the fact that I could be unemployed shortly and you're talking about commitment on almost every level. It's too much."

He looked sheepish. "Okay, sorry, message received and understood. It's not going to be all awkward in the office now, is it?"

"Not as long as you keep buying the coffee and cakes."

"I don't know about that. Times are hard; we may have to share."

She smiled. "I can live with that."

Dana sat in the darkened conservatory, a glass of champagne in her hand.

Ryan touched her hand. "Maybe I should go."

She looked up at him, realizing that her mind had wandered, again. She didn't seem to be able to concentrate on anything at the moment — anything other than the past, that is. "I'm sorry, Ryan. I've been terrible company this evening, haven't I?"

"That's okay. But now that you've finally finished your book, I thought you'd be happy."

"How can I be happy? It's rubbish."

He raised his glass of champagne. "At least you drown your sorrows in style."

She smiled. "Ed thinks I'm a lush."

"Where is big brother tonight?"

"Off photographing some moonlight shots for the calendar he's working on."

"You're such a creative family."

She looked surprised. "It's strange you should say that. My father had no time for Ed because he showed no interest in art or literature."

"Your dad sounds like a hard man."

"He was," Dana said. "He humiliated my mother and bullied my brother. He'd shout and scream at them and took his belt to Ed on a regular basis."

"And what about you?" Ryan asked.

"Oh, he never touched me. I was his little princess." Her eyes filled with pain. "Have you any idea how awful it is to be loved so much by someone who's hurting the people you care about? When I was young, I adored my father. He was my hero. It wasn't until I got older that I realized what a tyrant he was and understood how he used me to exclude my mother and punish my brother."

"Don't blame yourself, Dana. You were just a child."

"Yes. I suppose I was." She yawned.

He smiled and stood up. "I can take a hint."

She allowed him to help her to her feet and kiss her. "I'm sorry. I've been so miserable."

"I'm flattered you feel you can talk to me." He kissed her again, this time harder and longer. "I am so looking forward to you getting that cast off," he said with a groan when he finally pulled away.

She smiled. "Not long now."

When he'd gone, Dana went into her office and continued to tap out her story with one hand.

As I parked the car and got out I looked around nervously. I hadn't gone to the house — couldn't bear the thought.

340

Instead I headed straight to the funeral home. I was early, deliberately, so that I could have time on my own with my mother. I had never seen a dead body before but then this wasn't a body, this was my mum. Hurrying across to the entrance, my face buried deep in the collar of my coat, I prayed Father wasn't here. I knew I was probably safe, though. He'd be receiving mourners in a suitably solemn manner, and playing the part of the grieving widower.

When I went inside, a young man came from behind a desk to greet me with a gentle smile.

"Can I help you?"

His voice was soft and pleasant, but solemn; perfect for the job.

"I've come to see my mother, Rosemary O'Carroll."

"Of course, come this way."

I followed him down a corridor and he stopped by a set of double doors.

"Would you like me to stay with you?" he asked kindly.

I tried to smile but my face felt frozen. "No, I'll be fine."

"The other guests are expected at five."

"I'm sorry, is it a problem me being early?" I asked.

"No, of course not! I'm sure your mother would appreciate the time alone with her daughter." He smiled again, opened the door and stood back.

Straightening my shoulders, I walked in. As I approached the coffin in the centre of the room I realized I was holding my breath. Maybe it was all a mistake; maybe it wouldn't be my mother at all. But, sadly, it was. Her tiny figure looked even smaller than I remembered but other than that she looked just the same as she did when she was asleep. I half expected her to open her eyes and smile. She was dressed in the customary habit — she would have much preferred one of her pretty lace blouses — and someone had joined her hands and wrapped rosary beads around them; Father no doubt. I felt like snatching them away, they would have meant nothing to her. My mother had not been a religious woman. Father had turned us all off religion. The fact that he could be such a monster at home, and then attend the sacraments regularly, had been hard for us all to bear.

I felt guilty for not having come straight home when my father phoned. I should have been here to make sure he didn't abuse her in death as he had in life. I only realized I was crying when a tear fell on my mother's face. Horrified, I wiped it away with my finger. Her skin was cold and felt like paper and it hit me like a slap in the face that my mother was gone forever. I would never hear her voice again or see her smile. I would never feel her kiss on my cheek, or know the comfort of those thin arms around me. She was gone. I was crying noisily now, my shoulders heaving as deep waves of sadness engulfed me, and I clung on to the side of the coffin for support.

It took me a moment before I realized there was a hand on my arm. I turned to see it was the young man who had let me in.

"Come and have a cup of tea," he said.

"But I can't leave her," I protested.

"You can come back in," he promised. "Just take a little break."

This unleashed more tears and he had to almost carry me from the room. He led me to a small sitting room further down the corridor. A table was already set with a pot of tea, a plate of biscuits and two cups and saucers.

"Would you like some company, or would you prefer to be alone?" he asked.

"No, please stay." I struggled to get my tears under control. "I'm sorry about this."

He shook his head as he poured the tea. "Don't apologize, it's your mother."

"Whose decision was it to put her in a habit?" I added milk to my tea and raised the cup to my lips using both hands for fear that I'd drop it.

"Your father and brother made all the arrangements together."

I stared at him. "Ed's here?"

He nodded.

"But how did he know she was dead?"

"I don't understand —"

I shook my head. "Sorry, it's just my brother left five years ago and hasn't been in touch since."

"He must have kept in touch with someone. Many people do, you know. And it's quite common for reunions to take place in a funeral home."

"Don't you find that rather pathetic?" I said bitterly. "What's the point in coming, once they're dead?"

He shrugged. "At least you and your father get to see him again, and, hopefully, stay in touch this time."

The phone rang outside — a hushed muted tone — and he excused himself. I sat there for a moment and then realized I couldn't face my father. I didn't trust myself not to strike him or scream and shout. And I couldn't do that to my mother. There had been enough of that during her lifetime. She deserved to at least be buried in peace.

I stood up and went back down to the room where my mother was laid out. Going to her side, I dropped a gentle kiss on her cold lips. Then I hurried out of the room and back out into the reception.

"Thank you for your kindness," I whispered to the funeral director.

He looked up, surprised. "Aren't you going to wait for your family?"

"I'll see them tomorrow. That's time enough."

I went back to my car, moved it to the other end of the car park and waited. It wasn't long before a black stretch limo drove in, and the driver walked around to open the door. I slid down in my seat and held my breath as I watched my brother step out, looking handsome in a dark suit. He leaned into the car and offered his arm, and I gasped in surprise when I saw my father emerge. They paused on the step for a moment before going in. Father looked hunched and thinner than I remembered. He pulled a snow-white handkerchief from his pocket and blew his nose. Ed put an arm around his shoulders and squeezed them in a comforting manner. Father nodded as Ed said something and, taking his son's arm, Father went with him inside.

I pushed frantically at the car door, swung my body around, and bent over just in time to vomit on the grass verge. When I'd finished I cleaned my face and hands with some tissues and then, dazed and shaken, drove the short distance to my friend's house.

CHAPTER
THIRTY-TWO

"You're working very late."

Dana whirled around to see her brother in the doorway. "For God's sake, Ed, don't creep up on me like that."

"Sorry, I didn't mean to startle you. What are you so engrossed in anyway? I thought the book was finished."

"Just playing around with an idea," she said vaguely, saving the file and closing down her machine.

"Drink?"

She nodded. "There's a bottle open in the conservatory."

"Oh, right. So how is lover boy?"

"Stop calling him that," she snapped, cradling her arm as she stood up and followed him outside.

Ed raised an eyebrow. "You're touchy tonight. What's up?"

"I'm tired and sore."

"Poor you." He poured the wine and handed her a glass. "You shouldn't be working so much. The doctor said you were to rest."

That was Ed; whenever he was being really annoying or irritating, he'd turn around and say something nice.

"So did you get any good shots?"

He nodded enthusiastically. "Yeah, I went down to the canal and got some great mirror images."

"You've been gone hours, you must be freezing."

"I don't notice the cold when I'm working. Anyway, I went prepared." He peeled off two jumpers and sat down.

"You really love your work, don't you?" Dana remarked.

"I do," he said, taking his glass and stretching out in the armchair beside her. "Just like you."

"I'm not so sure any more," she murmured. "Sometimes I think I'd like to do something completely different."

"Like?"

"No idea," Dana admitted. "I've never really done anything else."

"You're one of the lucky ones. Many people chop and change jobs and never actually find anything they love to do."

"Strange. I don't feel very lucky at the moment."

"Look around you," he snapped. "You don't have it so bad."

She glared back at him. "How dare you judge me? You're the last person who's entitled to do that."

He sighed. "Have another drink and cool down, will you? Maybe you should go into acting," he added under his breath.

"You think I'm acting?" she said, growing angrier.

"I think that you're too quick to pick a fight," he retorted. "It was supposed to be a joke, Dana."

"Well, you're not funny. Stick to the day job."

346

"I intend to. You know," Ed added thoughtfully, "we should do a book together."

Dana shot him a curious look. "What kind of book?"

He shrugged. "I don't know. Maybe a history of Wexford. Or a look at the nature in our home county. Or," he winked, "the old man's biography."

"Write about that old bastard? Are you mad?"

"It would be the ultimate revenge," he pointed out. "We could say what we want, and everybody would believe us because we're his kids. And we could put in all the worst photos we could find. Now that would really piss him off. He was always so vain."

They sat in silence for a moment and then Dana sat forward, her face curious. "Can I ask you something?"

"Sure."

"When did you lose your stammer?"

He smiled.

"What?"

"Nothing, it just wasn't the question I was expecting."

"Well?" she prompted.

"I worked for a very nice man in a pizzeria for a while. I started off washing up and preparing vegetables, that sort of thing, but he wanted me to work out front. He said I was a good-looking lad and would draw in the girls. I told him I wouldn't be able to handle it — my stammer was always worse when I was with strangers. I said that with my stutter it would take half the night for me to tell them the specials, and he'd end up losing customers. But he wouldn't take no for an answer. At first he just put me on the till. Then, as I got more confident, he let me serve and take orders. The stammer got better and better, and after about a year it disappeared altogether."

"What a good person," Dana murmured, wondering if she would ever take the time or have the patience to help another human being. "How old were you then?"

He frowned. "About nineteen."

"I never noticed at the funeral."

He raised an eyebrow. "I'm not surprised; you hardly talked to me at the funeral."

"Sorry, but —"

He held up a hand. "It's okay. We've been through all that. Anyway it was stupid of me not to realize how you would feel at the time. I suppose I wasn't exactly thinking straight."

"Neither of us were."

He reached over to pat her good hand. "I'm glad we've had this time together, aren't you? It's great that we can finally lay these ghosts to rest."

She forced a smile. "Yeah. It's great."

"Dana? Are you okay?"

She nodded. "Sure. I'm just tired. I think it's time I went to bed."

"Let me help you." He stood up and held out his hand.

"No, that's okay. I can manage."

"Goodnight, then."

"Goodnight, Ed."

Ed watched her slow progress up the stairs, and when she was safely in her room he went into her office and quietly closed the door behind him.

★   ★   ★

Walter didn't read *The Mile High Club* immediately. First, he cancelled his last appointment, then he slid the bulky manuscript into his briefcase and went home. After pouring himself a very large G & T, he put on the answering machine and settled down to read. He wanted to be sure that there was no hope for this book before he talked to Dana. He also needed to think long and hard about what to do next.

As he read he got more and more upset. He felt he was witnessing the premature demise of an author who had so much more to give — much more than she had produced so far, and yet even that had brought her huge success. On a personal level he felt that Dana was lost. She'd tried to tell him, of course, but he hadn't listened. He'd been convinced that it was just a rough patch that he would be able to jolly or bully her out of. But he'd been wrong, he conceded. As he read and drank, he felt like phoning Gus Johnson and giving him an earful. In fact that's exactly what he was going to do. Walter hurled the pages across the room and picked up the phone.

Gus and Terry were back on track. They had just had a lovely dinner in a romantic Italian restaurant around the corner from his rented flat, and when Gus asked her back for a drink, she'd agreed.

He had just fetched their drinks and sat down beside her on the sofa, when the phone rang.

Terry kissed the side of his mouth. "Don't answer it," she murmured.

He groaned. "I have to. There are a couple of guys at the office working late. It could be them and with Tom on leave —"

"Okay, okay, go on." She sat back on the sofa and started to slowly open the buttons of her shirt.

"Hello?" Gus croaked, his eyes following her fingers.

"Well, I hope you're proud of yourself."

"Excuse me? Who is this?"

"You know damn well who this is, Johnson. I'm the man who's been trying to keep your poor wife from going over the edge. I'm the one who's been trying to hold her sorry career together while you screw around with a teenager. I'm the one who's going to have to tell her tomorrow that she has fuck-all chance of getting a new contract, because her latest book is drivel."

"Oh, Walter." Gus sighed. "Is it really that bad?"

"Like you care," Walter cried. "This is your bloody fault. So, what have you got to say for yourself? Well?"

Gus turned away from Terry's questioning gaze. "Walter, you're pissed."

"Not half as pissed as I'm going to be," the agent retorted, and hung up.

"Sorry about that," Gus said, staring at the phone.

"It didn't sound like it was work."

"No."

"It was about Dana, wasn't it?"

He nodded.

Terry gently touched his cheek. "Gus, she's not your problem any more."

"No," he agreed.

"Why did you ask me here, Gus?"

He shrugged. "I wanted us to have a nice evening together."

"Then let's do that," she said, kissing him.

He kissed her back, but his heart wasn't in it.

She pulled back and stared at him. "Gus?"

"I'm sorry, Terry."

She sighed and started to button up her shirt again. "So, what is it? What's wrong?"

"Dana's got problems."

"Don't we all?" she mumbled.

"It's serious, Terry. And I need to try to help her before it's too late."

She looked at him in silence for a moment, then nodded and stood up.

"Terry?"

She picked up her jacket and bag. "You've been messing me around, Gus."

"No, honestly, I haven't!" He tried to pull her into his arms but Terry side-stepped him. "Terry, please. Just give me some time. Maybe when this is all sorted —"

She paused at the door and shot him an incredulous look. "And maybe you should just go to hell."

Ed was still reading when the doorbell rang. He started, surprised by the sound. No one could get to the door unless they had the code for the gate. The only person it could be . . . He hurried out to the hall. He hoped Dana was asleep. He eased the door open and stood back to let Gus in.

"Come through to the office," he whispered and led the way.

"You don't seem surprised to see me," Gus said when they were in Dana's inner sanctum with the door closed.

"Nothing surprises me these days."

Gus walked to the window and turned around to look at his wife's desk and chair. "It feels strange being in here without her." He turned to face Ed. "I got a call from Wally. He was pissed as a newt, but I think he was trying to tell me that Dana's book is a disaster."

Ed flopped into Dana's chair. "She said she thought it was crap. I was hoping she was just being paranoid."

"Is this my fault, Ed?" Gus asked.

"Yes and no. Oh, please, sit down. You're giving me a crick in my neck."

Gus shook his head. "Not in here. I don't feel comfortable. Let's go to the kitchen or even out to the pool-house — I don't care, just not here."

"Okay, then, you head down to the pool-house and I'll get some drinks. Beer or something stronger?"

"Whiskey and soda, please. I'm not driving and I could really do with a drink."

While Gus quietly opened the french windows and slipped out into the garden, Ed went out to the kitchen to fetch the drinks.

"Sorry, you'll have to do without ice," he said, as he kicked the door of the pool-house closed after him.

"No problem, it's cold enough out here anyway." Gus raised his glass. "Thanks for letting me in. So, Ed, is it my fault?"

They sat down in two wicker chairs facing out towards the floodlit pool. Though Ed could see Gus's profile he could not see his expression or the look in his eyes. Maybe it was easier that way.

"There's no doubt that your leaving was the catalyst that set off this chain of events."

Gus dropped his head in his hands.

"But," Ed added, "it was only a matter of time before she cracked. She's been bottling up a lot of hurt and anger for years."

"But she did attend a psychiatrist, Ed. Surely she worked through her problems then?"

Ed shrugged. "Who knows? It doesn't really matter, does it? It obviously didn't work."

"And do you think it's all down to your father or her abortion?"

Ed shook his head. "I'm not sure. My father was an old-fashioned, bigoted, autocratic sort of man. His family were hugely important to him, but it was equally important that we fitted in with his image of what the perfect family should be. He was deeply committed to the Catholic Church and expected his children to follow his example without question. If I missed Mass or didn't go to Confession when I was supposed to, he'd take his belt to me. If he caught me out in a lie or I got into trouble at school, there was hell to pay. His relationship with my mother was complicated. I think he loved her in his own way but at the same time he didn't really approve of her. She wasn't as impressed by the Church, for a start. And she was way too soft on us for his liking."

Ed paused to take a drink.

"We were probably no different from other families when we were young. My father was working as a teacher and I was too small to cause that much trouble. The problems started when I got older. I couldn't do anything right, or so it seemed. That's when the shouting started and his belt became a regular feature in my life. My mother — small and gentle though she was — always stuck up for me. She used every trick in the book to distract him, and sometimes it worked." Ed stopped and swallowed hard. "And sometimes it didn't. And then, of course, there were times when she wasn't around and he would be free to make me as miserable and as terrified as he could. By the age of fourteen, I had developed a stammer, and he ridiculed me for it. He'd make me read my homework over and over again, trying to badger me into talking properly. Of course, the more upset I got, the more I stammered and the angrier he would get. Sometimes," Ed's voice shook slightly, "if I was really upset, I would wet myself. Then he would mock me and say I was a disgusting little animal, not worthy of the name O'Carroll. That I didn't deserve to live in the lovely comfortable house that he had worked hard to provide for us."

Ed stopped for another drink.

"He told me I was a weak, miserable excuse for a child and an embarrassment to him and my mother, only she was too much of a lady to admit it."

"The old bastard," Gus murmured.

Tears welled in Ed's eyes and he was glad of the cover of darkness.

"What about Dana? Did he treat her the same way?"

"No." Ed shook his head. "Dana could do no wrong. She was his little princess. You see, she was pretty and clever and funny. And she was talented. By the age of eight, she was reading the classics and writing the most amazing little stories. Dad realized that she was a chip off the old block, and he gloried in that."

"Did you hate her?"

Ed stared at him. "No, of course not! She was a great kid and she thought I was the best brother in the world. Given the way my father treated me, you can understand why that meant a lot. We were close, despite the fact that there are almost three years between us. When my parents argued, she would cling to me, shivering like a frightened little puppy. She didn't know what was going on most of the time, and I did my best to shield her from the worst of it. Mum did too." He sighed. "Maybe that was the wrong thing to do. As she got older, though, she began to understand that he treated me and Mum differently and she was furious." He grinned. "She was a fiery little character, even then. When there was a major row, she would put herself in the middle of it, and scream at him to stop. Unfortunately it had the opposite effect. He saw her taking my side and it made him angrier. The rows got worse and more frequent. Then one day, I'd had enough. We were in the kitchen and he was in full flow and I just grabbed a kitchen knife and pushed him up against the wall. Mum screamed and Dana came in from the garden. They were both begging me to stop. Of course, they needn't have worried. Dad easily overpowered me. But I decided in that moment that I had to leave. I couldn't take the abuse any more, and I knew life would be better for both Dana and my mother if I left. So I did."

"And you didn't keep in touch?"

Ed shook his head. "I was afraid to. I thought it would just make things worse for Mum and Dana and as I wasn't there to protect them, I couldn't take that chance. But I kept in touch with an old school friend, Keith. He kept an eye on them for me."

Gus nodded. "So Keith told you about Dana's abortion?"

"No, he didn't know anything about that, no one did. He just said that Dana had left home and was finishing her secondary education in a boarding school. I just assumed that she had also had enough and left of her own free will." He looked up at Gus, his eyes full of pain. "I should have come back then, shouldn't I? I should have checked that everything was okay. Hell, I could have even found out where she was and written to her. Dad wouldn't have known."

"Don't torture yourself." Gus reached for the whiskey and soda, and silently topped up Ed's glass and then his own. He walked to the window and stared up at Dana's room. "Go on."

"That's about it, really," Ed said. "The next time I saw my father and Dana was when Mum died."

"When was this?"

Ed frowned as he tried to remember. "When I was about twenty-three, I think."

"How did she die?"

"She fell down the stairs."

Gus swung around. "Fell?"

Ed nodded. "Yes, I'm afraid so. She was quite sick, you see. She was on a lot of medication and sometimes she lost her balance. It was a straightforward, horrible accident."

"How do you know that?" Gus asked. "You hadn't seen her in years."

"Keith had told me she wasn't well."

Gus watched him, his eyes curious. "Yet you still didn't go back."

Ed looked down. "No. No, I didn't. And I regret it, believe me."

"I wonder whether Dana feels the same way. She left too, after all."

"I've no idea."

Gus sighed. "What a mess. How come you've got through this unscathed and she's so scarred, though?"

"Oh, don't be fooled." Ed laughed softly. "I've had my moments too. It took me a long time to find peace. I did all the usual things first. I drank and I experimented with drugs. It was many years before I found peace. You asked me if it was your fault that Dana fell apart and I said yes and no. That's because I'm equally responsible. When she came back for Mum's funeral, it was to find that Father and I had reconciled. That completely threw her. She hardly talked to me through the funeral. She wouldn't even look at Father. Then, at some point during the reception, I noticed she was missing. When I went in search of her, Judy told me she'd gone back to Dublin."

"You could have gone after her," Gus remarked, his voice sharp.

"I could have. I should have. But, like I said, I was a bit of a mess myself."

Gus was silent for a moment and then he came back to sit opposite Ed. "Didn't you ever wonder if your father had something to do with your mother's death? Who knows what he was capable of by then? He'd lost his princess, remember? Maybe he blamed your mother for that."

Ed shook his head. "He didn't do it."

"How can you be so sure? Ed, you have to face the fact that this is a real possibility —"

"Stop!" Ed rubbed his eyes and then looked straight at Gus. "I know exactly what happened, Gus. I was there."

CHAPTER
THIRTY-THREE

"You've got to tell her," Gus said again, kneading the ache in the back of his neck. Dawn was breaking and there was a light frost on the grass. The empty whiskey bottle rolled on the floor between them and Gus felt cold and tired.

Ed shook his head. "I can't. I've finally got her back in my life and I won't lose her again. Besides, she needs me."

"You can't build your future relationship on yet more lies, Ed, you must see that."

"If she knew the truth, she'd never forgive me."

"Have some faith in her. She's wise and kind and generous —"

"If she's so great then why did you walk out on her?" Ed snapped.

"Because when I found out how much of her life she had concealed from me, I didn't believe she could possibly trust, never mind love me."

"It was just her way of trying to deal with things. She closed the door on her past and started again. It was nothing to do with you really."

Gus nodded. "I realize that now."

"It's not too late, you know." Ed smiled at him. "Come on, I need to get some coffee before my head explodes."

"What if Dana's up?"

"She won't surface before ten, especially now she's writing so late at night."

"What's she working on?"

"Ah, well, that's a whole different story," Ed said with a wide yawn. "I'll tell you some of it, but not until I get a dose of caffeine."

When they were sitting at the kitchen table, a pot of coffee between them, Ed told Gus about the new book that his sister was writing. "It really brings home to me how much I underestimated her understanding of what was going on in that house. The poor kid must have been miserable."

"She'll kill you when she realises you've read it," Gus retorted.

"I don't care. I had to find some way to figure out what was going on in her head. I'm going to read all of it — well, as much as she's written — and then I'm going to sit down with her and talk about it all."

Gus raised an eyebrow. "Will you tell her everything?"

Ed sighed. "I can't —"

"You can and you should. It will be okay, Ed," Gus said gently.

"I wish I could believe that."

Gus glanced at his watch, and quickly stood up. "I'd better get out of here before she wakes up." He shrugged into his jacket. "Lord, I would kill for some sleep, but I need to shower and change and get into the office for a meeting. Tom is still on leave." He held his hand out to his brother-in-law. "Thanks for talking to me and for being so candid; it can't have been easy."

Ed waved away his empathy. "Please, at this stage I've had so much therapy I'd tell my life story to the postman."

Gus eyed him speculatively. "Now that I don't believe. Keep in touch, yeah?"

Ed nodded. "I will."

Ed tidied up, went to shower and change and was snoozing in the conservatory when the buzzer on the gate went. After the hysterical phone call Gus had received last night, Ed half expected it to be Walter Grimes, the agent he had heard so much about. With a wide yawn, he went out to the hall and pressed the buzzer. "Hello?"

"Hi. Who's that?" a female voice asked.

He smiled as he recognized the accent. "Who's asking?"

"Ed?"

"Hello, Judy. Come on in." He pressed the button to open the gate and then went to the front door to greet her.

"It's so good to see you again, Judy." He kissed her cheek.

She smiled. "Hello, Ed, you look wonderful. If I wasn't an old married woman with two kids —"

"You're younger than me," he said, and laughed. "And you look stunning. Now come in and have a cup of coffee and tell me how you've been. I hope you have photos of the family."

"I'm a mother," she reminded him. "I always carry photographs. Where's Dana?"

"Still asleep. She was working late last night. Let's leave her for a bit while you and I catch up."

Judy, initially cagey, opened up once Ed made it clear that he was here to help Dana. She told him how they had drifted apart over the years, but that when Gus left it had brought them closer again. "I suppose I was the only one she could really talk to."

Ed winced.

She touched his hand. "I'm sorry. I'm not trying to make you feel bad. You're here now and that's what matters."

"I'm not sure Dana would agree," he said, thinking about the manuscript he'd pored over the previous evening.

"Don't be fooled. She acts tough but she's still a softy behind it all," Judy said affectionately. "Tell me something, why did Gus ask you to come?"

"He was worried."

Judy shook her head irritably. "Then why didn't he just come back? Why the hell did he leave in the first place?"

Ed gazed back at her. "He had his reasons."

Judy's eyes narrowed. "So are you saying Dana did something to make him leave?"

Ed held up his hands. "I'm not saying anything at all, Judy. It's between the two of them."

Judy sighed. "It's strange, I only met the man a couple of times but I thought they made a lovely couple. What do you think of Gus?"

"I like him," Ed admitted.

She sighed. "I wish there was something we could do to help. I thought it would be good for her to get away for a while. I even asked her to come back to Wexford — just for a visit. She was horrified. It's almost as if she's afraid to come back."

"So Mother's funeral was the last time, the only time, she returned?" Ed asked.

Judy nodded. "And that was a disaster."

"Did she talk to you about it?"

Judy stared down into her coffee. "She came down the day of the removal. But she went to the funeral home early because she wanted to spend some time alone with your mum. When she came back, she was in a terrible state. She'd seen you and your father together and it seemed to send her completely over the edge. She wanted to go straight back to Dublin but I persuaded her to stay. I knew that if she didn't attend the funeral she'd regret it for the rest of her life."

"Thank you for that," Ed said quietly.

Judy looked at him. "Can I ask you something?"

He nodded silently but smiled his encouragement. She had a right to ask questions; Judy was practically the only family Dana had had for the last twenty years.

"Why did you forgive him?"

Ed couldn't look at her. "I had no choice, Judy."

"You should have followed her to Dublin," she persisted. "You should have explained."

"I know."

"It's all such a mess. You were both hurting and you could have helped each other. Instead you've spent all of these years apart."

"Oh, Judy. If I could go back and change things I would. I know now how much I hurt her. I'll never forgive myself for that." He buried his face in his hands. Poor Judy probably thought he'd completely lost it. But after reading Dana's account of events, spending the night talking to Gus and now being faced with Judy's reproach, he was an emotional mess. He felt an arm creep around his shoulders and, leaning his head against her, he cried. He had only just pulled away, and was drying his tears with some kitchen towel, when Dana walked in.

"Judy!" Dana was so happy to see her friend that she didn't notice her brother turn away and use the moment to pull himself together. As she greeted her friend, Ed took down a mug and poured her some coffee.

"Why didn't you wake me and let me know that Judy was here?" she said as he set the mug down in front of her.

"Sorry, we were catching up."

"My fault," Judy jumped in. "I've been quizzing him about what he's been up to all these years and how he's managed to stay single."

He shot her a grateful smile. "Love 'em and leave 'em, that's my motto," he quipped.

"How true," Dana mumbled.

Ed's smile faded. "Can you stay the night, Judy? Shall I make up a bed?"

Dana's eyes lit up. "Oh, yes, please stay, Judy. We could even go out."

Judy raised an eyebrow. "I didn't think you'd be able to spare me any time. Not now Ryan's on the scene."

Dana grinned. "He's away on business so you have me all to yourself."

"Then I'd love to stay," Judy announced. "Phil is taking the girls to visit their granny for the weekend, so I am blissfully free until Sunday evening. You know, leaving him to cope alone every so often has had quite a positive effect on him. I actually think he's beginning to appreciate how hard it is looking after the girls full-time."

Dana laughed. "Good. Then you must come up more often. Ed will be delighted. He can take some time off from playing nursemaid. Apparently I'm not a good patient."

"The worst," he confirmed. "But if you think you can put up with her for a couple of days, Judy, I would love to get some work done."

"Looking after this one will be a walk in the park after my two, I assure you. What are you working on?" Judy asked Ed.

"I'm putting together a nature calendar at the moment. It's to be a very stormy weekend so I'd like to get some grey sea scenes if I can."

"Sitting on a pier in the cold and wet — sounds great." Judy shuddered.

He laughed. "I'll leave you two to talk. Great to see you again, Judy."

"And you, Ed."

"You two looked very cosy," Dana remarked.

Judy just gave a casual shrug. "He's nice. He certainly seems to be looking after you very well, and look at this place." She waved an arm around her. "It's gleaming."

"He has been good to me," Dana admitted grudgingly, "except for when he opens his mouth."

"What do you mean?"

"Oh, he's always asking questions; he wants to know all about Gus and why we broke up — it does my head in."

"It's only natural he'd want to hear all about you," Judy reasoned. "You're his only sister."

"So? We haven't had a proper conversation in nearly twenty years; he might as well be a stranger."

"But you can put that right now." Judy leaned forward and took her hand. "This is your chance to get your brother back."

"We'll see."

Judy, knowing it was time to back off, changed the subject. "Anyway, forget about Ed for the moment. Tell me, how are things going with your new boyfriend?"

Dana visibly relaxed. "I'll fill you in on Ryan, if you wash and blow-dry my hair," she bargained.

Judy smiled. "Done."

"And then we could go shopping," Dana continued. "There's this fabulous new shopping centre just minutes away. And after that we could have a nice long, lazy lunch."

"Sounds great," Judy said, pleased to hear her friend so enthusiastic.

"I'm so glad you're here." Dana leaned across to give her friend a clumsy hug. "I didn't think you'd be able to come up again for ages."

"You've given me a taste of the good life, now. I can't stay away!"

"So when is Ryan back?" Judy asked as she combed conditioner through Dana's wet hair.

"Sometime early next week."

"You don't sound too excited."

"I am," Dana protested. "I'm just distracted."

"By?"

"A few things — Gus, for one."

"Oh?"

"He called me to see how I was and he was really nice."

Judy paused. "Oh!"

"It doesn't mean anything," Dana assured her.

Judy turned on the taps and rinsed Dana's hair. "How do you know?"

"I just do. We're past the anger and hate, that's all. Now we're trying to be civilized. I suppose divorce is the next step."

"Is that what you want?" Judy wrapped a towel around Dana's hair and helped her up from where she was kneeling at the side of the bath.

"I don't know." Dana walked through to the bedroom and sat down at her dressing table.

Judy stood behind her and dried her hair. "Liar. You want him back, admit it."

Dana met Judy's eyes in the mirror. "But what I want and what I can have are two entirely different things."

"So Ryan is just a fling, then?"

Dana sighed. "I wish he wasn't. He is everything you could want in a man, and more."

"But you don't love him."

"No."

"So what are you going to do?" Judy asked, fetching the hairdryer and plugging it in.

"I'm going to have a nice afternoon with my best friend."

Over lunch in a sushi bar in the city centre, Judy asked Dana how she was getting on with Ed.

"Better," Dana admitted. "I realize I've been very selfish and self-obsessed. Ed had to deal with our mother's death too. It was a difficult time for us both. I realize now that he never knowingly did anything to hurt me."

Judy smiled. "That must give you a lot of consolation."

"Yes. Yes, it does."

"How long is he staying?"

"He said he'd stay until my cast came off," Dana told her. "So I suppose that means I'll be on my own again in a few days."

Judy looked concerned. "I don't like the idea of that."

"I'll miss him but I'll be fine."

"Really?"

Dana nodded. "Really. Now I've finished the book, the pressure's off. Also, I've been working on something else."

Judy's eyes lit up with curiosity. "That's great. What is it? Another romance?"

"My autobiography," Dana told her.

"No!" Judy's eyes widened.

Dana laughed. "I know. I can't quite believe it either. It's hard going but it's proving quite therapeutic."

"You're not going to publish it, are you?"

"Probably not. Why, do you think it would be a mistake?"

"Well, if it's a completely honest version of events —"

"It is."

"It would rock a lot of boats. How do you think Ed and Gus would react?"

Dana rolled her eyes. "It's hard to say."

"You'd have to tell them everything up front."

"I think it's about time that I did that anyway, don't you?"

Judy reached over to take her hand. "I think you're doing the right thing."

"Well, what's the worst that can happen? I won't see Ed for another twenty years and Gus won't talk to me ever again." Dana smiled but there were tears in her eyes. "That's probably going to happen anyway."

"I'm sure it will all be fine. But whatever happens, I'm not going anywhere. Remember that."

Dana tightened her grip on her friend's hand. "You've no idea how much I'm depending on that, Judy."

CHAPTER
THIRTY-FOUR

Ed woke late in the afternoon, feeling only marginally rested. His dreams had been abstract and distressing, making him toss and turn. He finally woke in a sweat. Going into his bathroom, he splashed cold water on to his chest, neck and face and dried himself roughly with a towel. Throwing on a T-shirt and sweat pants, he went downstairs barefoot to find a note propped up on the kitchen table.

Ed,
Gone out for the day. Don't know when we'll be back.

Dana, Judy x

PS Enjoy your weekend off.

Deciding to take advantage of having the house to himself, Ed made a pot of coffee and some toast. He ate the snack quickly and then took his mug into his sister's office. Taking care not to move anything around on the desk, Ed crouched over Dana's laptop and opened the file. There wasn't a lot left to read and he only hoped he could find the answers he was looking for. His time was running out. Dana's cast was due to come off next week and she would probably want him out as soon as she was able to use her hand again. Still, he felt, despite her protestations, she had grown used to having him around. There were times when she forgot to be angry and actually seemed to enjoy his company.

He searched through the file looking for where he'd left off. Then he settled himself more comfortably and started to read.

After I had fallen into Judy's arms and told her what had happened, my dear friend led me up to her spare bedroom. Making sure I had everything I needed, she hugged me tightly and left. I lay awake long into the night, replaying the image of my brother handling my father with such obvious love and tenderness. I felt excluded, cheated and furious on my mother's behalf. If they were going to make their peace, why hadn't they done it when she was alive? How happy it would have made her. I could imagine the joyous phone call I would have received, begging me to come home to complete the perfect, reunited family. I sat up in bed, shaking, overcome with hate and fury at their joint treachery. My beautiful, kind and wonderful mother had done nothing to deserve the heartache that was her life. And whereas, before, my father had been the focus of all my anger, now I felt an almost equal fury at Ed. If he could find it in his heart to forgive Father, why had he not done it years earlier?

I was angry and hurt but also disappointed. This was not the brother I'd known and loved.

Ed gasped and pushed the chair back from the desk. He could feel the hurt emanating from the screen and he could completely understand it. My God, the poor girl had only been nineteen or twenty when she'd gone through all of this. She must have been distraught. Gus was right; it was time to tell Dana the truth. It wouldn't bring their mother back, but maybe it would help her to understand the rest of it.

He turned back to the screen and skimmed quickly through the rest of the chapter that dealt with the funeral. It was pretty much how he remembered it. They'd had tea and sandwiches afterwards in a hotel near the graveyard, and his father had sat in a chair in the corner and spoken to no one. Ed had gone around the room speaking to neighbours and friends and thanking them for coming, which was something else that had obviously irritated Dana. She had sat in another corner — as far away from her father as possible — flanked by Judy and her family. As soon as the first mourners began to drift away, she had left. When he'd gone in search of her, Judy had fixed him with a glare and informed him that she'd gone back to Dublin.

The chapters that followed were hard to read. They detailed Dana's misery afterwards, and how she had been devastated that her brother had made no attempt to contact her since the funeral. She had dropped out of college and turned to drink for comfort, but she had continued writing. The first book had been completed and she was working on the second. Judy had tried to keep in touch but Dana shut her out too, pleading heavy coursework and study. But despite everything, Dana met her deadline, and received what would have been in those days a generous sum. This she used to put a deposit on a small flat nearer the university and, after a lot of grovelling, she was allowed to return and complete her degree.

Ed realized he was on the last page, although it obviously wasn't the end of the story.

Shortly after the first anniversary of my mother's death, my first book, Silent Rapture, was published in the US. I had received a dozen complimentary copies in the post, and I sat in my flat surrounded by them. It should have been a very special moment but I felt nothing. Other than Judy, no one knew about my writing. I sent her a copy of the book but I still avoided her calls. I was too raw to talk. The only way to get through this was to put everything behind me. It was my only chance of survival.

I hoped that somehow, somewhere, my mother knew of my success. I hoped she'd be proud of me. I knew she'd forgive me for leaving Wexford behind. She had been the one to urge me to leave in the first place and make a new life. And that's what I planned to do. And yet, I would have loved to pick up the phone to my brother and tell him my news. Despite everything, I knew in my heart Ed would be pleased for me, and proud. But I couldn't call him, not now. When I thought of him, I thought of my father. Ed had changed sides and that hurt too much. In a way, I wished he'd never come back.

Ed sat staring at the screen for some time. Finally, realizing that it was late and that Dana could arrive back at any moment, he closed the laptop and took his empty mug out to the kitchen. He paced the room feeling tired and drained, and yet, he knew, sleep was not an option. His brain was full of pain and memories and he needed to do something that would require his full concentration and distract him totally. Going in search of his camera bag, he put on a heavy jacket and went out into the sanctuary of the garden.

Ian and Sylvie sat in the pub on Sunday afternoon eating a late lunch. While Ian was wolfing down his food, Sylvie was playing with her cottage pie.

"I thought we'd agreed that you'd start eating properly?" Ian said, not taking his eyes off the flat screen on the wall that was showing the Sunday game.

Sylvie rolled her eyes. "I do eat properly, I'm just not a fan of stodge."

"Good plain home cooking."

"Yeah, straight off a production line. If anyone eats badly in this relationship, it's you. Have you any idea of the amount of E numbers you must consume?"

He turned to look at her. "What is wrong, Sylvie? Are you worried that you're going to lose your job?"

She nodded, her face glum. "It's not a good time for me to be out of work. Mum's not been well lately and it's looking more and more likely that Dad will need another operation."

"Then you need to do something new and I know just the thing."

"Oh?" Sylvie eyed him doubtfully. Ian was always full of ideas and optimism, but that wasn't enough to put food on the table.

"You can be a virtual PA."

"A what?"

"It's basically what you're currently doing for Dana," he explained, "but instead of having a boss, you just have lots of clients. A lot of people that work from home need someone to do their admin work, take their calls, update their sites, that sort of thing. They can't afford to hire full-time employees and, even if they could, they wouldn't have anywhere to put them. So instead they rent the services of a virtual PA by the hour or for a specific job. I've already checked it out online. There are people doing it in the UK, and already a couple of companies here in Ireland. All you need to do is set up a seriously professional website and you're in business."

"It's that simple?"

He nodded. "Pretty much. And there's nothing to stop you doing it straight away. Even if Dana wants to keep you on, she's not going to have much for you to do for a while, is she?"

"No, but she always pays me anyway."

"Better again. You get paid twice and work the hours that suit you. And by the way, I'd like to be your first customer."

She laughed. "We're in the same room, there's nothing virtual about that."

"No, but I could use some help," he said seriously. "I'm thinking of expanding the business and, to do that, I need to portray a professional image."

"I don't need charity," she warned him.

"I had hoped we'd got past comments like that," he said, looking hurt. "You know how I feel about you, Sylvie, but that's a completely different matter. I need a PA and I'd prefer to work with someone I know and trust than give my hard-earned euros to a stranger who might be crap."

She smiled and leaned over to kiss his cheek. "I'm sorry, Ian. Sometimes I don't know why you put up with me."

He smiled. "I think you do. Now, let's go."

"Where?"

"To see Dana."

"What!"

"You won't be able to relax until you know where you stand." He stood up and held out his hand. "Coming?"

She hesitated for a moment then put her hand in his. "Coming."

Ed and Dana had just waved Judy off and retreated to the kitchen to clear up after their extended lunch, when the buzzer went.

"She must have forgotten something. I'll go," Dana said, and she hurried back out into the hall. She picked up the receiver and pressed the buzzer at the same time. "What did you forget, you silly woman?"

"Dana?"

"Sylvie? Come on in." Dana stuck her head back into the kitchen to explain to Ed.

"The things you do to get out of the washing-up," he drawled.

She smiled and went back outside to open the hall door. She had no idea what Sylvie and Ian were doing here but she was grateful for the interruption. It had been a lovely weekend, but she felt slightly uncomfortable being alone again with her brother. There was so much left unsaid between them.

She smiled as Ian parked the car and the two of them got out. "This is a nice surprise." She reached up to kiss Ian's cheek and then gave Sylvie an impulsive hug.

Sylvie looked slightly shell-shocked. "Hi."

"How are you, Dana?" Ian asked politely.

"Good," she said and led them towards the kitchen. "Come and meet my brother."

"Sorry for coming on a Sunday —" Sylvie started.

"No problem." Dana pushed open the kitchen door. "Ed, meet my PA, Sylvie Parker, and publicity guru, Ian Wilson."

Ed wiped his hands on a tea towel and came forward, smiling, to shake their hands. "Nice to meet you. Drink?"

Sylvie shook her head. "Oh, no, we don't want to interrupt —"

"You're not interrupting anything. We've just finished lunch and now Ed is going outside to photograph clouds and rain, or something equally depressing."

Ed smiled. "So, what will it be? Wine? beer?"

"Wine, please."

"Beer for me, thanks," Ian said. "So you've been minding the patient, then. How is the arm, Dana?"

"Much better, thanks. I'm getting the cast off on Tuesday."

"That's great news," Sylvie said.

When Ed had got the drinks, Dana led them through to the conservatory. After she'd settled herself in an armchair, she looked at them expectantly. "So, what did you want to talk about?"

Ian and Sylvie exchanged glances and then he looked back at Dana. "Sylvie is a bit concerned about her job."

"Ah." Dana nodded. "I see."

"I'm sorry, Dana," Sylvie added. "I know this hasn't been an easy time and you have enough on your plate. It's just that, well —"

"I completely understand," Dana assured her. "I don't have all the answers at the moment. I haven't heard from Wally yet, but I don't think Gretta will accept this book."

"I'm sure Walter could buy you some more time," Ian told her. "If anyone can, he can."

Dana shook her head. "It wouldn't make any difference, I just can't do it. I don't want to."

"But you've always wanted to be published in Ireland," Sylvie said.

Dana shrugged. "Let's say my priorities have changed slightly over the last few months."

There was a moment's silence as her two visitors absorbed this.

"So are you going to give up writing completely?" Sylvie asked faintly.

"I don't think so." Dana smiled. "I don't think I could even if I wanted to. I might try something different, though."

Sylvie's eyes lit up. "A different genre?"

"Maybe, or possibly even non-fiction."

"So do you think you'll still need a PA?" Sylvie asked in a small voice.

Dana knew she probably didn't, but understood now how important this job was to Sylvie. "I should think so," she said vaguely. "Even if I don't write any more books for Peyton Publishing, I'm still going to have to maintain the website for the existing fan base. And there'll still be the post to open and the VAT forms to complete. How would I manage without you?"

"But still flexible hours?" Ian asked.

"Yes, I suppose so. Why?"

Ian shot Sylvie a look and when she gave him the nod, he told Dana about his idea.

"I think that's a marvellous idea," Dana said, when he'd finished. Her eyes twinkled as she looked from one to the other. "And I think you two will make a great team in every way."

"We're just dating," Sylvie said firmly.

Ian grinned. "She's mad about me, really."

Sylvie rolled her eyes and stood up. "We should go. Thank you so much, Dana."

"For nothing. And I'm sorry I have been so difficult to work with lately —"

"Forget it," Sylvie said immediately.

Dana smiled. "So, let's put the past behind us and make a fresh start tomorrow. Is that okay?"

"Great." The girl nodded happily.

"You probably won't need my services, though, will you?" Ian said as they walked to the door.

"Probably not in the immediate future," Dana agreed. "The last thing I want now is publicity. But if or when that changes, you'll be the first person I call."

After she'd waved the two of them off, Dana went back out to the conservatory and sat down. The sky was already darkening and she could barely see the silhouette of her brother at work in the garden, oblivious to the wind and rain that lashed him. Dana closed her eyes and allowed herself to drift off.

She was asleep only a few minutes when the buzzer went again, pulling her back to consciousness. Who the hell could it be now? Dana dragged herself out of the chair, went out into the hall and lifted the handset. "Hello?"

"Hello, darling. Open this bloody gate, will you? And make me a G & T. I'm gagging for a drink."

CHAPTER
THIRTY-FIVE

Dana pressed the button and went to open the door. Wally was already stepping out of the taxi.

She held out her arms to him and smiled. "Hello, Wally. This is a nice surprise."

He looked at her. "You may not think that after you've heard what I've come to say."

"You're always welcome, no matter what." She pulled him inside and closed the door. "Now let's go and get you that drink."

"You know why I'm here, then?" Walter said, following her to the kitchen.

"I think I can guess." Dana got the drinks, fetched ice from the freezer and took a lemon from the fridge. "I'm afraid you'll have to serve yourself. My brother usually acts as waiter, but he's working at the moment."

"How is the arm?" Walter asked, as he halved and sliced the lemon.

"Fine." She watched as he made his drink and then led him back across the hall to the conservatory.

"Aren't you drinking?"

"No, I've given up."

"No!"

"No," she agreed, grinning. "There's a bottle of wine already open."

"Well, I'm glad someone can still laugh in the face of total disaster," he said dramatically, throwing himself down on the sofa.

"So you agree it's a disaster, then?"

"Let's say, this novel is not your best."

"Very sensitively put."

"I'm sorry, darling. I really thought we could rescue it. I wasn't listening to you, was I?"

Dana shrugged. "You were just doing your job. I'm sorry I let you down."

He waved away the apology. "Don't worry about me. But I have to figure out what I'm going to tell Gretta."

"Yes. She won't be impressed, will she?"

"No, but Gretta's no fool. I'm sure she has a Plan B."

"True."

"Still, we need to handle this carefully. She's not a woman we should make an enemy of."

"No." Dana agreed. Gretta could turn nasty, and life was difficult enough at the moment. "So, what do you think we should do?"

"That depends on you, my darling. Do you want to sign a new contract with Peyton Publishing?"

Dana thought for a second. Although her biography was painful to write, she was enjoying the fact that it was real and that there wasn't a heaving bosom or a chiselled jaw in sight. She looked up at him, her face solemn. "No, I'm finished with all that."

"Phew! I can't believe it." Walter dabbed his eyes. "I really thought you'd keep going until you were six feet under."

She smiled, feeling a little tearful herself. "Me too."

He cleared his throat and then he was all business again. "Very well then, here's the plan. I have a new author that I think Gretta might be interested in. I wasn't thinking of pitching her at Peyton Publishing, but it might be the politically correct thing to do. Hopefully it will help Gretta get over the shock of losing you."

"You don't think she'll try to sue me, do you?"

He shrugged. "Hard to know. She might settle for taking the book as is."

She frowned. "I don't mind that, but I don't want it used to launch Passion. I want my first book published here to be something completely different."

"Well, I'm relieved to hear that you do plan to continue writing." He smiled.

"I thought I mightn't at the beginning," she admitted. "But I'm over that now."

He looked at her through narrowed eyes. "You're working on something, aren't you?"

She nodded. "I don't think I'll ever do anything with it, though."

"Let me be the judge of that," he said, sitting forward and watching her with interest.

Her eyes met his. "It's my autobiography."

"Oh!" His eyes widened. "I see. Commercial or candid?"

She winced. "Very candid."

"Oh!"

"Stop saying 'oh'. I'm only writing it for me. I'll probably never show it to anyone."

"That would be a great shame," he said sadly.

"But if I do decide to do anything with it, you'll be the first to know," she promised.

"I'll hold you to that. So why are you writing it? Is it therapy?"

She nodded. "In a way."

"And has it worked?"

"I'm getting there."

He patted her hand. "You've always been a fighter, Dana. I'm glad that hasn't changed."

"I don't know about that. I've felt a total loser these last few months."

"Don't talk like that," Walter chided. "You've been to hell and back again. Losing the love of your life isn't easy for anyone."

Dana raised an eyebrow. "How do you know he was the love of my life?"

He smiled. "I've seen you together, remember?"

"He obviously didn't love me as much as either of us thought," she said, and sighed.

His smile faltered. "By the way, I have a confession to make."

"Go on."

"I phoned him the other night."

She sat upright. "Who? Gus?"

He nodded sheepishly. "I was a bit upset after I'd finished *The Mile High Club*, and very slightly

385

inebriated. So I decided to call him and tell him exactly what I thought of him."

Dana's lips twitched. "What did he say?"

"I don't think I gave him a chance to say anything. When he finally got a word in edgeways he just told me I was pissed and hung up. I'm sorry. Not very professional of me, was it?"

"You were acting like a friend and I love you for it," she told him. "Anyway he deserved it."

Walter leaned over to squeeze her good hand. "I'm so glad you're okay again."

"You think I'm okay?" She laughed, though her eyes were bright with tears.

"I think you're marvellous, darling. I'm very proud of you."

"Proud? Of what? I thought you would kill me when you read that book."

"Me too," he admitted, with a smile. "But I can see that you've come to a crossroads and nothing I can do or say is going to change that. I hope, though, that when you do produce your next masterpiece, you'll bring it to me."

Dana leaned over to kiss his cheek. "I wouldn't dream of going to anyone else."

"Oh, don't, you'll start me off." He pulled out a handkerchief and blew his nose. "We need more drinks." He filled her glass and then poured wine into his tumbler.

"Wally, you can have a wine glass," she said with a laugh.

"Don't worry, darling. Once it's alcoholic, I'd drink it out of a chipped mug!"

"It's absolutely freezing out there." Ed burst in through the french windows and stopped short when he saw Walter. "Oh, I'm sorry, Dana. I didn't know you had company."

"Ed, this is Walter Grimes, my agent and dear, dear friend."

Wally reached out a hand and smiled. "It's a pleasure to meet you."

Ed shook it warmly. "And you. I've heard so much about you."

Walter groaned dramatically. "I deny it all!"

Ed laughed. "It was all good, I promise."

"Have a glass of wine," Dana offered, amused to see that her agent was blushing.

Ed shook his head. "I won't, thanks. I'm not done yet. I only came in for some more film."

"A drink would warm you up," Walter pointed out.

Ed smiled. "You're right but if I stop for a drink, I'll lose the light."

"Oh. Pity."

"Nice to meet you, though." Ed held out his hand once more.

Walter grasped it. "And you."

Dana watched them both, mesmerized. Walter looked like a lovesick teenager. And Ed — Ed wasn't much better. How on earth had she not seen it before? How had she been so blind?

She talked on with Walter until they finished their drinks, and then she faked a yawn. "Oh, sorry, Wally.

It's just that it's been a very long day. I'm exhausted. Can we continue in the morning?"

"Of course, my darling."

"I'll call for a taxi." She went out to the hall to make the call and heaved a sigh of relief when she was told there was a car available immediately. She went back in to Walter. "That's lucky. There's a car around the corner."

He took her arm and they went out into the hall together. "I tell you what, darling. Why don't I take you and Ed to lunch tomorrow?" he suggested.

"Oh, I'm not sure —"

"Oh, go on. This is the end of an era. It will be fun."

Dana looked into his eyes and smiled. "Okay, then. But I'm not sure what Ed's plans are. What time were you thinking of?"

"Whenever," he said quickly. "You let me know what suits, and where. We could go to that Thai restaurant you took me to once. Or maybe Ed wouldn't like Thai —"

"I'll call you in the morning," Dana broke in, and was relieved when the buzzer went.

Walter gave a small, embarrassed smile. "Okay, then."

He opened the door and turned to her once more. "Goodnight, my darling."

She returned his kiss. "Goodnight, Wally. And thank you, for everything."

He hugged her, tears in his eyes. "It's been a pleasure — all of it. Talk to you tomorrow."

★ ★ ★

When he had gone, Dana walked back into the conservatory and sat down to wait for Ed. It was nearly an hour before he came in, and then he stopped and smiled when he saw her sitting there.

"Are you okay? Only, you don't have a glass in your hand." He grinned, his teeth shining white in the darkness.

Dana reached out a hand and switched on the lamp. "It's true, isn't it?"

His smile faded. "What?"

"I saw the way Walter looked at you. And I saw the way you looked at him. You're gay."

Ed's smile was nervous as he held up his hands. "Guilty. It didn't really come as that much of a surprise, did it?"

"It did," she told him, nodding her head. "I'm very dense, aren't I? It honestly never occurred to me."

Ed sat down in Wally's seat. "Sadly it occurred to our father long before even I realized it."

Dana put a hand to her mouth as realization dawned.

"Oh my God! Is that what it was all about? He treated you that way because you were gay?"

"I'm afraid so. He did everything he could to knock it out of me — literally. He even dragged me down to Father Flynn and made me confess. He asked him what saint we should pray to in order to turn me back to normal. If he caught me even looking at another boy he dragged me out to the shed and took the belt to me."

"Oh, Ed, I'm so sorry. I had no idea. Did Mum know that was the reason he treated you so badly?"

He frowned. "I'm not sure. We never talked about it. I'm not sure they ever did either — too disgusting to put into words. When Dad was angry or drunk, though, he'd refer to me as a perverted little bugger."

"When did you know?" she asked, tears rolling down her face unheeded.

"That I was gay?" Ed smiled. "I suppose it was a gradual process. I wasn't interested in the porn magazines that were passed around under the desks in the classroom. When I went to the school disco, I felt nothing for the girls I danced with. But," he grinned, "I had a young, handsome history teacher and every time he looked at me, or asked me a question, my mouth went dry and my heart skipped a beat."

She laughed softly. "For me it was my English teacher, but it was a guy."

"And that's why you were the princess. You loved writing stories. You were pretty and clever. And, most important, you were straight. You were perfect in every way."

"Why didn't you tell me?" she said reproachfully. "You must have known that it wouldn't have mattered."

Ed moved over to sit next to her. "Bless you, but it wasn't that straightforward. Dad made me feel dirty and ashamed. I thought that everyone would think the way he did. The revulsion in his eyes when he looked at me hurt so much, I couldn't have borne it if you'd looked at me the same way."

"You know I wouldn't have done that," Dana exclaimed. "What happened the day you left?"

He sighed. "I had been sitting at the kitchen table doing my Latin homework and Mum was cooking. He came in and looked over my shoulder, and saw that I'd doodled on the side of the page. He went mad. You know what he was like: didn't I know the price of text books? Had I no respect for anything?" Ed rolled his eyes. "Anyway he took it up in his hands and started to leaf through it, and a piece of paper fell out. It was a sweet, innocent little love note from a boy in my class. Dad went ballistic, calling me all of the names under the sun. Then he started on Mother, saying it was her fault that I was the way I was. She'd turned me into a nancy-boy, kept me too close to her when I should have been out riding my bike or playing Gaelic football." Ed's expression glazed over as he remembered. "He was only inches from her, screaming into her face. I could see his spittle on her cheek." He shrugged. "That was it. I flipped. I don't remember consciously thinking about what I was doing, I just grabbed the knife and, well, you witnessed the rest."

"I wish I'd known," Dana said sadly. "I could have helped you. At least you would have had someone to talk to."

"You were fourteen, Dana, and such a little innocent. How could I have explained to you that your only brother was a pervert?"

"Will you stop using that word?" she cried.

"Sorry, it's his word, not mine. And I grew to believe it. I was nearly twenty before I finally allowed myself to look at men romantically. And when I did, I always went for the wrong type."

"But you told me that there had been someone special," she said, remembering their conversation the day they went to see Ashling and her baby.

Ed's smile was sad. "I met a lovely guy soon after Dad died. But I was completely screwed up and not ready for a serious relationship. I kept pushing him away. Finally he left."

"Oh, Ed."

He smiled. "I'm okay, Dana. Especially now I've got you."

She sighed. "It makes sense now, why you left. But I can't begin to understand how you could forgive him. I saw the two of you arriving at the funeral home together and you were so close. Then I watched you the next day, the perfect son, his aide, his spokesman."

Tears filled her eyes and her voice shook. "I thought I'd lost my mind. That I had imagined the horrible way he'd treated you. I have to tell you, Ed, that day I hated you nearly as much as I hated him."

"There are things you don't know." Ed looked into her eyes.

"There can't possibly be more," she said with a nervous laugh. But her smile faded as she saw his solemn expression. "My God, there is, isn't there?"

CHAPTER
THIRTY-SIX

Ed stood up. "I'll get us more drinks."

"I don't want a bloody drink," she cried.

"Well, I do," he retorted and left the room.

When he returned, Dana watched him with anxious eyes as he poured the wine and sat back in his chair.

He sat in silence for a moment and then looked up into her eyes. "Mum was still alive when I came home." Dana opened her mouth but he held up his hand. "Let me explain, okay?"

She nodded silently.

"All the time that I was away, I kept in touch with my old school friend, Keith. I suppose I was always afraid that one day Dad might actually hurt Mum. Keith always had a contact number for me, and he promised to call if he was ever concerned. At the beginning everything seemed to work exactly as I had hoped. He saw you coming and going to school and Father going out for his walks. Later, after you left, his mother met ours at the shops and reported that she was quiet but seemed fine. Then a few days before Mum died, Keith phoned me to say that his mum hadn't seen her for a while. She'd asked around and soon realized that it had been weeks since Mum had been seen out. That scared me so I decided I had to come home."

Dana was on the edge of her seat now, watching him anxiously.

He sighed. "My instincts were right but not in the way I'd imagined. Dad hadn't hurt Mum. She was sick, Dana."

"What was wrong?" Dana whispered.

"They weren't sure. She was due to go in for tests the following week. But she had a bad cough, shortness of breath and some chest pain. The GP suspected heart problems."

Dana shook her head. "But she fell down the stairs."

"I'm not finished," he said. "I asked Dad if he had contacted you, but he said he was waiting for the results of the tests. Mum didn't want him to worry you. I didn't talk much with him at all other than that. I sat with Mum and he left us alone. She wasn't well. Her breathing was quite laboured and she looked frail. I told her all the things I'd done, the places I'd been. She seemed happy I was there. She drifted in and out of sleep and sometimes seemed disorientated when she woke. At one point, I'm not sure she even knew who I was."

Dana's heart went out to him as his eyes filled up. "She hadn't seen you for over three years and if she wasn't well . . ."

He nodded. "I know. So I asked her about you — where you were, what you were doing. She started to cry and said that Father had sent you away. I couldn't make much sense of what she said at first, but then she became quite lucid. She told me about your abortion."

Dana opened her mouth to say something, but found she couldn't. "I didn't think you knew," she finally whispered.

"Keith didn't know anything about it. Dad kept it very quiet. But, then, he was good at that." Ed looked at his sister. "I'm so sorry you had to go through that, Dana. I'm so sorry I wasn't here to help."

"Was Mum ashamed of me?" Dana asked, her voice shaking.

"No! No, she was just heartbroken for you, and furious with Dad. She said he was more worried about his image, and what people would say, than what his daughter was going through. She told me how he sent you away to that boarding school and found ways to stop you coming home in the holidays. She felt guilty that she'd let him send you away, but at the same time she'd known you might be better off."

"I missed her so much." Dana started to cry, great big heaving sobs. "She was the only reason I hadn't thrown myself under a train."

"Dana!"

"It's true. I thought I'd go out of my mind when I came home from London. Putting one foot in front of the other was such an effort. She was my only reason to live. And then he sent me away. I often thought about ending it all. Then I'd think of her and I knew I couldn't."

Dana had to stop, her tears choking her. After her sobs had subsided, Ed handed her a tissue. "Are you okay?"

"Yeah."

"She loved you so much, Dana. She told me about the few weeks you had together in Dublin. She enjoyed every minute of that."

Dana smiled through her tears. "That was just before I started university. She spent a fortune on me. I said Dad would go mad but she didn't care. It was a very special time. It really made me realize — made us both realize — how little time we'd ever had alone together."

"That's sad."

She nodded, unable to speak.

He looked down into her face. "Will you tell me about what happened in London?"

"Later. But I want you to finish your story first."

He hesitated. "I'm afraid that by the time I've finished, you'll never want to talk to me again."

Dana stared at him, wiping her tears away with her hand. "You have to tell me, Ed."

"Okay then. Mum fell asleep again and I went to find Dad. I was furious, really angry. It was like that moment in the kitchen all over again. I couldn't believe that he'd even managed to hurt you, his princess. He was in the hall talking on the phone to Father Flynn when I found him. He was arranging for Mum to receive the Sacrament of the Sick. I knew she wouldn't want that and I took the phone out of his hand, and told the priest his services would not be required."

Dana stared at him, her eyes wide with shock. "You didn't!"

"I did! Dad was livid. He started to hurl abuse at me — it felt just like old times. I told him he was a hypocritical, evil and pathetic old man. I told him he'd managed to hurt every member of his family, even you." Ed shook his head. "He went berserk."

"So what happened then?" Dana prompted when Ed stopped.

He stared into space. "We kept roaring and shouting at each other and the next thing I knew, Mum was at the top of the stairs, screaming at us to stop. Father told her to shut up and stay out of it. And —" he swallowed and looked at Dana — "I hit him. It was like everything happened in slow motion after that. Father fell back against the wall and Mum screamed and stepped forward. Then she was falling down the stairs. I rushed forward to catch her, but I was too late. I turned her over and I knew, instantly, that she was dead."

"Oh my God," Dana gasped and put her hand to her mouth.

"So you see, Dana. I killed her."

"No!" She shook her head. "It was an accident."

"If I hadn't been there, it wouldn't have happened," Ed insisted. "If I hadn't antagonized him, she wouldn't have come to the top of the stairs."

"If, if, if . . ." Dana shook her head impatiently. "It was an accident." Dana poured him more wine and pressed the glass into his hand. "Have a drink."

He did, and she filled her own glass and drank. "What happened then?"

"It was like Father went on to automatic pilot. He called an ambulance, although he knew as well as I did that it was too late. And he called the priest, of course. I was a mess at this stage and he dragged me into his study and sat me down. He told me to tell anyone who asked that we were in the kitchen when we heard Mum cry out. That we rushed out to find her at the bottom of the stairs, dead. I said no, we should tell the truth. Dad said if *he* told the truth, I'd end up in jail. He said it was my fault and that if I had any decent bone in my body I'd go along with his story for Mum's sake. He said this was my opportunity to do the right thing. To make up for all the hurt I'd caused both him and my mother over the years. And he asked me what I thought it would do to you if you learned that your brother killed your mother."

"My God, he was manipulating you even then," Dana fumed. "You didn't kill her, Ed! Please tell me you know that?"

He smiled slightly. "Most days I do. But then I was a mess, Dana. I was shaking, I couldn't string two words together. I didn't know what to do or what to think. So, God help me, I did and said exactly what Dad told me to."

They sat in silence for a while, both engrossed in their own private thoughts until finally Dana asked him the question that she had wanted to ask since the first day he'd got here. "Why didn't you follow me to Dublin?" she asked, her voice trembling. "Or, at least, pick up the phone?"

He sighed. "I was in a terrible state, Dana. I did what he asked: helped with the arrangements, talked to the neighbours, acted like the perfect son. He said it was about time I did. He told me I had to be a man, and keep a grip on my emotions until the funeral was over.

He said if I didn't, I might let something slip and I'd end up in a cell. And once the funeral was all over, he told me to get out and never come back."

"And I thought you had reconciled and put the past behind you." Dana shook her head.

"I had to let you think that. If you realized I still hated him, you'd have talked to me and I knew I'd have ended up telling you everything. Dad had convinced me that you'd be devastated if you knew what I'd done." He shrugged. "So I did what he told me to do. And I hoped maybe you would find comfort in the fact that Dad and I had managed to bury the past."

She shot him an incredulous look. "I would only find comfort if you managed to bury him!"

"I did that too," he reminded her. "Eventually."

"So why did you go back?"

"Father Flynn had taken me aside at Mum's funeral to tell me that Dad was sick too. I talked to the doctor and he confirmed that Father had prostate cancer and was refusing treatment. So I gave Father Flynn my phone number and asked him to let me know when Dad was near the end. I felt, rightly or wrongly, Mum would want one of us to be with him. Despite everything, I do believe she loved him."

Dana nodded in agreement. "Yes. It didn't seem to matter what he did, she wouldn't leave."

"Oh, it mattered all right," Ed retorted. "But she was his wife and had promised to stay with him no matter what. And that's what she did."

There was another lengthy silence and then Dana spoke again. "You said you asked Father Flynn to call you when Dad got sick. But you weren't with him when he died — were you?"

Ed went over to the window and stared out into the darkness.

"No. I was with him a few days earlier. I meant to go back but he went quicker than we'd expected." He turned to look at her. "Why didn't you come to the funeral?"

"I couldn't go and pretend a grief I didn't feel. To be honest, I didn't trust myself not to dance on his grave."

"I was going to come and see you then," he admitted.

Dana sat forward on her chair, her eyes searching his face. "Why didn't you?"

He shrugged. "I still felt so guilty about Mum. I didn't think I'd be able to look you in the eye without blurting out the truth. And I didn't want to do that. You'd had enough pain in your life. And, by then, you were a published author." He smiled. "You'd become Dana De Lacey. Nice touch, by the way. Mum would be so proud that you'd taken her name."

"I certainly couldn't use his." Dana shivered. "Oh, Ed. We've wasted so much time."

"I know. If it wasn't for Gus, we might never have found each other again."

Dana thought about her husband's role in all of this and wondered what had led him to the truth. "Do you know why he left me?" she asked suddenly.

Ed looked at her and nodded. "He found your letters."

Dana froze. "Letters?" she said faintly.

400

"The ones you wrote to us all and never sent. I wish you had, Dana," he said with feeling.

"They weren't real letters," Dana explained. "I never intended sending them anywhere. I was supposed to destroy them. They were a part of my therapy."

"Therapy?"

"After Mum died, I was in a bad way too," she told him. "Walter persuaded me to talk to someone."

"Good for Walter," Ed murmured.

"Dr Corcoran said I should write to you and Dad and tell you exactly how I felt. He said I didn't need to send the letters, but that the act of writing it all down would be therapeutic in itself. So I did."

"And you wrote to someone else too," Ed reminded her. "Your son. Gus read it and thought you had a child stashed somewhere that you hadn't told him about. That's why he left, Dana. He couldn't believe that you'd kept such a huge secret from him."

She stared at him. "When did he tell you all this?"

"He contacted me soon after he left you. Walter told him where he'd find me."

Dana nodded. Of course, Wally had been around when her Father died. He had tried to persuade her to attend the funeral — he was concerned about bad publicity — and when she refused to go, he'd packed her off to the States. Then he'd put a death notice in all the papers and issued a press release saying that, despite their estrangement, Dana was very upset to hear of the death of her father. She was currently in the US promoting her new book.

"Dana?"

She looked up. Ed was looking at her.

"Sorry. So you told Gus about the abortion," she whispered.

"Yes. I'm sorry if I was wrong. But he was imagining all sorts of things. I thought it was better that he knew the truth."

Dana shook her head. "Why didn't he just ask me? Why didn't he tell me he'd found the letters? Ask me about the baby? Why would he talk to you, a total stranger, and not talk to me, his wife?"

"You'll have to ask him that, Dana. And I think you should. But, remember, if it wasn't for him, we wouldn't be here together now."

She stared at her brother. "So I'm supposed to be grateful to him?"

He shrugged and smiled. "I am."

Ed retired to bed soon after, and Dana went into her office. She stared at her screen, her fingers poised over the keys, but the words wouldn't come. Maybe there was nothing left to write. She had reached the point in her story where she was getting her life together. She had started her sessions with Dr Corcoran. She had almost finished her third novel. And Walter was in the process of negotiating a bigger, better deal for her next three books. The future was bright. Her world was complete. Her new life was established. Dana O'Carroll was dead. Long live Dana De Lacey.

And, Dana realized, that had been her mistake. She couldn't pretend the past hadn't happened. A day didn't go by that she didn't grieve for her aborted child.

Her mother was always with her, and she was often haunted by the terrible things her brother had endured at the hands of their father. And if she'd told her husband, he would have listened. If she'd explained, he would have understood. If she'd told him how her heart ached for her baby, he would have held her while she cried. And, she knew with certainty, he would have made sure that she had reconciled with her brother years ago. If only she'd given Gus the chance. It was too late now, she knew. There was no going back. But, at the very least, Dana owed her husband an explanation.

CHAPTER
THIRTY-SEVEN

The next day, Dana and Ed had lunch with Walter. She watched, fascinated, as the two men talked. There was an obvious, if conservative, attraction on both sides. Wally was fifty-two — twelve years Ed's senior — but Dana didn't think that would matter. They were both damaged people who would be sensitive to each other's background. She had thought it unbearably sad that Ed had never had a close relationship in all his adult life. It was such a waste. He had been a lovely boy and, despite everything, he'd turned into a wonderful man. It was a pity she was only just finding that out.

As the wine loosened their tongues and inhibitions, Dana and Ed told Walter some of their story.

"It's very sad," he said. "And, forgive me, but I still think you should publish it. The book would fly out of the shops."

Dana shot her brother a nervous look and noted the lack of surprise on his face. "Ed?"

"Yes?"

"You knew I was writing my biography, didn't you?" she exclaimed. "Did Judy tell you?"

"Of course not. I'm sorry, Dana, but I've been reading it," Ed admitted.

404

"What?" Dana dropped her knife and fork with a clatter.

"I'm sorry," he said again. "But I discovered it by accident. And when you wouldn't talk to me, I felt it was the only way I'd find out what was going on in your head."

"I can't believe this," Dana mumbled.

"He only did it because he cares," Walter pointed out.

"I know that." She shot her brother an anxious look. "So, what did you think?"

"I thought it was very moving and it made me realize that leaving probably wasn't for the best after all."

She shook her head. "No, Ed. Now I know the full extent of what Dad put you through, I'm glad you left. And it probably would have been better if you hadn't come back."

"Enough of this", Ed said. "There's no point in either of us beating ourselves up. We need to put the past behind us and be glad that we've found each other again."

"But publishing the truth might help too," Wally interjected.

"Walter." Dana glared.

He shrugged, unrepentant. "Once an agent, always an agent."

"It is quite a read," Ed acknowledged. "And it's a shame to see all your hard work go to waste."

"It wasn't wasted," Dana assured him. "It's helped me enormously. And I think it will help Gus too."

Ed looked at her. "You're going to let him read it?"

She nodded. "It's only fair."

"I'm glad."

"Of course, you could turn it into a novel," Walter mused. "If you change a few details here and there, no one would be any the wiser."

"Wally, shut up and drink your wine," Dana said, smiling.

Her phone rang and she excused herself when she saw the name that flashed up. "Sorry, I should take this."

"Lover boy," Ed told Walter. "He's always calling."

Dana rolled her eyes and walked out of the restaurant. "Hi, Ryan."

"Hi, Dana. How are you?"

She sighed as she thought of all the events of the last forty-eight hours. "Tired."

"Does that mean I can't take you out tonight?"

"You're home?"

"Just landed. I've missed you."

Dana closed her eyes at the tenderness in his voice. "Was it a good trip?"

"You were supposed to say, 'I've missed you too.'"

She groaned inwardly. "Of course I have."

"So, have dinner with me."

"Could we make it tomorrow evening instead?" Dana asked. "It's just that I've had a hectic few days and tomorrow morning I'm going to the hospital to get the cast off."

"Excellent. We can celebrate. Shall we say eight?"

"Perfect."

"Are you okay, Dana?"

"Yes," she reassured him. "Like I said, I'm just tired."

"I hope you haven't been out gallivanting with other men," he said lightly.

"No, I've just had lots of visitors. I'll fill you in when I see you."

"I'll look forward to it. Till tomorrow."

"Bye, Ryan."

Dana turned to go back into the restaurant, but stopped when she caught sight of Wally and Ed through the window. Their heads were close together and they were completely engrossed. She knew that she was probably the topic of conversation, but she didn't mind. It was nice to see these two wonderful men enjoying each other's company. It was probably too much to hope that it would grow into anything more. Living in two different countries wasn't an ideal way to start a new romance. But it would be nice even if they were just to become friends. Dana could foresee lots more lunches and dinners in the future, and the thought warmed her heart. It would be like being part of a proper family. She turned and strolled down the street. There was no harm giving them a little more time alone. And she needed some of that too. There was so much to take on board.

In one weekend, she'd had a lifetime's questions answered. Gus deserved the same. She understood now why he'd behaved as he had. Even though he was the only man she'd ever really loved, she'd always held something back. She'd shown him just one side of her, and hadn't even realized she was doing it. She'd destroyed their marriage single-handedly and she had to admit that. She didn't kid herself that doing so would bring him back. Apart from the fact that Gus had another woman, Dana was now a different person to the one he married. And then there was Ryan. Gus was a proud and jealous man. Even if they could get past everything else, could he ever forget that Dana had taken another man into her bed — their bed?

She sighed as she turned to stroll back towards the restaurant. What was she to do about Ryan? They had fallen into an easy, comfortable relationship but Dana knew it would never be more than that, at least not for her. But she sensed Ryan was getting serious and she didn't want to hurt him. It might be time to call it a day. It was such a pity. Ryan had made her laugh at a time when she thought she'd never stop crying. He'd also made her feel desirable and beautiful and that had boosted her ego and confidence enormously. And as for his lovemaking — she smiled — well, he knew what buttons to press. But, strangely, the closer they became, the more she found herself thinking about Gus. She'd even been dreaming of him lately.

"Dana?"

She looked up and saw that Ed was waving at her from the door of the restaurant. She hurried back to him. "Sorry, just needed a breath of air."

"We were getting worried about you. You're not cross with me, are you? For reading the book, I mean."

She shook her head. "No."

"You made me cry," he confided.

"I'm sorry. It must have brought back some painful memories."

"It did. But I cried when I read about you going to London. And then for him to send you away . . ."

Dana felt the tears well up. "It was probably as well that he did. It would have been impossible for us to live in peace together after that. Conall O'Carroll had finally realized that his darling princess was just an ordinary little girl after all."

A tear rolled down her cheek and he gently wiped it away. "There's nothing ordinary about you, little sister."

Dana tucked her arm through his. "We should go in. Poor Wally will think we're very rude."

"I think we're past formalities like that."

"You like him?" she asked.

Ed shot her a look. "Don't even go there."

"I don't know what you mean." She grinned at him and led the way back to their table. "Sorry, Wally. Did you think we'd got lost?"

"Yes and I had to order a stiff drink to console myself." Walter raised his brandy balloon in a silent toast.

She laughed. "Good man."

"So how's lover boy?" Ed asked, as they settled back down.

Her smile faded. "Eager."

"Isn't that a good thing?" Walter asked.

"It should be," she agreed.

"She still loves Gus." Ed told him.

Dana scowled. "How would you know?"

"It's obvious," Ed said with a shrug.

"It is," Walter confirmed.

Dana groaned. "I hope it isn't to him. I feel pathetic enough as it is."

"Why would it be?" Ed reasoned. "You're dating an attractive man."

"Not for much longer. I've decided to finish with Ryan."

Walter stared at her. "Oh, Dana, why? I thought you said he was great."

"He is. But I'm still too raw for a heavy relationship, and I get the feeling that's the way this is heading."

Walter shook his head. "The path of true love never does run smooth, does it?"

"It did for me," Dana said. "I just blew it."

"Don't be too hard on yourself," her brother said. "It's not your fault you turned out like that."

"I can't blame everything on Dad. You turned out remarkably normal despite everything he did to you."

"I feel like we're discussing a film and I've only seen the trailer," Walter complained.

Dana laughed. "You'll have to wait for the book!"

The agent pulled a face. "Don't tease me. It's cruel."

"If you're publishing, I'll want my cut," Ed warned her.

Dana shuddered. "I couldn't do it. You've no idea what it would be like, Ed. I'd have to do interviews to promote the book. And can you imagine the interest? The great Conall O'Carroll, a bully and a tyrant?"

Walter took out his handkerchief and patted his brow. "Oh, my, I'm seeing serious pound signs."

"Wally! This is my life — our lives." Dana gestured to Ed. "We're the ones who'd have to live with the fallout."

Ed shrugged. "If it would help you, I'd cope."

"And you think we'd feel better if we told the world about our problems? Do you want revenge? Is that it?" Dana asked.

"No," Ed assured her. "I'm past that stage. I just want peace. And you back in my life."

"I think I should go," Wally said, pushing back his chair.

"No! No, Wally, please. I'm sorry. We shouldn't be excluding you like this."

"It's the booze," Ed told him. "It gets us talking. I'm sorry, Walter. You take us out for this lovely lunch and we end up boring you with all this family stuff."

"Boring is the last word I'd use," Walter replied. "Sad, maybe. I remember the first time I met Dana. It was shortly after your mother died and she had signed her first contract. It should have been an exciting time of her life but she was miserable. That was natural, of course. Most people are devastated when they lose a parent. But Dana's misery was deeper and it worried me in one so young. And she seemed so alone in the world. I'm sorry," he added hurriedly when Ed grimaced, "I'm not making any judgements."

Ed nodded. "That's okay. I'm so glad that you persuaded her to see a doctor."

"Me too," Dana said. "I was in a very dark place back then. If it wasn't for Dr Corcoran, I'm not sure I'd have come out the other side."

Ed leaned his chin on his hand and studied his sister. "Was the depression due to Mum's death or because of the abortion, Dana?"

Walter spluttered out his brandy. "Abortion? What abortion?"

Dana froze.

Ed looked from the agent to the shocked expression on his sister's face. "I'm sorry. I just assumed —"

Dana sighed. "I didn't tell my husband, but you thought I'd tell my agent?"

Ed groaned. "I'm sorry. It's just when you said that Walter had suggested you get help, I thought you must have confided in him." He stood up. "Maybe I should go —"

"Oh, for God's sake, sit down, Ed," Dana said. She felt tired and drained. She'd had so many deep and meaningful conversations over the last few days — she couldn't remember who knew what. It was hardly surprising her brother didn't either. But, she realized, it didn't matter. Walter was a true friend and she certainly didn't mind him knowing she'd had an abortion. On the other hand — she suppressed a smile at the thought — she could always kill two birds with one stone. "I'm tired and I've drunk too much wine," she told them. "I need to go home."

"I'll call for the bill." Walter looked around for a waiter.

"No, you two stay. Please," Dana insisted. "Do me a favour, Ed. Fill Walter in on all the gory details. I'm not up to it right now, but I would like him to know."

Ed patted her shoulder and stood up. "I'll organize a taxi."

When they were alone, Dana turned to Walter. "Please don't be offended that I didn't confide in you before."

"Of course not! I'm as tough as old boots, you know that. And I know I've been going on about publishing your story, Dana, but I'll respect your decision, no matter what. I won't mention it again, if that's what you want."

"No, like Ed says, that's the mistake we've made in the past. Even if this manuscript never sees the light of day, I'd like my close friends to know the truth. And," she smiled, "you certainly fall into that category."

Finally, when she was in a taxi and on her way home, Dana pulled back her wrap and looked at the slightly grubby cast that would be taken off her arm the following morning. It would mark the end of Dana the invalid and the beginning of Dana the survivor. Because that was one thing she was sure of. She might be a bit bruised and slightly battered but she would survive.

CHAPTER
THIRTY-EIGHT

"Okay, Ms De Lacey. Do the exercises I've shown you and you should be absolutely fine."

Dana gingerly flexed her arm and fingers. "It feels so strange. I'm a bit afraid to use it."

"That's completely natural," the nurse told her. "But don't worry, it's mended and the more you use it, the stronger it will get."

"Thanks for everything." She smiled at the nurse.

Dana went out to the waiting room where Ed sat reading a newspaper. "Well?"

"I'm as good as new. Though it feels weird, and very light."

"So, what would you like to do?" he asked as they walked out to the car.

She laughed. "Have a shower."

"Straight home, then?"

She nodded. "Yes, please. And then, I have a hair appointment."

"Is this all for lover boy's benefit?" he asked as he opened the passenger door for her.

"It's to give me courage to finish with him."

He climbed in beside her and started the car. "Are you sure that's what you want to do? You've had an emotional few days. Maybe you should wait a while before making that decision."

"You think?" Dana thought about his words. It was true; her head was all over the place and she seemed to spend as much time in the past as she did in the present.

"I do." He swung the car out into traffic in the direction of home.

"Did Wally fly out this morning?" Dana had gone straight up to bed when she got home yesterday, though it had only been four o'clock. Amazingly she'd slept straight through till six this morning so she never even heard Ed come home.

Ed nodded. "Yes, his flight was at eleven."

"So how did it go after I left?"

"I told him about the abortion. He cried." Ed smiled. "That guy cries a lot."

"He's soft and kind. He's been good to me."

"I can see that. I'm glad you had someone to watch out for you."

"And then what did you do?"

"I told him a bit about me and my work. He told me a bit about him and his work. And about Giles — what a bastard."

Dana turned her head to look at him. "He told you about that?"

Ed glanced over. "Yes, why?"

"He never talks about Giles, not properly. He must really like you."

"Dana —"

"I'm just saying! Look, I know Wally. He was devastated when he found out that Giles had been cheating on him. And even so, he was ready to forgive the shit and carry on. When Giles walked out, Wally was heartbroken. And though I've seen him flirt a little and heard him talk about other men, I've never seen him open up as much as he has to you."

"Oh, Dana, I don't know . . ."

"I'm not saying you should hop on the next flight to London and ask him to marry you, Ed. I'm just saying there's nothing wrong in being open to the idea that maybe you and Walter have a future. And if not as a couple, then as good friends."

He shook his head, laughing. "I didn't know you were such a matchmaker."

"I'm not," Dana assured him. "But I saw something happen to you and Walter the moment you met. That doesn't happen often, at least not in my experience."

"And it's not there with Ryan?"

She sighed. "He makes me feel happy and sexy. He's attractive and kind —"

"But, no spark?"

Dana shook her head. "I don't think so."

"I'm sorry. Still, I haven't quite given up on you and Gus."

Dana looked mournful. "You haven't seen his girlfriend."

"No. But I have talked to him, a lot. He doesn't sound like a man who's moved on."

She turned in her seat and looked at him. "Have you been keeping in touch all the time you've been here?" she demanded.

416

Ed kept his eyes on the road. "Not all the time."

"Ed?"

"Look, he asked me to come here because he was worried about you. Obviously he was going to call me to know how you were doing."

"Did he ask about Ryan?" Dana asked.

Ed shook his head. "No."

Dana stared out of the window, afraid to hope that Gus was feeling anything more than guilt.

"I bet you he calls today."

Dana looked back at her brother. "What?"

"I said I bet he calls you. He knows you're getting the cast off."

"Oh. Yeah. Well, he might. But he'll just be being polite."

"If you say so." Ed pressed the remote control for the gates, and guided the car through them.

Dana climbed out of the car and stretched. "Oh, it's so nice to be able to do simple things without help."

"Go and have your shower," Ed said, opening the front door. "Call me when you're ready to go to the hairdresser."

"Oh, it's okay, I can drive —"

"No, don't start trying to do everything at once. Save your energy. You're going out tonight, remember?"

"I remember," Dana said and trudged upstairs.

She received three calls that day, from Walter, Sylvie and Judy, all checking to see how she'd got on at the hospital.

417

The call with Walter had resulted in tears on both sides as he sympathized with her on the loss of her child. No one had ever put it quite like that before and it had made Dana feel very emotional.

She had also chatted to Judy for a long time — there was so much to tell her.

"Poor Ed. He's had to cope with so much. And I can't believe your father made him believe your mother's death was his fault."

"He was not a nice man," Dana had replied.

"It would be wonderful if Ed and Wally got together," Judy had gone on.

"They're perfect for each other," Dana had agreed. "But I won't push it. Ed is very nervous, and Walter, after all, lives in London."

"It's only an hour away," Judy had pointed out. "And Ed can work from anywhere. Is he heading home now you don't need minding any more?"

"I don't know. I suppose he will. I'll miss him," Dana had admitted. "I've kind of got used to having him around."

"It's not far," Judy had reminded her. "You'll see him all the time."

"Not if he moves to London to be close to Wally."

"I think we're getting a step ahead of ourselves, don't you?"

"Yes, I suppose so."

The call from Sylvie had been a lot shorter. And that was it. No call from Gus. Dana was disappointed and annoyed with herself for caring. And annoyed with Ed for getting her hopes up.

"You look nice," he said when she came downstairs.

Dana's dark, blunt bob shone and she wore a red dress and matching shoes that made her feel very glamorous.

"Is that your 'dump 'em' outfit?"

Dana smiled despite herself. "No, but red always gives me confidence. Is it too much?"

"No, you look stunning. He'll be crying into his soup. Or will you wait until dessert to break the news to him?"

"It's not funny, Ed."

"You don't have to do it tonight," he reminded her.

"I think I do. He'll be expecting to come home with me, and if I let him . . ."

Ed grinned. "It would make you a complete tart."

Dana turned away to put in her earrings. "So much for Gus calling," she remarked.

"The day isn't over yet."

The buzzer sounded. "Maybe not. But I'm going out."

"If he calls, I'll tell him he'll get you on your mobile."

Dana grabbed her wrap and bag. "Don't you dare," she warned, hurrying to the door.

"Have a nice evening," he called after her.

"You look beautiful," Ryan said when they were sitting in the romantic French restaurant.

"Thanks." Dana managed a weak smile and wished she'd worn her jeans. Now that she was sitting across from him and he was looking at her like that, Dana knew it was over. She just couldn't let him make love to her again. They were no longer on the same page, and it would be wrong to let him believe they were.

"And the arm's okay?"

"A little sore but it's a relief to have the cast off."

They studied their menus, ordered and then sat back with their wine. "How was your trip?" Dana asked, for want of something better to say.

He watched her over his glass. "The same as all the other trips."

"Boring, then." She smiled.

He didn't bother answering. "Tell me about these visitors you've been having."

"Well, my friend Judy came up from Wexford and stayed with us for the weekend. And then she had just gone when Sylvie and Ian stopped by. Sylvie was a bit worried about her job and was looking for reassurances —"

"Why is she worried about her job?" he asked.

"She knew the book probably wouldn't be published so that made her nervous. But I've said I'll keep her on and she's going to do some other stuff as well."

"And is it definite that the book won't be published?" His eyes searched her face.

She nodded. "But I'm okay with that. Walter arrived just after they'd left — I told you it was a busy weekend — and we talked about it. It will probably be published in the States, but not here. Also I've decided not to sign a new contract."

"Wow. That's a big decision. Are you sure it's what you want?"

"I haven't given up writing. I've just had enough of this genre. It's time I tried something else."

"Any idea what?" he asked.

Dana thought about telling him about the biography and decided against it. She'd spent enough time talking about the past. She smiled. "I don't know, maybe thrillers?"

"Great. That's much more my sort of thing. I could be your first reader."

Dana's smile was strained. "I wouldn't have had you down as the bloodthirsty type."

He grinned manically. "Ah, there are lots of things you don't know about me, my dear. But we have plenty of time."

She looked down at her fingers and played with her wedding ring.

His smile faded as he watched her. "I see," he murmured.

She lifted her face and feigned innocence. "What do you see?"

"Oh, please, Dana. Don't do this. Not with me. We're beyond such games, surely."

"I'm sorry, Ryan."

"I suppose it beats a 'Dear John' letter."

She said nothing, wishing the meal was over instead of just starting.

"Is it Gus?" he asked, his voice quiet and controlled.

Dana shook her head. This was no time for honesty. He certainly didn't need to hear that she thought he cared more for her than she did for him. "I feel I need space. A lot has happened to me in the last few months and I've been completely lost. Now I'm ready to snap out of my stupor. And I feel that I can only do that alone."

He looked at her in disgust. "I take it back. Maybe a 'Dear John' letter would be preferable. How can you sit here and expect me to swallow this shit?"

She looked at him, alarmed. In all the time she'd known him, she'd never heard him use such a tone. "Please, Ryan, don't do this. We've had such a wonderful time. You've been the only light in my life —"

"Then why are you dumping me?" He reached over and grasped her hands, making her wince. "Don't do this, Dana. I love you."

"No, you don't." She pulled her hand away. "You don't even know me."

"I think I know you better than most," Ryan retorted.

"Are you having the steak, sir?" Dana looked up to see a pretty waitress with their dinners.

"I've lost my appetite," he grunted. "Take it away."

"Ryan, please," Dana murmured, embarrassed.

"Bring another bottle of wine, though," he said, ignoring Dana.

She shot the waitress an apologetic look. "I won't be eating either. But we'll pay, of course."

The waitress hurried back to the kitchen and moments later the maître d' arrived with the wine. "Is there a problem, sir?"

"There certainly is," Ryan replied, "but it's nothing to do with you or your food. Just open the wine. I'll pour."

The man shot Dana a concerned look as he opened the wine. She managed a smile but she was getting a little nervous herself. Ryan had emptied his glass while the second bottle was being opened and he poured himself another as soon as the waiter finished.

"Ryan, why don't we go home and talk about this?" Dana said quietly. She was aware that they were suddenly the centre of attention and that a couple of people had recognized her. Why had she dressed up tonight? And why had she let Ryan take her to one of the swankiest new restaurants in the city? She'd probably end up in the bloody papers again.

Ryan leaned forward and gazed into her eyes. "Why? Are you going to change your mind? Are you going to take me to bed? Are you going to do that thing you do —"

"Ryan, stop!" she hissed.

"Sorry." He spoke even louder. "Am I embarrassing you?"

"Yes. Yes, you are." Dana shook her head sadly and picked up her bag. "I'm sorry it had to end like this."

"Don't you dare walk out on me," Ryan warned her.

The maître d' was immediately at her side. "Is everything okay, *madame*?"

"Yes, I think so." Dana stood up. "Goodbye, Ryan," she said and walked quickly towards the door.

"Ms De Lacey?" The maître d' was hot on her heels. "If you like, you can use the side entrance. I took the liberty of calling a taxi."

"Oh, thank you." Dana smiled gratefully. "And please, look after him, won't you? He's not normally like this."

"I'll make sure he gets home safely," he promised.

"Thank you." Dana slipped out through the door and into the waiting car.

Ed looked up in surprise when he heard the key in the door. It wasn't even ten o'clock. He went out into the hall to see Dana leaning against the door, her eyes closed. "Dana?"

She opened her eyes. "Oh, Ed, what a disaster."

"He didn't take it well, then?"

She shook her head and kicked off her high heels. "It was awful. He turned into a completely different person."

"Did he hurt you?" Ed started.

"No. No, of course he didn't. He just got upset. The head waiter was fantastic, though. He got me out of the restaurant and into a taxi before Ryan knew what was happening."

"Well, if he turns up here, I'll be ready for him," Ed assured her.

"Great, thanks." Dana started up the stairs. "I'm going for a nice long bath. I need to relax after that."

424

"Don't you want your phone messages first?" Ed teased.

She turned to look at him. "Gus called?"

"He certainly did."

"Damn. What did you tell him?"

"That you were at a work do, of course."

"Oh, bless you." She blew him a kiss. "So what did he say?"

"That he'd call you tomorrow. I told him that you were out in the afternoon so he should phone in the morning."

Dana frowned. "I don't have anything on tomorrow."

Ed rolled his eyes. "I know that. But you don't want to spend the day on tenterhooks waiting for his call, do you?"

"Good thinking." She laughed. "Were you talking to him for long?"

"Not long. He just asked how you got on today and I said you were fine."

"Great. Thanks, Ed," she called over her shoulder as she went up to her room.

"No problem. Just call me your fairy godfather."

CHAPTER
THIRTY-NINE

It was eleven-thirty when Gus called. Dana had been up since eight. She was about to pounce on the phone, but Ed wagged his finger and answered it instead.

"Hi, Gus, how are you? Good. Yeah, hang on, she's around somewhere." And he held the receiver to his chest refusing to give it to Dana until he'd counted to twenty. Finally he handed it over and she turned her back on her brother, and went out to the conservatory.

"Hello?"

"Hi, Dana, it's me."

"Oh, hi, Gus."

"How are you feeling?"

"Pretty good."

"That's great. I'm glad."

"Gus, can we —"

"I just wanted to —"

They both started talking at once and laughed, selfconsciously.

"You first," Gus said.

"I wanted to ask you to come over for a chat. There are some things I need to tell you. I realize that you're probably busy —"

"No, actually, I'm free right now. Tom's back so the pressure is off."

"Oh. Great. What were you going to say?" Dana prompted.

"The same. I have something I want to tell you."

Dana felt her stomach flip. He wanted a divorce. He was going to marry his journalist.

"Dana?"

"Yes, okay. Why don't you come right over? I'll put on some coffee."

"I'm on my way."

Dana went back out to the hall and put the phone down. Immediately, Ed appeared from the kitchen. "Well?"

"He's on his way over."

"That's brilliant." Ed smiled at her and then frowned at the worried look on her face. "What's wrong?"

"He says he has something to tell me."

"That's not surprising. You have a lot to talk about," Ed reminded her.

"No, it's his choice of words," Dana argued. "He didn't say he wanted to discuss something or that he wanted to have a chat. He said he wanted to tell me something."

"For goodness sake, Dana, you're being pedantic. He's coming over, that's all that matters. Are you still planning on giving him the manuscript to read?"

She nodded. "Yes. I'd better go and print it off. Would you put on some coffee, Ed?"

"Sure. And do you want me to stay for moral support or will I disappear?"

"Disappear, I think. But —" she shot him a nervous look — "don't go too far, will you?"

He gave her a quick hug. "I'll go and do the shopping. You phone me if you need me and I'll be back here in five."

Dana was upstairs when her phone beeped. She picked it up to check who the text was from. It was Ryan. With some trepidation, she opened the message.

DANA, FORGIVE ME? BE HAPPY. X RYAN

She smiled as she sent him back a message.

THANKS, RYAN. YOU TOO.

She didn't add a kiss. No point in confusing the issue. But she was glad that he'd contacted her and they'd made their peace.

Her thoughts were interrupted by the sound of Gus's car pulling into the driveway. She checked her appearance, took some slow, deep breaths and went downstairs. Though he'd let himself in the gate, Gus rang the doorbell and waited patiently for her to let him in.

"You still have a key," she reminded him, as she opened the door.

He raised an eyebrow. "And you think I'd use it after the last time?"

She smiled and led the way into the kitchen.

"You look well," he said as she busied herself with mugs.

428

"Thanks."

"It must be a relief to have the cast off."

She nodded as she set the coffee down and fetched milk. "It is."

"Dana?" He waited for her to meet his eyes before he continued. "I'm so sorry."

She swallowed and smiled. "What for?"

He threw up his hands. "Everything? It's hard to know where to start."

"Yes."

"I found your letters."

"I know. Ed told me."

"It felt as if I was married to a stranger. And then when I read the one to your son —" He shook his head. "I imagined this whole other relationship you must have had, that you deliberately hid from me. I thought you were living a double life — visiting this boy somewhere, possibly even seeing the father."

"You should have asked me," Dana said.

"I know. But any time I'd asked you about your past, you had shut me down. I'm afraid this was the final straw."

She nodded. "I understand."

He looked at her. "You do?"

She laughed. "Is it that much of a surprise?"

"Just a bit," he admitted.

"The letters that you found were part of a therapy I did after Mum died."

"Was this when you were being treated for depression?"

"Yes," she told him. "Walter talked me into it. I was very down and on the road to self-destruction. He thought it was because of Mum, and it was, to a certain extent. But having the abortion was what I really found hard to live with. I was tormented by it day and night and Mum was the only one I could talk to. When she died —" Dana stopped, as she felt the tears bubble up inside her.

"It's okay. If this is too hard for you to talk about —"

"No." She pulled a tissue from the pocket of her jeans and blew her nose. "I have to talk about it. It's still a new experience for me, though, and I usually end up blubbering."

"That's allowed," he said softly.

"Anyway, when Mum died, I fell apart. I went home for the funeral to find Ed there and he and Dad were bosom buddies — or so it seemed. It was, to use your phrase, the last straw."

"And you never talked to anyone about what happened?"

"Yes. Obviously Judy knew and then, a year or so later, Dr Corcoran. I went off the straight and narrow for a while. I dropped out of college and drank too much." She shrugged. "But when my first book was published, I suddenly realized that I had something to hold on to. I had something that was just mine, and no one could take it away from me. In the two years after Mum died, I wrote two books. Writing saved my life. When I was working, I was too involved in my storylines to think about all that I had lost. And then because things were working out so well, and Gretta

430

was thrilled with my work, they started bringing me over there for promotions. It was wonderful. I couldn't believe the attention people paid to me; how complimentary they were." She rolled her eyes, smiling. "You know the Americans. They never do anything by halves. But I would probably still be a hermit if it wasn't for Wally. He was often in Dublin and he always insisted I partnered him to any of the events he was attending. And so I had a new life. He made sure I got some publicity here even though I wasn't published in Ireland. He was always thinking ahead."

"And will *The Mile High Club* be published here?"

She shook her head. "No. But then you must have suspected that after Walter's drunken phone call."

He smiled. "You heard about that. I've never heard Wally so furious. He obviously blames me for this. I'm sorry, Dana, if that's true."

"I'm not. I'm ready to move on and try my hand at something different."

"You weren't until I messed things up. If it wasn't for me, that book would be launching Passion over here, wouldn't it? And you'd be getting the recognition you've always wanted."

"I'm rather embarrassed by that goal now," she admitted. "In fact my entire career is a bit of a joke."

"Don't say that! You've worked damn hard to become so successful and you should be proud of yourself. I'm proud of you," Gus added.

"But I did it for all the wrong reasons," she explained.

"We've both made mistakes, Dana, but everyone does. That's life. My mistake was not trusting you. I'm sorry for that."

"No. I should have told you everything from the start," Dana protested.

His lips twitched. "Are we going to argue over who's more to blame?"

She shook her head. "No. I've had my fill of arguments."

"Me too."

"I have something for you." She stood up and went out of the door. Moments later she reappeared and handed him a thick manuscript. "This is my story. It starts when I was a child and finishes with the publication of my first book. I'd like you to read it. Maybe it will explain why I'm the annoying, frustrating person I am today."

Gus took it from her and set it on the table. He raised his eyes to hers. "Ed has told me some of the story."

"I know that. But this is from my perspective."

"Please don't feel you have to show it to me —"

"I want to, Gus, okay?"

He nodded and smoothed his hand over the front page. "Thank you. So, what now?"

She wasn't sure if he meant for them or for her and her career. She decided it was safer to assume the latter. "Walter and Ed think I should publish this or adapt it into a novel. I'm not so sure."

"You have to do what works for you," he counselled. "But remember, Dana. If you do publish it, once it's out there, you can't take it back."

"No," she agreed.

"It's been an eventful few months for you."

"And you," she retorted.

He smiled in acknowledgement. "So, this new guy —"

"Ryan?" Dana said and her heart skipped a beat at the pained look that crossed her husband's face.

"Is it serious? Is he going to be a permanent fixture in your life?"

"No. It's over."

He looked up, his eyes searching hers. "Really?"

She nodded. "And your . . . relationship?"

"Terry and I have split up."

Dana stared at him. "Really?"

"Really. So, where does that leave us?"

Her eyes returned to the book in front of him. "There's still a lot to talk about. But I'd really like you to read this first, is that okay?"

He nodded and stood up.

She watched him in disappointment. "Oh. Do you have to go so soon?"

He picked up the book and shoved it under his arm. "I have some reading to do. The sooner I get finished, the sooner I get back." He reached out his hand and touched her cheek.

The impulse to turn and kiss his fingers was huge, but Dana settled for covering his hand with hers.

"I'll be in touch." He stood smiling at her for a moment, and then turned to leave.

Dana stood watching until the gate closed after Gus, and the noise of his engine became indistinguishable from the other traffic. Reluctantly, she closed the door and went into her office. There was a note on her keyboard reminding her to call Walter. He would probably have told Gretta the bad news by now. That not only was *The Mile High Club* rubbish, but that Dana wouldn't be writing any more books for Peyton Publishing. Dana wasn't too worried about Gretta, though. As Walter said, she was sure to have a Plan B up her sleeve. She just hoped the editor hadn't given Wally a hard time. Dana should have had the guts to deal with the woman herself, but she hadn't trusted herself to say the right things. Wally hadn't either.

She picked up the phone and, moments later, was put through to her agent. "Hi, Wally."

"Dana, darling, how are you?"

"I'm fine. You? Did you talk to Gretta?"

He groaned. "Oh, Dana, that woman is impossible."

"She didn't take it well, then?"

"That's an understatement. Still, she was more annoyed with me than you. Deservedly so, I suppose," he acknowledged. "She said I should have come clean as soon as I suspected you were in trouble."

"But how could you? You didn't believe it yourself."

"True. I don't suppose you've changed your mind?"

"I'm afraid not."

"Well, not to worry. I've sent her the manuscript from that new author I was telling you about. That calmed her down slightly. So, tell me, how are you doing? How's the arm?"

"Fine. Everything is fine."

"Okay, out with it."

"What?"

"There's something you're obviously dying to tell me."

Dana laughed. "I just had a visitor."

"Who?"

"Gus."

"No!"

"Yes."

"And?" he prompted.

"Let's say it went well."

"You're back together?" Walter screeched.

"Not quite but it's looking good. I finished with Ryan — that's a whole different story — and Gus has broken up with his journalist too."

"Oh, Dana, I'm so happy for you."

"Well, it's early days," Dana cautioned. "We're not quite out of the woods yet."

"You'll be fine. Everything is going to be fine, I just know it. Oh, this is so romantic," Walter sighed. "You have your brother back in your life. And now your gorgeous husband too. You're a very lucky woman."

"I know."

"You have a proper family."

"Which you are an honorary part of," Dana assured him. "Whenever you're in Dublin, you have to come and see us. I know both Gus and Ed would want that as much as I do."

"Bless you, darling. So what will your brother do if you and Gus get back together?"

Dana smiled, delighted. Wally was trying to sound casual and indifferent, but she knew him too well. "We haven't talked about it yet, but I can assure you we're never going to lose touch again."

"That's wonderful. Oh, sorry, darling. There's a call holding that I really must take. Call me as soon as there's more news," he told her.

"Promise."

Dana spent the rest of the day alone. She wandered around the house trying to distract herself, but failed miserably. She eventually went to bed and was lying staring at the ceiling, when she heard the doorbell. Ed was out somewhere, and the side gate was locked. So, either it was a very polite burglar, or — Gus! Pulling on a robe, Dana hurried downstairs and smiled delightedly when she saw his familiar outline through the mottled glass. She threw open the door. "Gus!" Her smile faded when she saw the look on his face.

He stared at her from sad, red-rimmed eyes. "Dana. I am so sorry."

She swallowed back her tears. "Gus?" she whispered.

He opened his arms to her and, silently, she walked straight into them. As Gus held her tightly against his chest and stroked her hair, he kept murmuring, "I'm so sorry, my darling. I'm so sorry."

Dana drew him inside and closed the door. Without saying a word, she led him upstairs and into their bedroom. They were both crying as he undressed her, kissing each part of her body as it was revealed. Finally, when they were both naked, Gus took her in his arms. For a long time, they lay in silence, just holding each other. Then Gus took the palm of her hand and kissed it. "Please forgive me. Please take me back."

"Of course I will," Dana whispered.

And then he kissed her. And no kiss had ever been so sweet. She felt as if it were their first, only better. Through his fingers and his lips, he showed her how much he loved her and she closed her eyes and let him carry them both to a place where there was no pain.

They were sitting in their bathrobes, eating breakfast the next morning, when they heard the front door open. Gus buried his head in a newspaper, while Dana went to put some bread in the toaster.

Ed walked through the door, pulling up short at the domestic scene before him. "Hello!"

"Hi, Ed," Gus said from behind his paper.

Dana looked up. "Hiya. Want some breakfast?"

Ed lowered himself into a chair and looked from one to the other.

Dana poured her brother coffee, and put a plate and knife in front of him. "Did you get any good photos?" she asked.

"Don't give me that!"

She frowned. "Sorry?"

"When I left here yesterday, you were a separated woman who was planning an early night. Now you may well have had an early night, but you were obviously not alone." His eyes widened in fake shock. "Did you spend the night with your husband?"

Dana nodded solemnly. "I admit it. It's true."

"Ha!" A grin spread across his face as he looked from Dana to Gus and back again. "About bloody time!"

Gus put down his paper and smiled. "If it wasn't for you, I'm not sure we'd have made it."

"You certainly weren't helping yourselves," Ed agreed. "Maybe I should matchmake for a living."

"Stick with photography," Dana advised.

"So what did it?" he asked, wrapping his hands around the warm mug. "Tell me everything."

Gus shrugged. "Dana gave me her book to read."

"Ah."

"There weren't many surprises, but I suppose it was more heartbreaking having already heard your side of the story."

Ed nodded. "And then the London piece —"

"Don't tiptoe around it, Ed," Dana said. "We've done that all our lives. I had an abortion. Don't be afraid to say it out loud. I can handle it."

"I hate that word because I don't think it applies," Ed argued. "Saying you had an abortion makes it sound like you made a level-headed, informed decision."

"And you didn't," Gus agreed. "If you had, you wouldn't have been so devastated afterwards."

Dana sighed. "I did it to get back at my father. What does that make me?"

"What does that make him?" Gus retorted.

Ed's face darkened. "A monster."

Gus looked curiously at his wife. "I was surprised that your story ended with the publication of your first book. Why didn't you cover your father's death?"

438

She shrugged and stared into her mug. "He was already dead to me. Anyway, I wasn't even at the funeral."

"But what about his estate?" Gus pressed. "Forgive me, Ed, but if he hated you so much, how come he left you his house?"

"He didn't. The house was my mother's. Her father had built it in the forties and she inherited it from him."

Dana nodded. "From the day Ed left, Mum worried about him and how he'd manage. She knew that Dad would never give Ed a penny. So, with my blessing, she transferred the house into his name."

"But your dad couldn't have left you out of his will," Gus told Ed. "You're entitled to half his estate no matter what."

Dana laughed. "You underestimate my father. He took a leaf out of Mum's book. When he found out he had cancer, he started writing cheques for various charities and, of course, the parish got a large donation."

Ed took up the story. "Father Flynn told me as soon as Dad gave it to him. He was very upset. He told Dad there was no point in asking God to forgive his sins, if he couldn't forgive his own children's. But of course Dad wouldn't listen. Father Flynn wanted to tear up the cheque, but I told him to keep the money and put it to good use. I didn't want it and I knew that Dana didn't want or need it either."

"The royalties from his books go to an awards fund in his name," Dana continued. "He was determined to be immortal one way or another. But though his poetry was greatly admired and two of his poems even appeared on the school curriculum, he never earned huge money. It infuriated him that my first trashy novel earned nearly as much as he'd made in his entire literary career."

Gus stared at her. "You said you hadn't talked to him since your mother's funeral."

Dana looked like a rabbit caught in headlights. Ed sighed. "I thought we were finished with secrets."

CHAPTER
FORTY

"It's okay, Dana. Just tell us." Ed's smile was encouraging.

Dana braced herself, wondering what words she could use to make her brother understand.

"Okay, then." She took a deep breath and began the last, unwritten chapter of her story. "Father Flynn called me too when he knew Father was close to death. He said Dad wanted to see me and that I should probably come, if only for my own sake. So I did."

Ed stared. "You came back to Wexford? To our house?"

"Yes. I came down late one evening. Father Flynn was the only one there when I arrived. He said he had to visit another parishioner but he'd be back. He had a key so he said if he wasn't back before I left, to just pull the door after me." She smiled bitterly. "I assured him that I wouldn't be staying long. I asked him not to tell anyone I had even come."

"Why?" Gus asked.

She shrugged. "I suppose I thought that it would seem odd that I had come to see him and yet not turned up for the funeral. And I knew that no matter what happened between us that night, I probably wouldn't go."

"Go on," Ed said.

"Before Father Flynn left, I thanked him for his kindness to Dad. He said it was his Christian duty." She frowned. "I thought it was an odd choice of words. The way he said it, it was almost like an apology."

"Well, you have to remember that he was Father's confessor. He may have known everything that was going on all along."

"And done nothing?" Dana looked at him in disbelief.

"If it was said in the confessional, Dana, then his hands would have been tied," Gus said gently.

Dana shook her head in disgust. "Anyway, he left and I went upstairs. When I walked into the bedroom and saw Dad, I couldn't believe how he'd changed. He looked frail and pitiful. I thought how sad to be so successful and, at the same time, so alone." She looked up at them and smiled slightly. "That sounds familiar, doesn't it? I sat down next to him, and he opened his eyes and smiled." Dana turned her mug between her fingers. "He said he knew I'd come back eventually. For a few seconds I felt I'd done the right thing. Father Flynn was right and I was glad I'd come. And then he started." She shook her head. "First he asked had I managed to write anything decent yet or was I still making a living producing smut."

"The old bugger!" Gus fumed.

Ed's eyes never left Dana. "Go on."

Dana stared into her mug. "I don't remember everything he said. It was the usual stuff. I had shown such promise, and then I threw it all away. I'd embarrassed him and my mother by getting pregnant like some cheap little tart. And then I'd made things even worse by killing an innocent child." At this stage, tears were rolling down Dana's cheeks. She hardly noticed when Gus pushed a piece of kitchen roll into her hand. "And then the final insult, he said. With my talent, my background and education, I had chosen to make my living by peddling filth. I asked him how he knew what I wrote when he hadn't read it. He just said that he knew everything about my publishing deal with 'the Yanks'. He said they were an immoral lot over there, but I would never be published in a good Catholic country like Ireland."

"Crikey." Gus rolled his eyes. "Did all of this really happen only in the eighties? He sounds like a man from a different century."

"He was very old-fashioned," Ed agreed, "and bigoted and anti anyone different." His eyes went back to his sister. "What happened then?"

Dana dabbed at her face with the kitchen towel but the tears kept coming and soon it was a sodden mess. "He said I was as bad as my brother. I told him I'd take that as a compliment. I thought that would infuriate him but he smiled. He said I didn't know you as well as I thought I did. He asked if I'd seen you since Mum's funeral. When I said no, he laughed. 'Then you don't know,' he said."

"'Know what?' I asked."

"'That Ed killed your mother.'"

"I shouted at him and called him a liar. He swore it was true. I said if it was why hadn't he said something before? He said that it had been an accident, and that Ed hadn't meant to push her."

"I never pushed her," Ed exclaimed. "I was downstairs with him. The lying bastard!"

She nodded. "I know that, Ed."

Gus put a hand over hers. "Go on, Dana."

"Then he pulled himself up in the bed and looked into my eyes and said —" she paused, her voice trembling — "he said, 'If Ed hadn't been there that night, your mother wouldn't have died'."

Ed looked at her, his eyes full of tears. "And that's true."

"It was an accident," Gus said gently.

"How do you know that?" Ed challenged. "How do you know that I'm telling the truth?"

Dana's tears continued to fall. "Because you're a good person," she cried. "And I know what he was capable of."

His eyes held hers. "But you had your doubts, didn't you?"

"I'm sorry. But you know what Dad was like. He knew what buttons to press. Once I had a chance to think about it, I realized he was lying. His story didn't fit in with anything the doctor had told me."

Ed stared into space. "Why didn't you say something when I told you my side of the story?"

"I was too ashamed," Dana admitted. "I couldn't believe that I'd ever doubted you. I'm so sorry, Ed."

444

"Are you sure you believe me now?" He put out a hand and lifted her chin so he could look into her eyes.

"Yes! Honestly! That's why I never told anybody what he said." She shot Gus an apologetic look. "I didn't want to risk anyone blaming you."

"Thank you."

Dana went to hug him and he buried his face in her hair as she clung to him.

Gus sighed as he watched them. "I can't begin to understand why your father behaved the way he did. Even if he couldn't bring himself to forgive either of you, the least he could have done was reunite his children before he died."

"That's the last thing he wanted," Ed said. "He didn't want Dana to know my dirty little secret."

"And he wanted to punish me for the abortion and my books," Dana said.

"Why not blame your mother's death on Ed?" Gus argued.

"Because," she told him, "it would ruin his image. Father was always worried about appearances. He was the successful author with the lovely wife and the perfect children. When he found out Ed was gay, he went out of his way to hide the truth, even from me. Then I — his little princess — get pregnant and have an abortion. The icing on the cake was me making a career writing the type of books he abhorred. The way he saw it, Ed and I ruined everything for him and he wanted to punish us."

Ed nodded. "I think that's true. Imagine: his last act, on his deathbed, was to try to make sure that Dana had nothing more to do with me. Because of him, we haven't talked for more than twenty years."

"The man was sick in the head," Gus declared.

Ed shuddered. "I hate the thought that his blood flows through my veins. Sometimes I lie awake at night thinking about it. What if I've inherited some of his disgusting traits?"

"You haven't." Dana's smile was tender. "You're a sensitive and kind man. You're the complete opposite to him in every way."

Gus grinned. "Maybe your mum had a fling and he's not your father at all!"

Ed laughed. "Oh, what a lovely thought. It would be nice to think that she had had some love in her life."

"Why stay with him?" Gus mused. "She couldn't have been happy."

"She wasn't," Ed agreed. "I should have come back sooner and persuaded her to leave him."

Dana tore off another piece of kitchen roll and dried her face. "I asked her to come to Dublin and live with me. But she said her place was with him. I shouldn't have taken no for an answer."

Gus looked from one to the other. "What is this, a contest to see who's the guiltiest? If so, then I can join in too. When I went to university in Belfast, my mother was always asking me to come home at the weekend. But there was always some party I wanted to go to or a girl to chase. And before I knew it, she was gone."

Dana came and put her arms around him. "You never told me that before."

446

He shrugged. "No, but I do think about it from time to time. We all have regrets. But you can't spend your life beating yourself up. There's nothing you can do for your mum now. But you've got each other. You need to concentrate on that."

Ed looked at his sister. "Gus is right. Let's look forward, not back. And let's agree that nothing or no one will ever come between us again."

Dana hugged him. "Agreed." She pulled her husband into the embrace. "And that goes for you too."

Epilogue

Dana looked down the table and smiled at Gus. They were having dinner with their friends to celebrate the launch of her new book called *The Perfect Family*. There had been official launches in both Dublin and London, but Dana had wanted a more informal gathering, to show her friends and family her gratitude. And so she and Gus had invited a few people to their home in Cork and were delighted when everyone accepted.

Tom and Ashling were chatting across the table to Judy and her husband, Phil. Ed and Walter were in animated conversation with Angela Wiseman and her new partner. And Sylvie and Ian were quizzing Gus's sister, Annie, and partner, Greg, about New Zealand.

Gus tapped his glass with a knife and stood up. "Excuse me, folks, I'd just like to say a few words."

The group quietened and looked up expectantly.

"Dana and I are thrilled that you could all make it this weekend. I'm especially pleased to welcome my sister, Annie, who finally decided to come home for a few weeks. It's great to have you here, sis."

"Good to be here, Gus." She smiled.

Gus looked around the faces at the table. "I know some of you were surprised when we decided to make Bantry our permanent home. But —" he waved his hands at the huge window and the spectacular view beyond — "you can see the attraction."

There was a murmur of appreciation and nodding of heads.

"But you haven't got rid of us, I'm afraid. We'll be back on a regular basis. It's been an interesting couple of years for Dana and me." He met his wife's eyes and smiled. "And it hasn't always been easy. It's thanks to all of you, though, that we survived it. Your love and support have been truly humbling and we thank you for them. But that's enough from me. Pray silence for the author of *The Perfect Family*. Ladies and gentlemen, I give you my stunning and extremely talented wife, Dana."

Tom wolf-whistled and everyone applauded as Dana struggled to her feet. "What a marvellous introduction." She grinned at her husband. "Follow that. First, I'd like to echo everything Gus said. Thank you all for coming down this weekend. It's just wonderful to be surrounded by all the people we care most about in the world. Now this place really feels like home." She paused, and looked around at their faces. "This book only got published as a result of a lot of hard work and, this time, not all of it by me. A special thanks to Sylvie for all her help. And my apologies, Sylvie, I know I haven't been the easiest woman to work with."

"She told us," Ian said and everyone laughed.

Dana smiled. "Also, my heartfelt thanks to Angela, who is the best and most understanding editor in the world. I wouldn't have been able to get through this without you, Angela."

Her editor smiled and blew Dana a kiss.

"Of course, I can't forget my wonderful agent and dear, dear friend." She smiled at Wally. "I'm not sure why or how he's put up with me all these years —"

"For the money," Wally retorted.

She ignored him. "He pretends that he's tough but, believe me, he isn't. He got me my first contract all those years ago —"

"I was very young," Wally assured them, smoothing back his hair.

Dana laughed. "And he's stayed close by my side ever since. Sometimes I needed his professional guidance. Sometimes I needed a shoulder to cry on. Whatever I needed, though, Walter Grimes provided it. Thank you, my darling."

He surreptitiously wiped his eye, and waved away her thanks with a shy smile.

Dana paused for a moment and took a sip of water. "*The Perfect Family* hasn't been easy to write."

A hush fell on the room as Dana's voice dropped.

"It is a novel but, as you all know, it's been greatly influenced by my own experiences and, of course, my brother's. I want to thank Ed for giving this project his blessing and throwing himself into the publicity. Talking about any kind of abuse is hard, but talking about it with a journalist or in front of a camera or microphone is even harder. But when I asked Ed to do just that, he immediately said yes." She looked at her brother and

450

smiled. "For your eternal selflessness, love and support, Ed, thank you."

Ed inclined his head, his eyes bright with tears.

"*The Perfect Family* has been number one in Ireland for two weeks now —"

Everyone whooped and cheered but Dana held up her hands for quiet.

"And we just got word yesterday that it's entered the UK chart at number forty-nine."

The room erupted this time and there were hugs and kisses and a few tears too.

"It's too soon to talk about figures," she said, when everyone finally calmed down. "But let's hope we're going to make a lot of money for the ISPCC."

"Hear, hear," Gus called out.

Her eyes met his. "And finally, I want to thank my wonderful husband for giving me another chance. He is the love of my life and I intend to spend the rest of my time in this world making him happy."

He came down to kiss her and Judy reached for a tissue as everyone cheered.

Walter was immediately on his feet. "On behalf of us all, I'd like to say thank you for welcoming us to your beautiful home." He turned to look out at the view. "I can completely understand why you would want to live here, but don't forget us. You'll always be welcome in London and Dublin and," he smiled shyly at Ed, "Wexford."

"Hear, hear." Judy grinned.

Wally raised his glass. "To our hosts, Gus and Dana."

"To Gus and Dana."

"Will you really come back to Wexford?" Judy asked later, when she and Dana were alone in the kitchen.

Dana kicked off her shoes and flexed her toes. "I have to. Ed has made it his home."

"It will be fine," Judy reassured her. "You'll hardly recognize the house. Ed has done an amazing job. Do you think Walter will move in with him?"

"No, Wally's life is in London. But I think he'll be spending a lot of time in Wexford too. Ed insists they're taking things slowly, but it's obvious they're mad about each other."

Judy grinned. "It is, isn't it? I think for Ed to end up living in the family home with his gay lover is the ultimate triumph over your father's homophobia."

"I suppose it is. My mother would be so happy. Not only has Ed finally come home, but he's happy too."

"And you, Dana?" Judy asked. "Have you found peace?"

Dana put a hand down to caress her large bump and smiled. "Oh, Judy, I've never been happier."

Also available in ISIS Large Print:

The Betrayal of Grace Mulcahy

Colette Caddle

The life and marriage of Grace and Michael Mulcahy has all the signs of being a successful and fulfilled one: a daughter, rewarding jobs and plenty of friends. But when Grace discovers that her partner in her interior design business, 52-year-old Miriam, is embezzling her, the seeds are sown for Grace's bind.

When confronted with her betrayal, Miriam begs Grace not to tell anyone in order to preserve Miriam's marriage, which will fall apart if the truth outs. Grace agrees to keep quiet but finds it leads to all sorts of complications and misunderstandings that put a strain on all of her relationships both professional and personal. By the time she notices how close things are to crumbling, it could be too late to piece together the ties that bind her to those she loves.

ISBN 978-0-7531-7728-0 (hb)
ISBN 978-0-7531-7729-7 (pb)

Red Letter Day

Colette Caddle

Tipped as one of Ireland's top young designers and recently married, Celine Moore is relaxed, happy and looking forward to an exciting future. When tragedy strikes in the violent loss of her husband, the dreams she aspired to melt away and are replaced by aching loneliness and anger. In trying to bury the past, Celine embarks on an affair and attempts to make a new life for herself away from local gossip. But eventually she has to face her demons and to seek the happiness that was once hers.

ISBN 978-0-7531-7205-6 (hb)
ISBN 978-0-7531-7206-3 (pb)

ISIS publish a wide range of books in large print, from fiction to biography. Any suggestions for books you would like to see in large print or audio are always welcome. Please send to the Editorial Department at:

ISIS Publishing Limited
7 Centremead
Osney Mead
Oxford OX2 0ES

A full list of titles is available free of charge from:

Ulverscroft Large Print Books Limited

(UK)
The Green
Bradgate Road, Anstey
Leicester LE7 7FU
Tel: (0116) 236 4325

(Australia)
P.O. Box 314
St Leonards
NSW 1590
Tel: (02) 9436 2622

(USA)
P.O. Box 1230
West Seneca
N.Y. 14224-1230
Tel: (716) 674 4270

(Canada)
P.O. Box 80038
Burlington
Ontario L7L 6B1
Tel: (905) 637 8734

(New Zealand)
P.O. Box 456
Feilding
Tel: (06) 323 6828

Details of ISIS complete and unabridged audio books are also available from these offices. Alternatively, contact your local library for details of their collection of ISIS large print and unabridged audio books.